Pebble Cove

MAIREAD
O'DRISCOLL

POOLBEG

Published 2006
by Poolbeg Press Ltd
123 Grange Hill, Baldoyle
Dublin 13, Ireland
E-mail: poolbeg@poolbeg.com

© Mairead O'Driscoll 2006

The moral right of the author has been asserted.

Typesetting, layout, design © Poolbeg Press Ltd

13 5 7 9 10 8 6 4 2

A catalogue record for this book is available from the British Library.

ISBN 1-84223-267-3
ISBN 978-1-84223-267-5 (From Jan 2007)

Typeset by Type Design in Palatino 10/13.8pt
Printed by Litografia S.A, Spain

www.poolbeg.com

About the author

Mairead O'Driscoll was born in Co Offaly and now lives in Midleton, Co Cork, with her husband, Leonard. She works as a Public Health Nurse with the HSE. *Pebble Cove* is her first novel.

www.maireadodriscoll.com

Acknowledgements

With so many people to thank, it's difficult to decide whether to be very, very expansive or really, really brief. So I'll settle for brief.

Suffice it to say that *Pebble Cove* would never have seen the light of day if Len hadn't been there to resurrect all the lost bits and zap the viruses. Thank you for that, Len, and for much more besides.

Special thanks and admiration to my parents, Andy and Christina Hackett, for their constant support and encouragement.

Thanks also to my wonderful mother-in-law, Nonie O'Driscoll.

To all the gang at home – Declan and Tina, Delma and Seán, Lori and Aaron, Cora and Michael and the fabulous kiddies – Hazel, Rachel, Kira, Dermot, Kate, Grace and Emma.

To my agent Ger Nichol – sincere thanks for believing in *Pebble Cove* from Day One and kick-starting me into Number Two.

To Paula Campbell, Gaye Shortland and all the team at Poolbeg – thanks for giving me this exciting chance.

To all the gang at Midleton Health Centre – laughter is definitely the best medicine.

To my friends – you all know who you are and what you mean to me – I hope!

Most of all, to Len for your unwavering support and encouragement in everything. From proof-reading to saving things on that little key, your input to *Pebble Cove* has been phenomenal. For your dedication and love, thank you.

For Len,

My best friend,

Always and ever.

1

Number 1

Linda Colton folded her long slender legs into the MG, slammed the door and flung it into reverse. If her mother thought she was coming out here again on a charity visit to that old crank she could think again. The cheek of him, sitting there in his manky old armchair, philosophising about what was going to become of her! As if he'd know!

"Girlie, you'd want to settle down now when you're young. Plenty of good-looking girls spend half of their lives saying, 'Who will I have?' and the rest of it saying, 'Who'll have me?' I'm only advising you in time."

For God's sake, she raged, flicking back her straight, ash-blonde hair, anyone would think she was ninety the way he was going on! Well, her mother could bloody well go and visit him herself from now on – he was *her* father after all. Let her go and listen to him harping on about settling down.

Linda had calmed down by the time she got out of the shower an hour later. She caught a glimpse of herself in the cheval mirror as she rooted through the wardrobe for a pair of black Capri pants, and realised that the new bulbs in the sunbed had definitely been needed. Her tan was fantastic after only eight sessions and she was pleased to see there wasn't even a hint of cellulite on her well-toned bottom. White linen would really show her off to best effect. She threw the black pants aside and, turning back to the wardrobe, selected a classic white halterneck dress that would take the sight out of Charlie's eyes. Sometimes she caught him looking at her when he thought she didn't notice, and the power she felt at being on the receiving end of that kind of admiration was dizzying.

Of course it wasn't something that was new to her. From her earliest memories she had known she was special and, as the only child of Daniel Colton, she wanted for nothing, attention in particular.

Number 1, Pebble Cove, was nothing short of what she expected. Only she'd have to get rid of the "Number 1" bit. Her father had cleverly placed a stipulation on the sale of all the houses in Pebble Cove that they should have a name instead of numbers. This would give the development an air of exclusivity, justifying the above-average price bracket. Linda felt that whatever name she chose, it ought to reflect her personality and experience. Something understated and arcane that only a likeminded individual would appreciate. Not like the "Kusadasi" and "Limasoll" people on the Cliff Road, whose houses were named when it was considered posh to go on holiday to Turkey or Cyprus, and who were considered upmarket just because they could afford an annual fortnight in the sun and a pricey house.

Well, thanks to her father's foresight, the Cliff Road was well and truly *passé*. Pebble Cove was the place to be now, and most particularly Number 1, the showpiece, given to her by her father as a thirtieth birthday present – complete with a handsome budget to help her decorate it to her own undoubtedly exquisite taste.

And exquisite it was, mused Linda as she pondered the cream walls, cream linen drapes and bedlinen, coupled with cherrywood hand-made furniture, its glossy warmth reflecting the soft glow of the sunken ceiling lights. Linda's eyes rested on a cutglass Waterford Crystal clock given to her by Charlie's mother as a moving-in present. She still hadn't made up her mind about it so thought it safest to leave it in the bedroom – on display should Mrs Moorehouse ever decide to pay her a visit, but not sitting in her main reception room as evidence of her own style, when she hadn't yet decided if it was in keeping with her taste.

Anyway, that was a problem for another day, and it was almost six thirty. Her father would be hopping mad if she wasn't there on time to make a grand entrance at the Rotary Club annual charity bash, especially seeing as her mother had taken off to Kinsale on a golf trip with her sisters. Why her father couldn't just give whatever money he had in mind to these people she could never fathom. Why did he have to make a big palaver out of it every year, when everyone knew that he was the biggest contributor anyway? Still, Charlie would be there at the Coltons' table – her father liked to give an impression that he was a man who ran a close-knit business empire, a man who had not forgotten his roots, and who was happy to spend a night out in the company of his employees, albeit the senior ones who showed signs of going places.

Linda rummaged through a vast array of scents before finally alighting on a suitable accompaniment for her simple yet stunning ensemble. *Allure* by Madame Chanel. Warm and seductive. Not so popular as to be called common, yet popular enough to be called a classic. Perfect.

She swiftly descended the stairs, her heels sinking into the lush softness of the deep-pile Navan carpet. Most people had overshot the runway when it came to the latest trends in floor coverings. As soon as the whole Americanised notion of timber flooring had hit Ireland, everyone immediately ripped out carpets as if they were infected with bubonic plague. They then proceeded to replace them with all manner of wood, from solid maple for the more discerning, to the most dubious of laminates that click-locked into place like Lego blocks.

Not Linda, however, who maintained that the impact of a pure wool carpet in the right setting should never be underestimated, and who had carefully selected and ordered each individual piece to enhance the area in which it was finally installed. Of course there was a price to pay for the benefits of having good taste. The stair-runner that she commissioned to blend in seamlessly with the deep richness of *Tír na nÓg* from the new Dulux Heritage range had taken four months to materialise, during which time she'd had to clatter up and down what was to her a hideously naked stairs. Nonetheless, it was in place now, to her immense satisfaction.

She slammed the door behind her and zapped the remote central locking on the MG. The car always reminded her of who and what she really was: a female version of the strikingly handsome bachelor types that normally bought such vehicles. Last year, before buying the MG, Linda had carefully researched the image projected by different cars, and the type of lifestyle that their owners led. Linda's brand of research consisted of intense observation of the men and women in her own circle of acquaintance who could afford the kind of car that she would at least consider. Anything with more than two doors gave the impression that the owner might one day consider needing space for a buggy. Indeed, anything with a back seat left wide open the possibility of a baby car-seat. So these categories were immediately excluded. Anything remotely practical was also scuppered very early on. Linda liked to give the impression that she was a girl who could afford not to worry about practicalities.

Then there had been the question of colour. Yes, black, navy and Racing Green were classy. However, Linda felt that this was a given in her case and that she no longer needed to prove it. Red, of course, typified all that was overt and sexually confident, so red it was. What she really wanted to say was that here was a single lady who enjoyed her status and did not need a husband to either keep her or make her feel secure. She had all of these things anyway, and while her man was undoubtedly a useful and indeed fun appendage, he was certainly not a necessity.

The tyres crunched on the gravel as Linda reversed out through the squat limestone piers that stood at the entrance of her property. Gravel was the only job for a driveway in Linda's book. As with the whole wooden floor thing, the country had gone bananas over "cobble-lock" driveways, an alternative to the maintenance of a gravel driveway, yet a step above the "car-park" look of tarmac. As far as Linda was concerned, nothing could match the swish of gravel under the tyres, and so what if it necessitated hiring someone once a year for its upkeep?

She loved the way the still blue of Cork Harbour unfolded before her as she approached the automatic gates that guarded the four houses from the outside world. Admiring the panoramic view as she moved forward and the gates opened silently, she started violently and had to brake hard to avoid the navy Volvo that suddenly careered out of the next driveway, practically cutting her off at the exit.

"Stupid bloody idiot!" Linda yelled, her ice-blue eyes glinting with irritation.

The driver looked as if he hadn't even seen the MG. Where did he think he was living? Mondello bloody Park by the way he was carrying on! Well, she'd soon let him know that this kind of racket was not acceptable in a setting like this. Anyway, enough of that until she saw him again; the Rotary Club gents were plenty to deal with for tonight.

2

Evergreen

Amy Harkin wondered what the night would bring as she boarded the lift for the third floor. On night duty, the first night was always an omen for the following six. Start on a hectic note and it generally got even more hectic. At least Kim and Noreen were on with her, particularly as it was her first stint of night duty since she'd been promoted to Clinical Nurse Manager earlier in the month. Both of her colleagues were highly professional with years of experience between them and would be excellent in terms of back-up and assistance in the event of an emergency.

The door of the Neonatal Unit was propped open as Amy emerged from the lift, a bad sign if ever there was one. The door was usually locked and monitored from the inside, primarily to regulate the number of people entering the unit, for infection-control purposes. Of late, the threat of newborn abduction had become an equally valid reason for monitoring those admitted. Tonight, however, the open door suggested the imminent arrival of an ill baby, possibly premature, where speed was of the essence and a valuable component in the jigsaw that made up the eventual discharge of a live healthy infant.

Inside, the place was a hive of activity. Amy entered the Intensive Care Unit, where Sheila Forde, the day-shift CNM, was putting the finishing touches to the "landing pad", the preheated open incubator that would receive the expected infant.

"Will I take report on the rest of them or will I stay put in here?" Amy enquired. Under normal circumstances, each member of the day staff would sit down with their night-time counterparts to get a full report of the status of all the babies. Tonight, Amy imagined that they mightn't have the luxury of such a time-consuming exercise if there was a sick baby expected imminently.

"You may as well stay here. There's a twenty-eight-weeker on the way so it looks like you'll be tied up in here all night. Kim and Noreen will manage the little gang in the cubicles. Five growing prems, two jaundiced on 'lights' and three new ones from the post-natal ward." Sheila reeled off the list as she expertly ran normal saline through an IV line attached to a regulation pump. "They're all fairly well," she concluded, giving Amy a thumbnail sketch of the situation so that she could make her decisions on where to place Kim and Noreen for the duration of the shift.

"OK then," said Amy, "I'll take over here and let you start filling Noreen and Kim in on the others. See you in the morning."

Amy's heart rate quickened in anticipation of the challenge to come. Starting from scratch, her brown eyes flickered between pumps and monitors as she rechecked all the equipment that Sheila had assembled – overhead heater set at the correct temperature, resuscitation gear in working order and placed within hand's reach, leads for cardiac and temperature monitoring ready to place on the infant's chest at the moment of arrival.

Finally, she placed a soft Winnie the Pooh cot sheet on the radiator, to be placed on the weighing scales before the infant was weighed. The risks of dropping a premature infant's temperature were manifold – even the cool plastic surface of the scales would be enough to significantly contribute to hypothermia. However, weighing the infant would be essential to care over the next few weeks, as all medications and fluid intake would be calculated in relation to the baby's weight. Amy worked silently, mentally anticipating the needs of an infant that would be twelve weeks early coming into the world.

With the baby's new home now in order, Amy started on the paperwork preparation. With the level of care that would be needed over the coming days and weeks, documentation of almost every moment of the infant's life would be essential so that nothing was either missed or duplicated.

The rabble of voices in the hallway heralded the arrival of the transport incubator, the heated "mobile home" that ferried ill babies from Labour Ward to Neonatal Unit. A team of Labour Ward staff and paediatricians swarmed in its wake, followed by a bewildered- looking man, presumably the baby's dad.

"Alex Fleming, spontaneous delivery at twenty-eight weeks gestation, no steroids given," was the succinct introduction doled out by Jane Winters for Amy's benefit.

Jane was a seasoned midwife, her eye-sockets ravaged by black rings from decades of night duty and too many cigarettes. She was known by everyone for the fact that she'd actually delivered some of the hospital's younger staff members in her thirty-year career and was fond of saying that she couldn't possibly take any nonsense from young scuts whose bottoms she'd slapped as they were brought into the world.

Amy placed the warmed sheet over the scales, taking care to recalibrate to account for the weight of the sheet, as the door of the transport incubator opened to reveal the red-raw, wizened little creature, skinny limbs outstretched, ribs protruding like a famine victim.

"OK, chicken, out you come," Jane whispered as she lifted little Alex out of the incubator and onto the scales. "1 kilo on the button – that's 2 pounds, 2 ounces to you, Dad. Not bad at twenty-eight weeks. Amy, this is Marcus Fleming, Alex's dad. Alex's mum is still in the labour ward."

Amy smiled a welcome to Marcus. "I'm Amy and I'll be looking after Alex tonight. We'll get him settled and I'll explain everything to you."

Marcus looked terrified and Amy was quick to reassure him.

"All the equipment looks very frightening, but once you know what everything's for, it won't be so daunting." Amy settled Alex onto the open-table incubator with the radiant heater glaring above it. "If you don't mind, I'd like you to wait next door in the parents' room and I'll call you in about half an hour."

Twenty-five minutes later Amy went in search of Marcus to explain exactly what was happening with his new son and to bring him back into the ICU for a proper introduction.

"Is he alright?" Marcus's concern was evident the moment she opened the door. He was tall and thin, with wavy brown hair sticking out at all sorts of angles, as if he'd been running his fingers through it with anxiety.

Amy had seen this look before and was quick to reassure him. "Absolutely fine at the moment." She sat down in one of the reclining chairs provided to make the breast-feeding mothers more comfortable. "I'll start at the beginning and explain everything before we go back in."

Marcus nodded mutely, so Amy continued as gently and as clearly as she could.

"Because Alex is so early coming into the world, he

13

has almost no body fat to keep him warm. He'll need us to provide heat for him until he gets a bit bigger in size. At the moment, we'll care for him on a small open cot with a radiator above it – this is because he will need constant attention. Later we'll move him into the usual covered incubator. Some of the time we'll use clingfilm or bubble wrap to keep the heat in, so don't get a fright if you see him covered up," Amy smiled. "His other main difficulty is that his lungs are not mature enough for him to breathe on his own. Because of this we've placed a tube into his lungs to help him, with oxygen flowing through it. He'll have this until his lungs mature a little more – this can take from about forty-eight hours, up to a week or more. We've also given him some medication through the tube to speed up the process. Alex will be fed by a drip for the next few days until he stabilises because his bowel can't tolerate food just yet. They're the main things for the moment. There will be a nurse with Alex all the time so don't be afraid to ask plenty of questions. Now come on and get a proper look at him, and we'll take some Polaroids for his mum."

"Oh God, he's tiny!" Marcus exclaimed when he caught sight of Alex through the web of wires. "Will he live? Is he not too small to survive?"

"Believe it or not, babies as early as twenty-four weeks can survive nowadays. That's not to say that this will be an easy ride for him. It won't. There are complications that he could encounter, but our job is to anticipate them and head them off at the pass. We'll always tell you everything as it comes, and what *you* want will be important in any decisions. You can touch him if you like, and talk to him. He'll know your voice – he's been listening to it for the past twenty-eight weeks, remember!"

"Will he be alright eventually, I mean, will he get brain-damage from being born this early?" Marcus hated to ask and was terrified of hearing the answer but he needed to know the worst.

"If everything proceeds as we expect it to, I would hope not. The first forty-eight hours are crucial. Because the blood-vessels in the brain are immature, some premature babies suffer bleeding in the brain. We'll be keeping him as still as possible initially to prevent this – which is one of the reasons that you won't be able to hold him for a while. He'll be having a brain scan in the morning as soon as the X-Ray department opens. I know it sounds frightening but it's all part of the care that any premature infant would get."

"When will Deirdre be able to see him? Will we be able to hold him?" Marcus asked anxiously, only mildly reassured about the fact that Alex would need a scan to check that he didn't have a brain haemorrhage.

"As soon as Deirdre's epidural has worn off, the ward midwives will bring her up in a wheelchair. Unfortunately, you won't be able to hold him for quite a while but you can both spend as much time here in the unit as you want. Don't ever feel that you're in the way. Alex needs his parents as much as he needs us. So be here as often as it's feasible for you both."

Gently Amy folded down the Perspex sides of the open incubator.

"Now, hold Alex's hand for a moment so I can get a good photo."

Marcus could feel the heat radiating off the overhead heater as he crouched over his son and tenderly enfolded Alex's tiny hand in his own. The delicate skin was pale and waxy-looking and a frisson of terror coursed through Marcus. The camera flashed and he hoped that it hadn't captured the fear he felt at that moment.

"There you go!" Amy smiled as she offered Marcus the two photos. "One for you and one for Mum."

Poor Alex looked more wan than ever in the over-exposed snapshots and it occurred to Marcus that for Deirdre seeing their baby like this would be more frightening than seeing him in the flesh. Amy, watching him study the photos, seemed to understand how shockingly small Alex appeared and commented that the sooner Deirdre was able to come up to the unit and see her son properly the better.

"It'll be less frightening for her once she knows what's going on," she reassured Marcus as she flicked through a red plastic folder bearing Alex's name that already seemed to have a large number of pages in it. "Now, before you go down to Deirdre, I'd like to recheck all your details. With ten babies under our roof we can't afford to make mistakes! You're living in Coppingerstown, I see."

"Yes, Pebble Cove. Seefin is the house name."

"Really?" Amy's face lit up. "Well, you may have a new neighbour soon! I'm in the process of buying the last house there. All going well, I hope to be moving in over the next few weeks!"

"That's marvellous. We were wondering who was going to get the last one." Marcus sounded genuinely pleased. "What are you going to call yours? We thought it was a bit of a nuisance at first, having to name the houses first thing, but it's actually nice to have a name that means something rather than a number."

"I was thinking of 'Evergreen'. My grandmother lived in Evergreen Road in the city in a little terraced house. I always loved it there – I even lived with her during my training. She died last year, but she'd have been thrilled if she knew I gave the house that name. How did you come up with Seefin?"

"Deirdre's mother was born in West Cork," Marcus explained. "There's a mountain near her home and legend has it that Fionn Mac Cumhaill used to sit there looking out to sea. It's called *Suí Finn* in Irish – the seat of Fionn. 'Seefin' is the anglicised version so we're using that – easier on the postman."

"That's lovely," Amy smiled in understanding before running through all the other particulars that would go on Alex's chart.

"Well, Marcus, you can head off to the ward now and fill Deirdre in on everything. The consultant will be on rounds tomorrow, so he'll be able to see you at about two o'clock. The house doctor, Dr Ali, will be here overnight if we need anything. Alex is very stable, but if anything changes in the meantime, we'll ring you on the mobile, OK?"

"Do and I'll come straight in. It's only twenty minutes – so ring me if there's any change at all."

"I will."

"Bye for now, little fella," Marcus whispered to Alex as he left.

Amy turned her attention to Alex. He was really holding his own, despite the fact that his mother hadn't had time for any steroid injections before the delivery to help mature the lungs rapidly. Deirdre had delivered fairly quickly on arrival at the hospital, not an ideal situation in terms of Alex's progress.

Amy finished updating her notes and then went in search of tea and company. She'd barely poked her head out of the ICU, and it was almost midnight.

Kim and Noreen obviously had the same idea. They were just emerging from the tiny kitchen laden with tea and toast, the night-duty staple. The early feeds were done on the less ill babies and all cubicles were stocked with enough gear to last the night. Amy settled into one of the rocking chairs normally reserved for the mothers who, despite haemorrhoids, stitches and sore breasts, sat most of the day in the unit watching the progress of their little ones.

Because Amy was the senior nurse in the unit, Kim and Noreen started to fill her in on all the details of the other babies. Then, munching on her third slice of toast, Amy made them both familiar with Alex's condition. Now, in the event of another, more ill infant arriving in the unit, any one of them would be prepared to take over the care of any baby.

Amy smiled to herself as she rose from the desk ten minutes later and made her way back to the Intensive Care section to start the next round of observations on the new arrival – did people really believe that nurses slept on night duty?

3

Seefin

Deirdre struggled to move her legs but they felt as heavy as tree trunks. The midwife had told her not even to attempt getting out of bed. She'd also told her that as soon as the numbness of the epidural wore off, she would personally put her in a wheelchair and bring her upstairs to see little Alex. Meantime, she was to rest and recover from the traumatic journey she'd endured and the shock of going into labour so early.

"Easier said than done," Deirdre had informed her wistfully, still visualising the scrunched-up red face that had been held up for her inspection before being swooped away in the incubator. She wondered why Marcus was gone for so long. Did it mean that Alex was worse than she'd been told? Surely not? She trusted Marcus to come and tell her if things were really bad. He'd know that she'd want them to be together if Alex wasn't going to live. God, she couldn't bear that, now that she'd seen him. The little face was imprinted on her mind in a way that would be there forever. Tears sprang to her eyes at the thought of losing him, and she scrunched them closed to try and will him to live.

What had happened to make her go into labour so early? She thought back through the day, trying to pick out anything that might have later triggered the sudden flush of warm fluid that started as a trickle and then became a huge flood that drenched her thighs and made a large dark stain on the pale Axminster carpet. She'd been kneeling in front of the fireplace when it happened, arranging a collection of dried flowers, fir cones and candles in the empty grate. Afraid to stand up, she'd started to call out for Marcus when the first contraction had gripped her.

The midwife in the Labour Ward had kept telling her that she hadn't done anything wrong, and that very occasionally labour started early without any external trigger whatsoever. But Deirdre kept thinking that maybe she had overdone it in some way and the exertion had been too much.

Maybe it was the way she'd been stretching from left to right to pick the best of the flowers from the pile on the floor, leaning in towards the fireplace to get each piece just right. No excessive exertion, that's what all the books had said. And yet she had reached up to the top shelf in one of the kitchen presses earlier to get a jar of black olives for Marcus's favourite pasta dish. What good are olives and flower arrangements to me now, she berated herself, when Alex is fighting for his little life?

"Are you awake, Dee?" she heard Marcus whisper from the doorway.

She immediately burst into tears with the stress of it all.

"He's OK, Dee, he's alright. Sorry I was so long but I had to wait while they got him sorted out. Here, look at these, I've got some photos. They said he's stable at the moment, and that it's all about giving him time now."

"Oh God, he's so small! What are all the wires for? Why has he got a hat on? What's that in his mouth? He looks desperate." Deirdre was shocked at the appearance of her baby – he didn't look at all like she remembered him.

"Look, Dee, I'll explain what everything's for. That's why I was so long. The nurse looking after him – Amy's her name – wanted me to know everything so I could tell you before you go up. Most of the wires are for monitoring Alex's heart rate and oxygen levels. They're only stuck onto his skin. See that one there, with the shiny patch. That picks up his temperature so they know how much to turn up or down the heat on the incubator." Marcus struggled to remember it all. "The tube in his mouth is the most important one. That's helping him to breathe while his lungs mature. They'll explain everything again to you in the morning. The reason they have him out on this open incubator is because he'll need so much attention over the next few days. When he gets a bit better, they'll put him into an ordinary incubator. The nurse said not to worry if he's

23

covered in bubble wrap when we go up in the morning. It'll be to stop him getting dehydrated and to keep the heat in."

Marcus was doing his best to explain things with as little drama as possible but, if anything, Deirdre was looking more worried than ever.

"Will he be brain-damaged?" Deirdre asked tentatively, afraid of the answer but needing to know.

"I asked the nurse that and she said that Alex would be having a brain scan in the morning. They said it's routine, but because the blood vessels in the brain are so delicate they can sometimes bleed and cause brain haemorrhages. The nurse, Amy, said that we'll have to treat him very gently for the first few weeks to avoid that, so we won't be able to hold him for a while. He'll hardly be moved at all, only to fix him up every few hours. The quieter he's kept the better, she said."

Marcus knew that it all sounded ominous but, like himself, Deirdre always needed to know the full story, then she could deal with it.

"I wish this bloody epidural would wear off. I'd just love to see him and let him know we're there. What if he wakes up and we're not there?" Deirdre couldn't bear the thought of Alex being alone in a strange place.

"It's OK. He can't wake up for the moment. They've given him sedation to keep him relaxed. We can't do anything now only wait. Look, I'll lie down beside you for a while and we'll go up together when your legs are ready."

Deirdre inched over to make room for Marcus's

lanky frame, and he settled himself onto the edge of the narrow hospital bed, curled into her back. For a second it was as if they were at home in Pebble Cove in the big mahogany sleigh-bed, still awaiting the birth of their baby. They'd spent so many nights lying there together, planning their future as a family. Deirdre closed her eyes to shut out the fear that squeezed around her heart. Almost as if he'd felt her terror, Marcus's arms tightened around her in the darkness, and they settled in to wait.

* * *

Deirdre woke with a start, shocked that she'd actually fallen asleep at all. A shaft of pale light filtered through the slit in the curtains as she slowly slid her arm from under the blankets to look at her watch. Six o'clock. She tried to move her legs but they still felt as if they didn't belong to her. The left one shifted a little with great effort, the soles of her feet tingling. Frustrated, she closed her eyes and tried to pray for Alex. Pictures of the journey to the hospital kept flashing into her mind, blocking out her pleas that her baby would live until she was able to talk to him and let him know how much he was loved already.

Everything had been going perfectly. She'd been feeling great from the beginning. No morning sickness even. Her sister Hazel, a hairdresser, kept saying that she'd never seen Deirdre's hair in such good condition, her glossy chestnut bob gleaming with health. She'd been full of energy all along and had no reason to believe that anything would go wrong.

Even though they hadn't actually brought anything home, she and Marcus had spent hours in Babyfare picking out the furniture for the baby's nursery. They'd painted the room lavender so that it'd suit either a boy or a girl. Ava or Alex; whichever they were blessed with. Everything was just right for their baby to be born into.

Deirdre knew they were lucky to have been able to plan for a baby at a time when everything was secure in their lives. Attending the GP's surgery for her regular check-ups had been an eye-opener for her. Many of the women that she met there were on their fourth or fifth pregnancy and occasionally referred to the event as "getting caught again". Deirdre often wondered if the toddlers that played around their feet would absorb the fact that some of the pregnancies were clearly unplanned, an unfortunate accident that would inevitably incur extra costs that the household budget would struggle to meet. Deirdre sometimes asked herself if she read too much into the whole concept of being financially prepared for bringing a baby into the world. She'd been chatting to one of the younger girls in the waiting room in the early stages and had been shocked to hear her say that she'd "planned" her pregnancy in order to get a council flat.

"You'd be on the housing list forever otherwise. Me da can't stick me fella so I'll have to get a place of me own sometime."

Deirdre had been sorry for her, a pretty young teenager, sorry that she'd had to resort to such tactics before she was really ready for motherhood and sorry also for her expected baby who might not have the chances in life that her own baby could look forward to.

Marcus agreed with her that maybe they *did* set a lot of store by being ready for things, probably because they were dealing with other people's money all day long and could see the consequences of debt and the stress of overstretching and borrowing. Even though she now worked in Asset Management, away from the run-of-the-mill dealings with personal finance, Deirdre had never forgotten her days on the front desk in a small branch in West Cork.

At that time, Unified Bank had a policy of putting all members of the Graduate Entry System through all aspects of banking before they chose the area in which they would ultimately specialise. Deirdre, fresh from college with a BCom under her belt, felt that she would be well equipped for whatever she had to deal with in a small country branch.

Nothing could have prepared her for the young couples that begged for a few months' leeway before their houses were repossessed, or those people who were suddenly broke as a result of the closure of a factory where both partners were employed. Even the elderly people who found themselves penniless and alone, having handed over their farms to their children on the premise that they would be "looked after" when the time came. The three-month stint had bred in

27

Deirdre a strong sense of the need to be financially secure. This was something that Marcus too had developed from working at ground level with people whose lives could be shockingly altered by a failure to plan for the future.

It occurred to Deirdre now as she lay in her hospital bed with Marcus breathing softly beside her that all their forward planning hadn't done much good. They'd made some fairly good investments over the years, both their pensions were in order and their mortgage was small enough to be of no real stress to them, yet here they were with their plans askew and their future uncertain.

She felt frighteningly out of control, scared for Alex and terrified about her own ability to cope. What if she wasn't able to manage the breastfeeding? The nurse had explained to Marcus that it was important for a baby as premature as Alex to get the benefit of all the immunity that breast milk could offer. She hadn't managed to hold on to Alex for the full pregnancy. What if she couldn't feed him either? Tears coursed silently down her face, wetting the pillow. She felt Marcus stirring beside her and tried to hold back the tears. Breaking down was no use when Alex needed her.

"It'll be alright, Dee – we'll just have to take every day as it comes."

Marcus stroked her hair back from her face as he often did and the gesture somehow comforted her. Alex *would* be alright, she vowed, knowing that he'd be the centre of their lives, whatever happened.

4

Evergreen

"The birds are singing and it's only quarter past five."

Kim announced this with glee, causing Amy and Noreen to look up from their respective charts in surprise. Surely it couldn't be that time already? Hearing the first early-morning twitters in the ancient beech trees that surrounded the maternity wing of the hospital was always a signal that the night was drawing to a close.

"I'd better make a shape and get Alex's bloods done," said Amy.

She signed her name on the last of the charts and started to pick out a selection of minuscule blood bottles from the array displayed in the ICU. The night porter would arrive at six to collect the samples and transport them to the laboratory and would have a fit if they weren't ready and labelled for their trip to the basement. Nothing short of a bomb-scare was a good enough excuse for Joe missing his morning tea; even the arrival of a set of triplets at half past five was considered a poor defence for holding him up.

Amy raised the blinds a little and allowed streaks of the orange dawn to steal into the unit as she carefully opened one of the IV lines that had been threaded into the infant's umbilical cord earlier. Drops of blood plopped slowly into one of the tiny bottles that she held beneath it. Once three of the bottles had been filled, Amy slowly flushed the line with sterile water to prevent clots forming, before closing the line off.

Alex was stirring a little, she noted. Soon it would be time for his 6 a.m. drugs: antibiotics to prevent infection and a Valium derivative to keep him relaxed so that he wouldn't fight against the breathing tube in his throat and dislodge it.

It was almost six by the time she had the blood samples labelled and packed, with minutes to spare before Joe thundered through the double doors.

"Three in labour, one of them shouldn't be too long," was his greeting. "She was screeching her head off before she was even admitted!"

Oblivious of Amy's frown of reproach at his lack of decorum, Joe continued with his story. He was a state of high excitement, anticipating the work to be done before his shift ended, planning the transport of a mother and baby to the ward on a trolley.

By dint of manning the front desk of the maternity unit at night for almost thirty years, Joe considered himself to be something of an expert on the severity and duration of labour. Despite being a bachelor of indeterminate age, he was convinced that his expertise had more foundation than that of most of the midwives, particularly the newly trained ones whose qualifications he disparaged at every opportunity.

"There you are, Joe," Kim placated him, handing him the collection of plastic biohazard bags.

"You won't be so easygoing when you're landed with a premature one before the morning's out," he admonished.

Kim tried to look suitably chastened as Amy and Noreen smirked from behind the raised lid of the drugs trolley.

"One of the women had a very small bump," he added astutely, leaving as swiftly as he'd arrived, no doubt to spread the news of the influx to the remainder of the hospital.

"Good God, Matron Sloane has nothing on him!" Amy giggled, referring to the stern matron in one of the Australian soaps.

Noreen, who'd been working in the hospital for almost ten years, had often told them the story of how the present Director of Nursing and the Hospital Manager had tried to instil in Joe the idea of professionalism. Calling him to a meeting to discuss his less than discreet working ethos, they'd been stunned to find themselves "dismissed" by Joe after a few minutes.

"You're very new, the two of you," he'd told them. "Once you get the run of the place you'll be grand. I have my own way of doing things, you see. Now I'll have to go – I have three coming in for sections this morning."

Over the years, they'd made several attempts to knock Joe into shape, to no avail it had to be said. However, his reliability and trustworthiness more than made up for his loud, though harmless, personality so it seemed he would work out the remainder of his days "running" the maternity unit.

"Some fine day he'll get it right and a set of quads will walk in the door," Amy laughed, making her way back in to Alex.

Joe's dire predictions rarely, if ever, materialised. However, the gossip he created by simply getting things wrong kept the hospital in fresh news constantly. His most recent escapade involved seeing Mary Watson, one of the senior midwives, leaving the office of the Director of Nursing and presuming, from the way that Mrs Kelly was shaking her hand and congratulating her, that she was pregnant. It had taken Mary Watson two weeks of intense explanations to reassure everyone that she was very much non-pregnant but that she *had* been promoted to unit manager in the Labour Ward. Highly offended at the idea that people thought she was pregnant, she had immediately joined Weight Watchers and shed a stone in a matter of weeks.

The three nurses barely noticed the rest of the shift slipping away as they recounted Joe's myriad blunders and went about their last-minute duties with the infants in their care. It was almost half seven when they finally declared it a night.

"God, I look like death warmed up!" Amy wailed, catching sight of herself in the mirror over one of the sinks. Her face was pale, highlighting the dark circles under her eyes, and several blonde tendrils escaped from what had been a tidy knot at the nape of her neck twelve hours earlier. Normally, it fell to her shoulders in layers but was impossible to work with unless it was tied up. Producing a small make-up bag from her handbag, she started to do a repair job.

"This has to be the worst bit about night duty," Noreen complained. "It's all grand until the sun rises and the blinds are pulled up – then you're like something out of the 'Thriller' video."

Kim, pulling a brush through her unruly curls, grinned over at Amy who was attempting to reinstate her hairdo to its former glory. "Going to the library again this morning, are you?"

Blushing, Amy reminded her that she had an assignment to complete by the following Friday. In the second year of a Master's degree in Health Services Management, she was determined to maintain her grades in the face of a profusion of night duty. The hospital medical library was invaluable to her in terms of locating journal articles and textbooks. "I've a few things to photocopy but I won't be long. Peter said he'd have them ready for me."

"Did he now? How come he was never this helpful when I was doing the HDip?"

"Funny that," Noreen teased, having been filled in on the situation overnight by the irrepressible Kim. "I was in the library night, noon and morning when I was doing the Lactation Consultant course and there wasn't so much as a peep out of him. It's amazing the way people come out of themselves."

"Do you think there'll be any progress?" Kim was always interested in the state of people's love life and considered herself a sort of guru in terms of advice and information.

"Don't get carried away just yet." Amy was anxious that her colleague wouldn't lose the run of herself totally. "One dinner and you're practically expecting an engagement ring!"

"What about the Easter Ball? Are we not counting that?" Noreen, married to Ger for the past twelve years and the mother of three rowdy boys, was determined to get to the bottom of the budding romance between Amy and the handsome librarian.

"No, we're not," Amy countered obstinately. "That was more of a 'get to know you' thing. I was only sitting beside him by chance."

"So what's the story now?" Kim persisted.

"Well, Saturday night went well and we've arranged to go out next weekend as well, so we'll just have to see how it goes."

"But is there a spark?" Noreen wanted to know whether the relationship was looking likely before she got too excited.

"He's really nice, actually. The Mill Race was ready

to close and we were still chatting away."

"That's always a good sign," Noreen commented approvingly.

Amy declined to tell the girls that Peter Deasy had walked her back to the apartment she rented in Gilabbey Street and that they'd opened another bottle of wine. Although he hadn't stayed the night, she was sure that he had wanted to and she suppressed a smile at the memory of his fingers caressing her feet as they rested in his lap while they sipped from the heavy John Rocha glasses and laughed into the early hours.

"Plus you'll have a handy research assistant for your thesis and probably free photocopying thrown in as a bonus," Kim grinned, thrilled that the whole thing was falling into place so neatly.

Her own love life was somewhat erratic in nature, with a succession of men masquerading as "the real thing". She herself had spotted Peter in the library block long before Amy had but, despite several valiant attempts, she hadn't been able to secure a date. Never one to bear a grudge, Kim was only delighted that *somebody* was benefiting from his athletic physique and shy brown eyes. No point in having him go to waste, she'd advised Amy pragmatically when she'd spotted them engrossed in conversation at the hospital's annual Easter Ball earlier that month.

"There's more to it than free photocopying," Noreen teased with a knowing grin, having noticed the brief smile that had crossed Amy's face. She tucked her lipstick and hairbrush back into her handbag as voices in the corridor indicated the arrival of the day staff. "Now, you give the report on Alex first and get off to the library," she instructed. "We'll fill them in on the rest of the babies when you're gone."

"Thanks, Noreen. I've a load of stuff to look up on problem-solving and leadership."

"You're welcome," Noreen grinned. "Anything to further your love life!"

5

Number 1

Linda knelt over Charlie and slowly trailed her nipples up and down his chest. She loved the roughness as they brushed over the wiry hair. Charlie pulled her closer and softly bit into the hollow of her shoulder, raising his hips to enter her. Stubble grazed the front of her throat and Linda heard herself moan involuntarily. She held herself away a little, above him but barely touching him, pulling away and then lowering her hips as Charlie rose to meet her, teasing him, each time a little farther, until she could feel him just inside her. Her breathing quickened as she heard Charlie groan and with one movement he grasped her hips and pulled her towards him. Linda gasped and gripped his hands, leaning back and quickening her pace, all sense of control forgotten until she felt Charlie shudder and pleasure flooded over her, throwing her forward onto his chest where she felt his arms tighten around her and her face rested on the damp hardness of his shoulder.

"Charlie?" Linda whispered a little later, when she heard his breathing return to normal.

"Mmmm . . ." was the reply but Linda knew Charlie was still awake and she wanted to talk to him about her idea. She'd been twisting it about in her head for weeks but she hadn't had time to talk to him about it until now.

"You know I was saying about getting bored with work?" she began. "Well, I've come up with something that I'd like to do."

"Go on," Charlie prompted, finally roused from post-coital repose.

"Ages ago Dad bought a couple of acres of development land out in Rochestown. It was only about three acres. I think at the time he was planning to put five or six high-spec detached houses on it. But it's inside the High Density Zone so all he'll get now as regards housing is planning permission for maybe twenty-five townhouses and semi-d's. He's going to just sit on it but I have a better plan."

"Does he know about this plan yet?" Charlie enquired, knowing that no matter how much Daniel Colton loved his only child he was a shrewd businessman who wouldn't give in to a whim if it meant the loss of even a square metre of prime land in one of Cork's wealthiest suburbs.

"Kind of," Linda ventured, looking warily at Charlie. "I told him that you and I had come up with a development plan for it. But that you were still working on it so he'd have to give us a bit of time to come up with the drawings and stuff."

"Right. What exactly am I supposed to be working on?" Charlie chided mildly but with a hint of real reproach that wasn't lost on Linda. "Just in case my boss asks me about my plans for land that I didn't even know existed."

Charlie could see that Linda knew exactly how to play her father. She knew that while Daniel would never agree to hand over valuable land to someone with no experience of building and development, he would however trust Charlie Moorehouse, senior architect with Coltons and the company's newest director, to come up with a viable proposition. Linda would get her way, albeit by the back door as it were.

"For ages now, I've been bored with running the leisure centre. It practically runs itself," Linda said, referring to the exclusive leisure centre that her father had acquired as part of a land deal the same year that Linda had finished school. It still amazed her that he'd allowed her to take on something so big with no experience. Her mother had objected strenuously at the time, insisting that Linda could make nothing of herself if she didn't at least have a degree.

Little did she know that it was her father's tenacious pride in the face of her mother's snobbish attitude that had actually made the decision, rather than any of her own wheedling and cajoling. This was the first time that Daniel had realised that while his wife liked all the things that his money could buy, there was still a sense that being rich as a result of years of hard graft in the construction industry wasn't quite the same as being the rich wife of a doctor or lawyer. He'd felt diminished somehow and it placed a distance in his relationship with Frances that hadn't been there before.

Obstinately determined to prove to his wife that success wasn't all about having a piece of paper to prove oneself, Daniel had given in to Linda's wish to run the leisure centre, but on the condition that she enrol in a part-time course in Sports and Leisure Management.

Linda was oblivious to her father's real reasons for letting her manage Bodywork. She had got her way by wheedling many times before and as far as she was concerned this was no different. As it transpired, she had a flair for knowing what people wanted and how to provide it. In spite of herself, she actually enjoyed the intensive evening course that her father insisted she enrol in. It was only when she started running into the everyday problems of running a business that she started to appreciate her father's wisdom, as well as his many achievements. Now, however, Linda felt she had taken Bodywork as far as it could go and she was ready for a new, much bigger challenge.

"But I want to stay in the business," Linda continued eagerly. "I was thinking about a leisure complex. It'd have to be somewhere like Rochestown where people would buy into a sort of exclusive club. As well as a leisure centre and pool we'd have different complementary therapies, a café and a restaurant.

Everything needn't be under the same roof. It could be a collection of buildings on a campus. People could pay a subscription for the use of all the facilities, or they could just subscribe to a smaller package like gym and pool, pool only or therapies only. You could design the complex, I'd market it and run it. I know Dad will like it once he sees the full thing on paper. We could go three ways on it." Linda's face was shining with the excitement of what Charlie had to admit was a great idea.

The only thing that bothered him was her presumption of shared ownership. Surely she must realise that, despite the fairly serious salary that Daniel Colton paid him, he didn't have the means to get involved in such a development at that level.

"Linda, I think this is a seriously great idea. Planning permission shouldn't be a problem because there aren't enough amenities in the area as it is. Once the Carter development goes up in Douglas the place will be overloaded in terms of population, with a deficit in services. It could be sold to the planners as a means of pacifying any residents objecting to development on the grounds that the area doesn't have the level of services needed to absorb more housing."

"Do you think Dad will go for it?" Linda asked, secretly pleased that Charlie was so impressed with the project.

"I'd say he'll have no problem with it, once the design is good. He knows you can run it easily if you get someone in to manage Bodywork. The only problem is my part in all this. I can do the design alright if it's done as a Coltons job. But if you're thinking of setting up a separate company, you need to know now that I don't have that kind of money."

Charlie knew that he needed to be straight about this now. Linda didn't really think about money, didn't have to. As the sole beneficiary of all her father worked for, she'd eventually be pretty wealthy. The leisure centre had been placed in her name once it had started turning over a profit. If her father agreed to her plans, he'd probably put up Linda's share of the investment, possibly with some stipulations so as not to be seen to give in too easily. Like her having to do the management course when she took over Bodywork first.

"I thought you'd say that," Linda rejoined bluntly. "I don't have it either – well, not as such," she conceded, knowing that her position was altogether different from Charlie's. "But, I thought we could sit down with Dad and work something out. Maybe your fees in lieu of part of the investment, as well as overseeing some of the development. I'd probably sort something out in lieu of the actual day-to-day running of the place. But you'd be up for it if we could get around the financial stuff?"

Linda had seen the kind of work that Charlie had done since coming to work with Coltons four years ago, the kind of stuff that had taken the company on to another level, allowing them to command prices way in excess of what would previously have been considered high in housing development terms. Linda knew he would make a serious job of a challenge on this scale.

Linda had pre-empted any misgivings her father might have. She knew her father wouldn't hand this to her on a plate. She also knew that Charlie's involvement in this would guarantee almost automatic approval. Daniel trusted Charlie's opinion on most things and in Linda's heart of hearts she knew her father had hopes that he'd one day be his son-in-law. Linda hadn't thought about this too much, preferring to forge ahead with her own plans. If her father's expectations of her relationship with Charlie removed some obstacles from her way then so be it. At the end of the day, Linda knew this project to be a viable one. It was just a matter of getting it up and running.

6

Leadington

Shay Deegan couldn't get over the sight of the normally sensible-looking banker rolling out of his car at 9 a.m., looking like something the cat had resurrected. Usually it was the reverse, with Marcus shaking his head at Shay in a "been there, done that, definitely don't want to go there again" sort of way. This morning Marcus looked shattered, like he was coming down off something. Surely he wouldn't have done "E" or something? Shay approached his neighbour, more out of curiosity than concern.

"Jesus, man, you look rough. Were you up all night?" Shay enquired jovially. "I didn't have you down for a clubber!" He regretted his bonhomie immediately as Marcus's face crumbled.

"I'm coming from the hospital. Deirdre went into labour last night, twelve weeks early," Marcus informed him, tears springing to his eyes at the thought of having left Deirdre and Alex behind. "We have a little boy."

Earlier, Sheila Forde, Alex's nurse for the day, had advised Marcus to be sensible and go home to rest. Things were stable at the moment but Marcus could be called at any time. He'd be no support to either Deirdre or Alex if he was wrecked out of his brains. Marcus had to admit that she was right, and left reluctantly. But now he didn't want to be alone in the house without Dee.

"How did that happen? Are they alright? What size is the baby?" Shay had sat through plenty of girly films where tiny rat-like creatures clung to life in incubators, and felt that he had some knowledge of the situation.

"Deirdre's fine," Marcus told him. "Alex, the baby, is fine too. He's about two pounds in weight. He'll be there for a few months – as long as he gets over the next couple of days."

"Look, Marcus, why don't you come in and have a bit of breakfast?" Shay offered, not knowing what else to do but sensing that Marcus needed a chat. "You must be nearly dead. Did you have anything to eat all night?"

"What about work? Were you not on your way out?"

"Don't mind that. I have a meeting in Douglas at ten. I'll phone at quarter to and tell them I'm stuck in the tunnel."

Shay was referring to the Jack Lynch Tunnel that ran under the Lee, designed to ease the morning traffic chaos going into Cork city. However, massive increases in housing development on the east side of the city in recent years had led to serious congestion at the mouth of the tunnel every morning.

Shay sounded as if he'd used this excuse before but Marcus was beyond caring. He could do with a bit of company to take his mind off things this morning and maybe then he'd settle down enough to actually close his eyes. The way he was now, he couldn't imagine himself sleeping.

"OK so, if you're sure. I'll just run in and put on the heating and I'll be out in a minute," said Marcus, darting off towards his own house.

Shay opened his door again and punched off the alarm. So what about the meeting! Daniel Colton would hardly be aware that Shay would be late for their monthly update considering that he usually sent one of his minions to sort out the run-of-the-mill stuff these days.

Shay rummaged through the fridge, pulling out orange juice, sausages, rashers and black pudding. He'd actually been late this morning anyway, thanks to Carla, only arriving back in Pebble Cove in time to shower and shave for work. He'd missed his usual morning fry, so maybe meeting Marcus was God's way of leading him back to the right track, he comforted himself. He had the frying pan sizzling when Marcus arrived in, looking even more haggard than before. Shay passed him a glass of orange juice and waved him towards one of the leather-topped barstools at the breakfast bar.

47

"So, what happened? Why did Deirdre go into labour?" Shay was keen to have all the details for Carla, who he knew would be fascinated. Women always were.

While Marcus outlined the whole saga from the beginning, Shay expertly flipped eggs and microwaved baked beans, made toast and warmed plates. The morning-after fry-up was Shay's speciality, particularly on those mornings that he had some gorgeous girl curled up in the bedroom and he wanted her to stay the following night as well.

"Thanks, this looks great," Marcus said, breaking off from the story of Deirdre and Alex to tuck into a rasher.

"Will he be able to take bottles yet?" Shay asked, himself fascinated with the situation.

"Not for ages yet. He's on a drip at the moment but they said they might start feeding him over the next few days. They've asked Deirdre if she'd express some breast milk so that they can give it later through a tube down his nose. Imagine – he doesn't even have a sucking reflex yet! Jesus, I can't believe I have this amount of information already. I thought we had loads of time to think about all these things. Deirdre's not even on maternity leave yet. I suppose I'd better ring work and let them know we won't be back for a while." Marcus still couldn't credit how all this had happened so quickly.

Shay looked around his orderly, well-equipped kitchen with its granite worktop and stainless steel fittings and thought how far removed Marcus's life was from his own right now.

His mother had advised him to go ahead and buy the house before prices rose any further. In reality, she thought he was wasting enough money on socialising, with nothing to show for a fairly decent salary except a trendy wardrobe and the Saab. His mother had even taken it upon herself to choose a name for the house when Shay kept avoiding the foreman's pleas for the full address.

As it happened, women seemed to like the name. It was one of the first things a girl asked when she arrived on his doorstep. Shay thought it was the air of mystery, the idea that a house name had some deep underlying meaning for its occupant.

His mother told him that, when they first got married, she and his father had rented the gate lodge of an old estate house called Leadington. The lodge was Shay's first home, so Nora thought it fitting that Shay bring a little part of his history to the new house. Shay was only delighted that a name had been chosen without any great effort on his part. Knowing how sentimental his mother was, he was happy enough to go along with her choice. She'd even gone out and ordered the black wrought-iron nameplate for him.

"That one in the show-house is some wagon," Marcus was saying. "She ate the face off me when I came out of the house just now, for cutting out in front of her yesterday evening. I told her why I was driving like a lunatic but she wasn't interested in any kind of an explanation. She kept going on about driving like a madman until the boyfriend asked if Deirdre was alright. She's a bit of a witch, I'd say. I don't know what your man sees in her."

"Money and prospects," Shay informed him knowledgably. "He's the senior architect with Coltons. He was made a director last year, so he knows what side his bread's buttered on. Having said that, he's a nice enough sort. I got talking to him a few times when the house was going up, and he seemed OK."

"God, Shay, it's ten to ten – you'd better get going or you'll be fired," said Marcus, hopping off the barstool. "Thanks a million for the tea and sympathy. It did the trick. I was absolutely banjaxed but I feel a bit better now."

"No bother, man. Let me know how they're getting on. Sleep well!"

And Shay reached for his mobile to spin out another of his "I'm late" lines.

7

Evergreen

Amy was making her way towards the library block, having changed into jeans and a dusty pink Lainey Keogh sweater that her sisters had given her at Christmas. She caught Peter's eye as she pushed back the heavy tinted-glass doors and he smiled from where he stood by the large mahogany desk, surrounded by an enormous pile of serious-looking tomes.

"Hi," she greeted him, noticing appreciatively how well he looked in navy chinos and a pale blue shirt that set off his tanned good looks to perfection.

"How are you? You look great for someone who's been awake all night!"

"Thanks. The night was grand – busy when we came on but it settled down towards morning." She indicated the elderly volumes covering the desk and two large trolleys. "You look as if you're spring-cleaning."

"I am actually, would you believe. They came from the old library when St Michael's closed and I'm only getting around to them now. Most of them will have to go out for rebinding and suchlike."

"Sometimes I think I'd love to work in here all day – it's so calm and peaceful. No drama."

"You'd miss the drama of the wards after a week. *And* you'd have to put up with med-students getting excited about photocopying cards getting stuck and fellows hiding books in obscure places to stop other fellows getting better marks!"

"OK, the glamour has just worn off that idea. I'd better make tracks before I fall asleep."

"Oh, have a look at these first – I pulled out a few things that might be of some use to you. You'll have to give me your reading list the next time."

"A few things?" Amy laughed incredulously as he pulled one of the trolleys towards her. "I'll definitely give you the reading list if you're going to uproot the whole building. Thanks – you didn't have to, you know."

"It's no bother really. It gave me a break from the antiques. Go on – have a look before you need a stretcher. And don't go hiding things in queer places."

Forty minutes later Amy had sifted through the impressive collection he had put together for her and had decided on the ones that would be most useful to her.

"That was brilliant. A whole day's work done in less than an hour. I could get used to this kind of treatment," she smiled as he expertly zapped the five books with an electronic pen.

"I know you're working over the weekend," he said, "but are you still on for going out for a while on Saturday evening?"

"That'd be lovely. I usually get up around four so I could be ready for five. How would that be?"

"Brilliant. We could try Doc's – it's changed hands lately and it's supposed to be nice. And you'd be into work in five minutes from there."

"Great so, I'll see you on Saturday. And thanks for the books."

They stood there for a moment until an Asian doctor coughed discreetly to attract Peter's attention. Laughing quietly, they said their goodbyes, suddenly conscious that they'd been standing there just smiling at each other.

8

Seefin

Deirdre shifted uncomfortably on the high stool that enabled her to have a better view of Alex. Even though, on the midwife's advice, she had brought one of her pillows to the Neonatal Unit to sit on, she still felt the sting of her stitches and regretted refusing the offer of Panadol earlier.

Before Marcus left for home, the house doctor had filled them in on Alex's progress. His brain scan was booked for later that day, after which the consultant, Mr McNeill, would come and talk with them.

The ward midwife had advised Deirdre to come back to the ward as soon as Alex was settled and she could start expressing breast milk to store in the freezer until Alex was well enough to be fed. Glancing at her watch, Deirdre realised that she'd been in the Neonatal Unit for over an hour but she dreaded leaving her baby alone.

"You can come back up as soon as you've expressed and had your lunch," Sheila Forde told her gently. "I have the extension of your room, so I'll phone you straight away if anything changes. He'll be fine – I'll cover him over and he can have a sleep while you're gone."

Sheila, an attractive, middle-aged lady, looked completely capable as she unrolled a sheet of bubble-wrap and started to secure it around Alex's tiny body.

"Will he be able to breathe under there?" Deirdre asked anxiously when all she could see of Alex were the various tubes protruding from under the bubble-wrap.

"The ventilator is doing his breathing for him at the moment. He needs to be covered as much as possible for the first few days because his skin is so porous. Over the next few days it will toughen up and we'll be able to expose him a little more."

Wincing, Deirdre slid off the stool.

Noticing her discomfort Sheila advised her to take some painkillers when she went back to her ward. "Alex needs his mum in peak condition so make sure to take care of yourself. Also, your milk flow will be restricted if you're in pain all the time. No medals for martyrs here," she smiled as Deirdre shuffled towards the door.

"There you are," Cora Callely greeted as Deirdre emerged from the lift on the ground floor. "How's the little man?"

Deirdre filled the midwife in on all the details, marvelling at how much she had already learned.

56

"It's like landing in *Star Trek* and having to learn a whole new vocabulary. You probably don't even notice any more but it's all initials."

"You've obviously just had the 'ventilation' talk," Cora grinned knowingly. "Don't panic a bit – you'll be coming back to the ward in a few days telling me about SIMV and CPAP and giving out because the pressures are too high and the PCO2 is too low!"

"That's exactly the kind of thing I *was* starting to panic about. There's so much to know," Deirdre marvelled as they reached the private room that would be her home until Alex had stabilised fully.

"Just keep asking questions. And if you are going to panic, at least do it over something really complex like this thing." With that, Cora lifted a large blue box off a trolley and landed it in front of Deirdre.

"Now you'll know all about *Star Trek*," she quipped.

Deirdre had never set eyes on a breast pump in her life and was totally unprepared for the complicated apparatus awaiting her. The large blue motor sat on the bedside locker with two tubes attached. At the end of the tubes were two dome-shaped objects that looked like they might have to fit on to her nipples. Deirdre stared at it, her green eyes widening in horror at the thought of having to manage it.

"It's actually much easier than it looks at first," Cora reassured her, sensing that her patient was somewhat overwhelmed.

"I blooming well hope so." Deirdre was fascinated. It looked like an implement from a torture chamber.

"Sit down and we'll get started," Cora told her. "We'll help you until you're able to manage it yourself. You'll need to express milk every four hours or so to keep your supply up."

Deirdre opened her pyjamas tentatively, wondering if you did one breast at a time or both together. As if sensing her question the midwife handed her the two domes and instructed her to centre one over each nipple.

"Don't worry. I won't turn it on until you're ready. We'll start on the minimum suction and you can turn it up to medium or maximum if it feels comfortable. Ready?"

Deirdre nodded and immediately felt a gentle tug at each nipple. "Oh my God, that's mad!" She burst out laughing at the ridiculousness of it, as the pump began to slowly draw tiny drops of milk into two bottles attached to the machine.

"Not half as mad as the fact that it'll be the most important task of your life for the next few months. We'll organise a pump for you to use at home when the time comes."

"Is that all there is?" enquired Deirdre with disappointment ten minutes later, looking at what looked like a teaspoon of milk in each bottle. "I thought I'd fill the bottles."

"That's actually lots for the first time. I'll bring the pump in again at two o'clock and you can try again. I'll pop this lot in the freezer for Alex – it won't be long until he needs it."

Before she knew it the lunch had arrived but Deirdre couldn't face the thought of eating. She figured that Alex would be having his brain scan around now. Closing her eyes, she willed it to be clear. Both the neonatal nurse and the house doctor had warned Marcus and her of the risks that prematurity could bring. Even if the scan was clear today, Alex could still have a bleed tomorrow or next week, although the risks lessened with each passing day.

"Please God, let him be alright!" Deirdre prayed. "Just give him a chance to get stronger."

With that, Deirdre's mobile rang. Marcus was waiting outside the Neonatal Unit while the radiographer finished the scan.

"There's a man in with him as well – I think it might be Mr McNeill. I'll stay out here until you come up."

They waited together outside the door until Sheila Forde ushered them in ten minutes later.

"Mr and Mrs Fleming, I'm John McNeill, Alex's doctor."

Deirdre studied the competent-looking man before her and willed him to say the words that she wanted to hear.

"As you know," he continued, "coming into the world at this early stage is not an ideal situation for Alex. However, now that he's here, there's a lot we can do to help him survive these first few weeks. I know that Dr Ali and Sheila here have explained the risks facing him, and believe me, Alex *will* run into some problems initially."

Deirdre and Marcus could only stare at the man, both in too much fear of the scan results to be able to even speak.

"As far as Alex's breathing is concerned he's really holding his own, which is what we would hope for in the first forty-eight hours. Unfortunately," he said, lowering his voice gently, "Alex has had a small bleed on the right side of his brain, as is often the case with these small babies."

Deirdre felt as if iced water was drenching over her but she could still hear the voices through a haze.

"What does that mean?" Marcus interjected anxiously, his face now pale. "Will he have to have surgery?"

"No surgery. What we would hope is that the bleed will re-absorb over the next few weeks with no side effects. Fortunately, it's what we call a Grade 1 bleed at present – the least serious kind. All we can do is allow Alex as much rest as possible and repeat the scan next week. I'm afraid it means no cuddles with him for a while – he'll need to be kept as still as possible. We'll keep you informed of everything as we go along."

* * *

The following evening, Deirdre's parents arrived from West Cork. Marcus had phoned them, as well as her sister Hazel, the previous night to let them know about Alex's arrival, but had asked them to hold off on visiting until he was a little more stable.

Hazel had her own business in the city and had been in earlier in the day, promising to be back later with more pyjamas and toiletries for her sister.

Now Deirdre's parents were sitting on their daughter's bed in the postnatal ward, still in shock at the size of their first grandchild.

"How long will he be on the breathing machine?" Tom questioned, having been given a sketchy outline of the situation by Marcus before going in to see Alex. Deirdre had thought it best not to tell her parents about the brain haemorrhage until they'd got over the initial shock of seeing him, and Marcus had agreed, knowing how protective they were about their two daughters.

"It all depends on how he responds to the medication they've given him to mature his lungs," Marcus explained. "If his oxygen levels are good tomorrow, they might start weaning him off the machine to see how he gets on. But it could be a few weeks before he's fully off it."

He was beginning to feel like a broken record. He'd recited versions of the same story on numerous occasions that day; to his brother Vincent in Arizona, to the manager in the Unified Bank where they both worked, and to his parents in Waterford who were arriving in the morning.

Marcus knew that his parents wouldn't be able to take on the implications of Alex's situation in the way that Tom and Rose had. While Rose had immediately pitched in, helping Deirdre with the breast pump and advising her on how to avoid mastitis, Marcus knew that his own mother would just gloss over the realities by saying: "He'll be fine – before you know it he'll be out kicking a football."

Joe and Eileen didn't do problems, Marcus had often told Deirdre. Even with things like the Leaving Cert, they dismissed worries about failing a subject with a standard "Of course you'll pass it! Sure the whole thing will be over in a few weeks!".

As far as Marcus could see, by dismissing things as "fine" his parents never had to get involved with any difficulties that their sons encountered. The result was that Marcus and Vincent had to paddle their own canoes in life. That they both managed pretty well only served to assure Joe and Eileen that things actually *were* always fine.

It was only when Marcus met Deirdre at university and started going down to her parents' house in Clonakilty that he realised the interest other parents had in their children's welfare.

At first, he'd thought it intrusive when Tom would advise him on the best route to wherever he and Deirdre were going. Or when he'd said straight out one evening over dinner that the acre site down on the main road was for Deirdre and Marcus if they ever wanted to build a house. After a while, he realised that Tom was looking out for them both, not telling them what to do, and that Deirdre took this support from her parents for granted.

Marcus then began to be aware of the fact that his own parents had no idea of what their son's plan for the future entailed. Nor, he realised with a shock, had they any interest in whether those plans included Deirdre, the first girl that he'd dated seriously or brought home to meet them. He couldn't imagine Eileen inviting them to live at home in Glencregg while they saved to build or buy a place of their own, as Deirdre's mother had when it looked as if house prices were going through the roof.

Even though they hadn't taken Tom and Rose up on their offer, opting to buy the house in Pebble Cove instead, Marcus had felt a sense of security and back-up that he'd never before experienced. That Dee's parents had no hard feelings about the young couple's decision not to live near them in West Cork still amazed Marcus.

"It's up to yourselves. The site's still there if you want to sell it to make up a deposit on the new house," Tom had told them.

Marcus had been so choked by the generosity of this man whose daughter he was going to marry, that he persuaded Deirdre that they should keep the site in case she wanted to be near her parents as they got older. He felt a closeness to this couple that he had never experienced with his own parents, a feeling he was often secretly ashamed of.

Thankfully, the fact that they both worked with Unified Bank had meant that they were able to avail of the low-interest mortgage package that senior staff were entitled to as one of the perks of the job. Hanging onto the site in West Cork was a luxury that many couples would be unable to afford and both Marcus and Deirdre were very aware of how lucky they were. They'd even started to discuss the possibility of building a holiday cottage there, thinking it would be an ideal place to spend the summer weekends as a family.

Now that they were here at the hospital, Marcus realised that he was expecting Tom and Rose to stay. He just presumed that they would take up residence in Pebble Cove and be involved in whatever the coming weeks brought.

"Of course we will be, love," Rose exclaimed when Deirdre asked if they'd be there for the next few days. "We brought enough stuff for the week and Dad can pop down home to pick up the post and collect more clothes as we need them. Alex needs us all around him now to give him a start."

Tears came to Marcus's eyes at this, at Rose's belief that the power of their all being there for Alex would give him a reason to keep going. Marcus felt a strength come over him, banishing the sense of powerlessness that he'd felt since Deirdre's labour had begun.

"Why don't we make some sort of a plan for the next few days," he suggested. "We can't all be here all the time. You need to get some sleep, Dee, in case you have to express milk during the night. How about if we go home now and Tom and Rose can settle in and get a rest? We'll get something to eat and I'll come back in to see you and Alex before bed-time."

"Good idea," Tom said, impressed by his son-in-law's level-headed calmness. "We'll meet you down in the front hall, Marcus. Bye for now, love."

Deirdre's parents each gave her a quick hug before leaving, closing the door softly behind them.

9

Leadington

"I met Dee's mother getting out of the car and she says Alex is getting milk through a tube still. He's keeping all the feeds down now so they're delighted," Carla informed Shay breathlessly as she dropped two full bags of groceries on the worktop.

It was like a running commentary from some medical drama on television, Shay thought. Carla was fascinated by the progress of his neighbours' child and never lost an opportunity to get an instalment, which she then reported to Shay in glorious detail. There'd been numerous ups and downs with little Alex, and while Shay felt sorry for the trauma that Deirdre and Marcus were going through, he tended to forget about them unless Carla got an update over the fence. She was even on first-name terms with the granny and aunt by now. Apart from the morning that Marcus had come in for breakfast, Shay had never had more than a five-minute conversation with any of his neighbours.

As Carla unpacked the grocery bags, Shay wondered out loud where they'd go that night. Saturday night was always the pivotal night in Shay's week. It sort of set the tone for the seven days to come. A good night out followed by a lie-in on Sunday was the best way to precede any working week as far as Shay was concerned.

"I thought we could stay in and have a few drinks," said Carla. "I got stuff to cook for dinner. I'm going to do *darne of salmon* in a cream and chive sauce, with baby potatoes. We can have the rest of your mother's cheesecake for afters."

This was the second Saturday night in a row that they'd be staying in. Last week Shay hadn't minded because he'd been pretty shook after Ken's thirtieth and was too sick to go anywhere. He and Carla had thrown themselves on the couch, switching around the channels until they could go back to bed again.

To Shay's alarm, Carla had enjoyed the night in and was now organising a cosy dinner for two. He didn't like the sound of it but knew he was too late to do anything about it at this stage. Next week he'd have something planned to head any suggestion of a night in off at the pass. He made a mental note to consult Ken on the subject. As much and all as he liked Carla he didn't want to find himself railroaded into a pipe and slippers routine before his time.

But he had to admit that Carla was gorgeous – a mass of dark red hair, great legs, slim without being skinny. He hated bony women. Carla was sort of voluptuous and curvy, and she really enjoyed sex without being inhibited the way most women were. This turned Shay on more than he would have believed. Sometimes they didn't even make it upstairs after a night out. Once, they hadn't made it out of the car, ripping each other's clothes off in the passenger seat of the Saab when Shay had pulled up outside the house. Pebble Cove had been in darkness, not being the sort of place where people hung around outside at night. A picture of Carla lying back on the seat, her long legs wrapped around him and both hands gripping the headrest came back to Shay. He made his way back into the kitchen.

"Get off me or the whole thing will curdle," Carla shrieked as Shay slid his hands up under her top, his thumbs grazing her nipples through the lace of her bra.

He jumped back in disgust, his boyish good looks distorted for a moment with annoyance. It wasn't often that women gave him the brush-off. "Sorry for living and invading your space," he grumbled, any thoughts of passion that he'd had evaporating as Carla continued stirring with an implement that definitely hadn't been in Shay's kitchen that morning.

He plonked himself dejectedly in one of the armchairs in the den, with his legs thrown over the side, and flicked on the telly. Derek Mooney grinned back at him and proceeded to explain the vagaries of the weekly lotto game to an old fella from Mayo.

"Go on, Michael, Spin and Win!" Derek yelled, the

Mayo relations cheering in the audience.

"Christ Almighty, this is desperate," Shay cursed under his breath and flicked to another channel. *"Free bloody Willy!"* Shay zapped the friendly whale off the screen and tried again, this time getting King Henry the Eighth and one of his many wives. That was enough for Shay. He flung the remote control at the sofa opposite and headed back to the kitchen where Carla was expertly sprinkling the potatoes with freshly chopped parsley.

"Ready in two minutes," she announced, handing Shay a bottle of wine and a corkscrew.

Shay obliged, glancing at the clock to see if they'd be able to even go down to the local for a few after dinner. It was still only half eight. At least they'd be *out*. Maybe not exactly out on the town, but out somewhere.

* * *

Shay buried his head in his hands and cursed under his breath. It was bad enough to have turned up to a meeting completely unprepared, but to have Daniel Colton turn up without warning was disastrous. Shay had been totally thrown by the edgy queries fired at him by the older man and his usual tactics had, for once, let him down. By the time Shay got back to the office a note from his boss was already sitting on his desk asking that Shay come up to his office immediately.

This was the second time in a month that Joe

Kiernan had left such a message for Shay, the previous time also connected with the Coltons account. On that occasion, Shay had been pulled up for arriving at a 9 a.m. meeting looking dishevelled and stinking of booze. At the time, Shay had fobbed his boss off with a tale about losing his door key and not being able to shower and change before work. Joe himself had been at that particular meeting and, while he had filled in the gaps in Shay's work to save face, he'd been well pissed off at the younger man's attitude.

Shay knew he wouldn't get away so lightly today. For one, there had been no-one to cover for him. Also, Daniel Colton had known bloody well that Shay wasn't up to speed on matters concerning one of his businesses, the Bodywork leisure centre. Shay hadn't even been able to produce the related files, a situation that led to the holder of his company's largest account leaving the conference room in exasperation after what Shay knew was a pretty fruitless meeting. Colton promised to get on to one of the senior partners to see if they could provide the information he needed, nodding curtly at Shay on his way out the door.

Shay made his way to the lift, having first checked his appearance in one of the restrooms on his floor. He thought he was fairly decent-looking, despite the fact that he'd had barely two hours sleep. His streaky blond hair always had a tousled look but he smoothed it back to see if he could improve the situation, noting with disgust that his eyes were red-rimmed. At least he'd made it his business to shower this morning, even though it had meant forfeiting a precious ten minutes of sleep time. He'd rolled out of the taxi at quarter to six in the morning, barely having the sense to set the alarm clock before crashing out on the bed in his clothes.

"Never again!" he swore, as the lift opened and he faced the forbidding oak door of Joe Kiernan's office.

"Well, Shay," his boss began, eyebrows raised in anticipation of Shay's explanation, "why did I have Daniel Colton bending my ear for twenty minutes about spending an hour with one of our accountants and being none the wiser after it?"

Shay decided that the best policy was to come clean. He had already tried to bluff his way through one catastrophic encounter today and had failed miserably.

"Look, Joe, I admit I wasn't prepared for the meeting this morning and I certainly wasn't expecting Daniel Colton to turn up. I didn't have the stuff he was looking for about one area of the business. I know I made a mess of it. All I can do is apologise. I'll make a full report on the leisure centre side of things and fax it to him straight away." Shay looked up expectantly, hoping to gauge exactly how dissatisfied his boss was with his performance.

"And do you think that'll be enough to placate the firm's most valuable client? I don't think so," Joe answered for him. "This isn't the first time this has happened, Shay. How long do you think we can carry on like this? Actually, how long do you think you can hold down a job with this kind of carry-on?"

Shay felt himself break out in a sweat. He couldn't

tell if it was caused by the dehydration of the previous night or the very real possibility that his job might be on the line. Blast Carla anyway! It was only the whole claustrophobic Saturday night fiasco that had tempted him to go on the razz on a Sunday night in the first place. Ken had phoned earlier from some house in Douglas, not having made it to work at all.

"Are you with me, Shay?" Joe broke in on his thoughts. "You'll need to seriously look at your drinking before you can go anywhere near a client again. And you know I'll have to talk to Michael Murray about this?" he said, referring to the senior partner, an altogether more forbidding figure than Joe himself. "Do you realise that Daniel Colton threatened to withdraw his business from us if all he sees in front of him on a Monday morning is someone stinking of drink, who can barely stay awake?"

Shay nodded dumbly, apologising again for jeopardising one of the firm's most lucrative contracts. Joe Kiernan looked at him levelly before winding up what he considered to be a last-chance meeting with Shay Deegan.

"Shay, finish the report on whatever it was that Daniel Colton wanted, and let me run through it before you send it. Then take the rest of the day off and get some sleep. You can't go around the office in the state you're in. I'll talk to Michael this evening and see what the position is. You can take it that you'll be having no more to do with the Coltons account. And Shay, the next time this happens, you won't be dealing with me."

Taking the final comment as a dismissal, Shay left his boss's office, the beginnings of an unmerciful headache starting to throb at his temples.

10

Evergreen

Amy stretched luxuriously under the duvet, fanning out her limbs to the four corners of the king-sized bed in her new house in Pebble Cove. She lay awake admiring her surroundings, still not quite believing that all this was actually hers. She loved the way the white walls contrasted with the aqua of her duvet cover and cushions. She'd wanted simplicity for this room to make the most of the sun slanting through the two tall windows, dressed now in plain blue calico Roman blinds. Amy always left her curtains open in the summer so that she'd be awake early to make the most of the sunshine. This morning the blinds were pulled up to reveal a cloudless sky, and she could sense that today was going to be a scorcher.

She'd planned to have a lie-in, having arrived in from Cyprus at 2 a.m. but now that she was awake she was dying to get out and about. A week in the sun had been just what she needed after the whirlwind of moving into her first home. Everyone had told her that buying a house was one of the most stressful events of a lifetime but Amy had optimistically dismissed the warnings in her excitement to move in. The thrill of shopping for kitchen appliances and furniture was fantastic, her mother hovering with advice at every turn.

"Go for a gas hob and an electric oven, love," she cautioned. "That way you'll be able to manage if the power's ever off."

Amy had heeded most of the advice, having inherited her mother's practicality. She wanted a home that was functional and easy to manage, while still being comfortable and welcoming. Amy hated fussy things. Just as well, she often thought, considering that her budget wasn't exactly huge. Hardly a day went by that she didn't realise just how lucky she was to have had the cottage in Evergreen Road as a start on the property ladder. Selling it had been a wrench, her memories of her Granny Nolan holding her back until finally the lack of parking and the redevelopment of the inner city had made the decision for her.

Naming her new house "Evergreen" had been a sentimentality that would always remind her of the little terraced house where her grandmother had spent her whole life, a house that she'd willed in the end to her eldest grand-daughter. Three years later, with the price of property in the city rising at an alarming rate, Amy had decided to sell, knowing that she'd have to do so sooner or later anyway. Finding the house in Pebble Cove had been like a dream: a detached, four-bed overlooking the sea in a price bracket that she couldn't even have considered without the sale of the cottage.

Despite her large deposit, the mortgage was still hefty, yet it was manageable enough to allow at least some luxuries. Normally she'd have enjoyed a full two weeks of sunshine, yet her week away with her sisters had been a compromise that her harbour view more than made up for.

She hopped out of bed, catching sight of herself in the full-length mirror attached to the wardrobe and stopped for a moment to admire her newly acquired tan, her shoulders golden against the shoestring straps of a short cotton nightdress. She was delighted with her legs. A decent tan early in the summer meant that she could get into shorts and dresses without the fuss of fake tan.

After a quick shower, she smothered herself in body lotion to stop her skin peeling, slipped into a light cotton dress that showed her tan off to best advantage, and tied her golden-blonde hair away from her face with a scrunchie. She was already excited at the thought of the afternoon to come and wanted to have her unpacking done and a few groceries got before Peter arrived. He'd promised to call over and bring lunch, having taken the day off to welcome her back.

Amy had been amazed at how much she'd missed him while she'd been away considering that they'd been seeing each other for such a short time. Sorting out the sale of the house in Evergreen Road and buying her new home in Pebble Cove, as well as keeping up with the work on her thesis, had left precious little time for her relationship with Peter to develop.

Yet it had done just that, even though the physical side of things had been somewhat slower in getting started than she might have anticipated. A fortnight sharing Kim's bedsitter in Blarney Street between giving up her apartment and the new house being ready, coupled with an extended run of night duty hadn't helped, but the night before her holiday had more than made up for the wait.

Peter had stayed over in order to drive the three girls to the airport the following morning. They'd had a relaxed dinner after which Amy's younger sisters had insisted on going out on the town, determined to start their holidays as soon as possible.

"At this hour? I haven't even packed yet." Amy had only finished her twelve-hour shift at eight and had a huge pile of ironing to tackle before she even contemplated pulling out a suitcase. It was gone half nine as it was.

"Why don't you start sorting your things out and I'll drop the girls into town," Peter had offered. "You'll have it done by the time I get back."

Thrilled, Denise and Laura had belted up the stairs to top up their make-up and upscuttle their cases yet again to find something glamorous enough for a night out in the city.

"Thanks." Amy had wrapped her arms around Peter

and rested her head on his chest. He smelled of *Cacharel Pour L'Homme*, a warm, spicy scent that made her glad that her sisters were going out.

"It'll be nice to be on our own for a bit, especially when you'll be gone for a whole week," Peter had whispered as his lips caressed her hair and found their way down to her ear, causing her to moan softly in anticipation.

"Hurry back then and I promise I'll have my suitcase in the hall," she'd whispered huskily, wishing that he didn't have to leave the house at all. "I'll light the fire and open a bottle of wine while you're gone."

Within minutes, the twins came clattering down the stairs dressed to the nines, obviously well accustomed to dolling up at short notice.

"Jesus, girls, Pana won't know what's hit it when I drop you two off," he'd teased appreciatively, using the Cork slang word for Patrick Street, the city's main thoroughfare.

Delighted with themselves, the girls had assured Amy that she'd picked "a right fellow" before exiting in a wave of exotic scents that would cause an explosion if anyone had the bad sense to strike a match.

Deciding almost immediately that a night of passion was higher on her agenda than sorting out a pile of holiday clothes, Amy had quickly lit the fire in the sitting room and switched on the terracotta Stephen Pearce lamps that threw a gentle light around the room. That done, she'd resurrected the travel iron and its adaptor and threw them into her case followed by the heap of sandals, shorts, T-shirts and cotton dresses. Underwear, swimwear and toiletries slotted into the side compartments and the whole thing was zipped shut in under ten minutes. Satisfied that if she'd forgotten anything one of her sisters would surely sort her out, she'd lugged the heavy case down the stairs and made a quick dash to the shower. Her sisters wouldn't be back for hours and she was very definitely looking forward to having Peter to herself.

Dressed comfortably in pale linen trousers and a fitted khaki top with shoestring straps, Amy had padded into the kitchen barefoot and collected a bottle of Australian Shiraz and two glasses, amazed once again as she looked around the kitchen that it really was all her own. The cream painted units were set off by a solid mahogany worktop, into which a miniature Belfast sink was set. The kitchen in the show-house had been all stainless steel appliances with a granite worktop that Amy felt lent a harsh, cold feeling to what after all should be a warm and comfortable part of the house. After lengthy negotiations, the foreman had agreed to let her pick her own kitchen, provided it was within the price range specified in the marketing brochure. As it transpired, her choice had come in at such a competitive price that she'd been able to include the genuine terracotta tiles for the floor, which were far more expensive than the ones specified in the original plans.

Mahogany French doors opened into the sunny dining room, where a solid mahogany table and chairs and ivory walls complemented the décor in the kitchen. Amy always loved the roughness of the sisal flooring under her bare feet as she sat at the dining-room table in the mornings with the sun warming her face.

Returning to the sitting room, she'd poured the wine and settled herself in front of the fire, resting her back against the sofa as she imagined the evening ahead.

She felt warm all over now as she remembered the feel of Peter's hands on her skin that night, his lips grazing her nipples as they lay on the rug in front of the fire, the flames making his skin look like bronze before she closed her eyes and lost herself in the feeling of his hands and mouth touching her everywhere.

Afterwards, she'd pulled a cushion off the sofa for him and she'd lain there with her head resting on his chest, listening to the steady beating of his heart as his fingers massaged the muscles at the top of her shoulders.

Pulling herself together now, Amy started to methodically sort out her luggage, dumped unceremoniously in the hall the previous night. Reflecting on the week away as she worked, Amy realised that she'd needed it to wind down. She felt rejuvenated and had really enjoyed spending seven days in the company of her twin sisters. Denise and Laura, a year younger than Amy, were the babies of the house at home, despite the fact that they would be twenty-seven next month.

The girls had planned the holiday on the spur of the moment, the night of Amy's housewarming, and egged on by their older brother, Robert, had insisted she come with them to chill out. They'd never been on a holiday together before as adults so Amy had agreed, stipulating a week only to keep the cost down. At one point, Robert had even announced that he too would come but the suggestion was quickly shot down by Denise and Laura on the grounds that he'd deter any men that might be interested in them. Robert, fresh from a year travelling around Australia, was determined to continue the party life-style that he'd become accustomed to but conceded that he might indeed be a liability to his sisters.

They'd had a ball, out all night and sleeping on the beach during the day. They'd hired a car for two days and explored the tiny island, fascinated by the bitter divide between the Greek and Turkish populations.

As well as picking up a hardwood chess board with tiny porcelain figurines for Peter, Amy had purchased numerous bits of pottery as well as a few bottles of Commandaria, the local dessert wine that she'd developed a taste for over the week. She unpacked these now along with some duty-free perfume and a mountain of laundry. She always brought more clothes on holiday than she needed but in this instance they came in useful for the twins, one of whom was as disorganised as the other. Luckily, they were all more or less the same build, petite and curvy, so the communal pile of clothes had benefited everyone.

Once she'd loaded the washing machine and sorted out her work clothes, she had a quick sconce around the kitchen to see what she needed for the rest of the week, planning a quick trip to the village before Peter arrived.

As Amy was getting into her car she saw Marcus, her neighbour, waving at her from across the green. She approached him, wondering how little Alex was doing. Because of the holiday, Amy hadn't seen him in well over a week and she was well aware of how much could change, even in a day, for a child like Alex.

"Well, how was Cyprus?" Marcus greeted her, and by his jovial form Amy presumed that all was well with his son.

"Great," Amy responded. "How's Alex? Still keeping down the feeds?"

"Yeah, he's going brilliant, thank God. He's up to 10mls per hour now."

Marcus was referring to the volume of milk being pumped slowly into Alex's stomach each hour, around the clock. The last night that Amy had cared for him, Alex had been on a mere 2mls per hour. Generally, the goal was to increase the volume by 1ml each day, so Alex seemed to be tolerating the increases pretty well. An infant as premature as Alex needed to be fed tiny amounts every hour, as his body couldn't cope with the amount that a normal baby would take.

"He'll probably start to gain weight soon, if he keeps going on the feeds," Amy told him.

To date, Alex had never been weighed, being too ill to be lifted onto a weighing scales. The neonatal staff kept warning Marcus and Deirdre that he'd probably lost quite a bit, but they weren't too concerned about it, allowing him to lose a certain amount of weight while feeding was being established.

"Kim says he might be getting weighed on Sunday. All going well, he'll be going into an ordinary incubator. Deirdre's terrified something will go wrong. It's amazing, isn't it? Most people would be in bits seeing their baby in an incubator, but to us it's a step forward. I just hope he's ready for it."

Like all parents of "prems", Marcus was on the alert for the downturns that he'd been warned could happen in a flash.

"All you can do is wait and see how he is on the day. I'll actually be working with him on Saturday and Sunday – on day-shifts. If he's well enough we'll be able to let one of you hold him while he's being transferred from the open incubator to the closed one," Amy told him.

Tears sprang to Marcus's eyes at that. Neither he nor Deirdre had ever held Alex, despite him being almost a month old. The brain haemorrhage that he'd got in the early days had meant that the "minimal handling" policy was strictly enforced and his parents were actually *glad* not to hold him if it made him any safer.

Since the first horrific brain scan, Alex had had two repeat scans, the first of which was unchanged. Deirdre and Marcus had been both relieved and disappointed at the same time. Relieved that the bleed hadn't progressed any further, disappointed that it hadn't started to reabsorb as everyone hoped. The third scan had showed some improvement but Mr McNeill, the consultant, was still cautious in his approach, reminding them that even if it disappeared completely, the haemorrhage could still have caused some damage at the time.

Now Marcus made up his mind that if one of them would be allowed to hold Alex on Saturday it would be Dee. She'd been through so much between the whole shock of early labour and now the exhausting task of using the breast-pump every four hours to provide enough milk for Alex. Deirdre spent most of the day in the hospital, even though she'd been discharged a week after the birth. She drove in every morning and Marcus joined her after work.

"That'd be fantastic," Marcus gulped, heading off to work a happy man.

Amy saw him stop again to talk to the man in the first house. Tall in an athletic sort of way and always dressed in a well-cut business suit, she'd noticed him before this, coming and going with the gorgeous creature he lived with. She didn't think they were married, as the standoffish blonde didn't seem to be wearing any rings. Handsome, she thought, as she pulled her Golf up behind his BMW at the exit pillars of the estate.

11

Number 1

Linda was sitting anxiously on one of the soft brown leather sofas that faced each other on either side of the white marble fireplace in the lounge, the early summer sunshine slanting in through the timber-slatted blinds. She was amazed at how nervous she felt. Daniel was due any minute and she felt as if she was facing a firing squad rather than sitting down with her own father.

She could hear Charlie's footsteps upstairs and wished he'd hurry up and get dressed before her father arrived. He'd only just put the final touches to the draft costings for the leisure complex this evening, dropping the slim package of documents on the granite coffee table before heading up to shower and change. She wanted him to be there when her father came in. She knew how direct her father was. He'd cut straight to the chase, postponing ordinary conversation until the business issue was dispensed with.

Linda flicked through the preliminary costings again, now so familiar with them that she could recite the details word for word. Both she and Charlie had put enormous work into the proposal and while the whole thing was still very much in the early stages, Linda felt that their basic estimates would be enough for her father to go on. Daniel Colton would see at a glance if this project would work. Linda knew that no amount of wheedling would entice her father to get involved in a venture that was only a pipe dream. She hadn't had a chance to look at all of Charlie's sketches but what she had seen was exactly how she'd envisaged the complex.

The only fly in the ointment was Charlie's reluctance to get fully involved in the overall picture. He felt strongly that Daniel would indeed be all for going ahead with the complex, but he could see no reason why it couldn't be done by Coltons with Charlie himself doing the full design.

Linda however felt that this was her idea and wanted to be involved at a different level, on the development side. Otherwise she'd just wind up being the manager of yet another of her father's concerns. The challenge of getting Bodyworks off the ground had burnt itself out. Developing the leisure complex from scratch would be her first venture into a much bigger arena. She just hoped her father would give her the entry point she needed.

As predicted, Daniel got straight to the point, sitting back to listen to them outlining the project as they saw it. Linda did most of the talking, with Charlie going through the drawings for each building afterwards. When Charlie had located the site maps it had transpired that there was more land than Linda had initially thought. The plan had escalated into a village-type complex to include a sports injury clinic and a number of self-contained chalets for weekend breaks or corporate use.

Once Daniel had heard the full pitch he sat back on the sofa sipping his brandy, looking thoughtfully into the empty grate. Linda knew he was formulating questions and queries about the overall proposal so she decided to sit back and wait. She had foreseen this, so she and Charlie had spent the last few evenings brainstorming to anticipate as many of Daniel's concerns and objections as possible.

Linda was fully prepared for a certain amount of opposition or at least debate.

When her father finally did speak, she was stunned to hear him say:

"So when would we hope to get started on this?"

12

Leadington

The following Saturday, Amy saw that Alex was indeed in good shape. He was now off the ventilator and was breathing on his own with the help of two little oxygen prongs in his nose. He was getting caffeine through his IV twice a day to stimulate regular breaths, something that had fascinated his parents when they first heard about it.

The unit was pretty quiet, something Amy was glad of on her first day back. She needed to update herself on all the infants, particularly the new ones that had arrived in the past week. Blood results from this morning would be arriving from the laboratory soon and Amy would peruse these with the house doctor in order to make any adjustments needed to the infants' care.

Because Alex was now much more stable, the person caring for him was able to look after a second baby. In

Amy's case, as well as Alex she had charge of a little guy with a heart defect who, while being quite well, would need to be transferred to the cardiac unit in Dublin for surgery as soon as a space became available.

The afternoon had passed uneventfully so far. Alex's next feed was due in five minutes so Amy had the little bottle of defrosted breast milk ready on the workstand, allowing it to come to room temperature before giving it to him. His evening medications were prepared so that she could carry out all his care at once to avoid disturbing him again. She'd also change his position to make him more comfortable as he wasn't yet able to do this himself.

Deirdre, sitting on her high stool beside Alex, was in the middle of a sentence when she noticed Amy's face become suddenly serious. Horrified, she noticed that her baby's face had gone a strange shade of dark blue. Amy reached over her and adjusted the oxygen dial, flicking Alex's heel with the fingers of her other hand to stimulate him.

Deirdre's heart stood still as the nurse waited for a response to the increase that she'd made in the oxygen. Amy reached for a mask attached to a soft plastic bulb, which was in turn attached to the oxygen supply. She stimulated Alex's feet with her fingers again, the mask hovering over his face. Deirdre realised that Amy was watching the machine that monitored Alex's oxygen levels.

Shocked, Deirdre could see that the usual figure, somewhere between 95% and 99%, was replaced by

84%. As the number started dropping lower, 75% and then 70%, Amy clamped the mask over Alex's face and gently started to squeeze the bulb, forcing oxygen into Alex's lungs.

Almost immediately, Deirdre could see that Alex's face was coming back to its normal colour and the reading on the monitor crept back up to 95%. Once it reached 99%, Amy stopped squeezing the bulb but left the mask hovering over Alex's face. Deirdre's eyes were glued to the monitor, willing the levels not to drop again.

Eventually, Amy laid the oxygen equipment down on the table beside her and turned to Deirdre to explain what had happened. Deirdre was white with shock and too terrified to speak.

"It's alright, Deirdre, he's OK now," she said gently. "Alex has just had what's called an apnoea attack. It means that he stopped breathing for a few seconds and the oxygen levels in his blood dropped below the normal levels. It's back to normal now but we need to look at why it happened."

"What would have happened if you weren't with him? Would he have died? What could have caused it?" Deirdre was frantic with questions and her words tumbled over each other in her need to find out just what had happened.

"If we hadn't been here the monitor would have alarmed when his oxygen saturation dropped below a certain level," Amy explained calmly. "That's why we keep checking the monitors at the start of every shift.

There are a couple of things that could have happened, so we need to look at all of them."

"What kind of things?"

"For instance, if Alex has gained weight, the levels of caffeine in his blood may have become too dilute. I can check that with the lab now. That's why we take blood for caffeine levels every week. The other thing is Alex's iron level. Iron carries oxygen around the body. If it's too low, then not enough oxygen is being brought around the body and the baby's breathing is affected. The other possibility is infection. Premature babies are more prone to infection, so we'll have to do a chest X-Ray and some bloods to rule that out."

What Amy didn't tell Deirdre about was the possibility that Alex had had yet another brain haemorrhage. Because he was due a routine brain scan the following morning, Amy decided not to burden Deirdre with this just yet. If nothing else came to light then it would have to be discussed. However, now was not the time to overload Deirdre with more information than she could assimilate.

While Deirdre digested all that the nurse had told her, Amy phoned the house doctor to come and review Alex. She also phoned the lab to request that the results of Alex's caffeine and iron levels be faxed to the unit as soon as possible, and paged the radiographer about the chest X-Ray. She then proceeded to take the set of blood tests recommended in cases of suspected infection.

"Should I phone Marcus and tell him to come in straight away?" Deirdre queried. "He said he'll be coming at half six anyway."

Amy had often seen parents arriving in the Neonatal Unit after such calls, having driven at dangerous speeds in their haste to be near their baby. On this account, she advised Deirdre to hold off on phoning Marcus just yet as Alex had now stabilised. The blood results and chest X-Ray would shed some light on the situation, so by half six they would have more information for Marcus without the danger of a frantic dash to the hospital. Deirdre saw the wisdom in this and agreed with Amy, who told her that it was unlikely that Alex would stop breathing again since the oxygen flow through his nasal tube was now increased.

Deirdre sat silently by Alex's side as he was examined by the house doctor and had more blood tests taken. The results of the caffeine levels were normal so that was ruled out as a possible cause of the apnoea.

The house doctor explained that Alex would have to have antibiotics, just to be sure, until the results of the infection screening were available, possibly in forty-eight hours' time. However, his iron levels appeared to be low to the point where a blood transfusion was necessary. Deirdre would need to give a blood sample to cross-match blood for Alex. After that, the blood would be available for transfusion by nine or ten o'clock.

As she wrapped a tourniquet around Deirdre's arm, Amy explained that a baby of Alex's size would only get a tiny amount of blood, about 10mls as opposed to the "pint" that adults got. It would be given through a drip over four hours.

Deirdre had got over most of the shock by the time Marcus arrived. At that stage she was able to tell him calmly, with Amy's help, that Alex was anaemic and would have to have a blood transfusion.

"How did you know he was anaemic?" Marcus wanted to know, so Amy explained the process of Alex's sudden cessation of breathing and the subsequent tests, taking the drama out of it insofar as she could to minimise the shock to Marcus.

Deirdre saw this and appreciated Amy's concern, not only for Alex, but for her and Marcus as well. Even the fact that Alex might not now be making the transition to a closed incubator the following day as planned was broached, but in such a practical way that they were able to see it as a temporary setback rather than a major disaster.

Deirdre knew she'd never forget Amy's face as she breathed life back into their baby, the impassivity and calmness that had made Deirdre believe she'd succeed. Not a glimmer of panic had crossed her features, just a studied concentration as she purposefully carried out each step. Amy's gentleness afterwards and her acknowledgement of the shock were exactly what Deirdre needed to help her deal with this new blow to Alex's progress.

Before Amy finished her shift that evening, Alex's transfusion was underway. He'd had no further apnoeas and his parents' relief was palpable as she bade them goodnight. Deirdre and Marcus, aware of the unit's "continuity of care" policy, were glad that Amy would be caring for their baby for the next two days.

Typical to have a bit of drama on the first day back after holidays, Amy mused as she headed towards the car park after what had transpired to be a fairly hectic shift. Glancing at her watch she quickened her step, wanting to shower and change before Peter arrived for the evening.

He'd called earlier in the week as promised with a selection of goodies to welcome her back from her holiday and they'd eaten a Greek salad and thick slices of grilled Halloumi cheese on crusty bread, sitting in the sun on Amy's makeshift patio. She'd resurrected the two wrought-iron chairs from her parent's garage and had teamed them with an old wrought-iron sewing-machine table that her grandmother had used in the 1940's. The hours had flown by as Amy described her holiday, filling him in on Denise and Laura's more civilised antics, and promised him a half-share in a bottle of Commandaria if he was free to stay over. As she'd imagined, the night was as wonderful as she'd expected. They'd made love into the early hours, only to wake up and start all over again before Peter had had to leave for work.

Tonight, they were heading to the Opera House to see Des Bishop, a madcap comedian that Peter adored. While Amy was definitely looking forward to hearing the foibles of life in Ireland as chronicled by the irrepressible American, her sights were more firmly set on having her boyfriend all to herself for the rest of the weekend.

*　*　*

She woke with the first of the morning sunshine filtering at an angle across the duvet cover. Only five o'clock, she mused sleepily, enjoying the Sunday morning feeling even though she had to work later. Plenty of time for a snooze before the alarm went off. She shifted lazily, loving the weight of Peter's arm thrown across the middle of her back. Flashes of the previous evening flooded over her, her mind relishing the memory of their lovemaking. Peter was a surprisingly passionate lover, his gentle, almost shy nature masking the more ardent side of his personality. She loved this about him – the thoughtful, patient way that he'd never pushed her at the beginning of their relationship, in contrast to the enthusiasm with which he now approached it.

"Hello there," he mumbled sleepily, rolling onto his side and drawing her towards him.

"Hello, yourself." Amy stretched languorously as he began to softly bite the nape of her neck and her shoulders, his hands sliding down over her hips, making her almost purr with pleasure.

"This is the best wake-up call I've had in ages," she teased, her body already aching to be touched all over.

"I can call again tomorrow morning if you like."

"That would be so nice," she told him, her legs

instinctively wrapping themselves around him as his lips trailed along her ribcage. This is just amazing, she thought distractedly, her mind separating from everything else as the bliss of their being together took her over.

*   *   *

Later that day, she mused on how she felt about Peter as Kim quizzed her expertly during their lunch break in the hospital canteen.

"Is there potential there, do you think?"

Kim was always bothered about what she called "time-wasting" with men. If there wasn't a definite sign of either potential or progression she felt that moving on swiftly was the wisest course of action. No point in wasting six months or a year on a fellow who hadn't a notion of settling down.

"There's potential alright," Amy admitted, trying unsuccessfully to suppress a smile. "We're getting on great. But it's early days yet," she cautioned, immediately spotting the expression that heralded Kim starting to look out for hats and wedding outfits.

"What's he like . . . you know . . .?"

"Jesus, Kim, is it an article in *The Examiner* you want?"

This was typical. Kim thought that a straightforward question deserved a completely straightforward answer, whatever the question.

Then, unable to help herself, Amy's face broke into a

huge smile. "He *is* gorgeous. When I used to see him in the library before, he always seemed sort of quiet-looking. I think you kind of assume that librarians are serious or something, but he's not a bit. He's great *craic* actually."

"*And* he's a fine thing. He's like your man Dean Cain in *Superman*. I'm assuming he's great crack in the *leaba* as well." Kim came from an Irish-speaking family in West Cork and was prone to throwing in the odd word at appropriate moments.

"Assume away," Amy smirked, knowing that Peter would kill her if he thought she was broadcasting his sexual prowess around the canteen of all places. "Now come on, will you, before the Nagle twins start to lodge complaints about not getting fed on time. It's nearly half-past."

He is fairly handsome, Amy mused to herself as they made their way back to the neonatal unit. Peter wasn't so much tall as big and solid, fit from playing soccer as many times in the week as he could. He tanned easily in the way that brown-eyed people always did and he had the kind of thick soft hair that it felt great to run your fingers through, no matter how short it was cut. Even thinking about him now gave her a feeling of warm anticipation that she'd never felt before they'd ended up sitting next to each other at the Easter Ball.

At least she had only one more shift to go before her day off, she thought, as they entered the lift. While she liked shift work for the freedom it gave her to come and go during the week, Amy knew that it wasn't a situation that could go on indefinitely. Day duty was fine, although working the weekends was a bit of a drag. Getting up at seven after a Saturday night out had to be the most depressing thing ever. Too many nurses ended up retiring early due to the burnout associated with combining weekend and night work with the demands of raising a family.

Of late, she'd been looking into the options that would allow her to work regular hours while continuing in a career that she enjoyed. Nothing had presented itself as yet but she was keeping a watching brief on the "Appointments" pages of the weekly newspapers. Even though it was tough trying to study and work, she knew that having a Masters in Management would make a huge difference to her career options in the long run.

In the meantime, she was making the most of the few "split weekends" that she did have free. While it was almost impossible to engage in any activity that required regular participation, due to the unpredictability of shift work, she was a keen hillwalker and spent as many weekends as she could walking, especially during the summer. She'd joined the local group when she moved to Pebble Cove and although it was smaller in numbers than many of the city clubs, the members were friendly and there was no pressure to go on treks every weekend, which suited Amy perfectly.

On Sunday, some of the group were going on a hike

in the Gilcrenan Hills as part of an annual walking festival. Peter had some sort of league match on so a walk was a good opportunity to get a bit of exercise, despite warnings from the others that it was a pretty demanding route.

Life is good, Amy thought to herself suddenly. A job that I like, which is more than most people have, a home that I love, great friends and now, out of the blue, Peter. With that, the doors of the lift opened on the third floor to reveal a swarm of labour ward personnel and paediatricians moving *en masse* towards the open doors of the Neonatal Unit, the transport incubator almost hidden in their midst. So much for life being good, Amy thought with a wry smile, as she and Kim quickened their steps in anticipation of yet another challenge.

13

Leadington

Shay glanced at the clock again. It was nowhere near lunchtime and he felt as if he'd been in the office for a week. After the whole Coltons debacle, things at work had settled down to some degree but Shay knew he was treading a thin line. Joe Kiernan was now treating him in a totally professional manner, with no trace of their former easy-going working relationship.

To be fair, Joe had smoothed the waters somewhat with the senior partner, who had informed Shay matter-of-factly that there was no place in the firm for the kind of behaviour that had been exhibited of late. However, he was willing to give Shay time to straighten himself out, adding that this was on the recommendation of Joe Kiernan who seemed to believe that the younger man had enormous potential. Shay returned Joe's professionalism, regretting the loss of his boss's respect but realising that nothing would regain that – only time and a hard slog.

He had gratefully accepted the fact that he would no longer be involved with clients on a day-to-day basis, and would instead be relegated to mere paper-pushing. Realising that his present position didn't merit the fairly substantial salary that went into his bank account each month, he considered himself fortunate that the issue hadn't even been raised by Michael Murray.

Shay knew he had to keep his head down and go through the motions of re-proving himself, all the while cracking up with the boredom of the mundane tasks facing him with each working day. This had been fine when Shay started work as a junior accountant, but now having reached a certain level of responsibility and then having it withdrawn suddenly, he felt bereaved. Initially, he'd actually felt hard done by and had even considered changing jobs. But the reality of his present position ensured that references would certainly be a problem should he decide to look elsewhere for work. No way would he be able to command a similar salary. Indeed his present one was high by any standards.

No, he'd have to take his medicine and bloody well like it, he decided. He was making a conscious effort to confine his social life to Fridays and Saturdays only, speaking little of his activities to his colleagues. That wasn't to say that his lifestyle had suffered as a result of his unfortunate work situation.

When he thought about it, Shay realised that it was Carla and the sense of feeling trapped that had led him to go a bit mad. Things had been pretty cool at the beginning, with Carla joining in to whatever he and

Ken had planned. She was up for anything and well able to handle her drink, so it became a regular occurrence to meet after work on Fridays and go on the razz for the night. Ken generally met someone and either they both came back to Shay's at the end of the night or Ken took off to her place if luck was with him. They would meet again on the Saturday night, sometimes with Ken's new *beau* in tow, other times just the three of them, with Ken regaling the others with tales of the previous night's exploits.

Sometimes Carla would moan about having to entertain Ken's latest conquest while the boys threw back shots at the bar, a little tradition carried over from their college days. Shay felt he could put up with the odd grumble as long as it was only the entertaining she was giving out about. And once he made sure to pay her a bit of attention before the night was up, Carla usually softened up, particularly if Ken and his companion headed for the hills.

Sex with Carla was dynamite, but not if they had an audience at the other side of the bedroom wall. Despite her uninhibited nature, Shay's girlfriend drew the line at making love while the giggles and moans from the next room were as loud as if the couple were in the room with them.

Lately Carla had started to suggest having dinner out as opposed to going on the tear two nights running, citing PMT or an exhausting week at work. She felt it would be good for them to spend some of the weekend sober, just so they could do something normal on a

Sunday instead of being thrown on the couch in bits.

Shay hadn't liked the sound of the "normal" bit, whatever it meant. He had this vision of himself and Carla in a garden centre, surrounded by the kind of couples who called out to each other to draw attention to a particular species of clematis or pyracantha: "We'll have to get this one, darling! It would cover the pergola in no time!"

Even the thought of being in such a situation enveloped Shay in a sense of panic. He was happy enough with Carla the way things were, but she was already showing signs of what Ken called "settlement cracks", a sure sign that Shay would need to redirect the course of their relationship before it was too late.

"Start as you mean to go on" was a fairly straightforward principle as far as Shay was concerned and he had no notion of spending another Friday night watching *The Late Late Show*.

On that note he punched in Carla's work number and told her he'd be in Counihans at six. Better get in there first before a film and a bottle of wine was suggested.

In his satisfaction at heading Carla off at the pass, Shay didn't even notice Joe Kiernan standing in the doorway.

"Don't let me disturb you, Shay," he commented caustically. "You can get those invoices up to me as soon as you finish organising your social life."

His expression of disbelief said it all, an expression that remained imprinted on Shay's mind for the rest of the day.

14

Number 1

Around the same time as Shay was being eyeballed by his boss, Linda was sitting at her desk staring out the window. She knew her mind wasn't on work at all today but for once she didn't care. Since they'd submitted the plans of the leisure complex to the council for approval, she had been on edge, watching the post every day. She was running out of patience. Today she was tempted to phone the planning office to see what stage the application was at but she was terrified it would be a "no".

She jumped as the door opened behind her and an envelope flew across her shoulder and landed on the desk in front of her. Her father stood in the doorway, laughing at her confusion, as it was only the second time he'd come to see her at Bodywork since she'd taken it over.

Linda grappled with the envelope, tearing it open in

105

a panic when she saw the Cork County Council stamp on the front. Relief washed over her when she read the words she had so longed to see. Full planning permission for the leisure complex had been granted. She would have imagined that she'd scream with delight at this news, but what she actually felt was a deep sense of satisfaction that the first part of her plan had been executed so swiftly and successfully. On many occasions, she'd heard her father grumble about the planning officials' misplaced sense of power, resulting in endless amendments before planning permission was finally granted. Sometimes the end result only vaguely resembled the original plans, so extensive had the alterations been in order to eventually get the approval of the council officials.

Daniel settled himself into the leather swivel-chair behind his daughter's desk and studied her as she made coffee for them both, evidently too stunned at the speed of progress to get excited and jump around squealing as she usually did when she got her way. With a stab of pride, he recognised how much she was like him, despite inheriting her height and her pale blue eyes from her mother.

"I guess we'll have to sit down with Charlie and work out the logistics of this thing soon," her father said, meaning, Linda knew, whether Charlie was going to be involved as a major player or merely at the level of an employee of Coltons.

Linda's face darkened a little. She'd been at Charlie to meet with her father and have this discussion, but he kept wanting to hold off until they knew if they would get planning for such a venture. She knew her boyfriend wasn't one hundred per cent sure about the wisdom of their setting up a separate company to develop the leisure complex. His main concern wasn't the success or failure of the project. Indeed Charlie was almost more convinced than Linda herself that it would thrive in view of the current economic climate. It was more that he felt he didn't have the same financial contribution to commit as Linda and her father did.

Linda could understand this, knowing Charlie's strong sense of pride, and longed to tell him it didn't really matter. Her father fully expected that Charlie would one day be his son-in-law and this in Linda's eyes negated any argument about each person having to subscribe to a certain level. Very much aware of her status as the eventual recipient of her father's business concerns, Linda was practical enough to see that she and Charlie were ideally placed to continue the running of the company when her father decided he no longer wanted to do it.

However, saying this out loud to Charlie was difficult, particularly when he hadn't ever actually mentioned marriage to Linda. She knew it would be on the cards at some stage. They were perfect together: his brilliant creativity and originality, her sharp business sense and the drive that she'd inherited from her father. Even physically they suited each other, with Charlie's powerful physique and dark good looks complementing her own tall svelte frame perfectly.

Intellectually and sexually they were a good couple. But it was just so hard to put it to Charlie like that, so that he'd forget about his pride and throw himself wholeheartedly into something that was going to be theirs as a couple anyway.

However, until Charlie made up his mind about the part he was going to take in the project, there was nothing stopping them continuing with the initial plans. Daniel and Linda chatted away about some of the finer details, discussing advertising and looking at how best to market the complex.

"Even choosing a name," Daniel teased pointedly, very much aware that his daughter's house was the only one in the Pebble Cove development not to be named yet. This was despite her approval of his attempt to create an air of exclusivity when the houses were being built.

After Daniel left, Linda rang Charlie on his mobile to tell him the good news. She could barely hear him over the noise of the machinery on the site he was visiting but he sounded as stunned as she'd felt at getting the first step over so quickly. Charlie rang off, promising to call in to Bodywork on his way back to the office so they could talk properly.

Linda felt an uncharacteristic nervousness take hold of her. If Charlie decided not to go in on this with her, some of the gloss would go off the whole thing. She liked the idea of them planning and working together, but mostly she was afraid that her father would be swayed towards proceeding with the complex as a

Coltons development if it was just going to be the two of them anyway. Linda knew that her father wouldn't see the subtle difference in her being an equal partner in a separate company as opposed to a hanger-on at Coltons. This was her idea and she wanted it to advance as such. She'd just have to do her best to bring her boyfriend around to her way of thinking.

*　*　*

"Congratulations, Ms Colton," Charlie exclaimed proudly later that day, hugging her on his arrival at the leisure centre.

Linda tried to read his face for any sign that he'd made his mind up, afraid of pushing it too much. Linda could be subtle when she wanted to and, unlike her father, Charlie didn't respond to wheedling and the female forms of persuasion. He was quite serious when it came to making decisions, weighing things up carefully before jumping in. Linda sensed that this was why her father had such faith in his opinions, and also why he thought him an ideal match for his headstrong daughter.

"Let's go out somewhere after work to celebrate. I'll try to book somewhere when I get back to the office. The Mill Race would be great if it's not full. At least we'd be able to talk properly there."

This sounded optimistic, Linda thought, and agreed to meet him in the foyer of the Coltons office at five. Most Friday evenings they went out for dinner with

Linda generally staying in Charlie's place afterwards. He'd bought the penthouse apartment in Longshore Quay, a development that was going on when he first came to Coltons, four years ago.

Daniel always gave employees an opportunity to buy into the housing schemes as it ensured a certain degree of staff loyalty at a time when the building industry was in a boom. Workers at every level were being lured to other companies with the promise of huge wage hikes and incentives like paid health insurance that constituted a monetary gain in itself.

Charlie was long past the stage of being won over to another company, despite numerous headhunting attempts in the early days. After he'd been the recipient of the Turner Prize, one of the most prestigious awards in architectural terms, Charlie had had many lucrative job offers. He'd chosen to work with Daniel Colton, not just for the substantial salary, but simply because Daniel had an outlook that high-density housing could be produced to a certain standard of individuality, in keeping with the ethos of the small towns and villages that were often host to sprawling developments of boxlike monotony.

Many of the Colton estates consisted of collections of detached cottage-style dormers, stone-faced, with slate roofing as opposed to the much cheaper, mass-produced tiles. Even the layout of the recent developments were a new departure, allowing for as much green space as could be got away with, moving away from the lines of "Legoland", brick-fronted semis that were part and parcel now of many smaller communities. Charlie too was a believer that the idea of an estate could be merged with the more conventional Irish home, incorporating the modern with the traditional to superb effect.

As well as building stylish homes, Daniel Colton had, since Charlie's arrival, lifted what had been a moderate concern onto an altogether new level, tendering for more lucrative state contracts and large areas of private development such as shopping complexes in the faster-growing towns and cities. Charlie Moorehouse's designs always attracted attention in the right places, the blend of traditional architecture combined with modern individualistic touches appealing to both the conservative eye and to those with less than moderate tastes.

* * *

They'd settled into one of the back booths in Mill Race with their glasses of Merlot before Charlie brought up the subject that was closest to Linda's heart. The low hum of the restaurant faded further into the background as he tried to describe the feeling of ownership that he felt with the completion of a building, the sense that it would always be in some way his own, regardless of whose name was on the deeds. The feeling that he'd created something lasting that was an integral part of the surrounding environment, of leaving behind a mark that was his alone.

"I'm just not sure that I want to move beyond the whole creative thing of simply designing and drawing. I *am* excited about the leisure complex, but somehow it's in terms of seeing how each individual building pans out. I just don't think I'd be committed enough to the whole project to go into partnership on it."

Linda could feel the leisure complex slipping away from her with each one of Charlie's words and a determination came over her to convince him that the project would be the best ever advertisement of his talent. If Charlie were to be a full partner in the undoubtedly successful venture, then it would be an ongoing testament to the artistic vision of its architect.

Charlie returned to the financial facts of the matter, but Linda had thought of a plan of action.

"We could agree with Dad some deal that if he puts up the largest share of the finance, we'll administer the complex for, say, five years. After that time, it would revert to being divided three ways, in exchange for our having got it off the ground and continuing to run it. Dad need have no involvement in the running of it, just putting up the money initially and sharing in the profits after that."

The notion of his investing more time to compensate for Daniel's large financial investment swayed Charlie somewhat, as did the idea of his name being attached to such a high profile enterprise. A venture on this scale would ensure his visibility as one of the foremost architects in the country.

While Charlie didn't have a definite plan for his

future, he knew what he didn't want. Ambitious and competitive, he knew that he could command a heftier salary than his present one from any number of prominent architectural consultants and become part of a stable of equally talented professionals who would moderate their work to suit the general ethos of the particular company. Dilute it to fit in with what people expected from a top firm, slowly and inexorably losing any originality in a quest to provide wealthy investors with the look that *they* wanted.

Making a name for himself was, Charlie had realised, the only way to ensure that he could command leadership of a project without the necessity of bowing to the judgement of people who were only interested in raking in lucrative contracts. This was why he had remained at Coltons for so long. Daniel gave him free rein to design as he wished, acknowledging the contribution that Charlie made to the company by only interfering with designs if they encroached on the practicalities of the planning regulations.

Essentially, Charlie was his own boss with the freedom to create the buildings he favoured, without the hassle of dealing with all the other details that eventually brought a plan to fruition.

"So what are you saying?" Linda asked eventually, having listened to all the angles that Charlie had presented to her. She herself was inclined to go with her gut instinct on whether to move ahead with something or not. She couldn't understand her boyfriend's need to tease everything to death before making a decision. She watched him now, swirling red wine thoughtfully around the glass, almost as if she wasn't there at all.

"I suppose I haven't really decided yet. You know this would be a huge commitment for me? Not just financially but in terms of being tied to the business end of a project that may go on for years. I didn't think it would all get off the ground so soon. I'm sorry, darling, I know you want to forge ahead with the plans but I need a bit of time to think it through."

"What is it that's bothering you most?" Linda questioned seriously, getting bluntly to the heart of the matter, much like her father, Charlie noticed.

"The bottom line is that I can choose to continue as I am, working for Coltons, and do the full plans for the leisure complex. Full stop. Or I can take on all the aggravation that goes with having financial responsibility for the project as well. I know it'd be high profile and that I'd make more money if I was directly involved, but I'm on a decent salary as it is. And," he added, "I think it's going to be high profile one way or another."

Linda's disappointment was almost palpable as she waved away the dessert trolley and concentrated on Charlie instead. He sounded very negative but she knew she couldn't push him. All she could do was point out the advantages to him and leave him to mull it over.

"Look, Charlie, I think we need to sleep on it and talk about it after the weekend. You know we could make a go of this together. In the long-term, I mean, aside from Dad," she added, hoping that he would get her point that all of it would be theirs anyway in the future. "Actually," she continued coolly, wanting to move on so he wouldn't see how much his decision meant to her, "I'm half thinking of going on an information tour over the weekend, just to see what all the other health spas are offering. I booked a few treatments in Castlerose and The Greenery to see what they're charging. And I've phoned some of the Dublin places and asked for their brochures. It'll be a start on the marketing side of things anyway."

It always amazed Charlie how his girlfriend could dismiss a problem like it didn't exist and move on, despite the fact that for him it wasn't resolved. Regardless of the fact that her proposed partner was undecided as to the next course of action, Linda was ploughing on ahead with her plans as if there were no obstacles at all.

He wondered if Linda even realised what a big deal this was in his life, if she really understood what the financial implications were. Even though she worked hard and had well earned her success at Bodyworks, she conveniently ignored the fact that the leisure centre had actually been *given* to her. She sometimes forgot that Charlie hadn't had any such cushion in life, that if he failed in business then he lost everything. If Linda failed, then she only lost face in front of her father. Her house was paid for. Charlie had a mortgage to consider. Despite the pressure his girlfriend was exerting, he knew he needed to take his time on this one.

"In that case maybe I'll go up home to Tipperary for a few days to clear my head. We can talk more about it on Monday," he said, calling for the bill. He felt exhausted and for the first time since they'd met, he realised with surprise that he wasn't looking forward to making love to Linda tonight. It was probably only the fact that this was one of the few times that they'd let work carry over into the weekend, but it was disconcerting nonetheless.

Linda zapped the remote central locking on the MG and, almost as if she'd read his thoughts, said in what she hoped was a steady voice that she'd drop him off at his house and head on home to Pebble Cove. Relieved, Charlie agreed.

The journey was short, the silence between them punctuated by the odd comment. Normally they'd have talked on the short journey to Longshore Quay but this evening there was only the most perfunctory of exchanges.

Linda pulled up outside his house. Charlie kissed her briefly, lost in his own thoughts about the decisions to come, and stood to watch her reverse out the driveway. This was the kind of night they should be together, he knew, to work out their plans. Not each going back to their own little world to think things out separately. He wondered now why he hadn't encouraged Linda to stay. Too late now, he thought, as she disappeared in a swish of gravel.

15

Leadington

"Fuck him, the prick!" was Ken's immediate response when Shay told him about the incident with Joe Kiernan later in Counihans. "What business is it of his what you do after work?"

They'd already had three pints and Shay was beginning to see Ken's point. It was no concern of Joe Kiernan that Shay actually had a life.

"Fuck him is right!" Shay declared and headed off to the bar, sealing the thought with a shot of whiskey as he waited for the pints to settle. Out of the corner of his eye he could see Carla watching him and he chose to ignore her pointed stare. Ken had abandoned her and was now at the far end of the bar chatting up a shapely brunette in a fairly revealing halter-neck top.

"You don't think Joe had a point, do you?" Carla queried when Shay settled himself in with the drinks.

"How do you mean?" Shay was shocked that his

117

girlfriend would think his boss was somehow justified in having an opinion on his social life.

"Well, you *were* organising your social life on company time. I know it wouldn't be a big deal ordinarily, but when you're supposed to be on some sort of trial you can see how he might think it's a bit much. You might need to keep the head down and look as if you've changed your tune. That's all they need to see."

Carla's tone was practical as she outlined what Shay knew to be the facts of the matter, but he didn't want to hear it right now. With a few drinks inside him he really couldn't be bothered, and he resented what he saw as disloyalty in Carla.

At least Ken was supportive, Shay thought, casting an eye around the bar for his friend. He spotted him over by a fire exit, chatting up a different girl, obviously having been blown out by the first one. Shay decided to go over and give Ken a good slagging and wind him up in front of his new friend. They often did this to each other for the laugh, to see if one could hang on to a conquest despite the best efforts of the other. Shay was well pissed off with Carla. No harm to let her cool down on her own for a while. It was her round anyway, he reasoned, heading off in Ken's direction.

He was just warming up on Ken and the lovely Ruth when he felt a tap at his shoulder and turned to see Carla, jacket on and bag over her shoulder.

"I'm heading off now," she informed him, obviously in bad humour. Over her shoulder Shay could see their vacated table with two full pints left for himself and Ken. Weighing up the situation, he decided it was best to leave with Carla seeing as his friend was absorbed in his mission to crack the stunning redhead who was not giving in as easily as Ken would have liked.

Ignoring Carla's protests, Shay got his jacket and winked knowingly as his friend gave him a discreet thumbs-up sign.

The taxi-driver chattered incessantly for most of the journey, Shay egging him on while Carla stared silently out the window into the blackness. Quietly she directed the car to her own apartment, a one-bedroomed affair in the basement of an old townhouse. It was only about ten minutes' walk from Pebble Cove, but Carla usually stayed at Shay's place after a night out.

Instead of heading straight to bed, Carla decided to make coffee, announcing that she wanted to talk. Shay knew enough about women to know that this was the big commitment talk and he was damned if he was going to be bullied into producing an engagement ring. Even moving in together wasn't on the cards for them as far as he was concerned, if that was the route she wanted them to take. Taking a deep breath, he decided to get his bit in, just in case his girlfriend was intent on getting him to capitulate.

"Before you start, Carla, I might as well tell you that I think we're getting too serious. So if you're going to say we should settle down a bit or whatever, then you need to know that I'm not ready for all that yet."

Shit, he berated himself; I shouldn't have mentioned

the word "yet", feeling that it implied he might be ready in the near future.

"You know, Shay," Carla answered softly, "I think you're right. There's no way you're ready for any sort of commitment. Nor am I, at the moment. But I *am* interested in a fairly mature relationship, and I don't think you're able for that at all. I don't mean to be bitchy or anything, but we're just at different levels right now. We're going nowhere really. Fine, I enjoy going on the piss now and again, but every weekend is a bit much. To be honest, I think we'd be better off calling it a day. I'm sorry, Shay, but that's how I feel."

Shay looked at her in stunned surprise. Normally the combination of his tousle-headed blond good looks and cheeky, upbeat manner ensured that women clung to him like limpets. No one had ever finished with him before, and here was he thinking she wanted to move in with him. And she didn't look as if she was playing games, he realised with a shock.

"I thought we were getting on OK," Shay blustered, confused by what he saw as an about-face from Carla.

"Look, Shay, the *craic* was good while it lasted, but I couldn't carry on like this all the time. It's up to you if you want to risk your job and your mortgage repayments for a constant session, but I'd like to meet someone who doesn't need to be plastered to have a good night out."

"Jesus, you're making me sound like an alcoholic!" Shay threw back defensively, not knowing exactly how to deal with the situation.

"Look, Shay, can we do this without picking and poking at each other? I've thought about it for a bit and I know that splitting up is what I want. I'm sorry."

"So, is that it?" was all that Shay could think of to say. It was dawning on him that he'd have to take his leave soon, as Carla seemed to have made her mind up.

For the last few weeks he'd been irritated with his girlfriend for getting too cosy, now he was kicking himself for not having acted in time. Annoyed that he hadn't got in there first, Shay began to say that he'd been thinking about finishing it himself.

"Come on, Shay, let's just finish our coffee." Carla suddenly sounded like a tolerant teacher who knew that a pupil was fibbing.

More irked than ever, he finished his coffee in a single gulp and left ungraciously without even saying goodnight.

* * *

Shay barely made it to the bathroom before throwing up. The doorbell kept ringing insistently, his brain throbbing inside his skull with every peal. Why in the name of God he had let his mother install the stupid, pretentious thing in the first place was beyond him. He was going to ignore it, when it occurred to him that it was probably Nora arriving to do her monthly clean-up to ensure that her son wasn't living in squalor.

Dragging himself off the floor of the en suite, Shay opened the bedroom window to see his mother looking up at him, perplexed.

"Are you alright, Shay? I've been ringing the bell for a full five minutes. Are you going to let me in?" she said in irritation, as her son stared dumbly at her from above.

"I'll come down," was all Shay said, rushing to the bathroom to be sick again before descending the stairs.

"Were you out late last night?" Nora queried, noticing her son's pallor. "You'll have to settle down a bit and not let yourself get run down from being out all night."

"I was in bed before twelve," Shay informed her wryly, neglecting to mention polishing off the best part of a bottle of whisky and collapsing in a heap on the bed. Fucking Carla, he thought again, remembering his brief visit to her apartment last night with disgust.

He'd been well cheesed off walking home and had tried phoning Ken to see if they could meet up in town and go on a session. Ken's phone had been turned off – a sure sign that he'd scored with the redhead and would have no interest in Shay tagging along. This annoyed him even more and he'd gone disconsolately back to the house, galled by the fact that it was still only eleven o'clock. Normally it was at least 2 a.m. before a night out turned into a disaster, so this was actually a record. He hadn't been in the mood for just going to bed, so he'd flicked around the channels and downed the whiskey in defiance of Carla and her sanctimonious attitude.

Shay came out of his reverie to find a cup of tea in

front of him, and his mother rooting in the fridge for the makings of a breakfast.

"God, Shay, you'll have to do a bit of a shop. There's nothing in here that wouldn't give you salmonella. I'll make a bit of toast, that's all the bread's fit for."

Thank heavens there wasn't enough in the fridge for his mother to make a fry-up, Shay thought, his stomach turning at the idea of it. He fought down the nausea and tried to sip the tea while Nora went on about her plans for the morning.

Nora loved coming over to put her son's house to rights once a month or so. She liked the idea of her only child living in a housing development as exclusive as this one. Most of her friends' children had bought into the bigger estates nearer the city, and while the location of Pebble Cove was probably a little outside the boundaries of convenience for those working in town, the magnificent views and the quality of the houses more than made up for it. Also, the fact that there were just four houses only added to the select tone of the development.

Secretly, Nora felt that she had done rather well for her son, considering that she'd been left a widow in her mid-twenties, with a toddler to raise alone. The years of struggle were worth it when she saw her handsome boy with a good job and his own home.

Admittedly Shay was looking pretty shook this morning but he must get out and about and have a life of his own, she told herself. Nora always tried to guard against cloistering her only child for fear of pushing him away. She had made a good life for herself, her evenings filled with bridge and the book club, with the odd game of golf at the weekends.

Thinking of the golf club put Nora in mind of Gertie Lynch's enquiry about the possibility of Shay organising a summer job in Murrays for Patrick, her youngest. She put this to Shay now, to see if he'd be able to help.

"Probably not," her son responded quickly. "It's usually only the directors' kids who get summer work there when they're off college for the summer."

Shay suddenly felt panicked by the fact that his mother thought he was a person of influence in Murrays, when as it stood he was barely hanging in there by the skin of his teeth. For the first time since his superiors had called him to order, Shay felt the enormity of his situation hit home. The thought of explaining to his mother that he'd been fired was enough to make him feel dizzy.

"You look desperate," his mother chided. "Go on back to bed and have a bit of a lie-in. You probably had a busy week. Gertie told me that Coltons are looking to start some big development in Rochestown – it was on the *Examiner*. I suppose you'll have all that to contend with soon."

Shay felt weak as he mounted the stairs again. His mother prided herself on keeping abreast of his career and he could imagine her boasting subtly to her friends about how high up her son was in Murrays, the most prominent accountancy firm in Cork. He now regretted any little titbits he had let slip when his mother had questioned him about work in the past. The fact that it obviously meant so much to her made the possibility of failure all the more frightening.

He lay on the bed but couldn't settle enough to sleep, the sound of Nora clattering around the kitchen jarring his nerves with every second. Maybe taking a shower and getting out of the house would clear his head. He certainly wasn't going to lie around fretting about work all day.

"You're up already?" his mother exclaimed in surprise when she saw him coming down the stairs again.

Explaining that he was off to do a grocery shop, Shay disappeared and left her to her own devices.

Everyone in the Cove was industriously employed this Saturday lunchtime, or so it seemed to Shay. Marcus next door was hurrying out of the house with an elegant, tallish girl, a cooler box wedged under his arm. Carla had told Shay that this was how they transported Deirdre's breast milk to the hospital for the baby. The perky nurse across the way was packing the boot of her car, stopping to wave at Marcus and then at Shay when she spotted him getting into the Saab.

Jesus, they were like Shiny Happy People, all waving and smiling at each other, Shay bitched silently as he acknowledged the greeting with a nod. He just didn't feel particularly neighbourly this morning. The tea and toast had settled his stomach somewhat, but the sooner he had the shopping over and done with, the sooner he could have something more substantial and start to feel human again.

The supermarket was a nightmare so Shay dashed around as fast as he could, flinging stuff into the trolley at random, mostly ready-made meals that he could just throw into the microwave when he ran out of the stocks that his mother would have loaded into the freezer while he was out.

He suddenly felt guilty at all the effort that Nora put in to keep his life ticking over, and recognised that he should bring something for a proper lunch to acknowledge her hard work. While his mother sometimes annoyed him with her fussing, Shay knew that it was only because he was the centre of her world since his father had died. All of Shay's achievements were proof that she had managed more than well when push came to shove. Once Shay was in school, Nora had gone back to work in the solicitor's office that she had left on her marriage, to supplement the income that she received from her husband's pension.

Returning to the deli counter, Shay put together some salads and cold meats that his mother would like, finally reaching the checkout to land behind the noisiest kid he'd ever encountered. His head was still throbbing, despite the two Neurofen that he'd swallowed before venturing out. The child's mother ignored his yells for some sort of crisps and chatted away to the checkout girl as Shay glared at her back.

* * *

It was almost five o'clock before his mother left, the house spotless in her wake. She'd actually suggested to Shay that he get someone in to do a few hours housework every week to stop the place getting into a state.

"I'm only too happy to come over and do it, love, but I don't want to cramp your style, as they say."

Shay knew that she'd love to be telling the bridge ladies that her son had a cleaner, a sure sign that he was too important and busy to be bothered with such mundane things as hoovering and dusting.

"Or maybe it'd be cheaper to get a wife instead," she joked, fishing for any news that would indicate her son settling down. Shay never brought his girlfriends home, but Nora supposed he would when he met the right one. In one sense, she hated the thought of losing him, on the other hand a wife and children would be ties that would bind them together as a family unit. She often thought on this, picturing herself as a doting grandmother, going out to Sunday lunch with Shay and his perfect wife and children.

However, by the grunt that Shay gave at the mention of a wife, Nora accepted that her little fantasy was far from becoming a reality.

16

Number 1

Having slept badly, Charlie had eventually decided to get up and head off immediately for his parents' home in Tipperary on Saturday morning. Once he was on the road, his distracted humour had started to dissipate and he rolled down the window to enjoy the scent of the whitethorn bushes that lined the country roads.

An hour later he was pulling into the yard at home in Gilcrenan, the familiar whitewashed farmhouse ablaze with colour.

His mother had surpassed herself with the window-boxes this year and Charlie wondered in amusement how many hours his father had spent trimming and watering the ones on the upper windowsills. Margaret was always determined to better the previous year's display, resulting in CJ having to spend every spare moment up the ladder attending to them while she instructed from below.

"You just missed your mother," his father greeted him as he got out of the car.

While theirs was not a relationship for hugs, CJ greeted his son warmly with a clap on the back as he led him inside. The kitchen table was overflowing with rhubarb tarts and plates of sandwiches, sponge cakes and scones.

"Is there a funeral on that I don't know about?" Charlie exclaimed, reaching for a queen cake and scoffing it in two bites.

"I've instructions to keep you away from the table until Maura Quinn comes to collect the rest of the baking. Your mother left a plate of sandwiches in the fridge for you, and a bowl of rhubarb crumble."

CJ was filling the kettle as he outlined his wife's orders affectionately. Even though it was only ten o'clock, Margaret had catered for her son's hearty appetite before she left the house.

Charlie went and claimed his sandwiches and rhubarb crumble. The mention of Maura Quinn reminded him that it was "walking weekend", the local name for the popular walking festival that the village played host to every summer. Margaret had been on the organising committee since it started twenty-five years previously and the whole family had somehow got roped in over the years.

CJ had always led the less difficult family-oriented walk on both Saturday and Sunday, with Charlie tagging along once he was old enough to keep up. He remembered walking along beside his father in the sunshine, listening to the older man pointing out areas of interest to the walkers, waiting patiently every half hour or so for the slower ones to catch up and have a rest before moving off again. Then it would be back to the community centre for tea and sandwiches, served up on paper plates by his mother and the committee ladies. Charlie had loved sitting up on the red plastic chair beside his father and the other walkers, feeling as grown-up and important as if he'd just ascended the Andes.

Maeve, his older sister, would be helping behind the counter, lining up the polystyrene cups and asking people in the long queue if they'd like milk and sugar.

Even though CJ was almost seventy now he was as fit as he'd been when Charlie was a boy. He still led the lower walks on the festival weekend, as well as going for a more brisk walk himself most weekends. His mother had no real desire to participate in the actual hillwalking, preferring instead the buzz of planning registration details and fees, organising buses to ferry the more experienced walkers up into the foothills and ensuring that the refreshments area ran smoothly.

"Are you walking at all this weekend?" his father asked now, assuming that his son's visit was timed to coincide with the festival.

In truth, Charlie had forgotten all about it and hadn't come prepared. He said as much to his father.

"Well, if you even have your trainers you can come on the lower walk with me. Your mother said there was a huge crowd booked so I could do with another pair of hands. You know that Jimmy got his hip done last week?" He was referring to his long-time walking partner who would now be unable to help guide the family walk.

"I suppose I'd be alright in tracksuit and runners. It'd be no harm to get a bit of fresh air anyway when I'm stuck inside all week. What's Maeve at this weekend? I suppose she's down below in the community centre?"

Like Margaret, Maeve was heavily involved with the organising committee, having the same love of list-making as her mother, not to mention her considerable culinary skills.

"Dan's mother is down with them for the weekend to keep an eye on the kids, so Maeve's up to her ears in it. All the rooms are full so she's really under pressure this year."

Since giving up her job in the Civil Service to raise her children, Charlie's sister had extended her house for use as a Bed and Breakfast. The festival weekend was usually her busiest, with walkers arriving from all over the country to trek the Gilcrenan Hills. The fact that Maeve was so tied up with the festival committee never impinged on the running of the B&B, as she'd fortunately been blessed with a marvellous mother-in-law who was only delighted to take on a pair of unruly twins as well as the guests for the weekend.

"What time are you setting out at?" Charlie asked now, delving into the rhubarb crumble. His father was already dressed in his walking boots so he'd have to get a move on if he was going to accompany him.

"I said I'd be over at the pub at half ten but we're not leaving until eleven. You can follow me over. It'll take me a while to round them up anyway."

The family walk usually departed from Murph's with the group arriving back at the community centre about three hours later. People were advised to register at ten but there were always a few stragglers. After CJ left, Charlie unpacked and changed, enjoying the familiar feeling of being in his old room.

He hadn't lived at home since he'd left school and set off for college in Cork but very little had changed. The same quilt was spread across the end of the bed, no doubt shaken out by his mother when he'd phoned this morning to say that he was on his way. Charlie hung the few clothes that he'd brought with him in the mahogany wardrobe and headed off to join his father.

The tiny pub was buzzing when he arrived a few minutes later. It was a glorious day which probably accounted for the large number queuing at the small table manned by CJ and the local curate. Ten minutes later the horde took off in the direction of the forest park, an amenity area of some hundred acres of woodland, boasting a collection of log chalets and rustic holiday homes. CJ led the way, matching his pace to that of those at the head of the pack. A mile or so later, on reaching the farthest exit point of the park, he stopped to take stock of the situation and allow the slower walkers to catch up. Surprisingly the group had stayed pretty much together, mainly because there were no children on board, the youngest being a trio of local teenage girls in very short shorts and exposed midriffs. Knowing that many of the village teenagers had absolutely no interest in hillwalking and participated mainly to flirt with the groups of youngsters arriving from surrounding areas, CJ cast an amused eye at his son before moving off again.

"It's great when they're all at the same level, you don't have to worry about the slow ones getting tired. How's work going?"

Charlie hadn't intended to unburden himself to his father. Rather he'd hoped that the change of scene and an environment where he didn't have to talk about the leisure complex would give him a better perspective on things. But now that they were effectively alone, parted a little from the main body of walkers, he suddenly felt like seeing what his father's opinion would be on the issue.

While Charlie had always been fairly independent, even as a small boy, he valued his father's balanced approach to a problem. As far back as choosing what subjects to take in school, he'd thought about what it was he wanted to do before sitting down and discussing it with his father. CJ normally agreed with his son, and even when he didn't, he would only offer advice. CJ wasn't the type to force a point, preferring to let his children make up their own minds.

Now he listened carefully, occasionally asking a question to clarify a point. Charlie put the situation to him from both viewpoints, trying to weigh up the pros and cons as he spoke aloud what he'd been mulling over in his mind for the preceding weeks.

"If the money wasn't a problem, would you feel more secure about it?" his father wanted to know. "Is it the fact that you can't contribute an equal share that's getting to you?"

"That's a bit of it I suppose, but I know the fact that I'd be overseeing the building as well as designing the complex and running it with Linda could be said to balance out the financial side of it. Daniel wouldn't be doing any of that – his input would be solely investment related. Having said that, I would feel a bit of a poor relation if I did go ahead with it," he admitted wryly, a reality that he found difficult to discuss with Linda.

"Look, Charlie, your mother and I were going to talk to yourself and Maeve about the farm over the next few months, but I might as well tell you now what we've been planning. It might make a difference. It's getting to be a bit much for us to be honest and I know that neither yourself nor Maeve and Dan want to take on the running of it."

Charlie had always regretted that he didn't have more interest in farming. Indeed the sizeable dairy herd would have made a substantial living had either he or Maeve been willing to take it on. CJ, if he was disappointed that his son hadn't the same love of the land that he and Margaret had, never showed it and always encouraged Charlie to follow the path that he wanted. When he was younger and some of his friends were starting to get involved in the family farms, Charlie used to hope that maybe Maeve would meet someone who would share his father's passion for the land. Dan, when he came along, was town born and bred, a man whose idea of country living entailed not being more than two miles from the shops. Teaching in the local primary school, he'd settled into Gilcrenan remarkably well but wasn't at all interested in the hard slog of farm life.

"We wanted to talk it out with you both before we did anything, but we both think it'd be best if we sold it now when land prices are high. I'll be seventy next birthday so it's time I slowed down a bit. Or so your mother tells me," he finished, smiling wryly at the fact that Margaret actually *wanted* him under her feet all day.

"You know that this whole leisure complex thing isn't just about the money? I don't expect you and Mam to solve it for me, you know. I suppose I just needed to talk about it to someone who's not directly involved." Charlie was anxious that his father didn't think that this was the reason he had poured out the story to him.

"I know that but, at the same time, the place will need to be sold at some stage soon, so it may as well be now if it makes a difference to you. It belongs to you and Maeve anyway. Your mother and I are well sorted for the future and we wanted to give the two of you a bit of a leg up in life. We're ready for a change, son."

Charlie was overwhelmed that his parents had discussed this so completely, that they wanted to sort everything out now. He'd never thought of his father as being old. But maybe they were right to retire fully from the land and enjoy life a little while they were both well and healthy.

Charlie was only able to mutter a "Thanks, Dad" under his breath, so choked was he by his parents' wish to see himself and Maeve well provided for.

"Your mother and I were thinking of keeping an acre or so and maybe building a bungalow for ourselves. The house is too big for us as it is and before we know it we'll be having trouble getting up the stairs."

"And what about the house? Would that go with the farm, do you think?" Charlie knew he had no right to be so shocked at the thought of the farmhouse not being home any more. After all, he'd had the choice of taking over the farm and eventually the house when his parents could no longer manage it.

"Well, it'd be great if one of you wanted to keep it but I suppose Maeve and Dan are happy where they are, with the B&B going so well. And you'd never get the kind of job you have now if you were to move up here. We don't expect either of you to take it on. The estate agent said we could sell the farm as a whole, or sell the house separately from the land. We'll see when the time comes."

With that, they arrived at the Shrine of Our Lady, which, CJ informed the group, had been built in 1954, the "Marian Year", the centenary of the proclamation of the Dogma of Mary's Assumption into Heaven. This marked the halfway point of the walk and the walkers threw themselves wearily down by the roadside to open the packed lunches that the festival committee had advised them to bring. The sun beamed down as sandwiches, fruit and flasks were unpacked. Even though it was only a couple of hours since his mother's brunch, Charlie ate ravenously, sitting a little apart from the small gatherings of two and three people. CJ wandered from group to group, outlining the features of the remainder of the walk, checking to see if anyone was too tired to continue and generally chatting about the route so far.

Charlie closed his eyes, trying to assimilate everything that his father had talked about. The sun was warm on his face and he suddenly wished that he could stay here by the side of the road to just think. He actually felt emotional and a little bit drained by the conversation of the past hour. A lot had changed in his life since this morning. He could now afford to go ahead with a partnership in the leisure complex if he wanted to, the financial obstacle now removed. Somehow, this made the decision even more difficult.

His reverie was interrupted as the walkers prepared to restart, stretching their legs in anticipation. Father and son led the way again as the party rounded onto a country boreen that would lead them back in the direction of the forest park. All in all, the walk would be eight miles, with the leisurely pace and frequent stops stretching it out over four hours.

Almost as if they hadn't broken the flow of conversation with the lunch break, CJ resumed the discussion about Charlie's work situation. Despite spending much of the recess in genial chat with the walkers, he'd obviously been running the problem over in his mind.

"Say if you do go ahead with the project with Linda and her father, how will it affect the work you do already with Coltons? Will you carry on with all the other jobs you have on? You'd have a lot of responsibility and pressure to make the leisure complex work out so it might be tough to have the everyday work on hand as well. Or would you be thinking of quitting as an architect and going at the running of the complex full-time?"

Uncannily, CJ had hit on all the questions that had been buzzing around his son's brain since the news of the planning permission had come through. He had to admit that managing a complex on the scale of the one they were planning could be a full-time job. This was fine for Linda, whose career was rooted in the leisure industry. But for him, the whole operational side of business held no appeal. Charlie wondered if he was a bit wimpish to shy away from an opportunity such as this, particularly now that he had the money to back it up. Many a man would jump at this easy *entrée* into the world of big business and the social prominence that would follow. He said as much to his father who smiled at the notion that his son might be afraid to face a challenge.

"Is it that you feel you'd be letting Linda down if you don't join forces with her on this, or did you talk about how it would be if you decided not to get involved?" Again CJ had come very close to the heart of the matter, hitting on the one aspect that Charlie had been wary of giving too much thought to.

"You mean would myself and Linda still be able to get along if I choose to let her tackle this on her own?"

CJ had never spoken to his son about his future with Linda, but on the few occasions that he'd met her he'd been surprised that Charlie would go for someone so cool and distant.

"I've been thinking about that. I know she'd be disappointed if I wasn't interested, and it might even mean that Daniel actually would only finance it as part of a Coltons job. I can't see him handing over the land in Rochestown too easily when Linda has no experience of development at all. I think he'd be depending on me to put the reins on it a bit. It'd mean revising the whole plan really. I'll have to buck up and decide though – I can't be dithering forever," Charlie concluded as his father again drew to a halt by a stile to allow the stragglers to catch up.

"This'll be the starting point for the 'B' walk tomorrow," CJ told the assembled walkers, referring to the more difficult walk into the hills. "If any of you are considering going on it, the bus will be leaving Murph's at nine. You'll definitely need boots for it, and a packed lunch." Many of today's walkers would have done the easier "C" walk in preparation for the more difficult trek the following day.

The group moved off again after the short rest, many

of them munching apples and swigging from water bottles in the sweltering sun. Now that they were on the home strait a sudden burst of energy infected them, quickening the pace for everyone. Fifteen minutes later the gates of the forest park were in view, and the walkers strode out briskly.

"Tea and sandwiches in the community centre," CJ announced for the benefit of those who had travelled from afar and who would be facing a drive home unless they were staying around for the Sunday walk.

By three o'clock, CJ's charges were lined up at the counter accepting refreshments, some taking their polystyrene cups out onto the pavement to enjoy the sunshine and encourage the "B" walkers who were now returning after their more strenuous six-hour sojourn in the hills. Charlie propped himself at the end of the counter to chat to his mother and Maeve who were bustling back and forth in the apparently organised chaos surrounded by equally industrious ladies who all seemed to know what they were about.

"Hi, Charlie, no sign of you getting married?" Maura Quinn always teased Charlie mercilessly about his single state, chiding Margaret for having taught her son to cook so well that he now didn't need a wife.

"You'll get an awful hop when I do," Charlie responded laughing, abandoning the pandemonium of the refreshments area to locate his father on the street.

He felt energised by all the activity and looked forward to the evening ahead. Festival weekend was as much defined by the traditional music sessions in

Murph's as it was by the magnificent scenery and well-organised hill treks, and Charlie knew that Maeve and Dan would have booked a baby-sitter well in advance as always. There would be a long night ahead if previous festival weekends were anything to go by.

17

Leadington

Ken finally rang that same Saturday evening, waking Shay out of a deep sleep. He glanced at the clock as he picked up his mobile from the bedside locker. It was gone nine. His friend was full of his latest conquest, describing in detail his night as it had unfolded after Shay and Carla had left the pub.

"She's coming out tonight, only you'll have to leave Carla at home because Ruth has a friend staying and I sort of lined you up for her."

Ken often did this, making a date for Shay with the friend of whoever he was with at the time. Shay groaned. He'd almost decided to stay at home tonight and nurse his hangover. On second thoughts, it might be the very thing he needed to put Carla firmly in the recycle bin. Hoping that the friend would be halfway decent-looking, he arranged to meet Ken in The Watershed at ten, giving himself time to shower again and shave.

The place was hopping when he arrived, the floor actually throbbing with the force of the music blasting out from the massive speakers. Shay pushed his way through the crowds in search of Ken and his companions, squeezing through tight groups of boisterous patrons and feeling the coolness of the odd splash of a drink spilling on his shirt as the horde heaved almost as one. He eventually spotted them near the bar, the three pushed together in a huddle. He recognised Ruth from the previous night and was impressed with her friend, a tall blonde in a black strapless top, a bustier Carla had once told him they were called.

Ken waved as he made his way towards them, making the introductions as brief as possible over the music. Rhona seemed OK, smiley and interested. She tried to make conversation with Shay over the din when he arrived back from the bar with his first round, and he knew this was shaping up to be a good night. As good a night as he'd had in ages, he reflected now, considering how dry Carla had become in recent weeks.

Shay still hadn't had a chance to tell his friend about his girlfriend blowing him out, as he'd been still half-asleep when Ken phoned earlier. He knew his buddy would tell him that he was lucky to get out while the going was good, and while Shay knew this to be true in that he wouldn't miss Carla *per se*, he was pissed off at the whole notion of her finishing with him.

They eventually got an opportunity to chat when the girls went to the ladies'.

"Well, do you think you'll go for it?" Ken quizzed, referring to the fact that Shay and Rhona seemed to be getting on like a house on fire.

"Definitely. Carla's out of the picture now anyway, so I won't even have to feel guilty."

"Good man yourself!" Ken congratulated him, presuming that his friend had dispensed with Carla. "She was getting a bit clingy lately."

Shay let it ride, happy to have his reputation intact. Anyway, it was unlikely that Ken would bump into his ex and even more unlikely that they would discuss the details of the relationship break-up. Shay felt better already.

"Here's a little something to help you celebrate your freedom then," Ken said with a smirk, and Shay could feel his friend's hand slipping something into his pocket. "I picked a few up earlier before the girls got here."

The lads often did an 'E' or two if they were on a proper night out, so Shay wasn't surprised at his friend's purchase.

"They're new on the block," Ken told him now. "'Snowballs' your man said they were called. We can try them out later when we're on the floor."

With that, they could see the girls approaching through the throng, holding glasses and bottles aloft. They'd obviously detoured to the bar on the way back. Shay fingered the small tablet that his friend had placed in his pocket, relishing the thought of the abandon it would bring.

Shay always knew he was getting somewhere with a girl when she was leaning towards him enough for him to see right down between her breasts. This was the situation with Rhona now, so he tactfully ignored his friend's wheedling that they should all hit the dancefloor. Shay was damned if he was going to break the mood now, just when his companion was warming up. Ken took off, with Ruth clinging on behind him lest they get separated in the crowd. Shay now turned the full force of his charm on Rhona, turning his back on the dancefloor and leaning his arm on the wall above her shoulder.

Things were progressing nicely as they sipped their drinks and chatted as best they could. At one point, Shay could sense her losing interest and turned to see what she was looking at. Some sort of skirmish had started on the dance-floor and already three hefty bouncers were making their way towards the commotion. Rows always struck up in places like this where everyone was drunk and people started to push and jostle while others tried to dance. Losing interest, he turned back to Rhona but she was frowning, still taken up with the scene before her.

Suddenly she started to move towards the dance-floor, yelling at Shay that there was something wrong with Ruth. Indeed there was, he thought, seeing the screaming girl being held back by people as the bouncers tried to get in at the gang who were fighting.

Fuck's sake, surely Ken hadn't gone and started a fight? Shay knew how wild and wonderful his buddy's dancing was when he'd had a few pints, and he'd had more than a few already tonight. As he neared the mêlée, Shay urged Rhona to stay back. He knew it was possible that a few punches could be thrown when he came to Ken's defence.

With a shock, Shay realised that there was no brawl, only Ken lying on the ground surrounded by bouncers. They were waving the crowds back as his friend's body contracted stiffly, his head thrown back. Shay could see the veins in his neck standing out and froth flying from his mouth as the spasms clenched his body. He tried to tell the security men that he was with Ken but he just kept getting pushed back. One of them was speaking into a radio while another tried to control Ken's movements by holding his head to stop it hitting off the ground with every jerk of his body.

The crowds parted suddenly to allow two ambulance men through with a stretcher. Shay felt relief wash over him then as they both started to work on the convulsing form, blowing into his lungs with a mask clamped over his mouth and nose. A needle was inserted into his arm at some point and gradually the spasms lessened. Ken's face was now deathly pale, whereas it had been a florid red turning to purple before the ambulance crew arrived. He looked to be unconscious as they strapped him onto a stretcher that popped up onto wheels and transported him towards the exit. Shay followed them, trying to get their attention to know where they were taking him.

"I'm his friend, Ken's his name," Shay finally got to tell one of them as the still inert form was loaded into the ambulance.

"Then come with us in the ambulance," he was told by the burlier of the two. "We'll need you to give us his details and all once we get him stabilised."

The doors of the ambulance slammed shut behind them and Shay tentatively took a seat opposite the stretcher where his best friend lay unconscious, all thoughts of Rhona and Ruth forgotten. Just as they started to move away from the kerb, lights flashing, Ken's body again started to convulse, his face turning the angry red colour once more. The paramedic responded immediately, clamping the mask over Ken's face. His colleague, watching in the rear-view mirror, hit the siren as they sped away through the summer night.

* * *

The night had been endless and all Shay wanted to do was die. But he knew he had to phone his mother before anything came out in the morning papers. She answered the phone straight away, despite the fact that it was still only half eight.

"Is everything alright, Shay?" she asked immediately. She always asked this if he rang before 10 a.m. or after 10 p.m., and usually he laughed at her worried tone before asking her where to get a plumber or what wash to put a wool jumper in.

He decided not to tell her over the phone, just saying that he needed to talk to her and he'd come over straight away. The guards had offered to drop him wherever he wanted but he'd known that Nora would have died of fright if she'd seen a Garda car pulling up outside the house on a Sunday morning.

"I'm alright, Mam, honestly. I'll be over in a few minutes. Will you put a bit of breakfast on for me?"

Although he didn't feel much like tucking into the large grill that his mother would now make, Shay knew that it'd occupy her until he arrived. Otherwise she'd be out of her mind with worry.

"God, love, you look desperate," she greeted him on his arrival. "Were you in bed at all?" Nora made a mental note to talk to her son about minding himself a bit better but sensed that now was not the right time.

"I'm grand, Mam, but something happened last night." He knew she'd be shocked but he had to tell her before one of her cronies got hold of it.

"Tell me, for Jesus' sake, Shay!" He'd never heard his mother swear and realised how dishevelled he must look.

"I went out last night with Ken to a nightclub. He got some kind of a fit when he was out dancing and he was brought to hospital. Mam, they couldn't revive him. He was dead before they even got him into casualty."

Having been through the ordeal of hearing the exact same words said to Ted and Ina Roche only two hours

149

ago, Shay was beyond shock.

* * *

When Ina had opened the door in her dressing-gown and had seen Shay and the female Garda standing there, her face had told them that she knew immediately. As her husband Ted appeared on the landing above, she'd sunk to the ground, wrapping her arms around herself, her shoulders shaking with grief while Shay gently told her Ken was gone and repeated over and over how sorry he was. Ted stood stock-still as he watched his wife, a vibrant blonde and lady captain of their golf club, crumble before his eyes. He descended slowly and sat on the last step of the stairs, cradling his wife's head in his lap, unable to cry, and Shay knew somehow that they'd feared and expected this night.

Ken used to laugh at how his mother fretted over him, warning him about getting his drinks spiked with drugs and how easy it was to pick up sexually transmitted diseases.

"Mr and Mrs Roche," the Garda said at last, "may we come in?" She'd introduced herself to Shay as Angela and he now realised what a tough job she had, breaking news like this to people time and time again.

Ted straightened a little and looked at her squarely as if he was anxious to get it over with, to hear out loud what had happened. Shay was dumbstruck with shock and exhaustion, his heart contracting painfully when

Ina looked directly at him.

"What happened?" Her voice sounded abnormal to Shay's ears, tight and high-pitched.

"I think we need to go inside and sit down." This came from Angela who sensed the hysteria in Ina.

Slowly, Ted helped Ina up and supported her as far as the kitchen. Angela calmly asked Shay to make some tea. Glad of something to do, he plucked mugs off the mug-tree, the same green Denby ones that had been there in Shay's teenage years. He and Ken had always gravitated towards the Roches' home after a night out, knowing that Nora would sniff them for alcohol if they landed back to Shay's house.

Then Shay heard Angela explaining that Ken had been brought into hospital by ambulance following a collapse.

"What made him collapse?"

Silence hung over the table as Angela gave Shay the opportunity to answer. Unable to say out loud what he'd admitted earlier in the Garda station, Shay quietly laid two cups of tea on the table in front of the parents of his best friend.

Gently, Angela continued. "It seems that your son had come into possession of a 'Snowball' tablet. It's like Ecstasy, but many times more lethal. The fact that he'd had a few drinks before taking it meant that he may have been a little dehydrated. The combination appears to have caused a type of seizure. I'm afraid he didn't make it to the hospital. I'm so sorry to have to tell you this."

Shay admired her courage and the non-judgemental way that she was able to tell the Roches that their beloved son, born almost eight years after they thought their family was complete, had died of a drug overdose in the back of an ambulance. And that now his body was lying in the morgue of an inner-city hospital. It occurred to Shay that these people might never have been inside one of Cork's public hospitals, having had private cover for everything from maternity to tonsils to dental work.

"Can we go in to see him?" Ted asked this as if Ken had been admitted for a broken leg, and Shay wondered if he'd taken it all in. But it was very clear that he had taken it in as Angela nodded and Ted advised Ina to get dressed while he rang the rest of the family.

Shay sat dumbly at the kitchen table staring at his tea.

"Did you know he was taking drugs?"

Ted had waited until his wife had left the room before asking this. He didn't seem angry, more as if he was resigned to what had happened and just wanted to fill in the missing details. Shay wanted to cry with the shock of it all, from the horror of the nightclub to the terrifying ambulance and the utter panic when the paramedics eventually gave up the struggle to keep Ken alive. Now this man who'd been the only father figure that Shay had ever had was asking him if he'd been implicated in his son's death. Knowing that he'd lost one of the most precious things in his life, Shay felt he owed it to Ted to be honest.

"We'd often had a few Ecstasy tablets before, but neither of us had ever taken anything else. Usually the two of us would take them, but I was after meeting a girl and I was a bit taken up with her. Ken had got the Snowball off some fella earlier. I didn't even know he'd taken it until I saw him collapsing."

Shay had been through all this in the A&E department and later in the Garda interview room. He didn't know who had supplied the tablet, which was what the Gardaí really wanted to know. He could see the disdain in their eyes when they'd told him it would be better if he went with Garda Nolan to tell Ken's family the news.

"You know, Shay, myself and Ina always worried about Ken more than the rest of them. We always thought it was because he was the youngest and we still saw him as a baby. We knew he was a bit wild. People often gave me little hints to warn me, at the golf club and places. Ina was always trying to get him to calm down." He said this with a small wry smile, already reminiscing about his son. "But I'll tell you one thing, Shay. Whatever happens in this house, Ina and I have each other. Your mother has no-one. I remember her standing beside your father's grave with you in her arms. I'll never forget how strong she was and the way she kept going afterwards. She's a great woman, Shay, always was. Don't ever let her have to answer the door like Ina did this morning. Go on home now with Angela here. It wasn't what we wanted for him but I'm glad

Ken had a friend with him when he left the world."

Shay wished at that moment that Ted and Ina had screamed at him that he was the lowest of the low, that he was the worst thing that had ever happened to their beautiful son. How could he stand in front of these people as if nothing had happened? He didn't want to be let off the hook. The guilt and the misery were too great and he had no-one to share it with. This was one scrape that Ken wouldn't laugh off, nor would they look back on it together, wondering how they'd got away with it.

* * *

"I said, did *you* take anything?"

Breaking into his thoughts, his mother looked frightened. She knew nothing about recreational drugs and was afraid that Shay would get a delayed reaction and collapse in front of her.

"I took nothing," he answered flatly, aware that this was the first genuine thing he'd said in hours. "I'm sorry, Mam, I didn't mean for any of this to happen. It was a bit of a laugh and now Ken's dead. Oh God, this is desperate!" Feeling as if the whole world was falling in on his head, Shay put his head down on the table and sobbed from grief and loss and exhaustion.

Nora stroked his head, telling him over and over that it'd be alright, glad with all her heart to have Shay in front of her and ashamed at her selfishness in feeling this, her heart going out to the Roches who were today facing the worst ordeal of their lives.

After a while, Nora made him eat the breakfast that she been preparing when he came in. Shay did as he was told, incapable of refusing, and allowed his mother to take him upstairs to his old room.

"You get into bed, Shay, and I'll bring up a hot-water bottle."

As a child, even in the summer, her son had liked the comfort of a hot-water bottle going to bed. Nora knew that this would help him to settle.

Undressing in a daze and slipping under the duvet, the whole thing started to take on a surreal air. He felt as if he was detached from the scenes passing before his eyes and wondered was he losing his mind.

Nora came back with the hot-water bottle. Then she pulled the curtains and sat by the bed stroking his head until he fell into a deep sleep, images of Ken, waxy in death, floating around in his consciousness.

* * *

Closing the bedroom door on the sleeping form of her only child, Nora went back to the kitchen where she sat with her head in her hands and cried. The shock that this could just as easily have been Shay caught up with her and she sobbed in a way that she never had before. The day that Frank's boss had sat on the sofa telling her that her husband of four years had collapsed in the foyer of the bank after his lunch and was dead before the ambulance even got there, Nora hadn't cried at all.

The shock had been too great. That and the awareness of the responsibility of bringing up a small child on her own. She hadn't even known what their mortgage repayments were because Frank had dealt with that sort of thing. She hadn't had the luxury of sitting down and crying then, and afterwards it had seemed too late.

Now it was as if the shock of almost losing Shay had brought out all the grief that had been compressed somewhere inside her. Gratitude was what she felt most, thankfulness that her son hadn't been taken away from her. Nora knew with certainty that if Ken had been a regular user of drugs then Shay was also guilty. Maybe he'd been lucky enough not to have taken anything last night but how many other times had he put himself at risk? Not for the first time, Nora felt the weight of being both mother and father to Shay. If he'd had Frank growing up then maybe he wouldn't be in this situation now. But then, she reasoned, Ken Roche had had the benefit of a solid, gentle, tolerant father all his life and look where he'd ended up.

Nora washed and dressed quietly, afraid of waking Shay. She knew they'd have to go and spend time at Ted and Ina's house some part of the day and she didn't want her son to arrive looking as dishevelled and wild-looking as he had this morning. Somehow she felt that it would reflect badly on Ken's memory, as if they were a pair of druggies who'd got their comeuppance instead of two foolish young lads who went a step too far.

Ted Roche had been a great friend of Frank's and

had quietly done his best to support Nora in the years after her husband's death. Shay had been brought everywhere that the Roche children went, never missing out on anything because his mother had to work. Again, guilt at her own good fortune washed over her, knowing the grief of her friends at the loss of their child.

She made her way to Shay's house and let herself in with the keys that he'd left on the kitchen table earlier. The house looked almost exactly as it had when she'd left it the previous day, neat and orderly, surfaces shining in the morning sun. What good was it all, she asked herself. Swiftly she packed enough clothes to last for the next few days, knowing that Shay would need minding at home. Shirts that she'd ironed only yesterday, underwear and jeans that she'd folded, a suit that had come back from the dry-cleaners still in its plastic cover all went into the bag along with socks, ties and toiletries.

It occurred to Nora that a braver woman would go through the room in search of any drugs that might be hidden away but, in spite of her worry, she didn't have the heart to invade her son's privacy while he lay broken with grief at the loss of his friend. Recriminations could come later. All that mattered now was getting Shay through this.

18

Number 1

A beam of light was shining directly into his face and he had no idea where it was coming from. He tried to turn over on his front, but a tightness at the nape of his neck made him roll back again with a groan. He felt as if he was being smothered, his whole body bathed in sweat as he attempted to push the enormous weight off his chest. Panic struck him when he realised that he was bound tightly by whatever it was that was pinning him down.

Charlie's eyes shot open and he blinked against the ray of sunlight that focused directly on his face. He cursed the fact that he hadn't had the sense to close the curtains the night before. The eiderdown was wrapped around him like a sari so he struggled again to release himself, frantic in the need to reach the pint-glass of water that he'd wisely brought upstairs with him. He swallowed the contents in one go, his body finally cooling after the confinement of the bedclothes. It took him a few minutes to acclimatise to the fact that he wasn't in his bedroom in Cork. Familiar noises filtered up from the kitchen, his parents chatting over the noise of the radio and the sound of crockery rattling as his mother laid the table for breakfast. Charlie glanced at his watch and registered that the breakfast things were most likely being cleared away at this time. A car door slammed and the excited voices of Maeve's twins bursting into the kitchen filled the house.

Gingerly, Charlie sat out on the side of the bed and pulled on jeans and a T-shirt. He knew what would happen if he didn't appear in the next five minutes. And the last thing he was able for this morning was the sight of two little faces peering around the door looking to play "bouncy castle" on the bed. After a quick wash, he descended the stairs sheepishly, predicting the mildly disapproving glance that he'd get from his mother and the empathetic sigh of his father. Maeve, he knew, would have no sympathy for him in his hung-over state, occupied as she was with marshalling the troops for yet another food-fest.

"If you keep this pair occupied, I'll make you a fry," Maeve greeted him, indicating her children who had already flung themselves at Charlie's knees and were trying to drag him outside to see the chickens.

Marvelling at the energy of his sister, considering that she'd also straggled home as the pink dawn was hinting, he let himself be dragged out of the kitchen.

"You're on," he responded gratefully as he bent over

to admire the week-old chicks that huddled around their mother on the doorstep, steadying himself against the doorframe as a wave of dizziness passed over him.

"Will we try and feed them?"

This was from Dylan who'd already been warned by his grandmother to leave the feeding of the chicks to their capable mother. Dylan, however, was anxious to see if they'd pick at a crust of bread that he'd brought specially and was hoping that his Uncle Charlie was more adventurous than his grandmother. For his part, Charlie had learned the wisdom of not actually refusing a request from his nephew, who was likely to go ahead and do a thing anyway, having inherited Maeve's wilfulness.

"Never mind the feeding. Will we go and collect the eggs up in the top of the hayshed?"

Distraction and the promise of an even more exciting exploit won through and the six-year-old sped off in the direction of the hayshed, his sister trailing behind him and Charlie in their wake.

The heat trapped under the galvanised roof of the shed was intense, even at this early hour and Charlie began to regret his impetuous offer to search for eggs in its farthest reaches. This was an adventure of the highest order for the twins and the irrepressible Dylan was already scampering up along the neatly stacked bales of hay, Lauren waiting below to be lifted onto Charlie's back. Normally the children were prohibited from the hayshed, the risk of falling down between the bales too great to be hazarded. It was only when their uncle was home that the ban was lifted and the wonder of finding an egg nestled up near the roof became a reality.

Calling out to his nephew to slow down or he'd be sent back to the house, Charlie hoisted a timid Lauren onto his back and set off up the piles of bales, the hay pricking his arms. Dylan was already yelling that he'd found an egg, a warm one at that, meaning that it was freshly laid. Lauren slid off her uncle's back and cautiously crept along the top of the hay to join her brother.

Watching them closely for fear that they'd slip on a loose bale, Charlie was amazed as always at the differing personalities of the two children. Lauren's quietness reminded him of how shy he himself had been as a child, preferring to let the more boisterous Maeve take the lead. Lauren too followed her more confident sibling, even now watching as her brother explored the dusty corners for signs that a secretive hen might have ventured this far. Spotting a golden brown egg tucked in between two rows of bales, Charlie called out to Lauren to try over by the iron pillar, hoping that she'd have the pleasure of finding an egg as her brother had. With Dylan distracted in an even more secluded corner, she made her way over to where Charlie had suggested and methodically searched among the hay, squealing with delight when she discovered the prized object. Dylan immediately flew over to examine his sister's find, thrilled that they now had two eggs for their grandmother to boil for their breakfast.

Almost overcome with the heat of the hayshed and the after-effects of the previous night, Charlie gratefully descended, his niece clinging to his back and Dylan this time by the hand for fear he'd tumble onto the hard concrete floor in his haste to show off the delicate treasure.

Maeve was just putting the finishing touches to an enormous plate of sausages, rashers, pudding, eggs and tomatoes as her children burst into the kitchen bearing the eggs, followed by their frazzled uncle.

"Thanks for that," his sister smiled as Charlie began to wolf his way through the breakfast. "Are you going walking again today?"

"I'm after polishing up an old pair of boots in case you want to," his mother informed him.

Glancing over by the range to where his father's walking boots normally stood, Charlie recognised a pair of boots that he'd used when he first started college. He marvelled that his mother never threw anything out, always predicting a day when something would be needed in an emergency. She'd obviously somewhat forgiven her only son for acquiring a hangover the previous night and, being a teetotaller herself, had no idea of how formidable a six-hour hillwalk was after such a night, especially to Charlie, a moderate drinker normally. However, the substantial breakfast was working its magic on him and the thought of some fresh air was beginning to become more appealing.

"Thanks, Mam. I didn't know these even existed still."

Margaret responded that you never knew when you'd need a thing, adding that she'd also left out a pair of shorts for him.

Some things never change, he thought affectionately, entering his room to find an old pair of khakis laid out on the bed, again from his college days. A quick shower and Charlie was ready to join his father and sister for the drive down to the village, leaving Dylan and Lauren eating boiled eggs at the kitchen table with their grandmother.

* * *

Bidding goodbye to his father at the door of The Malthouse where he was supervising the registration desk before the "C" walk, Charlie set off down the main street towards Murph's to catch one of the minibuses that would ferry the more experienced walkers to the starting point for the "B" walk.

It was almost nine o'clock and small groups of two and three were converging on the tiny pub, equipped with compact rucksacks, sturdy boots and trekking poles. Thirty seasoned "A" walkers had left at eight from the same point to commence a fifteen-mile trek, a challenge for even the most competent. The festival committee divided the registration set-ups evenly between the two pubs in the village, ensuring that they both benefited from the inevitable surge in business over the weekend.

Nearing the pub on the corner of the main street,

Charlie's eyes were drawn to a pair of extremely shapely legs whose owner was rummaging in the boot of a VW. Straightening up and slamming down the boot, the petite blonde cast her eyes up and down the street before approaching him to ask where the "B" walk was starting from. "I'm heading down that way myself," Charlie told her. "They'll be leaving in a few minutes but you'll still have time to register."

"Thanks. I'd better start queuing," she laughed when she saw the crowds milling around inside the tiny building.

Charlie was very taken by her tanned prettiness and friendly manner, and felt a sense of familiarity that he couldn't put his finger on. Lined up behind the last of the arrivals, they ended up standing together for the short bus ride and continued chatting, with the blonde girl telling him that she was walking alone due to the rest of her small walking group opting out of the trek for one reason or another.

"I'm a bit the same," Charlie told her, explaining that while he was actually from the village, he'd totally forgotten about the festival until he'd arrived home for the weekend.

"This is my second year to come. I'm Amy, by the way. I walked on both days last year and it was great." When the reminder about the annual festival in Gilcrenan had arrived at her local walking club, Amy had marked it in her diary straight away.

Charlie too introduced himself before being hushed by the guide who was explaining the route to those new to the area. Eventually the group moved off, and they fell into step together, resuming general conversation until Charlie asked suddenly if she lived in Coppingerstown.

Amy reddened slightly when Charlie told her that his girlfriend lived in Pebble Cove, as it dawned on her that this fairly ordinary guy was the god that she'd spotted coming and going from the blonde princess's house across the way from her. Removed from the sharply tailored suits and indeed from the princess with the MG, he seemed different somehow, more relaxed or something. He was still handsome, in a rangy sort of way, his khaki shorts and well-worn boots showing off a pair of very hairy, muscular legs. Unbidden, a vision of Peter's tanned legs sticking out from under the duvet that morning sprang to mind, his arms resting behind his head as he watched her getting ready to leave for Gilcrenan.

Linda's neighbour, Marcus, had told Charlie that the girl in the last house was one of the nurses looking after his child in the baby unit, and he mentioned this to her now, asking how the little fella was doing.

"I can't actually talk about him outside work," Amy cautioned, referring to the confidentiality that was an inherent part of her job. "But he's grand," she added, realising that he'd only asked out of conversation rather than to hear any actual information.

"Sorry," he apologised at once. "Interesting job, though," he grinned, telling her of his astonishment when Marcus and Deirdre had once asked Linda if they could store some containers of breast milk in her freezer for a few hours while they defrosted their own.

Amy laughed, appreciating the fact that while the provision, storage and transport of breast milk were the constant topics of discussion in a Neonatal Unit, the whole concept was alien to those outside the loop. Responding to his interest, she told him a bit about the unit that she'd been working in for the past four years. Charlie was fascinated, as most people were, that babies could live despite arriving up to fourteen weeks early.

"Makes my job sound pretty boring," he laughed as they encountered the first of three steep woodland paths that made up the most difficult part of the day's walk. The group were forced into single file to ascend the narrow track, causing a welcome slowing of the pace. Amy took the opportunity to spray herself liberally with insect repellent, having felt the midges biting her skin as they wended their way through the shaded woods. Charlie slugged gratefully from a bottle of still water, glad that he'd had the foresight to stock up before he left Murph's. The group in front of them had dispersed to file uphill and now he indicated that Amy go ahead of him as he repacked the water bottle and zipped up his rucksack. Conversation had ceased with the effort of the climb, all of the walkers watching their steps over the uneven ground.

Finally, after a good twenty minutes' steep climbing, the ground started to level and the group emerged into an open field, home to a herd of startled cows.

"Five minute rest!" the guide called out to the sixty or so walkers who threw themselves down on the lush grass, careful to search out a spot that hadn't had a recent bovine visitor.

"I'd forgotten how tough that bit was, or maybe it's just that I'm a year older," Charlie exclaimed, knowing full well that the exploits of the previous night were to blame for his exhausted state.

Amy too was whacked after the hefty climb and rooted out her water bottle to cool herself down. Resurrecting a bigger scrunchie from the depths of the rucksack, she wound her ponytail into a tight bun, welcoming the cool breeze on the back of her neck.

Suddenly it was time to move again, many of the travellers groaning as they stretched their limbs gingerly.

Charlie was silent for the next few minutes, glad of the chance to clear his head. He'd been shocked to find himself studying Amy's movements as she tied her hair up, almost reaching out to touch one of the damp curls that escaped from the scrunchie and trailed at the nape of her neck. Realising that he'd better get a grip of himself, he reminded himself that this girl was Linda's neighbour, not someone to be gaped at like women were going out of fashion. Determined to behave like a normal person, Charlie started to tell Amy a little about the kind of work he did, including the fact that he worked for Linda's father.

"Does it work out alright, work crossing over into your outside life?"

While he knew that she'd only asked out of general interest, Charlie mulled this over before answering. "Normally the two don't actually clash at all, unless something in particular comes up. Linda runs a leisure centre so I don't see her at all during the day. At the moment Linda and I are trying to decide whether it would be a good idea to join forces on a project that she's planning. Until we decide what way we're going to work it, we'll inevitably end up talking about it a lot on our time off."

It occurred to him as he said this that, should he go ahead with a full partnership on the leisure complex, he and Linda would probably spend much of their time together in the evenings teasing out the daily ups and downs of the project. He wondered if this was such a good idea, but dismissed it immediately as overly pessimistic. Lots of couples they knew were working together, either in business or with the same company and it didn't interfere with their relationships.

Amy sipped water as she walked along, anticipating the next climbing leg of the trek. She noticed that Charlie was lost in thought and felt totally comfortable with him striding along beside her. They walked along in silence until their guide called out that they should be wary as they were approaching a boggy area that might have hidden dips. This was the kind of terrain that resulted in sprained ankles, hence the need for decent walking boots. Everyone in the group picked their way carefully, with only the odd squeal to be heard when someone felt the ground giving way under foot and the wet squelch of boggy water seeping in over the top of a boot chilled their ankle. Soon they were past the danger area and Amy was glad to get back on firmer ground, despite the punishing slope ahead. Again she went ahead of Charlie, her steps shortening as her chest tightened with the effort.

He too was finding the going tough, most likely due to the late night and also his recent lack of any kind of exercise. After this, Charlie told himself, I'm going to get back to the gym and as much hillwalking as I can. It's ridiculous to be this unfit at thirty-three years old. Relieved to see the top of this particular peak in sight, he was even more relieved when the guide announced that it was lunchtime.

Amy had reached the top before him and was perched on one of the many flat rocks that littered the surface, rummaging in her rucksack. Parking himself beside her, he was astonished at the amount of food being unpacked.

"Is it a buffet you're doing?" Charlie quizzed, amused that such a petite person could contemplate the selection of sandwiches, fruit, yoghurt and chocolate bars that were coming out of the bag.

"I'm always afraid I'll get marooned on top of a mountain without enough food so I pack loads. Then I have to eat it. Anyway, you're not short of grub yourself," she threw back at him, laughing.

"Well, I'd a bit of a hangover this morning," he admitted, "so my mother packed the lunch. She went a bit overboard alright!"

As well as four sandwiches, Margaret had packed fruitcake, scones and a bag of chocolate raisins. They chatted away for the next twenty minutes, sharing the fruitcake and chocolate while Charlie told her of the organisation that surrounded the walking festival each year. Watching the animation in his face, Amy was amazed at how different he appeared from the man she'd seen coming and going from the house opposite hers in Pebble Cove.

Apart from the final strenuous climb over heathery undergrowth, the remainder of the walk was glorious. The searing midday sun was tempered by a light breeze as the group savoured stunning views of the surrounding peaks and marvelled at the diminutive features of the village below them. Over the next two hours they wound their way back down through the forest paths, welcoming the shade and the green twilight beneath the magnificent firs. Conversation was easier now that they were on the home stretch and Amy talked about the experience of buying her first home. Charlie was impressed at her choice, considering that most single people working in the city would have opted for the convenience of an apartment or townhouse in the heart of the social scene.

"I lived in town for eight years and I loved it but I always knew I'd like to live out along the coast if I got a chance. It was the location that drew me first but when I went to see the houses I thought they were great. I think it's the way they're situated to catch as much of the view as possible that made me fall in love with them. I actually got the last one after the sale fell through for someone else."

Delighted with her enthusiasm for the design of the houses, Charlie told her of the battle with the planners over the fact that all the houses were different. Because they were situated in a crescent, he'd tried to position the windows of each house to best advantage, resulting in four similar yet very individual houses. Mostly, the planning department wanted as many identical houses as possible on each acre of land so it had been an uphill struggle for Daniel Colton to convince them otherwise.

Amy hadn't realised that he'd done the plans for Pebble Cove and it suddenly felt very intimate that this man had such a detailed knowledge of her home.

"You don't mind the drive in and out of town?" he asked her now, referring to the fifteen miles or so to Cork City.

"Only after night duty," she told him.

She did indeed dread the morning trip to Pebble Cove after a twelve-hour night shift and was terrified of falling asleep at the wheel. She nearly always drove home from night duty with the window down and the radio blaring. It was, she told him, the one aspect of her job that she was finding less appealing as time went on.

"And do you have to do nights or can you opt out? I must say the concept of working through the night and sleeping all day is alien to me!"

"You actually get used to it after a while, and the money's way better, which was great when I was buying the house. But it's not ideal for the long-term.

172

I've started to look around for a nine-to-five job. Hopefully something'll come up over the next year or so."

"Would you go into a different area altogether, or what?"

Amy explained that while she'd love to continue working with ill and premature infants, openings with sociable hours were few and far between. She might have to go into another speciality to get the hours she wanted in the long run.

The excited babble of the walkers at the front of the group heralded reaching the outskirts of the village. Charlie was amazed at how quickly the last two hours had passed and was baffled at how energetic he felt, bearing in mind the late night and frazzled sleep he'd had.

"Are you coming in for something to eat before heading off?" he enquired, knowing Amy had more than an hour's drive back to Pebble Cove ahead of her.

"I think I'll head off, thanks. Anyway, I couldn't possibly eat anything else this century," she said laughing as she threw her rucksack into the boot of the Golf. Charlie laughed too, and thanked her for the company and chat on the way around.

"Otherwise I'd have been dead before the halfway mark," he admitted, ruefully bidding her goodbye. He stood while she reversed out onto the road, unaware of his father watching him thoughtfully from across the street.

19

Leadington

When Shay opened his eyes he wondered stupidly what he was doing at home in his old room. His mother was standing over him with a cup of tea and she'd opened the curtains a chink so that a sliver of light fell across the bed. It was still bright outside even though he felt as if he'd been asleep for ages. Seeing the confusion in his face, Nora told him it was nearly four o'clock.

"Shay, I think we should go over to Ken's house once you have a shower and something to eat. I called over at lunchtime and Leanne told me that Ken will be brought home around six. People will start coming to the house around eight so I think you need to be there before the crowds arrive."

What Nora didn't fill her son in on was the fact that a post-mortem examination had been carried out on his friend's body almost as soon as Ted and Ina had arrived

175

to identify him. They'd sat for an hour in the draughty basement corridor, needing to hear from the young pathologist what it was that had extinguished the life of their precious boy.

It had almost broken Nora's heart to hear Ken's older sister Leanne saying that they were lucky that the body could be released so quickly. The fact that there had been no suspicion of foul play had contributed, as had the fact that the chemical had been identified immediately due to Shay producing an identical tablet for analysis. Ken's reaction, it seemed, had been typical of the drug's effect, with cerebral oedema or swelling of the brain being the cause of death.

She spoke gently to her son now, knowing that he wouldn't be able for seeing Ken for the first time in the middle of a huge throng of people. Word had spread quickly, and because the Roches had chosen to bring their son's body to lie in rest at home for a night before the removal to the church on Monday evening, friends and neighbours would arrive throughout the evening to support the family in their grief.

Nora had spent the afternoon making quiches and sandwiches, sponges and fruitcakes. All of the neighbours would do this today, to cater for the numbers that would call to Ken's home this evening.

Shay was still looking at her blankly, like a bewildered child waiting to be told what to do. Nora had read this somewhere ages ago, that some people go into a childlike state when they are unable to cope, ensuring that someone else would take over and look after them. At the time, she thought cynically that if she herself had reverted to childhood all those years ago, how would they have managed? But she could see now that Shay was lost.

"I've laid out all your stuff for you. I'll have the dinner ready when you come down. Come on now, you'll be alright when you've had a shower."

Half an hour later Shay looked almost normal. Dressed in navy chinos, a pale blue shirt and a navy tie with his hair still wet from the shower, Nora thought he looked like any young lad going out for the night, not someone who could have lost his life. Leanne had told Nora earlier that the drug her brother had taken was way more lethal than Ecstasy. The written post-mortem result would give them more information.

Nora knew that Shay mightn't have thought of his friend having to have a post-mortem. She also knew how much it would distress him if he heard it mentioned casually by some visitor at the house later. She'd try to mention it to him before they left home.

Surprisingly, he ate the lasagne and chips that she'd put in front of him, while Nora covered the plates of food she'd prepared and ferried them out to the car. Shay helped her to wash up, then sat down to watch the half-five news while his mother whipped cream and filled two large pavlovas. The news items ran unnoticed as he imagined Nora in the kitchen chopping strawberries, grapes and kiwis for the top of the dessert. Ken loved his grub and if he knew for a minute that Shay's mam was arriving at his house with the massive pavlovas he'd have met her at the door, cadging a slice by turning on the charm full blast.

This was unreal – traipsing over to the Roches with cakes and sandwiches as if they were going to a party. Where would Ken's body be situated? Working out the logistics of it, Shay figured that the undertakers would advise Ted and Ina to push the large dining table back towards the window and place the coffin in the middle of the floor. That way the mourners could come in the front door, turn right and say a prayer while filing around the body of his friend. They could then move in orderly fashion to either the living room or the good sitting room, depending on how close they were to the family.

People who were familiar with the house, like Shay and Nora, would automatically go to the kitchen to start the boiling of kettles and the laying out of china cups and saucers. How bizarre that people like Ted and Ina would wander from room to room dissecting the tragedy that had befallen their son, while neighbours took the run of their house, rooting in cupboards for tea-towels and tablecloths. This would go on all night, with a few elderly ladies, grand-aunts maybe, stoically keeping vigil by the coffin in the old tradition of never leaving the corpse alone. If this had been another time, he and Ken would have been nudging each other at the absurdity of the proceedings, the ludicrous rituals that were clung onto for generations.

Nora watched her son staring at the television and could see that he was in another world. She made a cup of tea and brought it in to him, knowing that it would soon be time to leave. Shay had been through a nightmare and was now facing another ordeal.

She herself could hardly bear to think of Ken laid out in a coffin and she knew her heart would break when she came face to face with Ina Roche, who'd been at the undertaker's when Nora had called earlier.

The drive seemed shorter than usual and in no time they were standing at the front door. It was slightly ajar and Nora pushed it in slowly. Everything was exactly as Shay had predicted. Ina came forward, and she and Nora clung to each other for a long time, tears falling unashamedly, both knowing that their roles could so easily have been reversed.

Shay stood in the doorway, the shame of what he'd brought on these broken people too much for him. He'd always been every bit as stupid as Ken, never once holding back or placing a word of caution on his friend's wilder schemes. They had backed each other up no matter what, thinking that this was loyalty of the highest order. What if he'd pulled back even once? What if he'd had the brains to see that buying stuff off some crook who was in it for the money wasn't such an intelligent thing to do? If he hadn't thought it was cool to act like a total eejit, would Ken be alive this evening?

Ted came over and put his arm around him then. "Come on, son, don't be afraid. It's still Ken, you know."

Realising that Ted thought he was fearful of seeing his friend's dead body again, shame swept over Shay at the generosity and kindness that a person could display on what must be the worst day of his life. Wondering if he himself could ever measure up to such a man, Shay broke down in sobs. "I'm sorry, I'm so sorry," was all that he could say, over and over again as Ted Roche held him against his chest, knowing in his heart that his own son would have been in the same state had he been spared to watch his friend laid out in a coffin.

"It's the suit he wore to my wedding," Leanne said gently, appearing from nowhere and placing an arm around his shoulder to turn him gently in the direction of the polished wooden casket.

Shay didn't know what to say – it wasn't as if he could say that Ken looked great or something. He didn't look at all great, despite the navy suit with its fine pinstripe and the trendy navy and lemon tie. His closely cropped carroty hair had been gelled back into a style that wasn't quite Ken but was probably an attempt by the undertaker to make him look like the young man that he'd been.

"His freckles are gone," he commented in a whisper to Leanne, noticing that the myriad brown dots that had covered Ken's face since childhood had now merged together to give his skin a smooth, pale brown appearance.

"He'd have loved that," Leanne smiled wistfully.

Almost without thinking, Shay reached out to touch his friend's face, his fingertips grazing the cool forehead. Ken looked as robust as ever, quite normal really.

"Will I leave you for a bit?

When Leanne said this, Shay realised that Ted, Ina and his mother had left the room, obviously thinking that he needed time alone with his friend.

"Just for a few minutes."

"Come out to the kitchen for a drink when you're ready," she told him as she left, quietly closing the door of the dining room.

Shay touched Ken's hair then, gently teasing the front into small spikes at the forehead the way he'd seen him do it before a night out. The gel that the undertaker had used was still wet. He noticed the light sheen of make-up that had been smoothed over Ken's face and realised it was this that made it seem as if his freckles had disappeared.

Eventually, having committed every inch of his friend's face to memory, Shay left the room to sip the brandy that he knew would be waiting for him, dreading the word goodbye as it escaped from him in a hoarse whisper.

The night passed in a blur with sympathetic glances and pats on the back for Shay being the norm. Over a drink, Leanne Roche told him that her parents had decided not to broadcast the details of her brother's death, only that he'd had some sort of seizure and that they'd have to wait on the post-mortem results. Shay could understand this and was glad that his friend's memory wouldn't be tarnished by the foolish lifestyle that they'd led. Shay assured Leanne that the facts of the previous night would never be divulged by him and that his mother would likewise respect their wishes.

"You know, Shay," Leanne continued, "you don't have to pretend to me that you and Ken were together in everything. I know that he was the ringleader and he could be pretty reckless when he wanted to be. He wasn't afraid of anything, least of all the consequences. If you'd been the one to die, I would have felt as guilty as hell because I didn't talk to Ken enough about the way he was carrying on."

Shay couldn't let this go. "I could have stopped him loads of times, but I just encouraged him. I thought he was great, and he was, but the way we went on was pure childish. This girl I was going out with, Carla, tried to tell me to cop on. She finished with me on Friday night because she was sick of us getting drunk and acting the maggot. She was right, you know."

"You looked wrecked," Leanne told him. "Go on home with your mother as early as you can. We all have a long few days ahead of us."

* * *

The following morning, Shay was awake early and he lay in bed thinking about what was ahead of him. Today Ken's family would sit with their son until his body was removed to the church. He and Nora would again spend the evening with the Roches, directing the mourners around the house until the hearse arrived to carry Ken the short journey to St Manchan's.

It felt like he'd been given a second chance. He could see his life for what it was and again he felt ashamed at his behaviour. His mother had worked hard to give him a good education and he'd barely acknowledged it. She'd put all her energies into getting him on in life, putting aside her own needs until he was old enough to look after himself. And he couldn't even do that much. He'd been lucky enough to get a decent job with a great salary and here he was on the brink of being fired for seriously unprofessional behaviour.

His heart skipped a beat when he realised it was Monday morning. He'd have to ring Joe Kiernan at nine and see if he could get some time off. He still felt kind of shaky, as if he had the flu or something, even though he'd slept for hours. Maybe it was best if he took a week of his holidays. Tears came into his eyes when he thought of Ken. He felt useless. His mother had organised all his clothes so that he wouldn't have to go back to his own house and he was glad of that because he barely felt able to get out of the bed.

An hour later he got through to his boss and explained his situation. He dithered when Joe asked if there was anything urgent that needed doing in his absence. He couldn't even think of what he'd been at on Friday, it seemed so long ago.

"Have you any meetings that need to be cancelled or rescheduled?" Joe sounded impatient, as if this was just one more in a long line of excuses.

Shay then realised that this *was* the case and attempted to pull himself together, trying to mentally conjure up the pages of his week planner.

"I was putting together some of the figures for the annual report for Manning Shipping. Jonathon is up to speed on that so he'll be able to pick up on it. The invoices for the July returns are finished as well. I left them on your desk on Friday evening."

Shay was acutely aware that these were the invoices that he should have finished early on Friday afternoon, the same ones that Joe had been looking for when he'd discovered Shay on the phone organising his night out in Counihans. As efficiently as he was able, he quickly outlined the other minor items that he'd been working on.

"Grand, Shay, we'll see you this day week. Take care of yourself." Joe's tone was that of an exasperated parent and Shay realised again that he was treading on thin ice as far as work was concerned.

The next two days passed in a blur as Shay gratefully fell in with the rituals that he'd thought were so macabre on Sunday night. He'd been asked to read a Prayer of the Faithful at the funeral and had mutely participated in the carrying of the coffin with Ted, his son Mike and Leanne's husband Barry as well as Ken's godfather and an uncle on his mother's side. He was glad of the opportunity to do this one last thing for Ken, but kept looking around for his friend's face among the crowd, as if it were someone else's coffin he was carrying. His legs still felt weak.

The whole group went to Maryborough House for a meal after the burial, the family's way of thanking people for their support. It occurred to him at one point that if Ken had ever decided to get married, the same exclusive hotel would have been a likely choice of venue. The same thought must surely have come to Ted and Ina as the sun shone in on their friends and family gathered together. Shay felt the now familiar flush of shame creep over him at the part that he had played in their being here.

He just wanted to be at home, away from all these people who kept questioning how a young healthy lad like Ken could be gone so quickly. The meal was over at last and he could see his mother near the door, chatting to a middle-aged man with silver grey hair, her face serious. She excused herself as she saw him approaching.

"Are you ready for home, love? It's been a long day for you."

He was glad that she hadn't lectured him about his wild ways and slowing down, even though he knew he deserved it.

"Will we call in to my house on the way?" he said. "I'll get a few bits and pieces to keep me going." The thought of staying on his own appalled him and he could see the relief on Nora's face that she'd be able to mind him for a while.

*   *   *

Shay woke on Wednesday morning with a blank feeling, a sense that everything was at an end somehow.

Ken was finished, gone. He was never going to see him again and even the ceremony of the past few days that was a link to him was now over also. There was nothing left. Unable to face it, he pulled the duvet over his head and willed himself to sleep.

20

Seefin

"Are you sure he'll be able for it?" Now that the moment had come for Alex to finally be transferred into his closed incubator, Deirdre was getting cold feet.

"There's never a definite answer around here," Amy reminded her. "But looking at everything, it really is the best move for him. He's been very well for over a week and the closed incubator will be a quieter environment for him."

"But what if he gets another apnoeic attack? Would you be able to resuscitate him in this incubator?"

Amy could understand her feelings of panic. The fact that she and Marcus had had a bad fright with Alex had made them more cautious.

"His haemoglobin came back at 12.1 this morning so it's unlikely that he'd become apnoeic again. But even if he did, we'd be well able to manage him. You'll see when we're transferring him over that the base of the incubator that he'll be lying on actually slides out to give us access to him."

"Look," Kim interjected, opening the door of the incubator that had been pre-heating all morning in readiness for Alex's occupation. As well as the two small portholes that Deirdre and Marcus had observed other parents using to reach their babies, the side panel of the incubator opened down flat. Kim then demonstrated how the base could slide out.

Reassured, Deirdre commented on the little mound of blankets that the two nurses had placed in the incubator.

"It's called nesting," Amy explained. "We'll be nursing Alex on his tummy mostly and it'll be comforting for him to feel that he has boundaries to touch his limbs off. The more comfortable he is, the more likely he is to start gaining weight."

"It'll be great to see whether he's gained anything up to now." Marcus was optimistic about the move now, especially as the promised weight check and cuddle were about to materialise.

He and Deirdre had been planning this with Amy and Kim since nine o'clock that morning. The nurses had advised them that it was best to carry out the move when the unit was in its afternoon lull so that they'd have maximum support to enjoy the moment properly.

Amy and Kim had pulled in the large incubator that morning and set the temperature gauge to 37 degrees. Marcus and Deirdre had watched over the next few hours as the digital readings had slowly risen until the temperature inside it was correct. The soft blue teddy-bear sheet was then wrapped around the mattress and the nest placed in the centre, awaiting Alex.

The weighing scales had been placed on a trolley, again with a soft sheet over it so that Alex could be lifted directly onto it as soon as his monitors were disconnected. Set in the middle of the floor between Alex's old home and his new one was the comfortable rocking chair that Deirdre was now sitting in, her green eyes anxious at the impending operation.

"Right then, are we all ready?" Amy waited until she got a series of nods from Kim, Marcus and Deirdre before starting to disconnect the temperature, oxygen and heart-rate monitors. Slowly, she wriggled her hands under Alex's small body and gently lifted him off the open incubator as Kim pushed the weighing scales a little nearer.

"This is fantastic," Amy exclaimed as soon as the digital reading settled. "He's 1.2 kilos – well above his birth weight!"

"That's great," Marcus exclaimed, "He's definitely absorbing his food!"

Deirdre meanwhile was holding her breath, having adjusted the fleece blanket that Kim had placed in her lap at least ten times. Tears threatened to choke her as she watched Amy lift Alex from the scales.

"Here you go, Deirdre, he's all yours," Amy whispered as she laid Alex delicately into the waiting blanket.

Deirdre could barely feel him, he was so tiny. The

tears poured down her face as she tried to settle him comfortably in her arms, terrified of hurting him.

"Oh, Marcus, look at him," she sobbed, trying valiantly to stop her body shaking. "He's gorgeous. He's just gorgeous."

Marcus, unable to stop himself from crying, put his arms around both of them and buried his face in Deirdre's hair, astounded as it crossed his mind that this was the best moment of his life to date.

Amy and Kim faded into the background as Deirdre spoke quietly to Alex, telling him over and over how special he was and examining his face in detail.

"God, Marcus, he looks like you now that he's sitting up a bit. Look at him frowning as if he's wondering what pension scheme to invest in," Deirdre teased. They'd only ever studied Alex when he was lying down and now it seemed that he had a whole different face.

"At least I've a bit more hair than him," Marcus chuckled, stroking Alex's sparse downy hair. "He does look a bit serious," Marcus admitted, leaning in to hold Alex's tiny hand.

Too soon, Amy touched his shoulder. "Will I take a quick photo before he goes in?"

"He'll love this in years to come," Deirdre laughed, trying to fix up her tearstained face. She smiled broadly as the Polaroid flashed, hardly able to believe that they'd been allowed this wonderful privilege.

"Time to be getting back into the heat for this fellow," Amy reminded them, putting the camera aside.

She now gently peeled open the blanket that was snuggled right around Alex's little head and, lifting him carefully from Deirdre's lap, turned towards Kim who was holding the door of the incubator open. All the equipment that had been lined up beside the open incubator was now attached to the new one. Marcus held his wife in his arms as they watched the two nurses re-attach Alex, expertly setting the alarms and adjusting the various probes.

"He looks like he's been in there forever," Deirdre declared when they'd finally finished settling him.

"You've a whole new learning curve ahead of you now, getting to know the temperatures and working through the portholes," Kim advised them.

"And his feeds will now be increasing on account of his weight going up," said Amy. "That'll really help him to progress. He'll be going on to two-hourly feeds soon rather than the continuous feed if he gains next week."

"That'd be a huge step," Marcus commented. "When will he get weighed again?"

"Normally it's Wednesday and Saturday," said Amy, "but I think we'll skip him this Saturday and leave him until next Wednesday. It'll give him a chance to settle into his new environment. The less disturbance he gets from here on in the better and the more rest he gets, the more weight he'll gain."

"Will Marcus be able to hold him when he comes out for the weight?"

"Absolutely," Kim promised, spreading a thick

green blanket over the incubator to keep the harsh fluorescent lights of the ICU off Alex's face, leaving him almost in the dark.

"Now, what do you think of this?" Amy had been searching through the drawer in the bottom of the incubator and now produced a large colourful sign that she stuck on the Perspex door panel.

"*Shhhhhhh… I'm growing!*" it read.

"Well that's telling us, little fellow," Deirdre smiled, her day complete now that she'd held her son.

21

Evergreen

By Saturday, Nora was becoming seriously concerned about her son. He'd stayed in bed all week, refusing to come down even for his meals. He already looked like skin and bone, in spite of her bringing small portions of things she knew he liked up to him and sitting with him while he ate. He never finished what she brought up. To her knowledge he hadn't showered since before the funeral on Tuesday. That very morning, she'd insisted on him getting out of bed while she changed the sheets but instead of taking a shower he'd just sat in the bathroom while she tidied the room.

Not knowing what else to do, Nora had walked down to Dr Daly to see if he could help. She thought Shay must be clinically depressed, though she didn't think it could happen so dramatically in less than a week. Maybe he needed medication to help him get over it. The elderly man had been their family doctor

193

for as long as she could remember, so Nora had no compunction in telling him the full story of Ken's death, hoping it would shed some light on the severity of her son's reaction to it. She knew that the doctor would never raise the issue again with anyone.

"Do you think the boy blames himself for what happened? Maybe he feels that he could have prevented it. As well as the shock of seeing someone close die in front of your eyes, he might be feeling a huge burden of guilt. I'll come and talk to him this evening, if you like."

Like most people who had known her over the years, Norman Daly had great admiration for Nora Deegan. She'd made sure that her son got the best of everything, at the cost of her own personal life, he often suspected. She could do without this.

Relieved, Nora set off for home, hoping that the prospect of the doctor's visit might motivate Shay to get up for a while, maybe even to shower and shave. She couldn't have been more wrong. He showed no interest at all, his eyes closing before she finished telling him.

Later that evening, Norman Daly delivered his diagnosis.

"He's in total shock and he can't stop focusing on the fact that he's somehow at fault. He's feeling guilty that he's the one alive. Things were always equal between him and Ken, so he feels that he should be dead as well. He's going to need a lot of time, Nora."

"Does he need medication or anything? Will he need to go to hospital? I can't just leave him in the bed. He's hardly eaten anything all week." Nora was beside herself that this should happen to her child.

Norman sighed, amazed as ever at the wonder of motherhood. This woman would go to the ends of the earth to get her son well again.

"Years ago, hospital might have been the answer, but not nowadays. I'll prescribe an anti-depressant now, mainly because they can take about three weeks to actually kick in. Nothing heavy-duty – those days are gone as well, thank God. Eventually he'll need to talk to someone professional to work through everything, but it's too early yet. He'll sleep a lot probably. Just treat him gently, see if you can get him downstairs some part of the day, even for his meals. His appetite won't be great so go easy on him."

"Norman, he wouldn't . . . you know . . . do anything, would he . . . ?" Nora's voice trailed off anxiously but she had to know if her son was in any real danger.

"I've talked to him about that and there's nothing on his mind in that regard right now. You know you can call me any time at home, day or night – I mean that. If you're worried at all, ring me and I'll come over straight away."

"Thank you."

"Don't be alone in this, Nora," he warned, knowing her strong inclination for independence. "As well as being your GP, remember that myself and Carmel are your friends as well."

Once the doctor had left, Nora felt her sense of

resolve return. She knew she'd have to phone Murrays first thing on Monday and tell them that Shay would be off work for a few weeks. There was no way that he could function in his present state and the look of him alone would frighten the life out of the clients. They'd just have to do without him.

She ventured upstairs again, having decided on her plan of action. She'd have to be firm but very gentle. Shay was as fragile as a baby right now. The room was in darkness and she spoke softly to her son, first putting on the bedside light.

"I'm going down for your prescription now. Will you come down and watch *The News* with me when I come back? We can have a bit of supper by the fire." Maybe if she gave him notice of doing things he might be able to perk himself up a little.

* * *

After she left, Shay just lay there, his mind vacant except for the feathery thoughts flitting in and out. How come Dr Daly knew all about Ken and what happened? How will I get down the stairs for the tea? What would the tablets do to him? He couldn't settle his mind on any of the questions for long enough. They kept coming and going in his head. His mother said she was going to the pharmacy. Why was she back so soon?

"Are you ready, love? I have the tea on? Just put on your dressing-gown. The fire's on downstairs."

Nora left the room but came back five minutes later

when there was still no sign of Shay. He was still lying in the same spot, staring at the ceiling. She'd have to actually help him for a while.

"Come on, love, put your legs out. Put your arms into the sleeves. Come on."

Shay responded to the persuasive tone in her voice, but felt dizzy when he stood up. His mother pressed him into a chair and pulled up the covers on the bed for fear he'd want to get back in again. She put her arm around his waist and guided him towards the stairs, her heart breaking at the sight of her son towering above her, his blonde hair matted from almost a week in bed.

He ate the small portion of chips and battered fish that Nora had collected on her way back from the pharmacy, hoping that his childhood favourite would spark his appetite. She'd discouraged junk food when her son was growing up, but this was what he'd always chosen whenever he was allowed a treat. Normally he'd have wolfed it down in minutes but tonight she had to remind him to take each bite. He had no interest in the news so Nora switched it off and tried to talk to him.

"Dr Daly says you're to take things very easy for the next few weeks. I'll sort out work and the house and everything. You just concentrate on getting better."

Shay just mumbled in reply.

Nora tried again. "The main thing is to take your tablets and get plenty of rest. You'll have to try and eat a bit more as well, love."

It was half nine. Maybe it was best to give him the sleeping pill and let him off to bed. He looked exhausted even though he'd only been up for half an hour. Dr Daly said that the tablet would allow Shay to have a proper deep sleep instead of just dozing day and night. When he got into a pattern he'd be better able to stay awake during the day. Nora prayed that this was true. At least she might manage to get him into the shower.

That night, Shay actually did sleep properly, without all the questions fluttering around in his brain. The following morning he still didn't feel ready to get out of bed. All his limbs were aching, and when he went to the bathroom and saw himself in the mirror, it felt as if he were looking at someone else through two holes in a mask.

Nora heard her son moving about and quickly mounted the stairs, determined that he'd at least get dressed. She'd been over to Pebble Cove early that morning and had collected some T-shirts and tracksuit bottoms that might be comfortable for lounging around in.

"I'll run a bath for you, Shay, and you can relax a bit." She could see that he was drowsy from the sleeping pill and hoped that it was the right thing to be giving him. The shower seemed too vigorous altogether, but she wondered was the bath safe for him.

She half-filled the bath and again helped him out of bed. "Don't lock the door, son, in case you fall asleep. I'll be outside if you want me."

Having listened to make sure he actually got into the bath, Nora opened the curtains and made the bed. She'd left his clothes and underwear in the bathroom and hoped he'd manage to dress himself.

When she'd heard nothing but the occasional small splash for ten minutes, she thought he must have fallen asleep.

"Wash your hair, Shay, and come on out!" she called. "Your clothes are beside the sink!"

Shay broke out of his reverie and realised that the water was getting cold. It was only up to his waist anyway. The shampoo felt cold on his scalp but with a huge effort he rubbed it in briefly and rinsed it off. The warm water from the showerhead was soothing and he sat there for a while with it flowing over his head and down his back, oblivious to some of it pouring over the side of the bath and onto the floor.

"Are you alright, Shay?" he heard again and the mood was broken. Slowly he climbed out of the bath and started to dry himself. The towel was rough, so he abandoned it and put his clothes on, conscious of his damp skin but not having the will to dry himself further.

He emerged from the bathroom unshaven but at least he was dressed. Nora felt a huge surge of satisfaction, as if she'd achieved something of enormous proportions. Now for the breakfast. The fire was lighting in the sitting room even though it was too warm for it really. She was struck again at how frail her son looked and couldn't believe it was barely a week since they'd had lunch together in his kitchen. That day she'd been fantasising about him getting married and now here she was minding him like a child.

After a very small breakfast, Shay lay on the sofa like an invalid and aimlessly watched the television. Nora's heart was breaking but she knew she had to heed Norman Daly's words and take things slowly. It would take three weeks before the medication kicked in. She had to keep focusing on that and do her best in the meantime.

Saturday and Sunday passed with Shay managing to stay up until lunchtime, retiring to bed after beans on toast, another childhood favourite. At least he was eating, Nora congratulated herself, even if it meant reminding and encouraging with every bite.

The phone call on Monday was difficult for her, not least because she didn't know who Shay's immediate boss was, nor did she know the title of his department so that she could ask for the head of that division. In the end she asked the receptionist to put her through to Michael Murray, the managing director of the company. She wasn't sure if it was the right thing to do but she didn't want to broadcast Shay's condition to some gossipy secretary who might spread it around that he was having some sort of nervous breakdown.

Michael Murray was sympathetic when she explained the situation, leaving out the bit about the drugs and focusing more on the shock that her son had had, and the fact that the GP had recommended complete rest. She didn't want to dwell on the actual condition that he was in, for fear that it might affect his chances of promotion in the future.

"I can post you in his sick certs and anything else you need. I think he'll be out for a month or six weeks. He'll be able to phone you himself once he comes around a bit."

"That's fine, Mrs Deegan," Michael Murray said eventually and Nora wondered if she'd imagined hearing a sigh. It *was* inconvenient for him, she supposed, to have one of his senior accountants falling ill so suddenly. However, she told herself firmly, if Shay was that important to them they'd just have to wait until he was ready to work again.

22

Evergreen

Amy sat cross-legged on one of the dining-room chairs while Peter typed out the references for her latest assignment. "Resolving Conflict" was a subject that had interested her immensely while she was researching and working on the project, but the listing of her sources and the collating of the titles in the correct order was a task that she'd been looking forward to with something akin to dread. Thankfully, referencing was one of her boyfriend's many talents so she was happy to give him free rein.

It amazed Amy that they had so much in common – a love for books among other things, although Peter had a more structured attitude to his collection that she did to hers. He'd enthusiastically explored her shelves, frequently telling her that he was tempted to start categorising her stash, exasperated to find JD Salinger lined up next to Brendan O'Carroll.

Amy was an avid reader and had a huge collection of books lined up on the shelves around the house. Having space for her books had been a major priority when she'd been looking at houses. The little house in Evergreen Road, while cosy and homely, had been tiny and most of her books were stored in her parent's house. The new Evergreen, however, had more space than she knew what to do with and once she'd been able to afford a few pine bookcases she'd been able to bring everything out of storage. As soon as they'd been in place, her new house had suddenly felt more like a home to her.

She usually had a few books on the go at any one time, alternating them depending on her mood. There was always a Maeve Binchy or a Marian Keyes by her bed. She loved both of the Irish writers, getting so involved in their plots that she often forgot that the characters weren't actually real. Patricia Cornwell, on the other hand, rarely made it upstairs because her gory post-mortems and rampant serial killers generally left Amy's head reeling long after she'd actually put the book down.

Amy knew her preferences were haphazard to say the least, with John Steinbeck and Tolstoy resting comfortably beside Joseph O'Connor and Pat McCabe. Although she wasn't generally a poetry fan, Patrick Kavanagh held an enormous appeal for her, his way of bringing out feeling and beauty in the bleakness of his subjects amazing her every time she picked up one of the volumes of his collected poems.

Peter admitted sheepishly to having his own books categorised under genre with each section in alphabetical order, blaming this on the brainwashing of working in a library.

As far as Amy was concerned, he could categorise her books any way he liked so long as he continued his referencing service, which he claimed he was glad to do in exchange for the odd evening of pampering.

Peter was always available for Amy's particular brand of pampering, especially on a Sunday evening after a soccer match. It usually meant an aromatherapy bath followed by a massage with a selection of fragrant oils that invariably led to the bedroom.

"Is the duty rota made out for Saturday the 29th yet?" he asked, looking up from Amy's handwritten list of references. "There's a dinner on in the Mount Vernon – it's an annual thing with the soccer club – it'd be great if you could come."

"That'd be great. I'm off the full weekend." She glanced at the calendar to double-check. "Is it dressy?"

Amy was immediately wondering what she'd wear and whom they'd be sharing a table with. In the short while that they'd been seeing each other she'd met a few of his friends, mostly the ones that he'd been to college with. The soccer club ones were a new departure, considering that this was the first "occasion" that she'd been around for.

"It's Black Tie apparently. I'll find out a bit more at training next week."

Thrilled that she had plenty of notice, Amy decided

that she'd go into town some morning after her night shift and have a look for something glamorous. Thank God for Cyprus – at least she had a bit of a tan. If she got her hair trimmed it would bring up the highlights a bit – plus she'd book a manicure for the day before. She'd be well sorted if she got something really nice to wear.

"There you go. All done. Though you'd better check through them in case I've left anything out." Groaning, he straightened his back, stretching his neck to either side to ease the tension from sitting hunched over the references for the past hour. "So now, what about that Turkish bath?"

Amy grinned back at him and slid off her chair immediately. "Right this way, sir!"

* * *

The following week, just as she arrived home after yet another busy night in the unit, Peter phoned. It was 9 a.m. and she was shattered after the drive home but as usual she was delighted to hear his voice.

"Just to let you know that it's definitely Black Tie for the soccer club thing. And I had a look at the table plan. We'll be sitting with Marcus Fleming and his wife Deirdre. Marcus says he knows you from work – I think they have a sick baby."

"I didn't realise you knew Marcus. Did you know he was living here in the second house? You know, Seefin?"

"I've known him for ages through the soccer but I haven't been talking to him for a while. We used to go for a drink after training every week until they had the baby. This evening was the first time in ages that he's been training."

"He's really nice and so is Deirdre," Amy said, thrilled that she'd know at least one couple at their table. "It's amazing that you haven't bumped into each other in the Cove at any stage."

"I think he spends most of the evenings in with the little fellow. He says he's a bit more stable these days."

Alex had indeed been fairly stable for the past few weeks, his feeding regime building steadily. It was good for Marcus to start getting out a little again. Deirdre was still on maternity leave and had brilliant support from her parents and sister who kept her company for much of the day by Alex's incubator. Marcus, on the other hand, held down a demanding job as a financial analyst with one of the major banks and was putting in as many hours as he could manage while Alex was in hospital so that he'd be able to take extended leave to support Deirdre when their baby finally came home.

Parental stress was a big concern in the case of very premature babies like Alex, as they'd sometimes reach burnout before their infant was discharged and found it hard to cope with the demands of managing outside the supportive atmosphere of the neonatal unit. An evening out in the Mount Vernon would do Deirdre and Marcus good.

Amy said her goodbyes to Peter and made her way to bed, already plotting the shopping trip that she absolutely had to go on come hell or high water.

23

Number 1

"Hold on, Charlie, Brona's just come in." Linda put her hand over the phone and looked up at Brona expectantly.

"Linda, I know you're not going to want to hear this, but the new lockers still haven't arrived. The guy from Keating's is here to fit them and he says he'll have to be paid whether they come or not. Apparently they turned down a job in Little Island to fit us in. He's going mad."

"Can't you see that I'm up to my eyes here, Brona? You'll just have to deal with it. If you're going to be in charge of the place you'll have to get used to sorting out this kind of thing." With that, Linda returned to her phone call, leaving a shocked Brona seething as she left the office.

If her boss had butted out in the first place this wouldn't have happened. What was the point in making her manager of Bodywork if Linda was unable to let go of the reins? She'd told Brona to book someone to fit the new, state-of-the-art lockers weeks ago while she ordered the lockers herself, wanting to maintain her connections with the major suppliers. But of course she'd forgotten all about it and had tried to cajole them into delivering at the last minute. Now the lockers hadn't materialised and the fitter was hopping mad in the reception area.

Brona couldn't blame him. He'd accepted the booking in good faith and naturally expected to be paid. Brona knew that it was she who'd get the blame when Linda spotted the invoice for two days' work that hadn't actually been done. Having pacified the fitter with assurances that his small firm would get paid, she poured herself a coffee and wondered, not for the first time, if her new managerial post wasn't a bit of a poisoned chalice.

Linda was supposed to be concentrating on the new Health and Leisure Village, hence the need for Bodywork to have a manager. Brona had been delighted with the promotion and the substantial salary increase. Her experience was good and she knew she'd be well able to manage Bodywork now, if only Linda would leave her to it. She'd managed a small leisure centre on the outskirts of Limerick city before taking the job as assistant manager under Linda the previous year and had been more than ready to take over as manager when the proposal had been put to her two months ago.

The reality was somewhat different to her expectations. Linda continued to use her own office as usual, so that when people phoned for the manager they were invariably put through to her. Then she'd come storming out to Brona's cubby-hole demanding to know why she as manager couldn't deal with whatever it was. Also the fact that Linda was in the leisure centre all day meant that the rest of the staff didn't know whom they were answerable to. Brona was becoming increasingly frustrated with the situation yet was reluctant to discuss it with her increasingly volatile boss.

Sighing deeply, she pushed away the coffee cup and pulled out the membership list. Serious forethought was required with regard to the subscriptions, considering that many of the more affluent members would jump ship once the pool and gym opened in The Sanctuary, as the new health and leisure complex would be called, the following year. Assuming that she'd still be manager of Bodywork then, Brona was aware that they'd need to plan ahead to recruit new members to fill the gap. She'd have to discuss with Linda the possible numbers of those who'd be able to afford the more expensive Sanctuary and plan an advertising campaign to keep the membership in Bodywork at its present level. Terrified of approaching Linda after the lockers debacle earlier, Brona pencilled into her diary a reminder to approach her boss on the topic the following Monday. It was Friday and she'd had enough hassle for one day.

24

Leadington

Nora had been watching the clock and listening out for any signs of movement from her son's room. It was like this all the time now but she was sticking to a routine of waking him at half nine if he didn't appear. She made plenty of noise as she ascended the stairs, hoping that some day he'd actually get up of his own volition.

She was thrilled to see him sitting on the side of the bed, albeit groggily, when she opened the bedroom door.

"Did you sleep alright, love?" she queried as she did every morning.

"Not too bad. I think I'll take a shower before I come down."

"Grand, love, I'll put the kettle on," was all she could say, grateful for any kind of a breakthrough. It was quite a while since he'd started the medication and she'd begun to despair of things ever getting back to normal.

Norman Daly had called the previous evening and had been surprised at how well Shay was doing. Nora couldn't see what there was to be glad about, with her only son stretched out on the sofa, unable to concentrate on the questions the doctor was asking him.

"But he's eating again, isn't he?" Norman had probed.

"Yes, but only if I keep him at it. He doesn't feel hungry at all, just eats because I put it in front of him."

Nora couldn't see any improvement and was terrified that her lovely son would be left in this traumatised state for the rest of his life. Who would look after him if anything happened to her? She panicked at the thought of it.

Nora had looked so distracted that for the first time Norman realised what a huge strain this must be for her. He'd always seen her as such a capable woman, one who'd made a good life for herself in spite of everything.

"He will come around, you know. But Nora, you'll have to keep your own life going as well." He hesitated before adding meaningfully, "Don't give up on things that mean something to you in the meantime."

Nora fiddled with the neckline of her blouse to hide the colour creeping up to her face.

"Shay has to come first at the moment," she said firmly, putting an end to any further discussion.

Hope now surged through her that today was the start of an improvement. She had the breakfast made

214

when Shay arrived down, toast and sausages, hoping he'd make a sandwich with tomato ketchup. She was running out of ideas but at least he wasn't losing weight any more. Keeping the meals small and frequent seemed to be the way to go and also served as a means of filling the day for him. Watching him now buttering the toast and slicing the sausages lengthwise she realised that she had been a bit pessimistic. Last week she would have had to do this for him.

"Will we take a drive over to your house later to see if there's any post or anything? You'll have to get a few clothes as well," she tried.

All this television couldn't be good. Maybe he'd get a bit of interest back if he went over to Pebble Cove.

"OK," was all he said but at least he hadn't refused.

Nora thought this was a major step, but thought better of it an hour later when she opened the front door of the house for him. Shay's face immediately crumbled and he sank down on the lower step of the stairs, sobbing.

"What is it, love, tell me?"

Shay's mother's voice sounded miles away and all he could feel was Ken's presence in the hall. He didn't want to be here in this place where they'd had so many laughs. Ken had thought it was a great idea, him buying his own place. They finally had somewhere decent to bring women back to – the "Taj Mahal" he used to call it. Now Shay wanted to be away from here, back in the security of his mother's house where the only memories were of his childhood.

"I want to go home – I don't want to be here."

"OK, love," Nora soothed him. "Take a minute to settle yourself and we'll go. You'll be alright, Shay, when we're home."

Sitting on the stairs stroking her son's back, she noticed with a shock that the light on Shay's answering machine was flashing. What if Michael Murray had been trying to get hold of him? Nora was terrified that her son's career would be destroyed and she hated to think of the disappointment it would cause him if his job were jeopardised.

"Before we go, love, do you want to listen to the messages, in case there's anything you need to answer for work. Will I play them for you?"

Shay listened mutely to a long list of condolences, mainly from the gang in his office who'd heard about Ken's death. Two were from Carla, the first apologising for not being in contact sooner, having been away the week of Ken's funeral, the second asking if she could call over some night. Nora's heart lifted hopefully at this and she felt even better when she heard a message from Michael Murray wishing Shay a full recovery. She decided she'd try to get Shay to phone him back the following day. Otherwise he might think that Shay had just ignored the call. But now she just needed to get him home.

Later that evening, she rang Norman Daly at home to let him know what had happened. He seemed to see the whole episode as progress, reminding her that crying was a wonderful way of releasing grief. Also, he thought that hearing all the phone messages would actually reinforce the fact that Ken was gone. Nora had been worried about this, wondering if it had been too much to subject Shay to the many messages of sympathy.

"Living with you for a while is probably a good thing. His childhood is a safer place at the moment. Ken's death is part of his adult life and he just can't face it right now. The new house is part of that as well. Being at home for the moment is like denying that Ken is actually dead."

Having this information comforted Nora. It made Shay's reaction seem acceptable and somehow normal. Tomorrow was a new day.

She wondered who Carla was and if a visit from her would make any difference.

The following morning Shay woke up in good enough form. Nora decided not to mention her conversation with the GP, knowing that her son was happy enough to stay with her for the moment.

"I was thinking of doing a few bits in the garden after breakfast – you could give me a hand if you like or even just keep me company."

The garden, her pride and joy, had been neglected over the past few weeks and the fresh air might do Shay good. She'd give him a simple job that he could manage without too much stress. Nora felt he needed to get a bit of activity back into his day or he'd turn into a complete zombie. She'd always hated that word but now she could see how it summed up the robotic appearance that was evident in her son.

It was half ten by the time they were ready to get started and the sun had come right over the house. The back garden was flooded in brightness with no sound other than the occasional twittering of a bird. Nora inspected the roses. It was time for their final feed of the summer and they needed dead-heading. She noticed a few greenfly clinging to the new buds and sighed. She had neglected them. Maybe Shay could spray them while she did the rest.

"They look great, Mam," Shay said, surprising her. This was the first time he'd commented on something without her initiating a conversation.

"They've been great this year. I keep snipping off the old blooms a couple of times a week to let the new flowers develop. They've been flowering since the beginning of June." Sensing his interest, she decided to rope him in. "You can nip off the old heads while I'm feeding them if you like."

Shay listened obediently as his mother explained which heads to cut off. There were ten bushes in all, bright red, with some of the stems bending almost to the ground with the weight of the flower heads. Armed with a bucket and the secateurs, he diligently began to snip off any flowers that were past their best. Nora was thrilled and settled onto her kneeler with a small fork, carefully placing handfuls of the grainy feed around the base of each bush, mixing it through the soil but judiciously keeping it from touching the actual plant.

Noticing a sudden silence, she glanced up to see

Shay staring into the bucket of rose heads, tears flowing silently down his face. Cursing herself, Nora wondered if she would ever get it right.

"Tell me what's wrong, love," she pleaded. "You were grand a minute ago. Are you thinking about Ken?"

Something about the tears coursing quietly down his face reminded her of when Frank had died, the way funny things like seeing an Argyle sock on a man at Mass had set her off. She couldn't imagine how something as sedate as the roses could have put him in mind of his madcap friend. She'd thought the garden was a safe bet as regards distraction.

For the first time since the funeral, Shay felt able to explain what was going on in his mind. "It's the way the roses were falling into the bucket, one after another. When Ken got the first fit in the nightclub, the ambulance men put a drip in his arm to stop it. Then on the way to the hospital he got another fit but he was jerking so much that the drip came out of his arm. These big drops of blood were falling onto the floor when they were working on him. Then they told me he was gone, that they couldn't get him back."

Nora was crying now, with the relief of understanding. She hugged him tightly, telling him that this was normal that he would see Ken in everything for ages and not to be afraid of it.

"I was like that when your father died. I couldn't go to the bank at all. Every time I saw a manager I used to wonder was that what Frank looked like at work, bending over a desk, going to lunch carrying a briefcase, talking to the cashiers now and again. Gertie used to do all the business for me."

Shay looked interested. His mother had never spoken to him about his father's death before, and it had never occurred to him how young she'd been at the time. She'd been about twenty-five, five years younger than he was now, with a small child to bring up. She'd only ever told him the good bits, he realised now, like how his father bathed him and put him to bed every night because he missed him all day. This had been unheard of at the time and Nora's mother had thought Frank was a bit of a "Nancy" when she found out.

"I remember a notice coming from the golf club, a receipt for his fees. I cried all one night over that because he would have been mad at himself for paying a year's subscription and not getting the value out of it."

Ever the accountant, Shay now asked if they'd refunded the amount afterwards.

"You know, I can't even remember whether they did or not. It was more about him missing out on the year's golf. Even things like aftershave used to bother me. I'd turn around expecting it to be your father but it'd be someone with the same aftershave. I think now that for ages I was expecting him to come back. I don't think I really believed he was gone."

"I know," Shay said now. "Yesterday was the first time I realised that Ken was gone for good, when we went into the house. I thought if I went back to Pebble

Cove I'd forget about it."

Nora could identify with this, and was glad that Shay was talking at last but, not wanting to tire him out, she suggested making a cup of tea.

"Grand, I'll finish these while you're getting it."

Now that he'd said it out loud, the red roses plopping rhythmically into the bucket, so reminiscent of drops of blood a few minutes ago, didn't seem so reproving. Shay had thought he was being reminded of the horrible way his friend had died as a sort of punishment. Now, though, he wasn't so sure.

25

Evergreen

The unit was buzzing when Amy arrived at work. Noreen, just finishing her day shift, was in the process of wheeling a set of phototherapy lights towards the ICU.

"Who's going sunbathing tonight?" Amy asked, pushing open the double doors to allow her colleague to push the bulky unit through.

"Kate McCarthy was looking a bit jaundiced earlier so I sent off her blood for a bilirubin level. I haven't said anything to her parents yet but I think she'll have to go on lights overnight. I'll leave her in the ICU with Alex. They'll be easier to manage if they're next to each other." She wheeled the phototherapy unit into a corner. "I'll leave this here for the moment," she added.

"I'll take the report on Alex and I can phone the lab when you're gone," said Amy. "We should have results by then. What time are Declan and Janet coming in?"

"Shortly. They rang to say they'd be in for the next feed."

Unless it was an absolute emergency, the parents were informed or consulted before any new procedure took place with their baby. In Kate's case, Declan and Janet would have been warned that jaundice could occur in the early stages and that, if so, it would be treated by placing a set of fluorescent lights over her incubator. However, hearing about a hypothetical situation was one thing. Landing in to find a baby bathed in eerie blue light and wearing a pair of black goggles was distressing in the extreme.

For this reason, Amy would wait for them to be present before telling them about the blood results and then letting them assist her in settling their baby under the lights. Meantime, she could listen to Noreen's account of the other issues concerning Alex and Kate, her two charges for the night, and start getting to grips with the rest of their care. Fortunately, there were only six other babies in the neonatal unit so Amy would be able to concentrate on her pair unless something unforeseen happened. Kim, her regular night-duty partner, had already taken over three of the less ill babies while their colleague Sheila Forde was in charge of the other three.

Kate's parents arrived as Amy was filling a large syringe with defrosted breast milk.

"Hi, Amy," Declan greeted her. "It's great that she's managing to keep the feeds down, isn't it?"

"Brilliant. I'll be with her for the night." Amy stood

aside while they peered into the incubator, letting them see first-hand that their little daughter, born six weeks early, was safe and well before she mentioned the jaundice.

"God, she looks so cosy. Just as well we don't have to take her out for the feeds." Janet opened the incubator porthole a little and stroked Kate's arm before shutting it gently again. There was no point in letting her get cold.

"Noreen says she's been great all evening. She thought she was a little jaundiced earlier so she sent a blood level to the lab to check. She may need to go on the 'lights' for a short while." Amy said this as casually as she could in order to alarm them as little as possible, giving them a little time to absorb the idea before anything actually happened.

"Where do the lights go? Will they actually be in the incubator with her?"

Neither of them looked too horrified, Amy noticed, glad that the possibility of jaundice had been mentioned in the past.

"No, we'll place them over the incubator, shining down on top of her. We'll have to put a little pair of goggles on her to shield her eyes from the brightness. Most babies don't even notice them."

"The lights won't burn her skin, will they?"

Amy reassured Janet that although Kate would look as if she was on a sunbed, the rays wouldn't harm her.

"Why don't you stay with her for a while and I'll chase up the blood results? Then we can get her started."

Half an hour later, Kate was stretched out in the incubator, the small black eye-shields looking for all the world like a pair of sunglasses. Because she had put up only the smallest of protests her parents settled themselves beside her, satisfied that she was in no way uncomfortable.

"She's like Stevie Wonder," Janet commented in amusement.

"Or Ray Charles," Declan threw in, relaxed now that yet another potential problem was being dealt with.

Amy smiled back at them, glad that the phototherapy lights hadn't caused too much alarm.

She'd just started to get Alex sorted out when Deirdre and Marcus arrived. As usual, they made a beeline for Alex, checking that all was well as they greeted Amy and inquired from Declan and Janet as to little Kate's welfare. There was an amazing sense of solidarity between the parents in the Neonatal Unit, a genuine concern for the well-being of the others' infants.

Often, another parent was the best source of reassurance for a couple who thought they'd never be able to cope with the demands that having an ill or premature infant placed on them. Many couples became very close, bonded by the shared experience that was almost impossible for their friends and family to appreciate fully.

As Amy left the ICU to collect Alex's medications from the drug trolley she heard Deirdre explaining to the other couple that Kate might get nappy rash while she was on the phototherapy but that it'd resolve after a few days. Deirdre had learnt a lot since she had come to the unit and this kind of reassurance would make the whole process seem somehow normal to Kate's parents, as if it was something that lots of babies went through, rather than a frighteningly abnormal and unfamiliar procedure.

Later in the evening, when Declan and Janet had finally waved goodbye to Kate, Marcus brought up the upcoming dinner dance.

"So, Amy, are you going to this do in the Mount Vernon? I only realised this evening that you were friendly with Peter."

"Well, I'll be off that weekend so it'll be something to look forward to. How about you two? Do you think you'll feel up to going?" Amy knew that they were both anxious to be on hand should Alex deteriorate in any way.

"We were thinking of going to the meal and leaving before the dancing and speeches start. We're all sitting at the same table, as far as I know." Deirdre smiled at Amy as she said this, adding, "At least I won't have to talk football all night!"

"I was thinking the same thing. It'll be great to have some like-minded company considering that I still haven't figured out the offside rule yet."

"I hope you don't either. It'd only put me to shame after years of Marcus trying to explain it."

Laughing, Amy left them to their own devices, knowing that the apnoea monitor attached to Alex's chest would alarm if he had any difficulty breathing. Although he'd remained stable in this regard since his one and only apnoeic episode, he would have to remain attached to the monitor until he was well enough to leave the unit.

* * *

Sunlight dazzled her as she made the short journey to the car park. The night had passed off peacefully, with only one newcomer joining Alex and Kate in the ICU early in the evening. Deirdre and Marcus had left early, only too aware of the shock on the faces of the new baby's parents and their need for privacy as they dealt with the onslaught of information that they themselves had had to cope with in the early days. Amy wondered now if they'd noticed the epicanthic folds at the corners of little Dora's eyes and the protruding tongue that gave away her diagnosis of Down Syndrome.

It had been an emotional night as the young couple from the inner city had come to terms with what they were being told: that their first baby would have some degree of intellectual disability as well as having a major heart defect. They'd eventually left the unit at 6 a.m., to start making the heartbreaking phone calls that should have brought news of a healthy newborn. Amy knew that little Dora would make the strenuous journey to the cardiac unit in Dublin later in the day, her future uncertain.

Shopping for something glamorous to wear to the upcoming night out had lost its appeal, yet Amy felt too restless to go straight home to bed. Breakfast in one of the many coffee shops along the recently refurbished Patrick Street might put her in the mood.

Two hours later, she was fully kitted out, having lost the run of herself once she got going. A long black silk dress with chiffon overlay, revealing a rather daring amount of cleavage, had been teamed to perfection with killer strappy sandals. The stylish sales girl, who looked like she knew what she was talking about, advised Amy to wear her hair "half up, half down". Thrilled with her purchases despite making an enormous dent in her credit card, she quickly added some costume jewellery before finally throwing her bags into the car as a wave of tiredness hit her. A lie-in until half six was definitely on the cards.

*   *   *

Amy slept like a log until the alarm clock went off. Normally she'd watch television for a bit while she ate her breakfast to help her wake up properly but this evening she'd have to make tracks or she'd be late getting to work. She hated rushing but it had been worth it to get her outfit sorted for the following weekend. Hopefully the unit would be fairly quiet. She had barely exchanged a word with Kim and Sheila the previous night.

The place was remarkably serene when she arrived,

the Nagle twins having been discharged home earlier in the day. Little Dora had indeed made the journey to Dublin, and had been replaced in the meantime by a pair of twins who were resting comfortably in their individual incubators. They'd been delivered five weeks early as a result of their mother developing pre-eclampsia, a condition where the blood pressure rose dangerously high. The twins, although quite small for their gestation, looked healthy and had already commenced small feeds. Alex, happy once his two-hourly feeds were on time and Kate, still under her phototherapy lights, slept contentedly oblivious to their new neighbours.

Despite the fact that none of the babies were acutely ill, the early part of the night flew by in a whirl of feeds, medications and documentation.

"Tea's up," Sheila called eventually, opening a packet of chocolate biscuits as she passed Amy a mug. "So now," she started immediately, "tell me about this Peter fellow."

"I'm sure Kim's told you almost everything," Amy grinned, making a face at their younger colleague.

"Only the major details, but it's the minor ones I want. We didn't get to talk at all last night so I'm getting in early before any kind of a rush starts."

Sheila Forde had been married for ten years before the death of her husband in a car accident. Her twin girls were now in college, testament to their mother's determination that they'd continue to have all the opportunities that they would have had if their father hadn't been unlucky enough to be in the path of a drunken driver the night before his fortieth birthday.

The girls, Rachel and Grace, had been seven at the time and Sheila now admitted that pouring all her energy into their upbringing had been her way of coping. Working full-time again, with her parents pitching in when it was needed, she'd managed to hang onto the old Georgian house that she and Martin had started to renovate, by leasing her husband's surgery to a newly qualified GP who was only too glad to walk into a ready-made practice.

Sheila had never remarried and as far as her colleagues were aware, had never been in another relationship since her husband's death. Yet she always had a lively interest in how the younger girls at work were getting on in the love department, claiming that she needed to keep abreast of trends so she'd be able to keep up with her daughters' movements. Amy filled her in now on the progression of her relationship with Peter, keeping strictly to the facts lest Sheila got as carried away as Kim appeared to have.

"An interesting profession for a young man," Sheila commented. "How did he decide on becoming a librarian?"

Careers were Sheila's particular area of interest, having guided her daughters through the Leaving Cert and spent endless hours deliberating with them over what college courses to choose. She fervently hoped that they'd be happy with their choices, having met many people over the years who'd ended up in jobs that bore no relevance to their real aptitude.

"I'm not so sure if he decided so much as developed an interest as he went along. He started out in UCC doing a Social Science degree and went to Belfast after that to do a Master's in Librarianship. He was there for a few years until the medical library opened here."

"And is he from Cork?"

This was the strange thing about night duty, Amy reflected. It was like being marooned on a desert island with a small number of people who clung together for dear life. It was a week out of life where conversations that would never take place during the day happened and confidences were exchanged that might not otherwise be disclosed. Generally, whatever was thrashed out during the night was left behind once the week was over.

"No, Waterford. He has an apartment in Douglas that he shares with a friend from home."

"What's the friend like?" Kim was always quick to grasp an opportunity, feeling that one needed to be proactive in an era when the number of women in the country far outstripped the number of men.

"Sam? Nice lad – has a girlfriend living in Scotland. He's moving over there once his contract at work expires."

Disappointed, Kim lost interest and started to prepare the one o'clock intravenous antibiotics. Sheila followed her, winking at Amy before advising her to keep an eye on Peter in case Kim got her claws into him.

"No chance," Kim retorted with a grin. "I've seen the way he looks at her. If Amy was chocolate, he'd eat her!"

26

Leadington

It was funny how the weeks had passed eventually, thought Nora. The night that Shay had been given the prescription for anti-depressants she had thought that they would never kick in. Three weeks had seemed endless. It was now a month since Ken's death and Shay was in much better shape than he'd been in that first night when Norman Daly had called. She'd consulted him the previous day about the medication and whether Shay could drive while he was on it. While he was nowhere near ready to go back to work, she thought it would be good for him to get back to the real world a bit.

"That should be no problem. He might feel a bit shaky so go with him the first few times. I was thinking of cutting back on the sleeping pill a bit in his next prescription, halve the dose maybe. He mightn't be so groggy in the mornings."

Nora was delighted to hear this. In the back of her mind she'd been worrying about Shay getting addicted. She knew he'd have to stay on the anti-depressants for six months or so and then start weaning off them slowly. But cutting down on the sleepers was a start at least.

He'd been getting out a bit more lately, but not enough in her opinion. She'd mentioned Carla, the girl on the answerphone, to him to see if he'd be interested in a visit from her but he was having none of it. He definitely didn't want the gang from work around and somehow Nora was relieved by this. He was still acting a little bit strange, something it might be wise to conceal from his superiors at work.

They'd got into a habit of going for a walk after lunch every day and he was certainly looking better for it. Shay had a natural tendency to tan and his fair hair had developed attractive streaks from being out in the garden for the past couple of weeks. He talked a lot about Frank, asking her about how she'd coped with the mortgage and keeping the house going. Nora wondered if she hadn't been too protective of her son in the past.

"What about my fees for college?" he'd asked the previous day. "Four years must have cost a lot."

He cursed himself for never having bothered with a job while he was in college. Most of his classmates had had to have one. He must have been thick to think that his mother had money to burn.

"It wasn't so bad. Your dad had been putting your

Children's Allowance into a special account from the beginning so it'd be there for your education. I never touched it. Everybody's doing that now but at the time it was considered a bit presumptuous to assume that your child would be going to college." She smiled as she thought about how far-fetched it had seemed at the time – planning an education for a three-month-old baby.

Thinking about this, Shay knew that the money would have been useful down the years for the more immediate things but his mother had probably just done without things herself. While he'd always known that he was the centre of her world, it had felt like a burden to him before. He'd often felt smothered by Nora's interest and her habit of wanting to make sure that everything was alright in his life. It was only now that he could see how much she had invested in him.

Ashamed that he'd been so ungrateful, Shay vowed that from now on he was going to pull up his socks where his mother was concerned. She hadn't been outside the door since he'd come back home and he'd been too selfish to realise that she might miss her golf or bridge. He didn't feel able to face living in his own house just yet, but his mother needn't be minding him all the time. Determined that he was going to make up for the years of taking everything for granted, he'd insisted that she start going out again.

Now it was Friday night and Nora was upstairs getting ready. He wondered for the first time what she'd told her friends about him. He couldn't imagine her telling the bridge ladies about the way he'd been at the beginning or that he was on anti-depressants. His mother was much too private for that. Yet she must have given them some explanation for her absence and he knew she kept in touch with them. Most nights after he went to bed he could hear her on the phone speaking quietly, no doubt so that Shay wouldn't be able to hear her talking about his condition. At the time he hadn't been able to care, it all went over his head. But now he wondered if Gertie and the others thought he was a basket case.

Nora eventually emerged, looking slim and attractive in a light grey trouser suit with a white top underneath. It struck Shay that she was still only fifty-three. If his father were alive they'd be in the prime of their lives, enjoying themselves. She was lucky to have had such good friends since she'd been widowed.

"Where are you off to?" Shay wanted to know. He'd never had any interest before, but now he needed to know if his mother's life was full or if she spent her evenings sitting in alone. The past month had been good for him in a funny sort of a way. He felt as if he was growing up at last and now acknowledged that he'd been a bit of a spoilt brat all his life.

"Just out to Ballycotton to The Gallery. They're after doing it up lately and it's supposed to be lovely. I'd better hurry up," she said, looking flustered as she rooted for her keys. "Don't wait up!" This was said with a grin and they both remembered the many nights that this had been Shay's parting shot as he left for a disco as a teenager.

The Gallery was a small but expensive restaurant perched precariously on the cliffs looking out at Ballycotton lighthouse. Shay had taken Carla there once in the early days and she'd been enthralled by the feeling of being so close to the sea, and the sense that the waves were crashing dangerously beneath them. His mother's friends must be pushing the boat out now that she was back on the scene.

27

Number 1

"So, how's Brona getting on?"

Charlie had overheard a number of fraught exchanges over the past few weeks and had been surprised at Linda's tone. They were on their usual Friday night out, this time tucked away in a corner of Umberto's, the new Italian restaurant on the Douglas Road.

"I can't figure her out. She was great as an assistant manager but I'm not sure if she's up to this job. She gets all sorts of things into a mix-up."

Linda had told him her version of the locker incident but even with her own slant on it, Charlie could see that Brona could hardly be blamed for it. It seemed as if there were too many cooks involved in Bodywork but Linda didn't appear to be able to see it.

"Would you think about moving over to Coltons altogether? You've enough on your plate with the groundwork starting on Phase 1."

Since Charlie had opted out of the opportunity to develop The Sanctuary with her, she'd forged ahead with it under the Coltons' umbrella. Her father had backed it financially without too much censure. He'd suggested that she abandon her office in the leisure centre and take up residence in the building that his company inhabited, reminding her that she'd need to be able to access and be accessible to the personnel involved in the project. Obstinately, she had declined the offer, refusing to be seen to arrive into her father's company as some sort of apprentice, preferring to act as project manager for The Sanctuary from her own premises.

"I think I'll have to until I get this thing off the ground. Maybe if Brona is left to her own devices she'll pull her socks up. I'll have to ask Dad about an office, I suppose."

Charlie could see that she felt she was giving in, whereas he thought it was a sensible move. He said so, reminding her that they'd be working in the same building as a result.

"That'll be nice – we'll get to do lunch most days." Linda was glad that Charlie seemed pleased about the prospect of her moving into the same building. At the time that he'd made his decision not to be involved in The Sanctuary at a managerial level, she'd tried to push him into changing his mind. Realising that she was getting nowhere, she'd had to rethink the whole plan and persuade her father to head the development, with her employed as project manager. After all, it was her idea and she knew exactly what was needed.

Daniel had agreed with the proviso that one of the senior project managers already employed by the company be consulted regularly in an advisory capacity. Linda agreed readily, thrilled to have the resources to move ahead with the project, and glad of the guidance of Luke Nolan, from whom she was already learning a lot. They now met every Friday to plan the week ahead and iron out any difficulties that had arisen during the preceding week.

Initially, she'd been angry with Charlie for not supporting her, and their relationship had reached a point where she'd accused him of being afraid of commitment. Patiently he'd reminded her that he was an architect and had no desire to become a property developer. That didn't mean he was bowing out of their relationship. Only that it was separate from work and he was happy for it to remain that way. He urged her to look at what she really wanted and she was forced to admit that developing The Sanctuary was her real goal.

What she didn't admit, even to herself, was that the only reason she'd wanted Charlie involved was with a view to selling the idea to her father and to get him to back her financially. The idea that she would manipulate her boyfriend like this was too much for Linda to acknowledge, particularly when she took for granted that they would one day be married.

However, the personal side of things would have to go on hold for a bit until she got the first phase up and running, and now that things had settled down between them again, she could see that Charlie had been right. He was much happier turning out great designs, without the headache of dealing with contractors and the like. The dynamic of their relationship was restored and even though they were both busy, they still enjoyed their time with each other in the same way they always had.

And despite the fact that he'd declined to buy into it himself, Charlie was supportive of the way she was running the project and was always there for her to bounce ideas off. Looking at him now across the table, she could see how he'd relaxed since his decision was made. From the time that she'd mooted her plan initially, he'd been tense and stressed with her, refusing to be pushed into joining forces on the project. He was back to his usual self now and Linda wondered if it wouldn't be a good idea for them to get away together for a holiday. They hadn't had a break since skiing in January, a first for Linda, who loved to get away to the sun, even for a weekend, every couple of months. Maybe I'll book something as a surprise, she thought, filing the thought at the back of her brain for Monday.

"Have you thought about what way you're going to work Phase 2 yet? The plans are done for the lot at this stage, you know."

Rather than build the whole complex together and have to wait years until the profits started to roll in, Linda had decided to carry out the work in four intensive phases. Work would start at the front of the site, commencing with the leisure centre, gym and swimming pool. This would include a medical wing with GP, physiotherapist, dentist and dietician. This had been one of Charlie's ideas, the concept of promoting health so that people incorporated it as part of leisure time rather than as a 'must' that they attended to reluctantly.

Linda was confident that the leisure centre would be heavily subscribed fairly quickly, generating an income at an early stage. The front of the site would be landscaped and the back cordoned off so that clients wouldn't be aware that they were on a building site. Construction work for the remaining phases would be carried out via a rear entrance opening onto a smaller road.

Linda had been mulling over the second phase and hadn't yet decided which of the options she'd go for.

"I suppose I have to look at whether we want to keep the income running as high as we can or the idea of setting an exclusive tone for the place. The beauty salon and hair studio would certainly start making money fairly quickly, especially where it's located, but I'm not sure if opening it before the complementary therapies would be wise."

Linda had been stunned by Charlie's plans for the complementary therapy unit when he unveiled them first. He'd wanted to ensure that the setting was conducive to relaxation so that clients could "tune out" while they were on the premises. Carnelian Springs was to be a long, low crescent-shaped building curving along the east side of the site. A moat surrounded it so that it had to be accessed via a stone bridge. A high bank would surround the moat, landscaped to give year-round views beyond the narrow expanse of water. The building would be effectively situated on an island and had been designed in such a way that all of the treatment rooms overlooked the moat and the garden beyond.

Linda had trawled the Internet to come up with a suitable name for the holistic centre, finally settling on Carnelian Springs when she came across a website detailing the properties of healing crystals. As well as liking the sound of the word, she was taken by the fact some healers used carnelian to clear negative energy. As clearing negative energy seemed, in Linda's limited experience, to be a good reason for attending a complementary therapist, she deemed it a suitable symbol for the holistic centre.

"I have an instinct to go ahead with Carnelian Springs once the leisure centre is up and running. If we expect to be considered one of the most exclusive resorts in the country we'd better start showing signs of it from early on."

"I think you're right, to be honest. A good advertising campaign will put the Springs out there in the whole 'oasis of tranquillity' sense. People *do* have the money now to consider prevention rather than cure so it'll catch on in that regard, as well as in the pampering aspect. I think it'll be good timing as well. The services seem to be limited enough at the moment in and around the area – I'd say it's nearly all small private practices. What does Daniel think?"

Linda laughed. "Doubtful about giving out the money for a slow starter when there's the possibility of raking in the bucks with a hair and beauty salon."

Charlie smiled at the succinct but accurate sketch of Daniel Colton. Always one to push the boat out on quality and innovation, he still remained cautious about getting in over his head on any project. Charlie agreed with him mostly but this time he thought that Linda's foresight would pay dividends, even if it meant putting the slower earner before the dead cert.

"What about Luke?"

Charlie had great respect for the senior project manager and thought that he'd be a good candidate for a directorship within the company. He was ambitious and driven in the way that Linda was but more cool-headed. In fact, Charlie himself had often wondered if he could do with a bit of that kind of drive, be a little more open to taking chances. There was no way that Luke Nolan would have turned down Linda's offer of a partnership in The Sanctuary.

"I talked to him about it today actually. He thinks that we should go ahead with it. It's not like him to be flowery but he thinks the plans for the Carnelian Springs building are 'inspired'." Linda waited with raised eyebrows for Charlie's reaction before continuing.

"That is fairly flowery for Luke," Charlie grinned, at the same time pleased that someone he admired as much as he did Luke had appreciated his work.

"The fact that the building is isolated by the moat and bank makes it easier to run it while the rest of the building is going on. The whole notion of being on a tranquil island can be maintained if we have good soundproofing from the outset. And you have that included anyway."

Charlie admired Linda's outlook on the project but could see that Daniel would be cautious in terms of financial management. He was a businessman at the end of the day and would be wary of being led into an unwise move by his admittedly headstrong daughter.

"Linda, your dad might be slow to appreciate your judgement just yet, when you have such limited experience. I *do* think you're absolutely right on this but do you think it would be better coming from Luke?"

"I suppose so," Linda conceded reluctantly, smart enough to realise that Luke's experience and previous record would convince her father almost immediately. "I'll give him a call about it on Monday."

"Good idea. Now, what about dessert?" Charlie surveyed the menu in front of him, finally settling on a rich tiramisu followed by coffee. Linda never touched sweets or pastries and was a serious devotee of Dr Atkins. A double espresso would finish off her meal nicely.

* * *

Charlie lay awake for ages after Linda had dozed off, thinking about their relationship. Although they'd made love and it had been as satisfying as ever in one sense, he now felt detached, as if it hadn't happened at all. He wasn't sure of what it was, but lately he kept thinking that something was missing. Looking at it factually, they were compatible in every way. They enjoyed each other's company and had a lot in common. Even sexually there still seemed to be the same chemistry that they'd had from the beginning. He wondered was this all any couple had. Maybe he was looking for something that didn't exist.

He didn't think his unease was related to the decision not to develop the leisure complex with Linda. It had caused a strain certainly and things had been pretty rocky for a while. At one stage they hadn't made love for two weeks, something that had never happened before even when they were tired or jetlagged. But they'd come past that once Linda had accepted that he wanted no part in the centre except in his capacity as an architect with Coltons.

In fact, Linda seemed all the happier now, whereas he had this mildly bleak feeling that wouldn't go away, no matter how hard he tried to push it to the back of his mind. Maybe all relationships became a little stale after a while, with couples getting used to each other's ways and even getting a bit bored. He couldn't honestly say he was bored with Linda but maybe the relationship was getting mundane.

Lately he'd begun to wonder where they were going

exactly but always shied away from the thoughts that followed. For other couples, it seemed to be engagement and marriage but he somehow couldn't see that happening with them. Their goals in life were too diverse for one thing. Linda was only getting her teeth into a huge project that was the start of what he thought would be a very successful career in property development, even if she didn't realise it yet. He couldn't see her breaking off to settle into family life with a husband and children.

Is that what I want, he questioned himself now. The fact that they'd never even discussed it said something in itself. The realisation that he'd never really considered Linda as a life partner shocked him. What was he expecting then? What did Linda expect? Did she have an understanding that they'd be together in the long-term? He didn't think that she'd have planned that far ahead but it made him feel guilty that she might envisage a future that included him, and that he'd led her to believe this unwittingly.

Suddenly it came to him that the proposal for the leisure centre would have further enmeshed them, had he been agreeable. Perhaps this is why Linda had reacted as she had. Never one to accept "no" for an answer, she'd been persistent in her bid to change his mind but Charlie had refused to give in to what he saw as her wanting her own way on a somewhat grand scale. Dope, he thought now, that he hadn't thought about what it would mean to them as a couple.

Sick at the thought that he'd somehow wronged

Linda while vacantly continuing with a relationship that might not be a hundred per cent right for himself either, Charlie tossed and turned for the remainder of the night, sometimes wondering if he was blowing the whole thing out of proportion. Their relationship was great. Maybe it was simply a matter of neither of them being ready yet. Nobody was putting a gun to his head saying they must get married or else. The fact that they had different goals didn't necessarily mean that they weren't compatible. It wasn't as if he wanted someone who'd stay at home to raise a family while he went out to work in the old-fashioned way.

Finally settling on the fact that there was nothing to decide on in the immediate sense, he willed himself to sleep just as the sun started to come up. Maybe now that it had dawned on him to really look at their relationship, he might be able to envisage what the future held for them.

28

Seefin

"OK, slowly now. He's going to cough a bit as it touches the back of his throat but keep going. Great, a little more, that's it. Now check to see if it's down far enough. Go by the measurement on the tube."

Marcus was out in a sweat, the perspiration dampening the back of his shirt. Despite having seen the feeding tube being inserted into Alex's nose on numerous occasions and having been talked through it for the last few days, the reality of doing it himself was something entirely different. In the early days, the feeding tube had been left in place all the time with a continuous flow of milk being pumped slowly into his stomach. Now that he'd progressed, his feeds had been broken up into three-hourly amounts, with the feeding tube being inserted on each occasion.

"What if it's gone into his lungs instead of his stomach?" He knew he was panicking but he couldn't help it.

"Just stick a little bit of tape on it to keep it in place while you check that it's in the right place. Here."

Amy handed him a sliver of surgical tape that she'd had ready and Marcus used it to secure the slim tube to Alex's cheek. Attaching a tiny syringe to the tip of the tube, he carefully drew off a small drop of acid fluid from Alex's stomach to test with litmus paper. He'd seen this done before each of Alex's feeds recently but it was odd to be doing it himself. Squeezing the little drop of fluid onto the strip of blue paper, Marcus prayed fervently that its colour would change from blue to pink.

"Well done," Amy exclaimed as the familiar pink tinge crept along the thin strip of paper. "The tube is definitely in the stomach so you know it's safe to go ahead and give the feed through it."

Marcus's hands were shaking as Deirdre handed him the container of milk. Relieved that her husband had inserted the tube properly on his first attempt, she wasn't dreading her turn the following day so much. They both wanted to be as competent at tube-feeding as possible in case Alex needed to have it for a while once he was allowed home. If they couldn't manage it, then Alex would have to stay in hospital until he no longer required the tube feeds.

As it stood, his sucking reflex wasn't as strong as the staff would have liked. He was able for some breastfeeds, or bottle-feeds when Deirdre wasn't available, but usually only lasted a few minutes before falling asleep exhausted. At this stage he needed at least three ounces at every feed to help him gain weight so the only solution was to keep giving him the milk through a tube every three hours.

Marcus sat back with Alex tucked securely in his arms as Deirdre slowly poured the milk down the tube. Alex dozed in the comfort of his father's heat, oblivious to the fact that he was having his midday feed.

"Great set-up, all the same, isn't it?" Marcus said, smiling. "No exertion whatsoever and he's as full as an egg."

Relieved that he'd managed to get the tube in first go, he was relaxing a little. The cubicle that housed Alex, his cot and all his accumulated belongings was stifling, though compared to the early days in the ICU it was like being in the Arctic Circle.

Initially, because he'd had almost no body fat and no shivering reflex to generate heat, Alex hadn't been able to maintain his body temperature at a normal level. At that stage, they'd been told, he could get hypothermia if they kept the tiny door of the incubator open for more than a few minutes. For Deirdre and Marcus, the most precious moments of the day had been when they felt Alex's little hand tighten around one of their fingers, yet once they realised that this necessitated opening the hatch and letting out some of the heat, they'd limited their 'cuddles' to a minute or so every few hours.

Marcus loved this about the staff in the Neonatal Unit. They never said "You can't do this" or "You're not allowed do that". A reason was given for every single thing that anyone did to Alex so that on many occasions they were actually delighted to stand back, knowing that it was benefiting their child.

And despite the fact that they were looking after babies like Alex every day of the week, the nurses never became blasé or failed to appreciate the shock that the smallest changes could have on the parents.

Marcus knew he would never forget the day that they came in to find one of Alex's legs encased in tinfoil, looking bizarrely like some sort of shiny, space-age wellie boot.

It transpired that the arteries in Alex's other leg had gone into spasm due to a special line that the consultant had inserted to take blood. The treatment was to warm the opposite leg in order to encourage the circulation in the affected leg to re-establish itself gently, hence the tinfoil. Once they knew what was happening, they were content to sit and wait as the colour slowly seeped back into the affected limb.

A week later it occurred to Marcus to ask what would have happened if the spasm hadn't eased. Kim, the nurse who'd been working with Alex that day, explained gently that if the blood supply hadn't returned to the leg, then Alex had run the risk of losing that limb altogether. This was the reason why they'd been so reluctant to insert the line in the first place, weighing up the need for it against the risks that it incurred.

Marcus had felt faint on hearing this, and blessed Kim for not telling them at the time. He'd noticed this skill time and time again. While informing the parents of everything that affected their baby, the neo-natal staff were able to filter the information in such a way that it came out in layers that could be easily digested without overloading people who were already at the far end of their coping limits.

Looking down at Alex, Marcus felt an overwhelming sense of achievement. When his first child had arrived into the world so suddenly, he hadn't been at all prepared for the enormity of what lay ahead and, at the time, he wasn't sure if he'd be able for it. He'd been spinning with the changes that every day brought and he kept hoping that he wouldn't crack up under the strain and let Deirdre down. She'd had more to deal with than him, experiencing all the fear and trepidation that Marcus did, only with the added strain of having just given birth and the pressure of producing enough milk for Alex to boot. Today he felt as though he was finally of some use and was thrilled that his first proper attempt at tube-feeding had worked out.

Once Alex was changed and winded, Amy advised them to go and have a coffee.

"You've had enough stress for one day, although if you're in tonight, Marcus, it might be a good idea to do the nine o'clock feed as well. Consolidate your skills, as the Americans would put it. See how you feel later."

"I think I will, Amy. Best to keep going while I have the confidence. And thanks for getting me through it," Marcus added, delighted with his new skill.

"You'll be nearly qualified to run the unit yourself if

you keep going at this rate!"

"Don't encourage him or he'll want to be put on the roster," Deirdre retorted, glad that it had been Amy who'd been on hand to instruct her husband in what was a terrifying task for both of them.

Since the night of the football club dinner at the Mount Vernon, a comfortable friendship had developed between them. Deirdre and Marcus had always liked and respected Amy in a professional sense but since Amy's relationship with Peter had developed, they'd got to know her in a social capacity as well. Marcus and Peter were great friends, both dedicated Arsenal fans, and could spend hours dissecting a game if they got an opportunity.

Deirdre and Amy, only mildly exasperated at the ongoing discussion about the possible transfer of Ashley Cole, had had ample time to get to know each other during the evening. Apart from their shared interest in Alex's welfare, the two women had much in common, having a similar outlook on many aspects of life. Like Deirdre, Amy was a book-lover, reading voraciously in between working and studying.

"If only Peter would transfer to one of the county libraries I'd be made up," she joked at one point during the evening.

Peter had winked at her, promising to apply if she'd consider transferring to the Accident and Emergency department so he could get his frequent soccer injuries treated at high speed.

Deirdre had met Peter on a few occasions in the past

and thought him to be a complete gentleman – great fun and engaging company. Seeing him with Amy at the dinner dance, she was struck by how comfortable they were with each other, even though they'd only known each other a short time.

She and Marcus had been reluctant to leave the hotel that evening, both enjoying the company and their first social event since Alex's birth. They'd spoken about it later that night and Deirdre was surprised to find that Marcus was as pleased as she was that Amy was living so near them. They both felt that she was somebody that would be a friend long after Alex was discharged from the unit, particularly if her relationship with Peter became permanent.

"If Peter has anything to do with it, it'll definitely be permanent," Marcus had laughed. "Every second sentence started with 'Amy says'. The lads from the soccer team were giving him a desperate slagging but he wasn't a bit put out."

Deirdre was inordinately pleased to hear this. Of their other neighbours, Shay Deegan was the only one they'd had much interaction with. However, even though he was friendly, he seemed to be on the go full-time with a different pace of life than she and Marcus had. Linda Colton in the first house was a stand-offish blonde who showed little inclination to get to know them, despite several overtures on Deirdre's part. Their most recent communication with her involved her eating the face off Marcus for his erratic driving the night that they'd rushed to the hospital, frantic with worry that Alex would be born before they even arrived. Marcus had attempted to apologise but to no avail.

Having Amy as a neighbour was therefore a bonus in Deirdre's eyes. Marcus agreed, teasing Deirdre about her vivid imagination when she wondered out loud whether Peter too would wind up living in Pebble Cove.

*　*　*

Later in the coffee shop, Deirdre wondered how she'd fare the following day with inserting the feeding tube.

"I was in bits until the time came," said Marcus. "I didn't sleep a wink all last night worrying. You're more calm than me, Dee, so you'll fly it."

Leaning over so as she could rest her head on Marcus's chest, Deirdre told him quietly that the only thing that had kept her going in the preceding weeks had been his way of quietly coping with everything that came their way, even when she herself was panicking. "And you have to deal with working and keeping everything at home ticking over as well. I haven't even asked about bills or sorting out the maternity leave or anything. Thanks for keeping it all going, love. Even today, you were brilliant. I feel as if the pressure's off me now, knowing that you can do it."

"God, Dee, it's amazing, isn't it? One minute we're an ordinary couple going about our business, and the next thing we're thrown into the middle of all this. You always hear about people having a premature baby but you think they just stay in hospital until they're big enough to come home. Simple as that. I had no idea that people went through this kind of stuff."

"Dad can't get over how you've taken to it. He thinks I got myself a fabulous man altogether. Apparently he keeps telling Hazel to keep an eye out for the same type of a fella as you."

Marcus laughed at the idea of his dynamic sister-in-law settling for someone as sedate as himself but was glad all the same of Tom's approval. His own parents didn't know if he was good, bad or indifferent in dealing with the situation that he'd so suddenly found himself in. While their approval meant very little to Marcus at this stage of his life, Tom and Rose's good opinion meant a lot. He valued their place in his life and hoped they could see how much he cared for their daughter. They'd both been brilliant since Alex had come into the world.

Rose managed the house with a precision that had Marcus reeling and he often joked that Deirdre would have divorced him after the first week if it had been left to him. No sooner had Alex been divested of a Babygro than it was washed and ironed and back in the "Clean Clothes" box under his cot. She'd insisted at the outset that Deirdre and Marcus had enough to cope with besides thinking of laundry and cooking.

"And anyway," she told them, "I can't do anything for Alex except to help his parents to be with him as much as possible. If that means cooking a few dinners and turning the dials on the washing machine, then I'll do it until this time next year if it's any good."

To Deirdre's amazement, Marcus had enfolded her mother in a bear hug, telling her that Tom was a lucky man if he'd got this kind of treatment for the past thirty-five years. To the best of her knowledge, her husband had never spontaneously hugged his own mother, and it meant a lot to Deirdre that he made such an effort with both her parents.

The house in Pebble Cove had fallen into a daily routine that ran like clockwork. During the week Tom drove Dee to the hospital straight after breakfast, while Marcus went to work and Rose tackled the day's jobs, as she called the housework. Deirdre and Tom usually came home for their lunch, with Rose going back in the afternoon to keep her company and bond with Alex. Deirdre wanted to spend as much of the day with her baby as she could but her mother insisted on her coming home for dinner at six with Marcus.

"It's no use to Alex if you get run down," she was fond of saying, and Deirdre knew she was right.

If her mother hadn't placed some kind of a structure on the day, Deirdre knew in her heart that she'd be like some of the mums in the Neonatal Unit who didn't even get to have a shower some days. Tales of having to be dropped into the unit every morning before their husbands went to work because they couldn't drive for six weeks after a Caesarean made her realise how lucky she was to have this level of support at her fingertips.

Some of the mothers could only get to visit their babies at the weekends because they lived too far away and had other children to look after at home.

Once, when Alex had been ill and Dee and Marcus had stayed the night, they'd been stunned to see a couple from Waterford appearing at 1a.m. with the familiar cooler box of breast milk. They'd got chatting in the parents' room and were told that the couple hadn't been able to leave for the two-hour journey to Cork until the last of the silage had been cut on their small farm.

"The contractors were booked to come so we would have had to pay them anyway. And we'd have had nothing to feed the cattle with for the winter if we didn't go ahead with it. Catherine here had the rest of the gang in bed and my mother came over to stay with them before we left."

This was told with not the slightest touch of how enormous a task it was for this couple to spend an hour with their baby. It would be at least four o'clock in the morning before Catherine and Joe got home to Waterford and, having lived in the country for most of her life, Deirdre knew that farmers often started work at five during the silage season in order to get as much done as they could in case the weather would break.

Amazed yet again at the sacrifices that other people had to make, Deirdre and Marcus had gone back to the ICU to sit with Alex and allow the parents of baby Joseph to have their precious time with him in private.

Deirdre felt guilty sometimes when she heard how

some of the mothers had to manage and she said so to Marcus as they looked around the hospital canteen, filled now with the familiar faces of the other "neonatal parents".

"I know, love. We have great support really. And it'll be great to have Hazel around when Alex gets home."

As well as Marcus and her parents, Deirdre had Hazel to talk everything through with. She called in after work most evenings, despite running a busy salon and being responsible for a workforce of ten.

Hazel had always wanted to be a hairdresser and had spent hours as a child trying to put ringlets in Deirdre's hopelessly straight hair. After serving her apprenticeship locally, she'd been determined to land a job in a busy salon in Cork. As usual, her determination won out and before long she'd built up a steady stream of regulars who were happy to pay what Hazel had initially thought of as extortionate prices.

Her big chance had come when an elderly aunt of Tom's had died, leaving her two-storey townhouse above a rackety grocery shop to her only nephew. Bewildered as to what to do with the city-centre property and terrified of it being vandalised once the city hoods realised that it was no longer occupied, Tom had decided to approach the local estate agent about letting it out or even selling it.

"Are you mad, Dad? Hang onto it for a little bit and rent it to me. If I can do it up a bit downstairs I'll be able to set up on my own."

Hazel's enthusiasm was enough to convince Tom,

who agreed to go to the bank with her for financing to set up her first business, first insisting that the property be rent-free. Delighted to be able to help his daughter with a start in life, Tom had thrown himself into the renovating of Aunt Kitty's musty shop.

Most of Hazel's customers had followed her to Talking Heads, ensuring a backbone of business to supplement the passing trade that the prime location provided. In three years, she'd repaid her starting loan and was now in the process of renovating the upstairs as her first home. Tom and Rose had transferred the deeds of the house into Hazel's name, having consulted Deirdre first. At the same time, they'd made a will leaving their own house and land to Dee and Marcus, happy to be able to provide for the future of both their daughters.

Hazel normally took Thursdays off from the salon to catch up with paperwork and meet suppliers and the like. Since Alex's arrival, she'd started calling into the hospital in the afternoons to take her sister out to lunch after spending an hour or so singing to Alex. Hazel was the only one in the family with a singing voice and it always amazed Tom and Rose that they'd produced a daughter with a note in her head. Hazel was convinced that there must be at least one other person in the clan who could raise a tune and was grooming Alex for the role.

Crazy about Alex, Hazel had offered to come and stay with them once the baby was allowed home, aware that Deirdre and Marcus would need help with the night feeds that would still be important to maintain his weight gain. She planned to give up her one-bedroomed apartment and lodge in Pebble Cove until her own house was finished.

"It'll be experience for when my own time comes," she told Deirdre, always adding, "if it ever comes."

Hazel maintained that there was a man out there for her who wanted a quiet life and would be happy for her to continue in the fast lane. She planned to open branches of Talking Heads in at least three locations in Cork city as well as in the outlying country towns that were expanding at a rate of knots since the housing boom had started. Marcus and Deirdre thought she was brilliant and frequently wondered if they themselves led a very sedate and cautious existence, but always came back to the fact that they loved the secure and easygoing nature of their lives, knowing it would be complete once they had Alex safely home.

"Do you think we should go into town and have a look at another chest of drawers for the spare room? Hazel won't have much storage if she's bringing all her stuff with her. We'd be back in plenty of time for the next feed."

Despite his earlier exhilaration, Marcus was feeling a bit anxious about putting down the tube a second time. A walk around the furniture shops would take his mind off it for a bit.

"Good idea, we could go into Argos as well and get one of those shoe racks. It'll be like living with Imelda Marcos."

Hazel loved shoes and was constantly ribbed about it by Deirdre who only ever owned a few pairs at a time.

*   *   *

Later that evening, Marcus managed to insert the feeding tube under the supervision of Kim, reassuring himself finally that the morning's success hadn't been a fluke. Kim advised him to repeat the performance as much as he could over the following days to build up his confidence. As the weekend was coming up, they decided to come in for all the feeds so that Deirdre could have her turn at tube-feeding with Marcus helping her.

They both knew it was best that they learn to manage the tube-feeding themselves so that if the need arose, they'd be self-sufficient.

That was another thing about the Neonatal Unit – anything they weren't told about by the staff, they heard anyway from the other parents. It had horrified them at first to see some of the older prems being discharged with a feeding-tube still in place. Some were even sent home on nasal oxygen.

But as the weeks had passed Deirdre and Marcus had come to understand the delight in the faces of those parents, despite the fact that they wouldn't be able to leave the house without an oxygen cylinder and that people would stare at the strange little tube snaking out of their baby's nose. They too, if necessary, would do all this and more for Alex.

29

Number 1

Things were really going to plan now that Linda had
taken the office in Coltons. The contractors had got the
groundwork for the new leisure centre underway and
so far there had been no major difficulties. Things were
moving so fast that she could hardly believe it had been
only a matter of months since the project had begun.
They'd been lucky in that the land had already been
zoned to their advantage and the planning permission
had come through without any objections.
Developments could be held up for years on account of
objections lodged with the council by individuals,
community lobbies and environmental groups so Linda
was well aware of just how fortunate they'd been to
date.

As a safeguard against local opposition, they'd
included in the plans a proposal to offer a set amount of
weekly swimming-pool hours to the two local

secondary schools and she felt that this alone might have ensured the smooth running of the planning process. Also the fact that none of the buildings were more than two storeys was a pleasant surprise to residents who were already adept at lodging objections to the many apartment blocks proposed of late.

Meantime, she had things like internal fittings, décor, equipment, advertising and particularly staffing to think about. As well as all this, she was planning ahead for the same issues regarding Phase 2. Following an energetic meeting with Daniel and the rest of the directors, she and Luke had succeeded in their quest to have the Carnelian Springs project start once the building work was complete on Phase 1.

Linda's experience and the contacts she had made as manager of Bodywork were proving invaluable now that she'd reached the stage of equipping Esprit, the leisure facility. She'd planned the complement of machines, weights etc with the fitness instructor from Bodywork and had already struck a deal with the supplier. Designs for the swimming pool were almost finalised, incorporating a kiddie's pool that would be fully supervised and a state-of-the-art Jacuzzi area.

The sauna and steam rooms were next on her hit-list and Linda was considering visiting a number of the top spas in northern Europe to get an idea of the latest in design and fittings.

The leisure centre would eventually sport a child-minding facility but this was something that would be put on hold until they were fully operational. The designated area would be fitted out from the outset but she reckoned that staffing and opening it would wait a few months until their membership warranted it.

Hoping to market the complex on several fronts, she felt that the backbone of their business would be local until the corporate chalets and holiday villas were functional. For this reason the childcare facility and things like swimming lessons would be aimed at providing a family-oriented service. However these features would have to be brought on stream when they had a better idea of the level of service required. This restraint on Linda's part had surprised her father, who'd been under the impression that she wanted everything going full swing from the word go.

As far as Linda was concerned, staffing was going to be the biggest headache. Wanting to avoid the teething problems associated with bringing a large number of new staff on stream at the same time, she planned to train them in via Bodywork. She'd already discussed this with Hugo, the senior fitness instructor, and had mooted the idea of him heading the gym staff at Esprit. Informing him that there would be a salary increase going with the move to Rochestown, Linda advised Hugo to groom his current assistant with a view to taking over the running of the Bodywork gym in the coming year. Impressed, Hugo promised to be ready for the challenge of heading up a much larger concern, planning immediately to start the process of training in his successor.

Brona was another staff member that Linda felt

would benefit the new facility. Since she'd been left to her own devices she'd come on in leaps and bounds and Linda wondered if she'd been a bit intimidated by having her boss around when she took over as manager first. Her initiative in wanting to plan for the fall-off in clients at Bodywork once the new leisure centre opened had impressed Linda, who hadn't actually thought of it herself on account of being so tied up with the new development.

Brona's plan was to target the "young adult" bracket as she called it. Having gone over the membership list with Linda they were convinced that the ones leaving to join the more exclusive facility would be those in the slightly older age bracket who were more established in life and could afford the substantial price increase. Bodywork was still pretty exclusive by any standards so targeting the upwardly mobile, young-guns set would still maintain the upmarket image.

Linda had considered the proposal and discussed it with one of the marketing executives in Coltons who thought it was just the way to go. Promising an increase in budget for pre-Christmas marketing, Linda commented that Brona was in need of an assistant manager.

"Are any of the present staff suitable or should we interview from outside? You'll be the one working with him or her so you'd have to sit in on the interviews."

Stunned that Linda was finally taking her seriously, Brona offered the opinion that many of the current staff were inexperienced, so perhaps it would be better to open up the post to outsiders.

"Fine, you can put the wording of the ad together and run it by me on Friday before you put it in the papers. We'll see what comes in before we set up the dates for interview." Linda planned to see how Brona handled the interviews and the type of candidate she'd be inclined to choose before offering her a post in the new leisure centre.

Bodywork was still Linda's primary source of income, so seeing that it was properly managed was as important as getting the new venture off the ground. Yet it was an ideal breeding ground for recruiting staff for at least one area of The Sanctuary. Areas like Carnelian Springs and the hair and beauty salon would prove more difficult but she was confident that when that time came she'd have the experience to deal with it.

30

Leadington

"Will we go over to Pebble Cove and get your car today, love?" Nora asked tentatively.

Shay hadn't been back there recently and she thought it was time to make a move in that direction. He was now acclimatised to the lighter sleeping pill so she wasn't as concerned about him driving. It would be a big step if he got back behind the wheel.

Shay saw the concern in her face and decided that he'd put his mother through enough this last while. Maybe he wasn't ready to face the house yet, but he could pick up his car at least.

Thrilled that he'd agreed, Nora didn't want to push too much nor did she want him driving on his own for the first time in case the medication affected his co-ordination.

"How about if we pick up your car and go to the Garden Centre? Your boot is bigger so we could get all the hedging in one go."

They'd been discussing putting a low hedge around the perimeter of the front lawn, with Shay promising to help with the heavy digging. The front of the house had been open-plan but lately a lot of the old neighbours had sold up, being replaced by families with young children. Nora loved that there were children in the crescent again but was loath to see her spectacular bed of Amber Queens flattened by footballs after years of feeding, spraying and pruning.

Shay did feel a little nervous getting behind the wheel but felt better knowing his mother was beside him.

Obviously unaware of Ken's death, Shay's neighbour Marcus had cheerfully come over to chat when he spotted him arriving at the house with Nora.

"Were you on holidays or what? You've been missing for ages."

Marcus's face was open and friendly but when Shay didn't reply Nora came in with a ready excuse.

"Just over minding his mother for a bit," she said with a smile. "I'll let him home soon once I'm back on my feet."

Annoyed at himself that his mother had had to bail him out yet again, Shay pulled himself together a bit and asked how little Alex was doing.

"Brilliant." Marcus was beaming and only dying to fill his neighbour in on all the details of the baby's progress. "He's been in an incubator for ages but they're hoping to get him into a cot if his weight is up on Saturday. He's still being mostly fed by a tube down his nose because even though we've tried a few times he's not strong enough to suck a bottle or . . . anything."

Marcus had been going to say "or the breast" but caught himself in time. Just because his own life revolved around breastfeeding didn't mean he had to offend the sensibilities of the middle-aged woman in front of him.

Nora, however, was fascinated and wanted to know more. Marcus was only thrilled to oblige, ending with "Of course Shay here was involved right from the beginning. He had to provide tea and sympathy the morning after Alex was born. I was in shock, but himself here sorted me out with a fine big fry. Thank God things are better than they were that morning."

Nora was impressed, firstly that this young man was so tuned in to the needs of his wife and baby and secondly that Shay had been so helpful at such a terrible time in their lives.

"So when do you think he'll be able to come home?" Shay felt that he ought to contribute to the conversation, now that he'd started it.

"Oh, it will be weeks yet. We just hope that he'll be finished with the tube-feeding before they discharge him. It'd be much easier if Deirdre was feeding him herself."

Marcus didn't mention that Alex's ability to feed independently would very much depend on how much damage had been sustained at the time of his brain haemorrhage. The possibility was that he would need to be tube-fed at home for weeks or even months if he didn't become strong enough to take a full breast or bottle feed.

"She's breast-feeding him?" said Nora. "Isn't that marvellous? He'll be all the better for it, I'll tell you that much."

Shay looked at her in surprise, amazed that his mother would be open-minded enough to discuss such a topic with a man, a stranger at that. There was a lot he didn't know about his mother, he decided.

After another few minutes with Marcus they sat into Shay's car, Shay trying to hide his nervousness as well as he could. They set off, Nora continued chatting as if this were an ordinary drive and not the first real step in her son's return to normal life.

Twenty minutes later they pulled up on the gravel drive of the Garden Centre and Shay felt as elated as if he'd just completed a marathon. His concentration was shot so he just wandered from stand to stand while Nora selected the slender saplings of green beech that they planned to plant the following day. The journey home was a bit easier but he found himself exhausted as soon as he'd parked the car in his mother's driveway.

"That was great, love," his mother commended him. "Are you glad you did it?"

"I suppose it's time I got back to normal a bit. I feel I've been lying around under your feet for long enough." Shay smiled as he said this, knowing his mother was only delighted to be fussing over him.

"Well, don't overdo it. You'll have to take your time

and make sure you're well before you go off the tablets or anything."

Nora, while eager for her son to get well, was anxious that he recovered properly. She'd discussed this with Norman Daly the previous week and while he too was happy with Shay's progress, he was adamant that Shay needed counselling in order to sort out the chaos of Ken's death and move on fully. Indeed, he felt that if he didn't have some form of psychotherapy, the risk of Shay having a repeat illness was quite high. He'd explained this to mother and son together in the hope that it would underline the necessity of being as strong as possible before attempting to come off the medication.

Nora understood the logic of this and trusted Norman's advice. She knew she'd have to give her son support and encouragement in proceeding with the restoration of his health. Anyway, she couldn't imagine him returning to his own house until he'd come to terms with the memories that his home evoked.

"Should we ring that fellow in Cobh about the counselling, do you think?" she went on. "Norman said he might have a waiting list. It might help you to get things straight in your head."

"I don't think I'll bother. It'll probably be all this 'tell me how you feel' business. I don't think it'd do me any good, going over it all with a stranger."

Nora had been afraid of this. "You had an awful shock, Shay. Things like that can stay with you for life if you don't get them out of your system. You have to open up to someone about it."

"Talking about it endlessly isn't going to bring Ken back," he retorted obstinately, surprised that his mother was so adamant about it.

"All the same, love, we should follow Norman's advice. He hasn't put us wrong so far," she reminded him. "And I'd be happier knowing you were out of the woods before you go back to work."

She felt a bit mean and manipulative in appealing to him to attend the counsellor for her sake but if he went at all, whatever the reason, it would be worth it.

"OK so," he said, softening. "I'll try him out, to see if he has anything to say. But if it's all airy fairy stuff . . ."

"Fair enough, just see how you get on." This in itself was good news and Nora reached for the phone immediately, in case he'd change his mind.

31

Number 1

Yet again, Charlie paused over the work he was doing and rested his elbows on the desk. The more he thought about it, the more he realised how juvenile he'd been in his relationship with Linda. How could he not have seen them as having a future together? They were practically living together, considering he spent most weeknights in Pebble Cove. Most of his work clothes were at Linda's house – suits, shirts and ties, socks and underwear. He even had his own wardrobe and chest of drawers. His toiletries were installed in the bathroom, a full set that stayed there, as opposed to coming back and forth in an overnight bag as they had at the beginning.

Lately he had begun to analyse the time they spent together and came to the conclusion that it was no different than the way that any average couple spent their lives.

Friday nights were usually spent at his house, with Linda leaving on Saturday after breakfast to go shopping and catch up on things around her house. Charlie normally spent the afternoon on grocery shopping and sorting out his laundry, even though the lady from the cleaning agency washed and ironed whatever was there on Friday mornings. He always cooked on Saturday evenings after which they'd go out for a few drinks with some of his friends or occasionally with people that they both knew through work.

Most Sunday afternoons were spent lazing around in the morning, sometimes going for a walk once they were up and showered. They usually had lunch with Linda's parents, the very odd time driving to Gilcrenan to have dinner with Charlie's parents.

He couldn't fathom why he had the sense that he was missing something, almost feeling that life was passing him by. He wondered was he having some sort of mid-life crisis that other people had when they were forty. He'd heard of men who no longer had anything in common with their partners, who felt that they had nothing to talk about any more. He felt that this certainly wasn't the problem with him and Linda. They had their silences, but they were comfortable ones that didn't create awkwardness or tension. And they never bickered or argued. Apart from the distance that had opened between them over the leisure complex, they'd never had a real disagreement.

He started to wonder if that was part of the problem. Surely if their lives were enmeshed enough with each other's, then they'd have more issues to tease out, important things that required discussion and decision. As it stood, they each took care of their own concerns – mortgages, finances and bills were separate. Maybe these were the things that bound other couples together, sharing worries as well as just time.

He jumped when the door opened suddenly, spilling the remains of a mug of coffee all over the report he was supposed to be reading.

"Were you asleep?" Dermot Nugent questioned him. "I knocked twice." Dermot was grinning at the confused expression on his colleague's face. Charlie was renowned for being on the ball in any situation so it was a bit of a novelty to see him looking in any way distracted.

"I might as well have been," he admitted. "One of those days where you read a thing ten times and still can't remember what it's about."

"Try living with a colicky baby and going to work the next day. I'm doped up to the eyeballs with coffee most of the time. I came in to ask you something but it'll wait until tomorrow. Will we knock off and go for a pint instead?"

"Good idea. I might as well be sitting in The Cosy as sitting here."

It was gone five and Linda had a meeting with Luke Nolan so she'd be late home anyway. He pulled on his jacket and followed Dermot down the corridor, glad of a distraction to take his mind off the recurring theme of himself and Linda.

"So what's up with you? You're very bothered-looking the last few weeks."

Dermot had the office next door to Charlie and they were in the habit of having their morning and afternoon coffee together. He was a nice guy, easygoing, and Charlie got on well with him. He was married to Tina, a primary school teacher, with three small children who were the topic of many of their tea-break conversations.

"Nothing in particular. I probably need a holiday. We didn't get away at all this year with the Rochestown thing starting."

Dermot was just the sort of person that Charlie would like to have talked to about the things that were bothering him. He was completely family-oriented and despite being excellent at his job, still seemed to be able to prioritise his wife and children over it. But there was no way that he could shelve his loyalty to Linda to get relationship advice from someone who was also *her* colleague. He'd have to figure this one out on his own.

They chatted about general things for a while and even the fact of being away from his usual routine made Charlie relax a little. He was probably stressed without realising it. Maybe he *did* need a holiday.

They were just about to order a second when Dermot's mobile rang. Glancing at the screen he told Charlie it was Tina. "Better answer it and see what's up," he said smiling. "Hiya, love!"

Charlie could only hear Dermot's side of the conversation but it seemed that some crisis had arisen, with Dermot promising to go home straight away.

"Everything alright?" he asked, concerned, once Dermot had hung up.

"Big drama – I'm afraid I'll have to head off. Something about angel wings and wire coat-hangers. Rebecca's roaring her head off because they're the wrong shape and Tina's after bending every hanger in the house to get them right. I'll have to make it to the craft shop before six or there'll be murder. Rebecca has a school concert at eight and she has to have wings – or else . . ."

Laughing, he departed, leaving Charlie wondering if this was what life was all about. Acutely aware that he'd never considered whether children would be a part of his life, it dawned on him that he had no idea if they were to be a part of Linda's either. Debating whether to order another drink or not, he decided against it. He knew he'd only sit there pondering the same things again and again, as he had all day. A good run along the pier will shake me up, he thought, throwing on his jacket again and heading for Pebble Cove.

* * *

What most people described as "the pier" was really a narrow path that ran for two miles along the coast between Pebble Cove and the neighbouring village of Carrowkeel. Because it ran parallel to the main road with breathtaking views across the harbour it was a favourite spot for walkers and joggers. The wide grass verge between the path and the road ensured that small kids on bikes were safe even if they did wobble and fall, and the constant flow of cars between the two villages rendered it secure for lone walkers.

It was pretty quiet as Charlie pounded along, even though there was still plenty of daylight. It dawned on him that he'd been pretty slack about exercising lately, probably due to late evenings at work. He went to the gym a bit but it wasn't the same as being outdoors. Anyway it was better than nothing, he told himself, surprised at how fit he was considering that he hadn't been out running in weeks.

He veered into the side of the path as he spotted a walker coming towards him in the distance. As they neared each other he recognised her as Amy, the girl that he'd met at the walking festival in Gilcrenan. He'd noticed her coming and going from her house since then and had waved over at her occasionally but hadn't actually been talking to her since the day in Gilcrenan. He pulled up as they met, smiling a greeting.

"Hi, how are you?" she greeted him as he attempted to catch his breath.

"Great," he laughed, panting. "Apart from the exhaustion of running a few miles. You?"

"Grand, I'm afraid I'm not as energetic as you – power-walking is all I'm fit for. Have you done any hillwalking since?"

"No, though I keep saying I will. My father's seeing more of the hills these days than I am. What about you?"

"Not much either, to be honest. I seem to be on night duty all the time at the moment."

"I noticed you weren't around much." Once he'd come out with this, Charlie wondered if it sounded like he was spying on her or something but she didn't seem to have noticed. "Any luck on the jobs front?" he asked now. "You were thinking about looking for something without nights that day we were talking."

Surprised that he'd remembered, she filled him in on the latest. "The papers have been terrible for jobs lately so I was beginning to give up on the idea, until a few weeks ago our unit manager decided to take a five-year leave of absence. I've applied for her job so I'll have to wait and see how I get on."

"Will you have to be interviewed for it, considering it's internal?"

"Yes, because it's more managerial than nursing. It's open to the other departments so there'll be plenty of applicants. I'll be called for interview over the next few · weeks, I imagine."

Amy had been secretly excited since Rhona Day, the current unit manager, had announced that she was heading off to Africa to work with a voluntary organisation on a massive immunisation programme. She'd sent off the application and was hopeful that she'd be in with a chance.

"It would be great to get it. What are your chances like, do you think?" Charlie couldn't imagine someone as young as Amy managing such a high-powered unit. He'd been listening to Marcus, Linda's neighbour, talking about it for the past few months and it sounded like an enormously pressurised place to work.

"Fairly good, I think, but it's hard to tell. I'll just have to wait and see, I guess."

"Well, good luck with it. I heard that Marcus's little fella will be home fairly soon, though I haven't seen either him or Deirdre in ages. How's he doing?"

"Great, by the sound of things. Deirdre's talking about staying out of work for a while, I think."

"Well, they've had a long haul so they might as well enjoy him when he finally gets home." Noticing himself starting to shiver, Charlie realised that he'd held her up for ages.

"I'd better keep going or I'll perish. And good luck with the interview."

"Thanks," Amy smiled, crossing her fingers. "See you."

* * *

Charlie arrived back from his jog feeling better than he had in ages. His head felt clearer although he wasn't sure why. After a quick shower he decided to nip down to the small shop in the village and get a film for the evening, something light that they wouldn't have to put too much brain power into. He'd open a bottle of wine and they could put their feet up for the evening. A break from their usual Friday night routine wouldn't be any harm.

Maybe he'd become complacent with Linda or took

her for granted. He wasn't sure of this but he was going to make an effort anyway, he thought, pulling two steaks out of the freezer. Popping them in the microwave on defrost so that they'd be ready for cooking later, he let himself out of the house and headed off to the village.

Browsing through the video and DVD selection he realised that he wasn't exactly going to have an extensive choice. New releases arrived in Pebble Cove when they were obsolete elsewhere, he thought wryly as he scanned the shelves in front of him. *Shrek*, an animated film that seemed to be aimed at children, caught his eye. Oh, what the hell, he thought, tucking it under his arm. He'd been meaning to get it out for a while as his niece and nephew were always raving about it. Charlie had watched numerous animated films with them while baby-sitting on the weekends that he went home to Gilcrenan and was always impressed with the twins' choices. Not sure if Linda would be in the humour for it though, he picked up a copy of *Love Actually* just in case.

Turning to make his way to the counter he collided with someone coming around the corner of the aisle, causing a shopping basket to crash to the floor. Apologising profusely, he bent to retrieve the contents, coming face to face with Amy again.

"Imagine bumping into you again," she quipped, already piling crisps, snacks and chocolate back into the basket. "Just as well I hadn't got as far as the wine yet."

"Sorry," he said again, "I wasn't looking where I was

going. Are you OK?" She was tiny compared to him and he'd practically mowed her down.

"Fine," she replied cheerfully, thanking him as he laid the last item, a DVD of *Pride and Prejudice* on top of the rest of her things.

Noticing the title, he smiled incredulously. Maeve, his older sister, had a copy on video that she watched repeatedly, especially if she was sick or sulking with Dan.

"Do women ever tire of watching that?"

"Well, it's more a matter of whether you can have a girls' night in without Colin Firth or not. It wouldn't be the same without him at this stage," she told him, her eyes twinkling as he threw his up to heaven. She made her way to the wine section then, leaving Charlie smiling after her.

He again made his way to the counter, stopping off to pick up a few nibbles and dips along the way. He reached the queue just as Amy did and indicated to her to go ahead of him.

Standing behind her he now noticed that since their encounter on "the pier" she'd changed into a floaty floral top that just met the waistband of her jeans. Her hair, tied up earlier, was down now and he could get a faint scent of perfume when she moved to settle the basket on her arm. He couldn't help but notice how great she looked in the Levi's.

Horrified to feel himself becoming aroused, he dived out of the queue and back to the security of the video section. This is fucking ridiculous, he told himself, remembering feeling the same compulsion to touch her the day they'd met at the walking festival. Finally, she left the shop, giving him a little wave on the way out and he once again made his way to the counter, blindly paying for his rentals and feeling like a right fool. Maybe he *was* going through a mid-life crisis.

* * *

Dinner was just coming together when Linda arrived in. He'd decided to experiment with doing the potatoes in a cheese sauce and they were bubbling away nicely in a casserole, along with roasted parsnips tossed in oil and a sprinkle of Parmesan. The steaks were sitting in their marinade, and the wine was breathing on the worktop.

"Hi there," he greeted her, planting a kiss on her forehead. "Are you wrecked?" It was gone eight.

"Not bad. What's all this?" She looked around in surprise at the table, which had been set earlier while the food was cooking.

"I thought we'd eat in for a change, especially when you were working late. You don't mind, do you?" he asked, seeing by her face that she wasn't exactly over the moon.

"No, I don't mind not going out. It's just that I ate earlier. We had loads to do and Luke was starving so we nipped into Rooney's when we were finished. What?" she asked defensively, in response to his raised eyebrows and incredulous expression.

"And you didn't think of giving me a ring to let me know?" It didn't bother him in the least that she'd stopped off and had dinner with one of her colleagues, especially Luke, as he knew that they had a lot to get through on Friday afternoons. But that she didn't think to cancel their own dinner plans really pissed him off.

"How was I supposed to know you were cooking dinner?" That was typical of Linda, never being in the wrong about anything.

"Well, we would have been going out for something to eat anyway. The least you could have done was let me know." Hurt that she didn't seem to appreciate the fact that she'd effectively stood him up, Charlie threw one of the steaks on the grill pan and put the other one back into the fridge.

"Look, sorry, OK? I should have rung you," she gave in ungraciously.

Charlie accepted that this was as much of an apology as he was going to get out of Linda. Usually she was obstinate in her belief that she could do no wrong. "Grand, so. Do you want a glass of wine?" He seared the steak briefly, preferring it so rare that it was practically raw.

"So why were we staying in anyway?" Linda was leaning against the granite worktop, sipping her wine, as Charlie dished up his own meal. Eating in on a Friday was a new departure as far as she was concerned.

"No reason. I just thought it would be nice to put our feet up after work for a change. I got a DVD for later." Charlie was sick of the topic now and felt a bit deflated that Linda was so disinterested in a night in together. "How are things with Luke?"

"Great, actually. We'll have enough topsoil from levelling the front of the site to make up the bank around the Island. We thought we'd have to bring it in from outside so it'll save a lot of hassle. The local residents would have been going mental to see loads of soil being dragged in from outside because the road would have been a right mess for a while. Plus the time and expense."

"Have the extra lads started on the first phase yet?" Block-laying had practically finished on the leisure centre building and Daniel had promised to put a bigger team on it to speed things up, as soon as he was able. An apartment complex that Coltons were working on in the city was nearly completed, so that would free up more of the construction workers.

"Monday," she said, picking a crispy parsnip off his plate and popping it in her mouth.

Charlie glanced up at her and smiled in response to her "Do you forgive me?" look. Didn't he always?

"I'd love to get things done as quickly as we can considering that we'll be depending on the locals for a lot of our business. Anyway, the sooner it's open, the sooner we'll be making money. What film did you get?"

"You've a choice – *Shrek* or *Love Actually*."

"I suppose I'll have to watch *Shrek* to get back in your good books?"

She hated animated films but she was feeling a bit

guilty for having forgotten about Charlie earlier. She and Luke had started chatting as they left the office and when he'd asked if she fancied a bite to eat she'd immediately said yes. Luke was good company, a little less serious than Charlie and ruggedly handsome to boot. Tearing her mind away from a picture of him loosening his tie once they'd settled into a booth in Rooney's, she went upstairs and changed into a pair of velour jogging pants that she'd bought after seeing them on J-Lo in *Vogue*. Charlie had refilled their wine glasses and pulled one of the leather sofas closer to the gas fire. He'd opened a bag of nachos and a sour cream dip as well as a small bucket of Minstrels.

"You went all out," she said, eyeing the goodies spread out on the coffee table. Pushing the nachos back near Charlie she scooped up a small handful of the Minstrels.

"That's me done," she announced, curling up at the far end of the sofa. She'd already had her evening meal and spending her evening watching a kid's film was bad enough without filling herself with carbs as well.

This was a great idea, Charlie thought sardonically, sliding *Love Actually* into the DVD player, knowing he'd be getting bored sighs from Linda all night otherwise. He could always watch *Shrek* with the twins the next time he was baby-sitting. Anything for a quiet life.

32

Seefin

Saturday mornings were always a big deal on the Neonatal Unit. Any of the babies that were past the critical stage were weighed and any of those that were gaining steadily were afforded the privilege of a bath. Alex hadn't reached the bathing stage just yet and Deirdre and Marcus sorely envied the other parents as they lifted their wriggling babies tentatively into the yellow plastic bathtubs before the nine o'clock feeds. Most of the babies had to be rushed in and out in a matter of minutes, as lingering too long would contribute to hypothermia and burn up precious calories. Yet they longed for the day that Alex would get even the most brief of dips, seeing it as a sign of enormous progress.

As it stood, his weight gain was so slow that he really couldn't afford to lose even an ounce, so they were half-glad to wait until he was more robust. Very

early on in Alex's tenure, Marcus had asked Sheila
Forde about exactly how much weight a baby like him
should gain every day. Once Marcus knew the facts he
was always content to stand back and wait for the
results. After first laughing good-naturedly and giving
him a dig about being a "typical banker", Sheila had
given him the old-fashioned rule of thumb of "an ounce
a day and a rest on Sunday". On average, the babies
were expected to gain about six ounces per week,
amounting to 25-35 grams per day.

So far, Alex had been putting on only three or four
ounces a week and became exhausted halfway through
his bottles of breast milk. Deirdre had tried to
breastfeed him a few times but he usually fell asleep
after a few minutes. For this reason, the staff had
decided to give the breastfeeding a temporary rest and
continue with mostly tube-feeds to save his energy and
allow him to soak up all the calories from his food
without expending any energy sucking. A week later,
Deirdre and Marcus were dying to see what his weight
gain was like.

Back on duty after having Thursday and Friday off,
Amy had opened Alex's chart at the page with the
graph that monitored his weight. The Centile Chart was
designed to track the weight gain along average lines
but so far Alex hadn't reached the expected milestones.
Finally the weighing scales became available and
Deirdre undressed Alex carefully, holding a woolly
blanket around him as Amy disinfected the scales with
alcohol wipes. Deirdre could feel her heart beating

frantically as Alex was lifted gently from the cot. The digital reading on the monitor showed the new weight in kilograms, which meant very little to them and the wait while Amy consulted the conversion chart seemed like hours rather than seconds.

"He's getting the hang of it at last. Ten ounces, would you believe," she announced, smiling.

Deirdre immediately burst into tears, the worry of Alex's slow weight gain only showing now that he seemed to be over the hurdle.

Marcus hugged her, laughing with the beginning of tears in his eyes. "You've been giving out about putting on the pounds since I met you – now it's all the rage."

Marcus was giddy with delight and marvelled yet again at the new world that they'd found themselves in, a world where an ounce, the weight of a box of matches, was the most important thing in their lives.

Deirdre's attention was glued to Amy, bent over the Centile Chart plotting Alex's weight gain with a series of dots on the graph.

"See here," Amy explained eventually, "Alex had fallen below the 'average' line but he's made a huge jump today. If he gains the same amount next week he'll be back on track. It looks as if he needs to be mostly tube-fed for the moment. I know it's disappointing not to be able to give him the breast, but once he's gaining regularly we'll be able to reduce the tube feeds gradually. How about if we do maybe one breast-feed every day and give him the tube the rest of the time? If he puts on a good bit of weight next week we can make a new plan."

Delighted with this, Deirdre and Marcus agreed, happy now that there was a plan in place for them to follow.

"You can put a note on the cot every night to say what time you'll do the breast feed," Amy advised Deirdre. "That way we won't end up giving him a feed before you arrive."

As far as Marcus was concerned, this was one of the best aspects of care in the Neonatal Unit, the way the parents were always included in the making of any plans. Despite having up to twenty sick and premature infants on the unit at any one time, the staff treated every one individually, catering for the varying life situations of each baby's family.

He'd noticed that one of the mothers was a single girl who appeared to have very little support. Marcus had got talking to her in the parents' room one evening and she'd told him that she sometimes stayed in the hospital overnight if she had no transport to and from Mitchelstown where she lived.

"And is there accommodation available for the parents or what?" Marcus hadn't heard any of the other parents mention this.

"Not normally," the girl, Michelle, told him, "but there's a Day Ward downstairs where people come in to have minor surgery done. It's empty every evening at six so one of the nurses persuaded the matron to let me sleep there sometimes. As long as I'm up and out by half eight there seems to be no problem. It's great because I couldn't afford to stay in a B&B all the time."

Like Deirdre, Marcus had really begun to appreciate how lucky they were compared to some of the parents. While they still had all the worries about whether Alex would be able to live a normal, independent life, at least they didn't have to wonder if they'd be able to see him every day or if the mortgage would get paid if Deirdre took more time off when Alex got home. And more important than anything else, they had each other. The thought of going through all this alone overwhelmed Marcus, who felt enormously sorry for the young Michelle sitting alone by the incubator day after day.

Once they'd settled Alex back into his cot, praising him profusely for getting so big, they decided to head over to Hazel's rented apartment and collect yet another load for ferrying back to Pebble Cove later on. Phoning first to demand that Hazel put the kettle on, Deirdre informed her sister of the latest achievement in the life of her nephew.

"Little savage!" Hazel exclaimed, delighted with the news. "He's definitely taking after his aunt in the grub stakes. Hurry on and I'll have sandwiches ready. I presume I'm not getting a Removals Service for nothing." With this, Hazel hung up, laughing.

Laying into doorstep sandwiches, Hazel's speciality, Deirdre and Marcus recounted the latest details of Alex's care. Although she acknowledged the practicality of having to tube-feed her nephew for the time being, Hazel was disappointed that the bottle-feeding opportunities were so limited. On one occasion that she'd been passing the hospital on her way home from a meeting, she'd popped in for a quick visit and found herself helping with Alex's feed. He was being fed by one of the nurses who asked if she'd like to have a go. She'd never forget feeling the warmth of little Alex in her arms and the way he sucked industriously on the teat before dozing off with two ounces to go. She'd immediately phoned Deirdre to tell her, amazed that she'd been allowed to even hold her nephew. Now it looked like she mightn't have the opportunity to feed him for a while again.

By the time their brunch was finished and they'd packed as much of Hazel's stuff as they could into the back of the car, it was time for them to head back to the hospital for the one o'clock feed. This would be Deirdre's first attempt to insert the tube and while she was looking forward to knowing how to do it, she was nonetheless terrified of not being able to manage it.

Because they were a bit early, Deirdre decided to go directly to the parents' room to express some breast milk for the next few feeds. One peek inside the door revealed three mothers already expressing so Marcus decided to go ahead into Alex's cubicle for a cuddle, aware that while most women were fairly comfortable with using the breast pump in the presence of other women, having to do it in front of someone else's husband was a bit much.

His heart stopped when he opened the door of the cubicle that Alex had inhabited since he graduated from the ICU. The tiny room was empty, with no sign of

Alex's things. Marcus's legs turned to jelly as he realised that Alex must have deteriorated while they were out. He headed for the ICU, sick at the thought of seeing him back in the incubator attached to drips and the heart monitor again. Please God let it not be another brain haemorrhage! Alex was supposed to be well past that stage by now.

Glancing up as the door of the ICU opened, Amy could see the alarm on Marcus's face. He was white with shock as she started to explain, knowing he was thinking the worst.

"It's alright, Marcus. Alex is fine, nothing's wrong at all. We had to move him into Cubicle 8. Come on over and I'll show you." Amy's voice was calm and reassuring but she could see that Marcus wouldn't believe her until he saw his son himself.

Shaking as he followed her across the floor to the corner cubicle, Marcus nearly cried with relief when he saw Alex tucked up in his cot, wedged in beside another cot containing what he figured was a baby girl, judging by the pink bonnet peeping out from under the layers of blankets.

"There's a set of triplets about to be delivered in theatre so we had to jig everyone else around to clear the ICU. We needed Alex's cubicle so that we could move a baby in an incubator out of the ICU. I tried ringing you on the mobile to warn you but Hazel answered it. You must have left the phone in her house earlier. Sorry you got a fright."

"*I'm* sorry for overreacting, Amy. I thought he was

after having some kind of a turn. I'll go down and tell Deirdre in case she faints on you when she comes in."

Now that he knew that Alex was safe, Marcus realised just how real the possibility of something going wrong was.

Deirdre was just coming out of the parents' room with her bottle of milk when Marcus arrived. She'd already heard from the other women that the triplets were expected so she wasn't too surprised to hear that Alex had been "doubled up" with another baby. One of the mothers had told Deirdre that her little girl had had a boy moved into her cubicle and they now wondered if this Cathy was Alex's new friend. They'd find out later no doubt.

"Will we go down to the oratory and say a prayer that the triplets will be alright?"

Deirdre knew by now that with multiple births the babies would be smaller and sicker than the average premature baby and felt an enormous affinity for the mother who would soon be waking up to the same nightmare that they themselves had woken up to a few months ago.

"Good idea," Marcus said, slightly less concerned than Deirdre for the welfare of the unborn triplets after the shock that he'd just had over Alex, but nonetheless wishing them well. However, a prayer of thanksgiving was first on his own agenda, grateful as he was that his son was now considered well enough to be moved along to make way for the newer arrivals.

The whole place was a hive of activity when they got back. They made their way into Alex's cubicle, aware that Deirdre's chance to tube-feed him might now be off the agenda. Marcus spotted Sheila Forde arriving, obviously drafted in at the last minute to assist with the expected arrivals.

"Alex will be changing hands for a while because Amy's going to be caught up in the ICU. If you like, Deirdre, you can take the opportunity to breastfeed Alex this time and we'll help you with the tube-feed later in the evening."

"Thanks, Sheila," Deirdre said with a smile of relief. "I'll be only delighted to postpone the ordeal."

They were amazed as always at the way that the Neonatal Unit seemed to run like clockwork even when something big was happening. None of the babies or their parents were ever neglected – the plan just changed to accommodate whatever was happening.

Suddenly, the transport incubator was pushed smoothly into the unit, the usual trail of nurses and paediatricians swarming behind. Deirdre and Marcus were used to this by now and it never failed to bring tears to their eyes, both remembering Alex being taken from them in the labour ward to go on his short journey to the unit.

Amazingly, all of the triplets seemed to have been transported together. Gently they were lifted out and weighed before being placed on their individual open incubators with the radiant heaters above them. All of the cubicles had glass partitions between them while the ICU section was completely open-plan, so it was inevitable that parents attending to their own babies could see any drama that was unfolding. Deirdre and

Marcus got on with the business of feeding Alex, happy to be past the days when *their* child had been the centre of attention in the ICU.

Almost as if he knew that there was drama going on around him, Alex fed like a dream for a full twenty minutes. By the time he was changed and settled, the unit had returned to its former state of calm. Amy, Sheila and Kim were scribbling furiously at the large central desk, obviously updating the new babies' charts before the evening staff arrived to take over their care.

Vaguely, Marcus noticed the door of the unit opening to admit a nurse, dressed in what looked like theatre scrubs. Something about her expression caught his attention. She approached Sheila Forde and drew her towards the door, her face serious. Deirdre, rummaging in the laundry basket under Alex's cot, looked up when Marcus touched her shoulder and saw Sheila turn to Amy and take her arm, leading her quietly from the unit.

"I hope everything's alright," Deirdre said quietly to Marcus.

Amy had been so kind to them in the weeks since Alex's birth that neither of them liked to think that anything might upset her. They'd both seen the meaningful glance that Sheila Forde had cast in Kim's direction as she left the unit with Amy. Kissing Alex goodbye, they let Kim know that they'd be back at nine before leaving quietly. They'd often heard the staff describe the unit as "the goldfish bowl". Today they could see what they meant.

33

Leadington

Shay woke with an overwhelming sense of dread. It took him a minute to register that it was only a few hours until the appointment. He wished now that he'd made the phone call himself, so that he'd have had some sense of what Will Moore would be like. He couldn't bear it if he was the type to insist on him putting Ken's death behind him. Shay knew he was responsible in no small way for what had happened and he didn't *want* to forget it.

"Are you all set?" Nora was terrified he'd back out at the last minute.

Even though Cobh was only fifteen minutes away, she was anxious for him to leave on time. If he was late at all or had trouble finding the house it would be an excuse to turn around and come home.

"Are you sure you don't want me to drive over with you?" she asked now, fussing in her eagerness that he

303

at least try the counselling.

"Are you sure *you* don't want to go altogether?" Shay was irritated and hated himself for snapping, but it was bad enough being forced to go, never mind being hassled about it all morning as well.

"Well, there's no point in wasting money just to please me – you may as well get some value for it." This was said with as much spirit as she could muster. Norman Daly had warned her about starting to treat Shay like an adult again now that he was starting to come around a bit but Nora was so terrified of him not going to the counsellor that she found it hard to resist babying him. However, she now realised for herself that there was nothing to be gained by placating him and treading on eggshells around him.

Stunned at this uncharacteristic forcefulness, Shay got his jacket and left in a huff.

Nora was shaken when he left, unable to deal with the shortness of temper that her son was displaying over the last few days. Thank God for Norman, who'd warned her about the different stages of grieving. Knowing that it was normal in its own way, and that it was a positive sign in terms of recovery made it a little easier. And anger of any sort was definitely better than the awfulness of the stupor that he'd been in for the first few weeks after Ken's death. She knew she'd be able to deal with anything once it was part of Shay's road to recovery. She just hoped that he'd open up to the counsellor and not just go for the sake of doing what he was told. When Norman had warned him of the risk of a lingering depression, Nora felt that he hadn't really taken it in. She'd have to keep reminding him of how ill he'd been until he became conscious of the fact that there was still a way to go.

* * *

Standing on the steps of the three-storey red-brick townhouse, Shay pressed the bell nervously and prayed that it wouldn't be answered, that he had the wrong house and that it was now too late to find the right one. But while the shiny brass numbers told him that he had indeed found the correct house, he still jumped with fright when the door opened.

"Hello, come on in."

Will Moore looked like one would expect a counsellor to look, Shay thought. Sort of calm and studious-looking with an air of stillness about him. Nervously following him into the hallway, he noted the sense of neutrality that pervaded the place and some of the anxiety left him. It wasn't like any house that he'd ever been in. It was more like the passport office or a dentist's surgery. Will showed him into a large airy room with two sofas facing each other near the fireplace. As well as the sofas there were a few armchairs, a beanbag and a small aromatherapy burner that accounted for the headily sweet fragrance that settled around him as soon as the door was closed. Shay, determined not to be taken in, remained sullenly silent, studying the man before him. He had the air of a monk about him almost – small and thin with soft white hair that made him look ancient.

"Your mother told me on the phone that you'd lost your best friend recently."

This seemed to Shay to be neither a question nor a statement and he was at a loss as to how to answer, so he just grunted as if to confirm that this was indeed the case. Will seemed to be satisfied with this and appeared to digest the information before speaking again. "I'm not sure how helpful talking to me will be."

Shay thought he sounded as if he were making a disclaimer, particularly when he continued with, "Talking about it won't make you forget it, I'm afraid, nor will it stop you being reminded of him by all sorts of everyday things."

Irritated, Shay felt like asking him what it was that counselling *would* do for him in that case. He'd only come here to please his mother and humour his GP, and now he was being told that none of the things they expected to be done for him were possible. He had a feeling that this man was telling him that he wasn't a suitable candidate for therapy, yet he knew that if he arrived home without some sort of result his mother would only insist that he find another counsellor. The thought of having to face all this with another stranger was too much and Shay was suddenly determined to insist that a few sessions was the least he should get, having come this far.

"But Dr Daly said you specialise in this type of thing. Can't I at least come a few times?"

"Well, it really depends on what you want from counselling and whether you feel it would be of value to come here again," Will explained. "Tell me a little about yourself first, apart from losing your friend."

Feeling slightly triumphant at having got this far Shay filled the little man in on the general details of his life. Home, work, his mother and the fact that his father had died when he was small.

"And you still live at home?"

This was asked with such a lack of interest that it was obvious that Will Moore had no intention of keeping him on as a client. How Norman Daly had recommended this eejit was beyond him and Shay felt like standing up and walking out. Only the thought of his mother looking up counsellors in the *Golden Pages* was enough to keep him in his seat.

"No, I have my own house out in Pebble Cove but I've been staying with my mother since the accident."

A pause followed before Will spoke and again Shay got the feeling that he thought there wasn't much that could be done for him.

"And how does she feel about you coming to a psychotherapist? Some people might be inclined to think that it's overdoing it a bit, that you have to get on with it anyway."

"That's what I think myself but Dr Daly seems to think I need it, so Mam insisted that I come. She thinks I'll have a relapse and have to stop working again."

"Are you finding work manageable at the moment?" Will asked now, throwing Shay a little when he had to admit that he hadn't actually returned to work at all yet. Almost as if it were an interview for a job that he badly wanted, Shay knew that he had to say something that would convince Will Moore that he would benefit from another few sessions.

"I'm not sure that I'm ready for work yet to be honest," he said, aware that he was only saying it to let the counsellor know that he wasn't fully cured, but feeling somewhat relieved to have said it anyway.

"How come?"

Will asked this with interest, forcing him to come up with a plausible answer. It took ages to explain exactly how poor his concentration was and the fear of being unable to focus on accounts or messing things up altogether.

"But surely they'd understand that you'd be a bit slow getting back into it after what you've been through?"

Will sounded as if he were trying to brush over the fact that going back to work was a big deal but Shay was intent on making him see that he needed to be in the full of his health.

"You see, before Ken died I'd had a few run-ins with my boss. If I go back too soon and I'm not able for it he'll think I'm useless altogether. I need to be well sorted so I can redeem myself a bit."

"I see your point," Will conceded. "Look, I think we've done enough for today. If you think it'll help at all, come back next week at the same time. We can talk a little more about work, if you like."

Stunned that the hour had passed so quickly and glad that Will appeared to be taking him on, Shay assured him that he would indeed be back the following week and took his leave gratefully.

Later, when Nora tried to draw him out about the visit to Will, Shay found that he couldn't tell her exactly what they'd been talking about. It wasn't that he didn't want to tell her. It was more that it sounded ridiculous to have spent a whole hour talking about himself to a stranger.

Once she'd been assured that he had actually gone, Nora was satisfied and didn't press the issue for fear of putting him off. Listening to him clattering around the kitchen making sandwiches for their lunch, she felt relief wash over her that at last he was turning a corner. Deciding to move on from the topic of the therapist, she told Shay that she was going out in the evening.

"Why don't you see if any of your friends want to come over for a bit?" she said. "Or maybe go out for a drink even? You must be getting bored with watching telly with me every night."

Nora was worried that Shay's whole social life had been tied up with Ken and that he wouldn't be able to pick up a normal life again. If he'd had a girlfriend it would have been easier but she knew there was no point in wishing for what didn't exist.

"I'm grand. I'll be seeing enough of the lads when I get back to work." Secretly, Shay was terrified of facing the world without Ken but knew he could never admit that, especially to his mother who was worried enough about him already.

"Where are you heading tonight?" he asked now, more to deflect the conversation away from himself than out of actual interest.

"Oh, there's a show on in the Everyman that the girls are mad to see. Some John B Keane thing. I suppose we'll go to Isaac's after it for something to eat."

Shay was impressed that his mother and her friends had such a busy social life and felt a pang of regret that she'd missed out on a lot while he'd been ill.

"Sorry I cramped your style for a bit there," he said sheepishly. "They must have thought you'd gone to ground altogether."

"Shay, love, as long as you're all right again, the going out will wait. You know, there's something I was going to chat you about before everything happened but I suppose things got a bit hectic and I never got around to it."

Nora was fiddling nervously with her wedding ring and Shay looked up expectantly, waiting for her to continue.

"Last year, just before Christmas, this man called to the door one day looking for your father. He was home from America and was looking up the lads he'd been in college with. Of course he didn't realise that Frank had died so young."

Shay was interested now, the reality of just how tragic his father's death had been dawning on him yet again.

"Anyway, I told him the situation and – "

With that the doorbell rang, startling Nora and annoying Shay who was just getting into the story. Lately, everything about his father interested him, now that he'd started to see him as a person rather than just a face looking out of the many photos that Nora kept around the house. It was almost as if Frank was a new person in his life, rather than a man who'd been a shadowy figure in the background all the time. Now he had a personality. He'd been a young man going out to work just as Shay himself was.

He answered the door now, hoping that it was some Internet salesman that could be easily got rid of so that he could get back to the story of his father's old friend but it transpired to be Norman Daly, paying his weekly visit to see how he was doing.

Delighted that his patient was doing so well, Norman came in, accepted a cup of tea from Nora and enquired how Shay was doing with the counsellor.

"I've only been once, today actually, and it was mainly taking my details and finding out a bit about me. We didn't really talk about what happened or anything. He's a bit unusual, isn't he?" Shay was interested to know if the serene little man was an ex-priest or a monk or something.

"He has his own way of going about things alright, but most people tell me he's the best thing that ever happened to them. Are you going again?"

"Yeah, I'm going next week for definite and he says we'll see from there if I need to go any more. I suppose it'll do no harm anyway."

Shay had decided that he might as well give in gracefully to a few sessions, knowing that he'd be bullied into it by the GP anyway. And he could see that Nora was relieved. He felt guilty about being narky with her about small things but he somehow couldn't help it.

"We can see how you're getting on over the next few weeks before we think about going back to work. How do you feel yourself? Are they happy enough for you to stay off for a bit longer?"

Shay wasn't exactly sure what his boss thought about him having all this sick leave – he'd just sent in the sick notes every week, or at least Nora had. The thought of going back frightened him. What if he wasn't able to keep up with things? He kept wondering whether Michael Murray had already decided to fire him and would only be waiting for the first slip-up. He'd be under pressure to have things under control and he wasn't sure if he could manage that just yet. His concentration was desperate still, even for watching a TV programme.

"They know I'll need to stay off until I'm fully better though I haven't been able to say how long. Is it the medication that's making my concentration so bad?"

"That and the fact that you have so much going on in your head. That's where the counselling comes in. Once you talk things through a few times your mind won't feel so restless. We'll be able to start weaning you off the tablets then. It'd be a bad idea to stop them suddenly."

Shay found it hard to believe that recounting the horror of Ken's death over and over could make things any better, but at the same time he was afraid of what would happen if he stopped the tablets without doing everything that the doctor was recommending.

"Do you think I could get addicted to all the medication? I know I'm nearly off the sleeping pills – but the anti-depressants?"

He'd been thinking a lot about what it would be like without the medication considering he was barely coping as it was.

"Shay, you probably don't realise how far you've come. Nora here had to do everything for you in the last couple of months. You're almost back to normal but you have a bit to go yet. Don't be too hard on yourself by rushing things. Being on medication won't stop you going back to work at all."

"But what if I'm not able to manage without it ever?"

"You managed before all this happened, didn't you? It's only a matter of time before you're well enough to stop it. Believe me, Shay, I won't keep prescribing them for you anyway. The drugs that you're on aren't actually physically addictive. But you *can* get psychologically dependent, which is the point of going for the counselling. So that you won't need a crutch."

This was said pointedly and Norman Daly was watching him as if he could see right through him. Shay reddened under his scrutiny.

"You know, Shay, you can go to Will Moore to please

your mother or to keep me quiet but in the end of the day it's you that needs to get value out of him. It's very easy to sit in front of him and pretend to participate. Your mother's after being very strong since all this happened, but you'll have to pull your own weight from here on in."

"I said I was going to keep going, didn't I?" Shay felt as if he were being treated like a child and was defensive about it, yet he knew that Norman Daly had seen how poor his intentions were.

"Well, have a good think about what I said. Just sitting in front of him isn't enough to make a difference to your health."

Shay knew that despite the stern tone the GP meant well and was warning him that his mother had been through enough. And regardless of how chastened he felt, he knew that he'd have to make an effort the next time.

"I know," he said as the doctor stood up to leave, "And thanks again for everything." Having it brought to his attention that he *had* been trying to fool his mother into believing that he was having counselling made Shay realise how childish he'd been for so long. He needed to think about where his life was going once he got back to normal. And the sooner he started the better. A bit of fresh air would clear his head and let him get his head around it.

"I'm just going out for a walk," he told Nora now. "I'll be back in a while."

"Are you going far? I'll be leaving around half six so

I was going to put the tea on a bit early."

Nora was anxious to get back to the conversation that she'd started before Norman had arrived, but Shay had obviously forgotten about it.

"Don't worry about me, I'll get a sandwich later." Now that he'd decided to move on with his life, Shay wanted to get away to think about things. "See you in the morning – enjoy!" he called out and slammed the door behind him.

34

Evergreen

If it hadn't been for the grave expression on Sheila Forde's face, Amy would have rolled her eyes in a "not again" sort of way when Brenda Loftus told her hesitantly that Peter had been admitted to the Accident and Emergency unit earlier.

"I'd heard that you'd been seeing each other for a while so I wanted to come up and tell you before you heard it in the canteen or something," she continued gently, aware that Amy was looking at her strangely.

"Amy, love . . ." Sheila paused, wanting her to ask a question, anything that would make it easier for their colleague from the A&E department to disclose the news that she'd whispered urgently to Sheila earlier.

Brenda started again, this time explaining that Peter had taken ill in the library block, falling the short distance to the ground from a small ladder. Two medical students sitting nearby had witnessed the fall and had stated that he didn't trip or stumble, just fainted in front of their eyes. Sally Deering, working alongside him all morning, had said that he'd been complaining of a headache and had planned to go home once the busy part of the day was over.

"The CT scan shows an intracranial bleed, Amy, most likely due to an aneurysm."

"Where is Peter now, Brenda?" Sheila asked when she realised that Amy still wasn't going to speak. "The ICU or still in A&E?"

"In theatre at the moment. Then it'll be ICU, all going well."

Amy looked up when she heard the last bit. Brenda didn't sound too convinced that Peter *would* arrive in the ICU, something that alerted her to thinking that the bleed was extensive, that there was a high risk that he might not return from theatre at all.

"Was he conscious at any stage?" she asked.

"No, Amy, I'm afraid not. The bleed was a large one. It seemed best to try and relieve the pressure on the brain as soon as possible."

"Will he be long more?"

"He's been gone almost an hour now. Do you want me to walk you down to theatre? Peter's parents are on their way from Waterford. They've been told to go to the waiting room outside theatre."

It dawned on Amy then that people would presume that she'd met Peter's parents. She'd seen photos of them in his apartment, taken at his graduation. She'd probably recognise them but what would they know about her? Very little, she imagined, considering that she had only been seeing their son such a short time. Peter hadn't met Amy's parents either. He'd only met her sisters because they'd stayed over in Pebble Cove before the holiday to Cyprus.

"Thanks, Brenda. You go back inside, Sheila, or Kim'll crack up. Who'll take over my gang?"

"Don't worry about that. The afternoon staff'll be here in a few minutes and I'll hand over all the details. I'll put you down for sick leave for tomorrow and get someone to cover the shift. Go on now," she said gently, "and take care."

35

Leadington

Now that he'd accepted that he needed to have meaningful interaction with Will Moore, Shay's mind was full of questions. Suddenly he could see all the obstacles that he had to get through before his life would be back on track. He knew that not being able to face the house in Pebble Cove wasn't right, yet he couldn't bring himself to do the simple thing and just go over there and open the door. He knew there was nothing sinister waiting there for him. It was just as if his mind closed up every time he contemplated it. He'd have to go back there sooner or later but he wanted there to be a sense that this was his home, not somewhere that he dreaded.

The other thing he needed to plan for was how to redeem himself at work. He had to acknowledge what an ass he'd been for the past year. It hadn't mattered in the early days because he'd been pretty junior and it had been easier to get away with slacking. Once he'd been promoted he should have had the sense to settle down a bit but it was easy to say that now. Cursing himself for his stupidity, Shay surmised that the best thing he could do was to talk to Will Moore about how he could address the precarious position he now found himself in. He wondered if it was best to come clean with Michael Murray, admit that he'd behaved poorly and state his intention of meriting his salary and position from now on.

He could see how the Americans were hooked on "therapy". Now that he'd copped on to what it was about, Shay could see that it was like talking to yourself except you could expect to get an answer, or at least an opinion. Things that he wanted to talk about started to tumble around his head, like some stopper had been released and he began to wonder if he'd be able to wait until the following week to get it all out. Maybe phoning Will to make an earlier appointment would be a good idea.

Shay was startled to find himself thinking like this but the combination of realising how his mother had put her life on hold to get him well again, and the fact that Norman Daly had seen through his carry-on with Will had jolted him out of his childishness. Earlier he'd been practically laughing at the idea of there being any value in recounting his woes to a complete stranger. Now he was only dying to get it all out of his system and start again fresh.

An hour later, Shay returned to his mother's house

having focused his mind on the main things. Firstly he was going to concentrate on sorting out his feelings about going home to his own house, with a view to moving back as soon as he felt comfortable. He'd decided that he needed a hobby of some sort to get out and meet new people rather than getting back into the routine of spending every weekend hung-over. He'd really had no life other than dodging work and socialising with Ken, so little wonder Carla had been pissed off with him. Work was going to have to wait a little until he was a bit more stable, he told himself, but at least he was focused on putting his head down and doing a good job when the time came.

Nora was gone by the time he arrived back so Shay spent the rest of the evening poring over the flyers on evening classes that would commence in the autumn. Normally he ignored the leaflets that came through the door every August but Nora kept all of them to go through with her friends, usually deciding on something like flower arranging or upholstery that would be an interest in the winter months.

Golf was the only thing that jumped out at him. He'd always resisted Nora's attempts to get him to join the local club, deeming it too fuddy-duddy for someone of his age. Nora herself was a member and always insisted that there were plenty of younger people who played regularly, but Shay had run a mile at the thought of his social life being tied up with that of his mother's generation. Now he decided he'd give it a go. The evening classes were for ten weeks, enough time for him to suss out the club and see if the game appealed to him. The lessons were so cheap that he could drop out if he really hated it, so he had nothing to lose.

Shay went to bed in a positive frame of mind for the first time in two months. It was only eight weeks since the night in The Watershed and the nightmare of the ambulance, the hospital, the Garda station and the terrible moment when Ken's mother had opened the door to him. He couldn't believe how much his life had changed in such a short space of time, but it had and he was determined to put his old ways behind him.

He knew he'd never forget Ken. But he'd always see his life in two stages, before and after, with the moment when the paramedic had looked up and said, "I'm sorry, son, we've done all we can," as the moment when everything changed. As he drifted off to sleep, Shay wondered fleetingly where he'd be tonight if his friend were still alive. His eyes had closed before he realised that this was the first time he'd really thought of Ken as part of his past and accepted that moving on with his own life wouldn't be a betrayal of all that they'd shared.

* * *

Waking with a feeling of hope was a new thing. Telling Nora his plans over breakfast, Shay felt as if today was the first day of the rest of his life. His mother would be able to rely on him for a change instead of having to look after him like a glorified baby. He could see the surprise in her eyes as she listened to his decision about the evening class in golf.

"High time too," she laughed. "You always said it was too boring for you."

"A man can change his mind, can't he? I suppose I'll have to go out and buy a set of clubs before the lessons start." Now that he'd decided to take up golf, his enthusiasm was growing. It might even benefit him at work. They were always looking for people to play for fundraisers and stuff.

"Would you think about using your dad's clubs to see how you get on?" Nora asked tentatively. "I never got around to giving them away. They're probably a bit old-fashioned but they'd do until you know whether you like it or not."

Shay couldn't believe that she'd kept a set of golf clubs for so many years, and was suddenly choked at the thought of holding in his hands something that his father had held so long ago.

"I'd love to have them, if you don't mind seeing them being used again. Especially by an amateur," he added with a smile, looking away in case she'd see the tears that had come to his eyes.

Somehow, it seemed as if he was getting to know his father a little better each day. He'd never realised before what he was missing out on – it was just a fact of life that he didn't have a father to bring him to football the way that the other lads in school had had. He'd taken Ken's dad for granted a bit, he could see that now. Shay had always gone camping with the Roches who were only delighted that their youngest son had a well-behaved, bright friend to pal around with.

"Finish your tea then and we'll go and fish them out of the attic. I hope they're not rusty or anything."

As a child, Shay had never been allowed to climb into the attic from the stepladder. It was simply too dangerous. In recent years, Nora had had a proper fold-down stairs installed so that things could be stored there and retrieved, rather than just being shoved up into the darkness never to be seen again. Stepping carefully over the trusses, Shay was fascinated by all the strong cardboard boxes placed neatly under the eaves and wondered why he'd never questioned where his toys and stuff had disappeared to when he saw the *Famous Five* peeking out of a box of books.

The golf clubs in their leather carry-bag were tucked away in a corner and he made a mental note to explore the attic another day as he dragged the heavy, clattering pouch towards the hatch and handed them carefully to his mother. Maybe there were more of Frank's things that Nora had been reluctant to throw out or give away.

"They're fine actually," Nora said once she'd examined each club in detail. "You'll have to get a new bag. This one's a bit shabby. They'll get you started anyway," she concluded.

"Thanks, Mam, they're great. Maybe I'll go into town after lunch and look at bags. I have to go down to the Community School tonight to sign on for the classes so I'll be all geared up then."

Delighted to see some of her son's old enthusiasm back, Nora told him to leave the clubs in the utility room and put the kettle on.

"I'll wash the dust off them later and have them ready for you." She felt as if she was talking to her son as an equal at last and was somehow grateful that they'd come full circle, despite the events that had led them to this. She knew it was time to start treating him like an adult instead of protecting him from everything. She'd started to try and explain about Anthony the previous evening but Norman Daly had distracted her. And this morning he'd been so full of his new plans that she hadn't been able to bring the subject up again. Tonight, she promised. It was silly having put it off for so long.

* * *

Shay finally decided on a dark green leather golf bag and even though it was a little on the expensive side he didn't care because he hadn't had to buy the clubs. Realising that he wouldn't be properly kitted out, he wandered over to the clothing section and started to browse among the rails of sweaters and polo shirts.

"Don't tell me you're taking up the golf at last, Shay!"

He swung around to see Gertie Lynch, one of his mother's friends, studying him in surprise. Shay laughed, knowing that his mother was always bemoaning the fact that he had no interest in golf.

"I had to give in sometime and it's a great excuse to buy some trendy gear," he said, holding up a particularly lurid tank top.

Gertie laughed, glad to see some of Shay's personality back. Nora had told her that he wasn't coping with Ken Roche's death at all so it was good to see him out and about. Not wanting to ignore the subject for fear of him thinking that she'd forgotten about his loss, Gertie mentioned that she hadn't seen him since the funeral.

"It must have been very difficult to have gone through all that, when you were such good friends."

"It was hard alright but I'm coming around a bit now. The golf will occupy me a bit over the winter, I suppose."

Shay wasn't sure how much his mother had told her friend about how bad he'd been and he didn't want to let her down. To change the subject and get away from any more chat about Ken, Shay asked her how they'd enjoyed the play the previous night.

"God, Shay, I wouldn't be into that stuff at all, but Nora's got very cultured since her new man came on the scene. Herself and Anthony keep telling me I'd love the shows if only I went . . . but there you are . . ." She trailed off as she realised by Shay's expression of shock that she'd made a *faux pas*. He'd paled before her eyes.

Surely it wasn't possible. But Gertie's panicked expression told him that it was indeed possible. Her new man! Sick at the thought that there was someone in his mother's life, a man that he hadn't known about, Shay felt faint. That something as big as this could be happening under his nose without him being aware of it was an enormous shock to him. He felt disgusted that his mother could even consider having a relationship after all the talk she'd had about how wonderful his father had been. Why had she kept his things? How could she even look at photos of him if she'd moved on to someone else? He felt betrayed, as if his mother had been just humouring him with stories about how she'd felt when Frank died. All of this flashed through Shay's mind in a matter of seconds as he stood dumbstruck among the rails of clothes.

He knew by her face that Gertie had thought he knew all about this Anthony. She was babbling now about buying a new putter as she tried to make her exit, knowing the damage she'd done and kicking herself for not keeping her mouth shut. Terrified that this would set Shay back again, she needed to escape from the shop and phone her friend. At least if she was warned before Shay arrived home, Nora might be able to salvage something from the situation.

* * *

Nora waited anxiously at the sitting-room window until she saw Shay's car turning the corner at the end of the road. Cursing herself for not telling him sooner, she knew how hurt he'd be that she'd contemplate a relationship after all the years on her own. Not for the first time, she wished she'd been the sort of woman to meet someone new and get married in the early years of her widowhood. At the time she couldn't even have

329

considered it, so great would have been the feeling of
betraying Frank's memory. Sometimes she wondered if
having a father figure was what her son needed, rather
than being reared as an only child with just his mother
for guidance. She often thought that she'd been selfish
to allow Shay the luxury of being totally devoted to
him. She could imagine his shock now to find that there
was someone other than himself in her life.

She felt physically sick as she heard the key turn in
the door. The thought that he might go back into the
same kind of shock that he'd been in after Ken died
made her feel faint but she knew she had to be honest
with him and face things as best she could. She felt
guilty that he'd found out about Anthony the way he
had, and wished as she had so many times in the past
few months, that she'd told him that Saturday she'd
called over to tidy the house for him. But it was too late
now for wishing the clock back.

"Shay, Gertie rang me. She told me about meeting
you in town." She hoped that Shay would at least attack
her for not telling him but he just looked pale and
bewildered like a child that didn't understand the
question, never mind have an answer. "We'll have to sit
down and talk about this, love. You were too sick up to
now and I was afraid of setting you back. I'm sorry that
you had to hear this from Gertie. I should have told you
sooner."

Shocked and all as he'd been to hear that his mother
was in some sort of relationship with a man, Shay was
absolutely stunned that she wanted to talk about it, as

if it was something that was going to continue indefinitely. All the way home in the car he'd visualised his mother apologising, saying that it meant nothing and that the whole thing was a mistake. Or even that he'd picked Gertie up wrong and was blowing things out of proportion.

"I don't *want* to talk about it. It's a bit late now for talking about it. It's none of my business who you go out with!" Angrily, Shay took off up the stairs and slammed into his room.

Nora stood at the foot of the stairs wondering if she should follow him and try to explain about meeting Anthony and, without having any intention of it happening, how their friendship had developed into something much stronger. Deciding that he needed a bit of time to digest the situation before he'd be able to talk about it and maybe even accept it, Nora made a pot of tea and sat at the kitchen table. He'd have to come down sometime.

After what seemed like ages, but in reality was more like fifteen minutes, Nora heard the bedroom door opening and Shay's footsteps on the stairs.

She could understand how shocked he'd be at this new development. Shay had never had any real interest in knowing about his father before Ken's death. He'd never really asked questions as a child and Nora hadn't wanted to build Frank up as some sort of hero that Shay would have to live up to. Subsequently, it seemed as if her son had only discovered his father in the last few months. She could imagine his horror that he was now

331

being replaced, almost as soon as he'd started to get to know a little more about him.

For Nora, the memory of how wonderful Frank had been had faded over the years. She remembered him as a young man, of a different generation even. Dread swept over her when she thought about how Shay would see her relationship with Anthony – that he'd see it as a betrayal of the man that he'd so recently started to see as a real person.

Bracing herself for what she knew was going to be a difficult encounter that would inevitably hurt her son more than he deserved, she looked up in anticipation as he came into the kitchen. Fear coursed through her as she caught sight of the gear-bag slung over his shoulder.

"Shay, there's no need for this, we can sit down and talk . . . I'll tell you everything. Where are you going to go?"

"Home, Mam," he said coldly. "Where I should have been for the last few months. Sorry you had to stay in and look after me. You can go out all you want now."

"Shay, love, it's not about going out. It wouldn't have mattered whether Anthony was there or not. I wouldn't care what happened as long as you were alright."

"It's time I went back home anyway. See you."

The sound of the door slamming after him reverberated around Nora's head as she sat on the stairs, the betrayal and disappointment that was written all over her son's face etched in her mind.

Knowing that she was the cause of it hurt her to the core, the thought of losing him unbearable. Yet, as she contemplated the alternative, Nora knew in her heart that losing Anthony instead was not an option.

36

Evergreen

Now suddenly everything was over, sorted out neatly as if had never happened. She'd stood with her sisters and Kim, Noreen and Sheila as the priest had talked about what an exceptional young man Peter had been, that even in death he'd reached out to help others. She'd known that he'd always carried a donor card, evidently his parents too had known and had acted on his wishes.

She'd filed along with the rest of the congregation to pay her respects to Peter's parents and family, introducing herself as a friend. Bizarrely, she was able to pick out each of his brothers from Peter's descriptions, their brown eyes achingly familiar in pale shocked faces.

Seeing Peter in his coffin at the removal hadn't been the enormous shock that she might have imagined. She'd sat alone with him for a few minutes after the

Deasys had left the hospital, probably unable to watch as their eldest son was wheeled back to theatre again, this time for organ donation. He was brain dead, kept alive by the artificial respirator until they'd said their goodbyes.

Amy had simply sat there, her hand on his heart, feeling the same strong beat that she'd heard when she'd lay with her head resting on his chest the first time they'd made love. That's what she'd remember, the strong, rhythmic beat that would stop, unbelievably, in the next few hours.

She still didn't know whether it had been a good idea to take the rest of the week off work. Everyone had been kind, especially Sheila Forde, who'd lost her husband many years before.

"It's not the same," Amy had reminded her sadly. "It must have been even more terrible for you. You were married. You had two small children together."

"And you think because you'd only just got to know him that your grief should be any less? It wouldn't have mattered if I'd known Martin ten years or ten days – I loved him from the beginning."

"We hadn't even got to that stage, of actually saying it out loud. There was so much time for all that. I feel such a fool to be crying like this. We hadn't even met each other's families."

"Amy, none of that matters. Don't try to make it smaller, as if it didn't mean anything unless everything was formalised. It meant a lot if you think you might have had a future together."

"God, Sheila, I really did think that we would have been together. He was just so right for me – I'd never met anyone like him."

"Is it that you think your whole future is gone now? I know that's the way I felt when Martin died. We wanted to have more kids. We'd always planned to buy a cottage in West Cork for the summers. As well as Martin being dead, all our plans were gone."

That's what kept going around in her head, that whatever had been laid out for the future was now gone. Somewhere at the back of her mind, she'd had a picture of herself and Peter living together in Pebble Cove. They'd spent more time there than in Peter's apartment in the city and he'd fitted in so comfortably that she must have got used to it. Even when she'd applied for the unit manager's post, she'd visualised herself, if she was lucky enough to get the job, being able to spend her evenings with Peter instead of always rushing off for night duty.

It was all so surreal. Her parents were desperately worried about her and had wanted her to spend the week at home with them. But she'd been adamant about staying in Pebble Cove, telling them that she was fine really and wanted to be on her own for a bit. What she really wanted was to be in the only place that she felt close to Peter. She hadn't wanted her sisters to come and stay with her either, knowing that they wouldn't know how best to deal with her and would only be more upset than they were already.

Deirdre and Marcus, Alex's parents, had called the

previous evening, having been unable to talk to her properly at the funeral. Amy knew she'd been stiff and formal with them, considering that they'd become such friends of late, yet she knew she'd feel foolish afterwards if she broke down in front of them. Marcus had held her hand briefly as he and Deirdre were leaving.

"I'll probably make things worse by saying this, Amy, but I'll say it anyway, in case it helps at all. Peter used to talk about you all the time and his whole face would light up. He really cared about you, Amy, so don't feel that you're forgotten."

"Thanks, Marcus," she'd whispered, closing the door gently before the tears came again.

37

Seefin

Two weeks of intensive tube-feeding had made a massive difference to Alex's weight. The previous week he gained so much that he'd finally had to move onto the normal newborn babygros. Although his feet still didn't reach the end and his little hands were lost inside the sleeves, Deirdre was thrilled that he'd at last grown out of the 'premature' ones. Now, for the third week running he'd gained well over the anticipated amount, passing the test for getting a bath, a reward akin to winning the Lotto for his parents.

"He's perished, the poor little mite," Amy exclaimed, smiling brightly as she placed yet another Polaroid picture face down on the work-stand. "One more for the grandparents and we'll get him out."

Ecstatic that they'd have photographs to mark the event, Deirdre and Marcus manoeuvred Alex awkwardly out of the little bath and placed him into the warmed towels that Amy held out for them.

"Try to get him dried as quickly as possible so that he doesn't get cold. His vest is on the radiator, Deirdre. I'll warm the milk a little while you're getting him dressed."

Amy left them alone in the cubicle to enjoy the moment of Alex's first bath together as a family. Little Cathy's parents had discreetly disappeared before they'd started, remembering how momentous it was when they themselves had first lifted their daughter into the warm sudsy water. Cathy was a few weeks ahead of Alex, well enough to be wheeled out to the parents' room in her cot to 'play' with her older brothers.

"Did we ever think we'd see this day? Remember when we used to look over at all the others getting the baths ready on the Saturday mornings?"

Marcus couldn't believe how lucky they were and was dying to show the photos to Tom, Rose and Hazel, knowing that they'd be as excited as if Alex was swimming in liquid gold. He planned to post the third Polaroid that Amy had taken to Vincent, his brother, aware that his parents would barely glance at it, unable to appreciate the significance of this important step in their grandson's life.

"It's great, love. He'll definitely be able to cut down on the tube-feeds a bit now. We'll ask Amy in a minute."

"She's still very pale, isn't she?" The concern in Deirdre's voice was evident, yet she knew that they couldn't infringe on Amy's grief unless it was what she wanted. Since the evening that Amy had resuscitated Alex during the apnoea attack, Deirdre had placed every ounce of her trust in her. Even though she knew that any one of the nurses would probably have acted exactly as Amy had under the same circumstances, the fact that Deirdre had witnessed her controlled capability and her kindness afterwards had created a memory that she felt would never leave her.

Coincidentally, Alex was allocated to Amy's care on many of her shifts, a fact that reassured Deirdre enormously, especially when she was leaving for home in the evenings and she knew that Alex would be in Amy's care overnight. Since Peter's death, however, both she and Marcus could see that she'd lost some of her spark and admired her all the more for her professionalism and the way that she did her job as efficiently and competently as ever.

Arriving back in the cubicle in time to see Marcus popping closed the last button on Alex's babygro, Amy consulted the feeding chart clipped to the end of the cot.

"I think we'll try him on a tube-feed every second time this week and see how he manages. His weight is very good so he should be well able for a bottle or breast feed in between tubes. How about if you alternate the breast and tube feeds during the day and we can use the bottle at night?"

"That'd be brilliant," Deirdre said, thrilled to be able to feed him so much herself. If he managed to maintain his weight while cutting down on the tube-feeds there was a very real possibility of him going home in the near future.

"Actually, it'd be a really good idea for you to have a night out together soon. I know you had the evening in the Mount Vernon but you only stayed for the meal that time. I mean a proper night out this time. He's pretty much out of the woods at this stage and before you know it, you'll be doing night feeds and wondering where your social life has disappeared to!" Amy looked inquiringly at them to gauge their reaction.

Marcus looked at her in admiration, aware of how much it must be costing her to act normally in their presence.

The staff in the Neonatal Unit were very much aware of the strain that was placed on even the strongest of couples, and the fact that relationships got designated to low priority in the face of dealing with a very ill baby. Sometimes the pressure caught up with them and the closest of couples found themselves bickering due to tiredness and the worry of coping with the baby at home.

"I suppose we could," Deirdre sounded doubtful. She was amazed that Amy had referred to the evening in the Mount Vernon, the first night that she'd been out with Peter in their company.

"No suppose about it, guys," Amy smiled. "Book yourselves a nice meal somewhere for next weekend. Maybe Hazel would come in for the nine o'clock feed in case Alex is lonely. You could even have a few glasses of wine, Deirdre, as long as you discard the first breast milk the following morning. You have enough milk in the freezer to last him until his first birthday."

They all laughed at this, as Deirdre did indeed have a healthy supply of breast milk.

"Amy's right, Dee. We can't have Alex thinking he has the most boring parents in Ireland. And Hazel will be doing a jig when she hears that she'll have Alex to herself for a whole feed. They'll have to sound-proof the cubicle."

"And don't forget that fairly soon you'll have a baby to mind full-time so you won't get the chance of a night out for a while," Amy encouraged, conscious of the fact that the average baby-sitter was reluctant to take on an infant that would still be quite small on discharge from the neonatal unit.

"OK then, you've persuaded me," Deirdre laughed, delighted that Amy thought of Alex as "out of the woods".

38

Number 1

Backed up at the entrance to the Tunnel, Charlie at her side, Linda's blood pressure was going through the roof. She normally swept down the less busy outside lane, bypassing the queue in the left lane smartly. Once she'd get near the roundabout she usually edged back into the left lane, nosing in ahead of cars that had been queuing for ten minutes. Typical that the occupants of the backed-up left lane were bumper to bumper this morning with no intention of letting her squeeze in at the last minute. Determined to get back into the left lane she tried to force the MG in ahead of a bloke in an Audi who obstinately clamped his car right up to the one in front.

"Fucking asshole!" Even though it was the end of October with a bitter east wind, she wound down the window to yell at the disobliging driver who ignored her studiously while inching his way towards the

Tunnel. The car behind him was as bad, its two female inmates giving her dirty looks for skipping the queue and clinging on to the Audi so as not to let her in. Linda made a face and gave them the two fingers only to have them burst out laughing. Fuming, she again tried to force her way into the lane but a middle-aged couple in a Micra were having none of it, sticking close to the bumper of the car in front.

"Take it easy, someone will let you in." Charlie sighed and beckoned politely to the occupants of the next car, mortified to be seen blatantly skipping the queue and then expecting to be let in at the last minute. Eventually an elderly lady in a Starlet responded to Charlie's beseeching expression and left a gap, indicating to Linda to go ahead of her. Charlie waved his thanks while drivers farther back the line hooted their displeasure at the traitor who'd allowed Linda to skip ahead of them.

Charlie and Linda rarely car-shared but they'd agreed to meet Luke Nolan for dinner that evening so it made sense for them to travel together. Surprised at how aggressive Linda was on the road, he hoped she wouldn't start the same carry-on at the next roundabout. If everyone hogged the road the way his girlfriend did, there would be complete anarchy.

Sensing his disapproval at her tactics, Linda turned to him boldly. "Don't be so bloody pious, Charlie! You'd be all day queuing for the Tunnel if you were going to act like Mother Teresa, for God's sake!"

"Did I say anything?" He was sick of her belligerent

attitude and her way of implying that he was somehow a wimp for simply following the same rules as everyone else.

Linda sulked the rest of the way to work, leaving him abruptly at the main door and stalking off down the corridor in a huff. Presuming that their usual lunch was out of the question, Charlie made for the coffee-room to grab a quick cup of tea, picking up a sandwich for later to have at his desk. Closing the door of his office after him, he sat with his head in his hands, wondering again what his relationship with Linda was about, and where exactly it was going.

Admitting that for him it was over was harder than anything, but he knew that this was the reality of the situation, however long it had taken him to be able to acknowledge it to himself. Suddenly it was very clear that Linda was just not the person that he wanted to spend the rest of his life with.

I don't love her. I don't love Linda. The words reverberated around in his head giving him an irrational urge to shout them out loud. Now that he'd got it straight in his head, the initial feeling of something like euphoria was replaced by a sinking feeling in his chest. He'd have to talk to her as soon as he could to put things straight. There was no way that he could continue as they were, not now that he felt like this. He couldn't believe that they'd made love the previous night. It seemed like light years ago. It had been silent and intense at the time but after Linda had fallen asleep, he'd lain awake listening to the clock feeling bleak and detached, as if the woman beside him was someone he didn't know at all.

The drive to work had been like a key turning inside him, as if he'd needed some catalyst to make him open his eyes to the facts. Everything was pointing in the one direction, telling him that things with Linda just weren't right but he'd been deluding himself that it was some kind of phase that would pass.

Cursing the fact that they were having dinner with Luke after work, he turned back to the desk to try and get some semblance of order on the day. He was meeting Daniel at ten and there was still some stuff he needed to have ready for him.

Daniel, he thought. How will he take the news that one of the company directors has dumped his daughter? Is that how he'll see it? Or that I've let Linda down, to use the old-fashioned phrase? Elbows on the desk, he again rested his head in his hands, raking his fingers through his hair. He was well aware that Linda's father saw him as a steadying influence on his daughter and a potential son-in-law at that. His attitude was bound to change now, and why wouldn't it? For all his gruffness and not letting her away with much, Daniel adored his only child, despite her headstrong nature.

Charlie couldn't get his brain into gear and knew it was because of the fact that he needed to act, now that his mind was made up. He always considered things for ages before making a decision but once he settled on something there was no going back. Wishing that he and Linda were going straight home after work so that they could sit down and talk was no good. Their arrangement with Luke had been made since Monday and there was no way that Charlie could cry off now without telling her the reason. He'd just have to sit through the meal as best he could and hope that they wouldn't be too late getting home. Determined to talk to Linda before the day was out if it was possible at all, he then started to contemplate again what her reaction would be.

Unable to picture her response when he told her that their relationship just wasn't working for him, he was amazed that he hadn't realised before how little he knew her. He felt a bit presumptuous in thinking that she might be devastated. It was more likely that she'd be outraged at the cheek of him, than hurt at the thought of losing him.

Reflecting on this he wondered if maybe Linda took *him* for granted rather than the other way around, as he'd berated himself over the past few weeks. She usually assumed that he'd fall in with whatever she had planned, like her idea for The Sanctuary, and was often stunned and churlish when he refused to go along with something. Before, he'd always let her sulk for a while, knowing that she'd accept that he wasn't going to be cajoled into agreeing with her but now he saw that this wasn't enough for him. Spending the rest of his life surviving Linda's demands and subsequent sulks wasn't a solid enough foundation for a marriage as far as he was concerned.

A picture of his parents flashed in front of his eyes. They'd always seemed to be able to reach a compromise in the situations that they'd come up against, without resorting to bullying each other. Acknowledging that this kind of relationship was more in the way of what he'd actually want for himself was a bit of a surprise. Most people spent their lives trying *not* to turn into their parents and here he was almost envying his own parents' comfortably solid life.

Charlie finished his tea and mentally shook himself. He was meeting Daniel in a few minutes and he didn't want to antagonise the man before he got wind of the deterioration in his daughter's personal life. Landing into a meeting unprepared was a sure-fire way to irritate him, despite the fact he had been such a loyal, hardworking and trustworthy employee to date.

Collecting the files that he needed for the meeting, Charlie took yet another deep breath and left the office before he had any more time to think about the situation that he'd found himself in.

* * *

The day dragged along endlessly until finally it was five o'clock. He'd hardly had time to ponder on what dinner with Linda and Luke Nolan would be like, considering that Linda obviously wasn't speaking to him. Normally they'd have had some contact during their working day but it seemed that she was still in a huff over his exasperation with her driving skills that morning. Another time, Charlie would have phoned her during the day to make peace but he was fed up with the whole game. All the same, he was reluctant to have any kind of scene in Luke's presence and hoped that Linda would be of the same mind. As far as he was concerned, their personal life was just that and a colleague being aware that they'd had a tiff just wasn't on.

Just as he was considering this, Luke made an appearance in the doorway.

"Are you right? I just met Linda in the lift – she said she'd meet us at the front door."

"Grand so," Charlie said, relieved that he didn't have to phone Linda in front of Luke. "Will we walk down or do you want to drive?"

"I think I'll take the car. I've a game in the morning so I'll be skipping the wine." Luke was big into rugby and spent his Saturdays training if he didn't have a game.

"I'll hang on for Linda then and we'll meet you there," said Charlie. "We travelled in together this morning."

"I'll get them to open a bottle of red for you," Luke grinned before disappearing towards his car.

Charlie watched Linda as she approached him down the corridor. Studying her dispassionately, he had to admit that she was gorgeous. But somehow any feeling that he'd had for her had evaporated, leaving him with a flat sensation that he knew wouldn't go away until he sat down and talked to her about going their separate ways.

Unbidden, a picture of Amy sprang into his mind, their eyes locked as he helped her to pick up the stuff that he'd knocked out of her basket the previous week. Something about her kept niggling at him, something warm and natural that made him aware of how brittle his relationship with Linda really was.

"Well, have you got over the stress of my driving yet?"

Linda's voice brought him back to reality with a start. She arched an eyebrow at him, trying to gauge whether he'd forgiven her or not. She knew that she was an impatient driver but Charlie's innate politeness riled her sometimes.

Giving her a half-smile, he told her that Luke had gone ahead to the restaurant.

"Right so. We'd better head off." Stalking in front of him, Linda zapped the remote central locking moodily, obviously put out that her boyfriend wasn't falling over himself to make up.

Doc's was buzzing when they arrived in. Luke waved to get their attention as soon as they entered, pulling up a chair for Linda and shifting his jacket off the one he'd been holding for Charlie.

"I hope the *Côte de Rhone*'s alright. This place is flying since the new crowd took it over, isn't it?"

Charlie's heart sank. Luke was obviously in vibrant form, so it looked like they had a lively evening ahead of them. He'd just have to go with the flow and forget about having a heart-to-heart with Linda for the moment. With that, the waitress arrived with their menus and outlined the specials in a cheery voice that did nothing to improve his enthusiasm for the evening ahead.

They chatted amiably while poring over the selection, with Luke and Charlie settling on the enormous steak sandwiches that the restaurant was famed for, while Linda eventually ordered a Caesar salad. Talk turned to the leisure complex as their starters arrived at the table. Luke, while generally overseeing the project and helping out with any difficulties that arose, was happy to leave the day-to-day running to Linda. Amazed at her capacity to get things done as and how she wanted it, he commented on the pace at which things were proceeding. Admitting that he'd been more than sceptical initially at the thought of someone with no project management experience taking on such an enormous job, he now conceded with a smile that Linda seemed to be more than equal to the task.

"You'd better get a move on and start rounding up the staff for the leisure centre," he said, "because it'll be up and running before you know it. I couldn't believe it when a quote for the bathrobes arrived from Pristine Linen. Needless to say, I directed it back to your office."

Luke glanced admiringly at Linda as he said this, a glance that wasn't lost on Charlie. He could understand his colleague being impressed with her. It was how he himself had been when they first met. The combination of statuesque ice-maiden combined with her forceful personality was a heady mix that had overwhelmed him until very recently. He watched Linda smiling back at Luke, knowing she was very much aware of his attention.

"Actually," she smirked triumphantly, "I've got that side of things pretty much sorted. The girl who's managing Bodywork at the moment has been training someone up to take over so that she'll be able to move over to Esprit when it opens. Ditto for the senior fitness instructor, so the senior staff are practically in place already. We'll start advertising for the rest after Christmas once the promotion for Esprit is underway."

"So when do you think the doors will open?" Luke was genuinely dazzled at Linda's dynamism, having had an impression of his boss's daughter as a spoilt glamour girl before he'd had the opportunity to actually work with her.

"I'd be hoping for Easter time, all going well. We've been lucky with the medical side of things in that the GP and dental practices are filled already. Dad happened to mention to a friend that we were going to incorporate the medical stuff into the complex and a few days later he got back to him to say that his daughter and son-in-law were hoping to move back from Canada and set up practice here."

"A doctor and dentist combination? Pretty convenient. And jammy!"

Luke laughed as he said this and Linda responded cheekily, "Jammy for them, you mean?"

"Well, it's another thing sorted. We'll probably use

contract cleaners for a while until we're able to recruit for ourselves. I've been looking into it and you'd be surprised how competitive the rates are."

Charlie watched the exchanges between them – Luke sincere in his admiration for Linda, and she in her turn flirting outrageously in response. Because he'd agreed to drive home, Charlie was making half a glass of wine last while Luke sipped a mineral water. Linda was already on her second glass, her cheeks flushed a little, the glow making her look even more attractive. In the early days, Charlie knew he would have felt a sense of possessive pride at his colleague's open appreciation of Linda.

Tonight he felt a bit detached from his surroundings, the interaction between his girlfriend and Luke having almost no effect on him. If anything, he was a little relieved that Linda was so obviously flirting. It made him feel better somehow about ending their relationship. And made him feel less guilty about the fact that he kept wondering whether Amy, whose surname he didn't even know, was involved in a relationship or not.

They lingered over coffee, with Luke filling them in on the details of his game the following day.

"I'm in it for the social life, if the truth be told. We normally go to Cudigans for a few drinks afterwards. You should join us tomorrow night. They're a nice crowd."

Noticing Linda's interest and terrified that she'd arrange for them to meet Luke the following night,

Charlie cast his eyes around for the waitress who obliged almost immediately with the bill. The distraction diverted his companions from their plans, temporarily at least. It'd be pretty awkward to have to phone and cancel in the morning once they'd dissolved their relationship in the meantime.

He was glad to bid Luke goodnight eventually, despite the dread he suddenly felt at opening the discussion that would end his relationship with Linda. Lost in thought, he didn't realise how quiet he'd been all evening until Linda commented on it.

"Are you still odd with me over this morning?"

He sighed deeply. This was it. "No, it's not that at all. I'd kind of forgotten about this morning, to be honest."

"Well, what then?" Linda was always one to get answers if she wanted them.

"God, Linda, this is hard. It's just that I've been thinking about us a lot lately." Pausing, he glanced at her to see her reaction. She was listening quietly, as if she somehow knew where this was going. He knew he had to continue now that he'd started talking. "I'm not sure that I'm all that happy any more, Linda. I can't say that it's anything in particular – I just know things aren't right for me." Pausing again, he hoped that she'd make some response. This wasn't like Linda. Knowing he wasn't handling it very well but not knowing what else to do, he continued as gently as he could. "I don't think we're right for each other, really. I think we want different things right now. I suppose I'm saying that I think it's best if we're not together any more." He paused. "Linda, say something."

"When did this come on?" She sounded a bit defiant, but at least she was saying something.

"It's been on my mind for a while."

Suddenly, they were pulling up outside the house in Pebble Cove and Charlie realised that he hadn't planned for this. He'd envisaged a situation where he and Linda would talk through their relationship, probably sitting in her house, with him leaving at the end of it. He hadn't counted on it being at half eleven at night with all his clothes still residing in her bedroom. In truth, he hadn't really thought it through at all, for all his mulling over it. He didn't want a big scene of packing and moving out, with all the stress it would bring to both of them.

"Look, we'd better go in and make some coffee," Linda said after a pause.

"OK," he said awkwardly.

Inside, Charlie sat uncomfortably in the lounge while Linda busied herself with the coffee in the kitchen. Once she'd settled herself into the sofa opposite him, he tried again to explain how he felt. Linda, however, wasn't interested in how he was feeling and for that Charlie could hardly blame her.

"Is this why you didn't want to get involved in The Sanctuary with me? Because you would have found it too hard to extricate yourself? Were you been thinking about it as far back as that?"

Charlie tried to answer as honestly as he could.

"Being honest, while I thought the idea for The Sanctuary was great, I never had an interest in the whole management side of it. I knew I'd start to think of it as hassle after a while, so it wasn't fair to get involved. It had nothing to do with us as a couple. Afterwards, when it was underway, I did start to think about why I'd backed away from it. I thought at the time it was because I wasn't ambitious enough or driven enough. I suppose that's what put me thinking about how different we are and how we want different things out of life."

"It's only work, Charlie. We could still have got on with our lives even if we had different career goals."

Linda said this as a statement of fact, yet Charlie could see that she was asking him what it was that had made their differing work ethics infringe on their personal life.

"I know," he said. "It sounds simple enough. But it's not just about work. It's more about us as a couple than anything. I'm sorry, Linda but that's the way it is for me."

He hoped that Linda would just accept that their relationship was over without probing it any further. He couldn't bear to have to say that he simply didn't love her. It would sound so harsh and stark to have to say it out loud.

"So, where do we go from here? We certainly can't go on working under the same roof. Have you thought about that?"

Charlie's heart almost stopped. Surely Linda didn't

expect him to resign from his job because their relationship had broken up? "No, I haven't thought about it," he said firmly. "We discussed this at the start and you were the one who said that we were adults and we'd be professional about it if things didn't work out between us."

They'd discussed this endlessly at the beginning and Linda had been adamant that Charlie's working relationship with her father would not be affected by a break-up. Now it seemed the goalposts had moved.

"Well, it's a bit different now," said Linda. "I'm working with Coltons in the same building as you. It was a different scenario when I was running Bodywork. Now we share a boss – and he's my father."

"Linda, forget about your father. This is none of his business. Lots of people who work together have relationships that split up and they just have to get on with it. I know people will speculate about it for a while but if we both act like professionals then they'll soon forget about it."

"That's fine for you to say."

Realising that Linda was more in dread of losing face than of losing him, he set about reassuring her. "Linda, why we finished up is no-one's business but our own. It's not like we have to make some kind of announcement. Most people probably won't even notice. And if they do, they wouldn't dare ask one of us what happened."

Charlie was trying to be reasonable, but Linda wasn't convinced. He had a vague feeling that she was trying to punish him in some way, to make things as difficult for him as he was making them for her. Trust her to be unreasonable about it. Even if she *were* upset, it wouldn't be her way to cry or appear hurt in front of him. It was more like her to sulk and not accept the situation, just as she'd done over The Sanctuary earlier in the year.

"I don't believe you don't think this is a big deal, Charlie. How are you going to work with Dad when he finds out that you've walked out?" So this was how she had decided it was going to be.

"Linda, this is nothing to do with your dad. It *is* a big deal, but for us – not him. If he wasn't your dad do you think we'd be considering our boss in all this? We have to be reasonable. What good would it do if I left Coltons? I'd be leaving a job that I love for no real reason and Coltons would be losing one of its directors. I'm not so sure your father would be impressed with that."

As he said this, Charlie was hoping that this was indeed how Daniel would think. Perhaps he would uncharacteristically agree with his daughter, particularly if he saw that she was devastated by the break-up. Charlie knew the kind of spin that Linda was capable of putting on something for her father's benefit. It was possible that Daniel *would* ask him to resign. He couldn't actually sack him but if their working relationship proved to be untenable then it might become the only option.

Linda appeared to be considering his words,

possibly trying to work out what way her father would look at this. Charlie knew he'd often surprised her with his firmness, especially where any sort of frivolity was concerned. Would Daniel consider it vanity on her part to expect Charlie to leave Coltons when he was the one who'd be at the loss of a senior employee? Charlie felt reasonably confident that his boss would expect them both to act logically and keep their private lives out of the office. Yet there was the possibility that he would support his only child if the matter was causing her extreme distress.

"Look, there's no point in talking about this all night." Linda sounded impatient and exasperated about the whole thing now. Bluntly she asked him, "What do you want to do about your clothes and stuff?"

Disappointed that it had turned so awkward and hostile, he decided that it was better to leave now and come back for his things later. "I'd better head off, I suppose. I could come by on Sunday, maybe, and pick up my things, if that's alright?" It was Linda's house after all.

"I'll probably be going home for lunch but you'll be able to manage on your own, won't you?"

"Linda, I'm sorry, truly I am. I know it's not going to be easy for us but we have to make the best of it. It'll be harder on both of us if there's animosity between us at work."

"I'll see you Monday," was all that Linda said as she waited for him to pick up his keys and leave her house.

39

Seefin

"This is mad," Deirdre giggled. "It's like being on a first date."

She'd already had two glasses of wine before leaving the house, egged on by Hazel, who agreed strenuously that her sister and brother-in-law should make the most of their big night out before Alex landed home. She'd dropped them at the door of The Mill Race and headed off to spend the night with a friend, insisting that they have the house to themselves for the first time in almost three months.

"Just be careful and don't get carried away with all the wine," she said as she waved them off outside the restaurant. "One baby is enough for the moment." With that she was gone, leaving Deirdre and Marcus in stitches on the footpath.

They were still laughing even after they were settled at their table waiting for their starter to arrive.

"She even bought me some sexy underwear to ensure that we enjoyed ourselves. She's really getting carried away with the responsibility of being a godmother."

Marcus grinned appreciatively when he heard this, finally feeling able to relax without the thought that they'd be called to the hospital at a moment's notice.

Deirdre, for her part, was enjoying her first few glasses of wine, but was slightly guilty about having to discard the breast milk the following morning. It had been so difficult at the beginning to keep up with Alex's needs that even now she felt that every drop was too precious to waste.

They lingered over the coffee, content in each other's company, and it was only when the restaurant was nearly empty that they realised that they'd been there for three hours. Walking arm in arm to the taxi rank, Deirdre thought that they must look like any ordinary couple on a night out. Nobody could imagine the steep learning curve that they'd confronted since Alex's birth.

Deirdre felt strangely stronger for all that they'd been through and even felt optimistic that they'd cope with all that was yet to come. She felt closer to Marcus than she ever had, even more so than when they were first married, despite the fact that they hadn't made love since Alex's birth.

Buoyed up by the wine, she cuddled up to Marcus as soon as he'd closed the front door.

"Will we try out the new underwear?" she

murmured, already opening the buttons of his shirt.

"Well, if you're offering . . ." he said, lifting her into his arms and proceeding up the stairs, all thoughts of the Neonatal Unit temporarily gone from his head.

40

Number 1

As soon as the alarm went off on Monday morning, Charlie felt a sense of dread envelop him. The whole weekend had taken on a surreal hue.

He'd gone and collected his clothes from Linda's house on Sunday, in her absence as predicted. The house had been eerily quiet as he'd folded his clothes into one of the holdalls that he'd brought with him. There was quite a lot, he realised, and he had to make a few trips to the car. Glad that it was raining, he managed to execute the removal of his things without being accosted by any of the neighbours, particularly Amy in the house opposite. He'd glanced over on his first trip from house to car but thankfully her Golf had been missing from the drive.

Once the car was packed, he'd glanced around to make sure that there were no remaining bits and pieces, but surprisingly there had been very little to suggest that he'd practically lived there once his clothes and toiletries were gone. He'd hated leaving the keys on the hall table and closing the door behind him but this was obviously what Linda wanted. If it made it easier for her not to be there, then that was the way he would play it.

Not relishing the thought of meeting her on Monday in the presence of their colleagues, he'd tried phoning her on Sunday night but both phones went to the answering machine immediately.

Jumping out of bed before he had any more time to think about the day ahead, he reflected on the sense of freedom he'd begun to feel over the weekend, despite the gnawing feeling of having hurt Linda in the process of gaining it. He'd spent Saturday evening alone, cooking for himself for the first time in ages, and had sat in front of the TV for the night, idly watching sports programmes that Linda had hated.

He arrived in work early, wanting to be prepared for the inevitable meeting with Daniel. Linda might choose to avoid him for the moment and that was her prerogative if it made the situation easier, but Daniel was a different matter. He met with all the senior staff every Monday morning to discuss the progress of the projects in hand, and to plan the outline of upcoming business. Aware that Linda would probably have told her parents about the break-up over the weekend, Charlie hoped that this morning's meeting would run smoothly.

He left it until the last minute to arrive in the

boardroom, to avoid finding Daniel there alone. In one sense he felt pathetic doing this, yet he knew that if they started a discussion about Linda before the meeting, the others would pick up the tension immediately when they arrived. As it stood, everyone else was in place when he arrived. He knew straight away from his expression that Daniel had been told. He nodded a greeting followed by a gruff "Charlie". Relieved that he didn't look too ferocious, Charlie responded in kind and took the nearest available seat.

The usual run of the Monday meeting followed a list made out by Daniel's PA on Friday evenings. Ongoing projects were discussed first, so Charlie often didn't have an input if they were running to plan. Following that, impending projects were looked at, many of which were at the drawing stage. Charlie was currently working on the detailed plans for the third phase of the leisure complex and knew that this would be one of the next few items on Daniel's agenda. Whatever way Daniel related to him while going over the drawings would set the scene for what was to come.

"Right. The Holiday Villas. Where are we at there, Charlie?"

Daniel met Charlie's eyes head on, with no hint of animosity or accusation. Relief flooded through Charlie as he responded in a businesslike tone,

"Nearly there. We can go one of two ways. All single detached dwellings, which would be in keeping with the whole luxury agenda. But we'd be looking at lower density in terms of occupancy and therefore income, as well as less efficiency in terms of upkeep. On the other hand, we could put in some semis and a mini-terrace with a courtyard. That would give us a higher number of dwellings but we'd probably have to look at charging less for anything that's semi-detached or terraced. I've drawn up both layouts – have a look and see what you think. Opinions welcome."

This last bit was said to the assembled group as he projected an overview of the first proposal onto the large screen in front of them. Having talked them through it, he moved on to the second proposal, using a pointer to outline the details. This done, he closed the screen and awaited the opinions of Daniel and the rest of the team.

Daniel was the first to speak. "What do Linda and Luke think?"

Charlie's heart was beating furiously but he willed himself not to colour at the mention of Linda. "We talked it over last week. Luke feels that, aesthetically, the detached format is the one to go for. Linda liked both of the designs but felt that, in terms of ongoing income, the higher density plan would pay more dividends in the long run. As for having to use different pricing scales for the various types, she felt it would give people a sense of choice. I'm inclined to agree with her."

"What do the rest of you think? Any ideas?"

Daniel had obviously decided to behave as if nothing had happened, and was going out of his way to appear professional and reasonable to Charlie.

Planning to take his cue from his boss and keep his personal life out of the office, Charlie was nonetheless glad that his own views on the matter of the Holiday Villas coincided with Linda's on this occasion.

The meeting continued in this vein for another half hour. Slowly the tension of the morning eased away and Charlie was able to engage fully in the order of business. He could acknowledge how difficult it was for Daniel to have to ignore the break-up of his daughter's long-term relationship and continue to work closely with the perpetrator. Charlie admired Daniel more than ever as a person and as a colleague.

Finally, the session ended. As the others drifted out of the room towards their various offices Charlie hung back, sorting through the files he'd brought in with him. He needed to face Daniel and show in some way that he appreciated the neutral stance that he seemed to be taking. Daniel too was obviously anxious for a word with Charlie, dawdling in the room until the last of the directors had left.

"Hard weekend, by all accounts?" This was said with raised eyebrows and accompanied by a deep sigh.

"It was. I'm sorry it turned out the way it has. I hope Linda's alright." His voice sounded flat and regretful. He could hear it himself and Daniel seemed to respond to it.

"Well, better now than later. Too many people find out after they're married that they're not right for one another. That's much harder. I thought the two of you would make a go of it, but there you are."

371

"I know, Daniel, and it would have been great if it had worked out. But it wasn't right for either of us. And I know it's going to be hard here at work, but we'll have to make the best of it now." Charlie knew that he had to acknowledge that there would be some awkwardness initially but that he and Linda would be able to keep their differences out of the office.

"Well, you're right there – it's no-one's business but your own. Now, what about a tea break? Have to keep the speculators at bay anyway."

"Grand, so. I'll drop these into the office and follow you down."

Daniel was right. There were gossipmongers in any company who would be only too glad to see discord among those in management. There was no point in them all avoiding each other and giving people food for thought. Grateful to Daniel for taking the lead, he grabbed his mug and made his way towards the coffee-room.

* * *

Linda glanced at the clock in her office on the third floor. She was dying for a cup of coffee but was terrified of approaching the coffee-room. If she was back in Bodywork she'd simply have asked one of the others to fetch her a cup. But here in Coltons she didn't have the luxury of having all the staff at her beck and call.

The weekend had been a nightmare. In a funny sort of way, Charlie bringing their relationship to an end hadn't been the worst part, even though it had precipitated the rest. She was more annoyed at him than anything.

He'd backed away from The Sanctuary project because he was afraid to admit that he wouldn't be able to cope with the demands it would bring. All the time she'd been trying to change his mind about it, he'd ignored her attempts to persuade him that he did indeed have the capacity to take it on.

And now he didn't seem to be able to deal with the fact that she was forging ahead successfully without him. Even though he'd cited all sorts of reasons for wanting to break up with her, Linda was very much aware that their meal out with Luke Nolan probably had a significant effect on his decision. Luke had been eloquent in his admiration of Linda's managerial skills on the Friday night, even going so far as to admit that he'd had his doubts where her experience was concerned, professing that he'd had to eat his words once they started working together.

The fact that this acknowledgement of her ability to succeed had so obviously made Charlie feel undermined, made her think that the dissolution of their relationship wasn't such a bad thing after all. If Charlie felt so threatened by her abilities then maybe they weren't right for each other. The fact that he couldn't admit to feeling inadequate really galled her. It was as if he needed to pretend that they simply weren't compatible to save face.

No, it wasn't the loss of a boyfriend that had upset

her so much. It was her father's pragmatic attitude that had really taken her aback. When she'd rung to say that she'd be over for lunch on the Saturday, he'd known immediately that something was wrong. She'd explained to him and her mother that her relationship with Charlie was off, with the minimum of emotion.

Her mother simply didn't do fuss, so she gave only perfunctory advice about settling down too young and there being plenty of better, more interesting men out there, before heading off to play golf with her friends. Linda hadn't expected any more than this, so therefore wasn't too disappointed with the short supply of empathy. Over the years, as she'd seen the relationship between father and daughter develop steadily, Frances had absented herself from the equation and made her own life with an ever-increasing circle of friends and acquaintances. She barely knew her daughter in any real sense, and had never warmed to Charlie who she saw as a little bit dry and serious for her taste.

Once her mother had left, Daniel and Linda had taken their coffee through to the den, a large room at the back of the house that served as a television-room-cum-office for Daniel. It was generally considered his territory and Frances rarely spent time there. Linda had brought the coffeepot with her, knowing that Daniel would want to get to the bottom of what had happened with her and Charlie.

Direct as ever, he didn't beat about the bush.

"Well, now. Do you think it's only a row or is it definitely all off?"

"Definitely all off, I'd say. Charlie thinks we have a different outlook on life, whatever that means. I think he can't deal with how well The Sanctuary is coming on and he just doesn't want to admit it." Linda sat back and waited for her father's response.

"So do you think you'll be alright at work? Would you think of taking a week's holiday or anything?"

Daniel's concern was evident. He knew how hard-headed his daughter was, yet she'd invested a lot into a fairly public relationship and he knew she was bound to be upset, whether she'd show it or not.

"Well, I'll be damned if I'm the one to hide my head! If anyone should be skulking away from Coltons it's Charlie. In fact, how can I be expected to look at him swanning around the office day in day out?"

"Well, love, remember we talked about this very early on? About what would happen if you and Charlie didn't work out?"

Daniel had cautioned Linda about going out with a senior member of the Coltons team when he'd first got wind of their relationship. He hadn't been ecstatic about it at the time but had trusted Charlie to keep a balance between work and social life. It was Linda that he hadn't been so sure about.

"Well, it's different now," Linda said mulishly, reiterating the argument that she had made to Charlie the previous night. "We're working in the same building now, for the same employer. *I'm* hardly going to resign."

"Linda, is there any need for anyone to resign? If I

wasn't your father, you and Charlie would be like any other couple having an affair at work. You'd just have had to keep your heads down until it had all blown over. And I think that's what you're going to have to do now. Charlie leaving would create a big fuss where there is none."

"It might not be a big deal to you, but to me it is."

Linda was hurt that her father didn't see this as the disaster that it was. Whether Daniel realised it or not, once people around the building heard that it was all off between them, someone was bound to find out that Charlie had been the instigator. Linda knew it was only her pride at stake, but she couldn't bear people pitying her. If people were to see Charlie leaving with his tail between his legs, then Linda would appear to be the one in control of the situation.

"I didn't mean it like that. I meant that it's important to you and to me as well if you're not happy, but other people won't see it as a big deal if you and Charlie don't make a drama out of it. And apart from anything else, from a business point of view, losing Charlie wouldn't be a particularly smart move."

"Oh, I see. It's what's best for Coltons that matters now, is it?" Linda had played this card before to her satisfaction, knowing that her father hated to admit that his business was often a substitute for family life.

"And who do you think is going to be running Coltons after my time? Linda, looking at the way that you're dealing with the leisure complex, and the way you turned Bodywork around, I hope you'll be taking over from me someday. It'll be *your* inheritance, so there's no way I'm running it into the ground over any boyfriend. And the day will come when you'll have to think like that as well."

Daniel was stern in his delivery of this directive and hoped that the emotion he felt at the thought of handing the reins of the business over to his only child didn't show.

Linda, for her part, was stunned. While she'd always had anything she wanted on account of her father's considerable wealth, she'd never entertained thoughts of taking over from him. Now, looking at the way that things had panned out, it seemed inevitable that she would do just that.

"Do you really mean that?" Linda asked, almost breathless at the thought of it.

"Of course I mean it. But only if it's what you want. I didn't mean to come out with it so soon, and I know it's a long way off but I'd love to see it happening. I don't want it to be a burden to you either, though. If something else comes your way over the next few years and you want to change direction, that's alright. We can always wind up or sell out to one of the bigger firms and put the money into something else."

"Somehow, I can't see that happening. I can't believe how much I'm enjoying the work I'm at now. I think I'll have learned a lot by the time The Sanctuary is up and running. Having Luke was a good idea." This she admitted with a smile, acknowledging the fact that Daniel was wise to insist on her having someone experienced to oversee the project from the outset.

"The biggest thing you're going to have to learn is to keep home and work separate," said her father. "I think I'm right about your having to keep a cool head over this thing with Charlie. I know it's not easy, but you made the decision to start seeing him, so you'll have to deal with the rest of it."

Linda sighed as her father held out his coffee cup for a refill. He *was* right, of course, but she was still pissed off at having to look at Charlie every day. She'd just have to play it cool, as if she'd been the one to blow him out. People would soon forget that they'd ever been an item. And wait until Mr Charlie found out that she'd soon be sitting around the table on the Monday mornings! *That* would give him something to think about.

* * *

However, now that she was marooned in her office longing for a cup of coffee to clear her head, the fighting talk had deserted her. She knew she'd have to face Charlie sometime, yet the fact that she'd had to acquiesce to her father's insistence that he stay with the company was galling. She was sorry that she'd ever drawn down the notion of him leaving. It wouldn't seem so much of a defeat now. Deciding, finally, that giving in gracefully was more dignified than maintaining her initial stance, she elected to forget about the coffee and take an early lunch instead. Facing

Charlie with some sort of olive branch could wait a little longer.

Deep in thought, she didn't hear the door opening until she heard the familiar voice. She looked up to find Charlie standing over her, his usual "Far Side" mug in one hand and a "Mr Men" in the other.

"Coffee?" He asked this tentatively, as if looking for permission to be there.

Linda, never one to be ruffled in the face of the unexpected, gave a wry smile before replying,

"I'd murder one."

41

Seefin

Deirdre and Marcus knew that the following days would be among the hardest yet, even though Alex would be going home at the end of it, all going well.

Deirdre was determined not to get her hopes up about the homecoming, having witnessed the disappointment of little Cathy's parents a few weeks earlier. They'd been all revved up for their "going home day" when Cathy had been diagnosed with a chest infection and needed to go back on antibiotics. Her parents, Steve and Norma, had been devastated to see her attached to the monitors that they'd thought were a thing of the past. Although it had been a temporary setback, it had shaken their confidence badly. The whole saga had had a sobering effect on Deirdre and Marcus, who were just starting to get excited about talk of Alex being ready for home.

As well as a brain scan, Alex would have to be

reviewed by the ophthalmologist before leaving the unit. Dr Ramsay had seen him on several occasions since his birth and so far had been pleased with his progress. It had been explained at a very early stage that many of the premature infants suffered from a disorder of the eyes called Retinopathy of Prematurity.

Dr Ramsay, a "jolly good old chap" type, examined each infant monthly and ordered laser treatment for those babies whose eyes were affected. Even with the treatment, some premature babies suffered with very poor vision all their lives. Thankfully, this was one problem that Alex hadn't run into, yet they were terrified that this final examination would uncover something. The eye specialist would review him on Thursday and would be able to tell Deirdre and Marcus immediately whether Alex was clear or not.

*   *   *

They arrived in the unit at the crack of dawn, nervous that Dr Ramsay would call on Alex before doing his rounds in the rest of the hospital. They'd missed his visit on one occasion but were determined to speak to him this morning to ask him about any future problems that Alex might have with his eyesight. Marcus had taken the morning off work in order to be there for the eye exam.

Deirdre hated anything to do with eyes and couldn't tolerate looking at the little implement that the specialist used to pull Alex's eyelids back. Marcus, on the other hand, was intent on going through Alex's discomfort with him as much as possible, standing there bravely and wincing as the small metal retractor was inserted to give Dr Ramsay as good a view as possible.

"Mmmm . . . good . . . yes . . . mmm . . . right . . . good . . ." was all they could hear as he peered closely at the right eye, then "Fine . . . OK . . . yes . . . good . . ." as he quickly removed the retractor and deftly inserted one in Alex's other eye.

"All done. Good news really – no sign of any damage at all. Marvellous considering how early he was. No need to see him for six months. Eye Clinic will send you an appointment. Any questions?"

After a brief discussion on the follow-up that Alex would receive over the next few years, the eye specialist strode off, leaving a faint trace of pipe-smoke in the cubicle. Emotionally exhausted at having received a positive outlook on at least one aspect of their baby's future, Deirdre and Marcus hugged each other silently, too drained to celebrate and very much aware that the next step in Alex's discharge plan might not be so straightforward.

His final brain scan was booked for 10 a.m. and they knew from past experience that the X-Ray department ran like clockwork. Methodically they prepared for Alex's 9 a.m. feed so that they'd be well finished before the portable scanner was wheeled into the cubicle.

"Will the results be ready by tomorrow?" Deirdre asked anxiously after the scan was done.

She and Marcus looked hopefully at the

radiographer, willing her to speed the results of the brain scan up if she could at all.

"Well, the fact that it's been done before lunch means that the report should be back to Mr McNeill tomorrow morning. Perhaps you could make an appointment to see him then."

The nursing team had already arranged this and once again, Deirdre marvelled at the level of co-ordination required to keep the unit running smoothly.

"And you can't tell from the scan if it's any better or not?" Marcus asked this, anxious for any indication of a positive outcome.

"I'm afraid not because I don't have an accurate picture of your baby's overall condition. It would be better to speak to the consultant once he's read the scan results." She began to push the bulky scanner out of the cubicle. "I hope the news is good," she said warmly as she left.

Now that Alex's discharge from the unit was imminent, the anxiety about the outcome of the brain haemorrhage had reared its head again. It was always there at the back of their minds but had taken a back seat to the feeding difficulties.

Alex's weight gain in the previous weeks had been excellent and he was now fully breastfeeding at last. He'd been almost a week without the need for a tube-feed and seemed to be managing well. This was partly due to having another blood transfusion, on account of his iron levels dropping again. This time it wasn't so dramatic. His listlessness and poor feeding combined with the weekly blood tests had led to the decision, much to Deirdre's relief. They were both amazed at the improvement in him the day after the transfusion, so much so that Marcus asked Amy why they hadn't given him the blood earlier.

"It's about trying to strike a balance between his need for a transfusion and the risks of infection. Even though all the blood is screened for viruses these days, there's still a risk involved because it can only be screened for viruses that we're aware of. So we avoid giving it if we can."

"And when he's at home with us how will we know if the iron levels are keeping up?" Marcus was anxious that they'd be aware of every eventuality in case Alex deteriorated once they got him home.

"Well, he's already taking the iron drops in his feeds and we'll be rechecking his blood levels before he goes home. He'll be on the drops for at least six months until he builds up his own iron stores. If you're fully breastfeeding you can put the drops directly into his mouth. And don't think that it'll be all down to you once you leave here. As well as your appointments with the hospital you'll have the Public Health Nurse calling to you. She'll be able to monitor his weight and advise you on feeding."

Deirdre was relieved that they'd have some back-up once they left the security of the unit even though Amy had reminded them that she was only a stone's throw away and would call over any time. They'd already been advised to spend a night in the unit looking after

Alex with no help from the staff, to give them confidence before they brought Alex home. They were going to stay in the parents' room the following night with Alex beside them in his cot. Deirdre was both excited and nervous, and was determined that they'd be as independent as possible in preparation for home.

If all went well, the plan was that Alex would be discharged on Wednesday. Rose and Tom were going to be there for the homecoming but had elected to leave for home once Alex had settled in, feeling that Deirdre and Marcus needed space to get their bearings with him. Anyway, Hazel would be there as back-up in case anything was needed.

They'd already discussed the possibility of Deirdre taking extended leave from work if Alex needed special attention at home to help his development. Speaking to Mr McNeill would give them a better idea of where they stood. Although Marcus was reluctant to make his wife feel as if *she* had to be the one to put her career on hold, Deirdre was adamant that she'd apply for leave of absence once they'd spoken to the consultant. Before Alex had been born, she'd always envisaged herself going back to work once her maternity leave was over. But now she couldn't imagine not spending every day with him as she'd been doing in the Neonatal Unit.

Tom had even reminded them that, as well as the house in West Cork, the land attached to it would eventually belong to them. If it needed to be sold now to help Alex in any way, then it was their choice to do so.

"Thanks, Tom," Marcus had said gruffly. "I hope it

won't be needed but thanks all the same."

* * *

Friday morning arrived and again they were up early, this time packing their things for the stint ahead in the Neonatal Unit. They'd be meeting Mr McNeill first thing to discuss Alex's progress and the scan results. Following that, they'd be taking over the care of their baby, starting with his morning feed and bath.

They planned to settle into the parents' room for the day, with Deirdre feeding Alex as he needed it. Their meals had already been ordered from the hospital canteen and would be dropped up to them by the household staff. The folding bed that doubled as a sofa during the day would be pulled out and Alex's cot parked beside it. Deirdre had bought pyjamas for Marcus and packed both their robes, just in case they had to go out to the main part of the unit during the night to get help if they weren't managing.

"At least it's a shorts and T-shirt set," said Marcus, surveying his new pyjamas. "I'd be like someone's grandfather if I arrived out in a pair of Paisleys."

First, however, they had to get the scan results and hopefully get some indication of how the brain haemorrhage would affect Alex in the long run. Thankfully the consultant arrived in the unit just as they were lifting him out for his morning feed.

"Good morning to you – I hope I haven't kept you waiting."

Deirdre cuddled Alex into her, searching the doctor's face for a sign that might prepare her for what they were about to hear. They were both mute, waiting for him to continue.

"I hear that the feeding has really taken off in the past few weeks. It looks like it may have been down to him needing the blood transfusion. His weight gain is excellent really."

Unable to wait any longer, Marcus came out with the question that they needed an answer to.

"How did the brain scan look?" Having asked, Marcus was now terrified of what he was going to hear.

"As you know from Alex's recent scans, the actual bleed had all but reabsorbed. This latest scan has improved in that regard, in that the remainder of the blood has soaked back into the system. However," he said gravely, seeing the look of hope that passed over their faces immediately, "there is what we call some residual damage to the brain tissue."

Deirdre felt the blood pounding in her ears as the words "damage to the brain tissue" reverberated around her head. She couldn't hear any more, only that Alex would have brain damage, with God only knew what effect on him. Marcus was still beside her, his arm around her shoulder. She clung to Alex for dear life, determined already to do everything in her power to make his life as wonderful as she possibly could, unaware that Mr McNeill had paused to allow them to assimilate what he'd just said.

"Dee, are you OK?" Marcus was whispering, his

voice full of concern and worry. This galvanised Deirdre and she relaxed her grip on Alex who was strangely quiet, almost as if he knew his future was being discussed.

Pre-empting their next question, the consultant continued. "There's no way of telling exactly how this will affect Alex. On the positive side, I can tell you that the damage to the tissue on the right side of his brain is very minimal, so I would hope that his development may not be affected at all. I'd be very optimistic due to the fact that he's feeding well now and his development is progressing well so far."

"How soon would we know if he's running into problems?" Deirdre was back in control now, a fierce protectiveness having replaced her initial shock.

"We'll be calling him back for assessment in three months' time to see how he's getting on. In the meantime, we'll refer Alex to a service called Grow, to which we refer all infants born before thirty weeks' gestation. It's based here in Cork and you should get an appointment in the next few weeks. Alex's needs will be assessed by a team of paediatricians, nurses, physios, social workers, psychologists etc and they'll decide from there if he needs any extra support."

"But do you think he'll need a lot of help? Are you saying that he could be physically delayed or mentally delayed?" Deirdre hated to ask but she knew that she'd be able to cope better if she had all the facts from the word go.

"The chances are that he'll be neither. His physical

milestones like sitting and walking will naturally be delayed on account of his being so early. The intellectual development is harder to measure in the early stages, which is why he'll need a larger amount of attention and stimulation. As I said, the residual damage from the haemorrhage is minimal but I feel it's important for you to be aware of it. The Grow team will be able to educate you on techniques to enhance development and they'll monitor him closely. Early intervention is the key to these things so make the most of these first few months with him."

"Do you think it'd make a difference if I gave up work for a while?"

"If you can afford to do that, then yes, it *would* help. If you're considering it, the team in Grow will be able to advise you about things like allowances and benefits that you can apply for to make it possible financially."

"In the worst case scenario, how do you think Alex could be affected? If we knew what to be looking out for, we'd be able to spot things early and get help." Marcus's thoughts were echoing Deirdre's. They needed to know, insofar as possible, what they were dealing with.

"Well, with any degree of brain damage there's a risk of Cerebral Palsy. This is where the functioning of one or more limbs can be diminished. In Alex's case, the fact that the bleed was on the right side of his brain would mean that the left side of his body would be affected. This is where the physiotherapists in Grow come in. Speech is another thing that's often affected so he'll be assessed by the Speech and Language Therapist there at a very early stage."

"So if anything shows up he'll be treated straight away?" said Marcus.

"That's exactly it. Most children who get early intervention go on to attend mainstream school and are discharged from the services. Their GP can then monitor their progress from there on. So I'd advise you to take up any services that are offered as early as possible because the outcome is always better if things are picked up early."

"So we just have to wait until the people from Grow contact us and go from there?" Marcus was satisfied now that they had a clear picture of how things would proceed.

"The main thing is to treat Alex like a normal baby," said the consultant. "Sometimes the stress can affect your own relationship, so get as much support as possible from friends and family once you get used to having him at home."

Accepting their thanks for the time and effort invested in Alex during his stay in the unit, the consultant took his leave, giving them a final reminder to "enjoy him" as he closed the door.

"It's hard to know what to think now, isn't it?" Marcus said thoughtfully, pulling Deirdre to him and kissing the top of her head. When brain damage had been said first, it had felt like the world was closing in on him. But by the end of the conversation with Mr McNeill things hadn't seemed so bleak.

Mairead O'Driscoll

All along, Marcus had focussed on the discharge date as being a point where they would know whether Alex would be a normal child or not. That hopefully he'd be deemed perfect as a result of the final round-up of tests. In his mind, it would be that or the devastating news that their son would never make a full recovery. He'd been prepared this morning for being told the latter and knew that Deirdre was thinking along the same lines, although they'd both been afraid to talk about it. It had been a fairly simplistic idea, he realised now.

As far as he could see, from what they'd just been told, there was going to be no black and white answer, no one time when Alex could be proclaimed as perfectly healthy. It seemed to be down to the matter of him being perfect for *them*, and Marcus knew that he was, no matter what deficits he had.

The concept of this being a journey rather than a destination became clear to him for the first time. They could only go from day to day and confront the problems as and when they arose. They would have to help him in every way they could to lead a normal life and hope that he'd be able to enjoy everything that any other child would.

"Do you know what, Marcus?" Deirdre looked more calm and resolute than he'd ever seen her. "I used to think that someone would have to tell us that everything was spot-on before we brought Alex home. But it doesn't really matter what stage he's at. We'll just have to find out as we go along. All we want is the best

392

for him and we'd want that for any child. We love him already. It's just a matter of helping him to get over as many hurdles as possible now. And if we've been able for it up to now, then we'll be able for whatever comes next."

"That's just what I was thinking, Dee. We'll meet the Grow people and find out all we can to help him. If it means you having to stay at home with him for a few years then we'll manage it as long as you're happy to give up work for a while. What do you think?"

"Definitely, now that we know where we stand a bit. When he said about there being signs of damage to the brain on the scan I thought we'd never be able to cope. But it's not like we'll be out there on our own. We'll just have to use all the services we can to help us."

"We'll be fine, the three of us, once we get going. And I love you, Dee. Now come on," Marcus said smiling, "Get out those boobs and feed the poor child before he makes a complaint to the unit manager."

42

Evergreen

That same Friday morning as Alex was starting his nine o'clock feed, Amy was sitting outside matron's office on the ground floor, staring into space. She wasn't even nervous when the door opened and Matron's secretary ushered her into the room. Normally, she'd have found the three serious faces in front of her intimidating but this morning she was beyond getting excited about a few questions.

The call for interview had come a few days after Peter's funeral and it was only Sheila Forde's encouragement that had made her accept.

"I know it's early days but you still have your own future to think about. And if you do get the job, the weekends off will be good for you."

"You make it sound like the job would be a doddle," Amy retorted, adding that the current unit manager, Rhona Day, wouldn't be inclined to see it like that.

"It'd definitely be a challenge but that wouldn't do you any harm," Sheila countered, anxious that Amy wouldn't give up this opportunity.

Now she was sitting bolt upright in front of Christina Kelly, the hospital's Director of Nursing, John Bolton the CEO, and Dr Louis McAllister, the Director of Neonatal Services.

"You're most welcome, Ms Harkin," Dr McAllister began after clearing his throat. Nearing retirement, he was rarely seen in the Neonatal Unit nowadays, so great was the level of administration attached to his job. Although Amy barely knew him, he was known as a gentleman by everyone, famous for his pipe-smoking which these days was confined to the outdoor smoking-shelter. His wife had died recently, Amy had heard.

"Now to begin with, what is it that has made you apply for this job?" he commenced.

Amy studied the three faces in front of her and wondered if any of them had any idea of how she really felt this morning. She'd had a bad night, tossing and turning with thoughts of Peter. Now she was wondering if she looked like the walking dead or whether her plaster-over-the-cracks job had been successful.

She thought that Mrs Kelly might have heard about her relationship with Peter on the nursing grapevine but doubted if the other two would be aware of it.

"Since I qualified as a General Nurse and then later as a midwife I've worked in a number of clinical areas. With the high standard of education and training that this country has to offer it would seem inevitable that a high standard of care would always be delivered efficiently and cost-effectively, yet this is often not the case. Good ward management, I believe, is the key to the provision of good patient care."

DrMcAlister nodded thoughtfully at this, allowing Mrs Kelly to continue the questioning. Christina Kelly was a single lady of indeterminate age, having been around for as long as Amy could remember. Her uniform of tweed suits and classic court shoes varied only in colour from browns to greys to blues and she seemed to have worn the same shade of lipstick for at least a decade. The modern title of Director of Nursing had never really caught on and people still referred to Christina Kelly as Matron.

"As a nurse, Amy, do you believe that you could successfully make the transition from the clinical area to a purely managerial role?"

"I've given this application serious consideration," Amy lied, making a mental note to tell Sheila how convincing she sounded. "Taking into account that I've taken over the management of the unit on a number of occasions in the past to accommodate Rhona Day's leave, I'm very much aware of how challenging it is, yet also that I have the capacity to handle it. Also, I've undertaken a Master's Degree in Health Services Management in order to underpin my clinical experience with a theoretical base."

"I'm aware of that, Amy," Mrs Kelly continued. "If you did get this post, how do you envisage the practicalities of completing that course of studies?"

Amy had known that this issue would be the real fly in the ointment. At the present time, her shift work had been organised to accommodate her classes in UCC every Wednesday. The unit manager's job was a 9-5, Monday to Friday deal.

"To date, the present unit manager has been extremely supportive with the organisation of shifts and this has allowed me to attend my lectures every Wednesday. As I'm now well into the final year, I would hope to come to some accommodation in order to complete this while obviously maintaining a full managerial service in the Neonatal Unit."

John Bolton, known as a taciturn number-cruncher who kept a tight hold of the hospital's purse-strings, was quick to interject at this point, anticipating a situation where the hospital would be out of pocket while the unit manager completed a degree that she might well use to further her career outside of his establishment. He was a stocky man with red-rimmed eyes and a sparse amount of straw-like hair that stuck out above his ears.

"And how would you anticipate the logistics of this panning out?"

"At the present time, the management of the unit is carried out on a five-day basis, taking into account that the structures put in place mid-week are sufficient for the smooth running of the unit over the weekend. I feel that this level of service could be achieved on a four-day basis if the manager were to make up the hours, for example, working from 8am to 6pm. This of course would be a temporary situation and indeed I would hope that it would be considered beneficial that the unit manager be highly qualified."

What next, Amy thought as sweat broke out between her shoulder blades. Now that she was actually in the middle of the interview it suddenly mattered to her that she got this job.

Mrs Kelly started off again and, to Amy's relief, indicated that this was the final question.

"And Amy, what personal characteristics do you feel you might bring to this post that would optimise your management of the Neonatal Unit?"

She *does* know, Amy thought, and she's asking me if I'll be able for it emotionally. Taking a deep breath and looking Mrs Kelly right in the eyes, Amy gave it her all.

"In my opinion, one of the key requisites in a manager is the ability to detach from matters outside of the job at hand and to be able to focus completely. Also to maintain professionalism at all times. It is a given that professional integrity and respectful interaction with one's colleagues are essential. I feel that, if offered this job, I can bring all of these qualities to bear on the management of the unit."

"Thank you, Ms Harkin. We'll be contacting all of the candidates over the next three weeks." John Bolton was brusque as usual and nodded a curt dismissal. Mrs Kelly smiled encouragingly and thanked her quietly. Ever the gentleman, Dr McAllister stood up to shake her hand and show her to the door.

"You'll be hearing from us," he told her gravely before gently closing the door.

Amy stood outside and waited for her breathing to return to normal. She hadn't realised quite how keyed up she was until it was all over.

I've done my best, she whispered in her mind, half to herself and half to Peter – now it's up to fate.

43

Seefin

Later that day, Hazel called to the unit to see how Deirdre and Marcus were coping with their first independent run as parents.

"How did you fare with Mr McNeill this morning?" They'd all been anxious to hear what the brain-scan result would be, hoping that Alex would be able to live as normal a life as possible.

Having discussed it throughout the morning, Deirdre and Marcus had taken on board the consultant's advice about treating him like a normal child.

"Much as we expected really," said Deirdre. "The original bleeding has reabsorbed but there's scarring left. He feels that Alex is doing well so far but can't guarantee that he won't have problems down the line." Deirdre recounted the rest of the discussion with as much optimism as possible, aware that their family and friends would take their cues from them.

"They have a service called Grow for monitoring babies who are born prematurely," Marcus added, "with things like physio and speech therapy laid on to catch any problems as soon as they arise. The liaison nurse will be in touch with us when we get home and Alex will have to go in for an assessment."

"That sounds good. Did you think any more about work, Dee? I was thinking that I'd be able to mind him one day a week if you wanted to go part-time." Hazel was looking at them hopefully, having already planned her workload to include a day in Deirdre and Marcus's house. She'd be well able to do a bit of work on the laptop in between chasing after her nephew.

"Would you really do that?" Deirdre was incredulous, knowing how much time her sister invested in her business.

"Of course I would. I know I said I was going to expand a bit but I haven't done anything about it yet. I was thinking it could wait another six months or so until the house is finished. In the meantime I'd be able to give you a hand."

"After talking to Mr McNeill we've decided that I'll take a year's leave of absence and see how we get on, but," she added quickly, seeing the disappointment on her sister's face, "I'll still need all the help I can get. The nurses on the ward have told us that Alex might have to go to Grow once a week at the beginning and he'll have other appointments in between. So don't get any ideas about being made redundant."

"And thanks, Hazel," said Marcus. "It's great to know that you'll be there to help if I'm not able to get time off work at any stage. You've been great to us all along." Marcus never ceased to be amazed at the generous offers of help from Deirdre's family.

"No problem! Fair exchange for the lodgings over the next few months and all that," Hazel said, then laughed as Alex blew wind noisily into his nappy. "Though if you think I'm putting up with that kind of thing you have another think coming!"

Hazel left before the 5 p.m. feed, knowing that Deirdre and Marcus wanted to concentrate on getting Alex changed, fed and settled before the tea arrived. The day was flying by and so far they hadn't had to call for assistance. Deirdre was enjoying the feeling of being in charge of her son, thrilled that he had settled after his earlier feeds. They'd been told that he could be "demand fed" overnight if he took all his feeds on time during the day.

This was a first for Alex, meaning that he could be allowed to sleep until he woke for his feed, rather than being woken religiously every four hours. This in itself was progress, as up to this he'd had to have a set amount of feeds per day to help him gain weight.

"This is like being on a camping trip," Deirdre giggled, handing Marcus a cup of tea from the flask that Hazel had brought. "Look, we even have chocolate HobNobs."

Even though there was only the fold-down bed that served as a sofa during the day and a portable television pinned to the wall, the little room felt like a palace to them. Spending a full day together as a family and not having to go home leaving Alex behind was like a dream. Even the theme music of *The Late Late Show* imbued them with a sense of homeliness.

As the credits rolled on Pat Kenny, Deirdre couldn't believe her excitement at pulling her cotton pyjamas out of her holdall. "It's mad, isn't it, getting ready for bed with a Neonatal Unit in full swing down the corridor?"

"As long as I don't go sleep-walking and end up down in the main Reception with the confusion of it all."

Marcus too was giddy with the idea of having their baby to themselves at last. Added to that, he was terrified that they'd be in a deep sleep and wouldn't hear Alex crying for his feed. He had visions of the nurses running in after hearing him crying for ages and refusing them a "pass" on their parenting skills. He set the clock on his mobile phone for half two, just in case. Deirdre thought he was mad, unable to visualise either of them falling asleep in the first place.

"We have to, Dee," Marcus warned anxiously, "or else we'll be half-stupid if anything happens during the night." He was determined that the night would go off without a hitch but loosened up when Deirdre grabbed him playfully by his pyjama-bottoms and pulled him into the bed, demanding her marital rights.

"Jesus, Dee, the whole unit would hear us groaning and moaning. They'd probably call the guards and have Alex put into care." The alarm on his face was comical and Deirdre collapsed in laughter, with Marcus following suit once he was sure she wasn't actually serious.

Lying together on the narrow bed, their child safely beside them, they both remembered the night that Alex had been born, when they'd lain together on Deirdre's hospital bed, frightened and powerless. Nothing could ever be as bad as that again, Marcus thought as he gazed at Alex.

"Will I turn the light off?" Deirdre settled the blankets around Alex and marvelled at the fact that it felt as if he'd been around forever. Lying there in the dark with Marcus's arms around her, she felt as complete as she'd ever felt in her life and thanked God for all that she'd been blessed with.

* * *

Deirdre stirred immediately on hearing the first gurgle out of Alex. She pressed the light on her watch, the tiny glow lighting up the sides of the cot. Quarter past two. He hadn't done too badly considering he was used to being fed at 1 a.m. by the nurses. Although she was dying to jump out and get him ready for his feed, Deirdre was conscious of Amy telling her the previous evening to let him enjoy his own company when he woke rather than picking him up straight away. He'd cry when he was ready for his feed, otherwise he'd want to be up in their arms all the time and would have problems settling in his own cot.

Sure enough, Alex mumbled and grunted contentedly for ages much to Deirdre's amusement, especially as he was accompanied by Marcus's light snoring. Eventually, at a quarter to three, Alex gave a little whimper, followed immediately by a high-pitched yell. Marcus shot bolt upright in the bed as Deirdre swung her legs out, turning on the bedside light at the same time. She'd switched off the alarm on Marcus's mobile earlier and he was shocked at how long Alex had settled for.

"I can't believe he slept this long." Marcus was all action, getting the nappy and baby wipes out from the drawer in the side of the cot and plumping up the pillows so Deirdre could get comfortable for the feed.

Alex too was all action, his head swivelling from left to right as if he couldn't believe his luck to be having yet another breast feed instead of the usual one o'clock bottle of defrosted milk. After feeding solidly for thirty-five minutes, he was changed and back in his cot, his first night feed completed successfully.

"No need to set the clock for the next one. Hopefully he'll last until breakfast-time." They settled down to sleep again, content that things were going according to plan. The next thing they heard was the rattling of crockery as Sandra, the chirpiest of the household staff, arrived with their breakfast.

"Is it that time already?" Deirdre asked, glancing into the cot to see if Alex was alright. Despite the fact that they'd settled him in cosily after the last feed, his cot was in a state of disarray, the blankets kicked back to reveal his skinny legs and arms. Deirdre beamed in at him, delighted that he looked so content.

"Don't worry, love," Sandra consoled sympathetically as she placed the tray noisily on the bedside table, "his legs will be grand once he puts on another bit of weight. Wouldn't it be desperate if he turned out like that!" She cast an amused glance at Marcus's long gangly legs sticking out over the end of the bed, the duvet at half-mast around his thighs.

"What?" Marcus demanded defensively, waking up to find the two women laughing down at him.

"Nothin', love, just saying little Alex is the spit of you." With that Sandra clattered out of the room, leaving Marcus with the distinct feeling that he should have set his alarm after all.

"This is the business," Deirdre exclaimed, sipping her tea as Marcus had a cuddle with his son. "Will I feed him now and we can bath him at lunchtime?"

Although he'd never had a bath two days running before, they'd been advised to make the most of their trial run to be as prepared for home as possible.

"Good idea. He'd be starving otherwise. He did brilliant during the night, didn't he? I didn't think he'd sleep so well between feeds."

"And at least we know now that we can manage without a major disaster. Maybe we should go home after this feed and have a shower and change. We could come back for the rest of the day and we'd really be into the swing of things."

"Grand so. I'll tidy up here while you're feeding him. And I can go out to the girls and let them know how we got on."

Grateful at the fact that the unit staff had given them the opportunity to spend such quality time with Alex, and at just how successful it had been in establishing their sense of confidence, he reported all the details of the night enthusiastically to Amy who was just arriving for the morning shift, the dark circles under her eyes only barely concealed by her over-bright smile. Marcus felt his heart go out to her yet again as he remembered her smiling across the table at Peter on the one occasion that they'd been out together.

"We're going to head home for a shower," he told her, "but we'll be back for the next feed. We might as well keep going when we're on a roll."

* * *

Tom, Rose and Hazel were having breakfast in the kitchen when they arrived home. All asking questions together, they were dying to know how Alex had behaved during the night.

"Like an angel," Deirdre pronounced. "Hope he carries on like one when he lands in Pebble Cove."

"I suppose we'd better pick up some of the stuff from Babyfare?" Marcus looked at Deirdre to see if she was ready for such a step. Up to this they'd been terrified to bring home any of the nursery things that they'd ordered early in the pregnancy, afraid to tempt fate when Alex was so unstable.

"I suppose we can't hold off any longer," she said. "We'll have to be some way ready for Wednesday, and most of the stuff comes in flat-packs so it'll have to be made up. We should give the shop a call and let them know we'll be calling for it."

"How about if you give them a call, Marcus," said Tom, "and I could pick them up later and make a start. It'd give me something to do." He had been under his wife's feet all morning, the garden having been tended to within an inch of its life and the garage tidied incessantly. A new project would be just the thing to stop Rose shunting him from room to room.

"No bother, you can gladly take over that little chore." Marcus had absolutely no affinity for DIY and hardly possessed a screwdriver. "I can hold the hammer for you or something when we get home later," he said, picking up the phone to ring Babyfare, hardly believing that they'd have a changing unit installed before the night was out.

* * *

"Would you ever go out to the boot of my car, Hazel love, and see if there's a bigger screwdriver in it? These ones won't do." Tom was determined to have everything just right for when Alex came home and cursed himself for not having thought to bring his toolbox back with him the last time he went down home.

Rummaging around in the boot of the Avensis, Hazel spotted the fine thing from next door pulling into his driveway. Hoping he'd look around so that she could get a good look at him and maybe even get in a friendly wave, she was disgusted when he made straight for the door without a sideways glance.

"No sign of one, Dad," she reported, to her father's disgust.

"And all the hardware shops close at one o'clock on a Saturday. What kind of a country is this when you can't buy a screwdriver at half three on a Saturday? The sooner we catch up with the rest of the Europeans the better."

"Cool down, Dad. I'll run out to the neighbours and see if they've got one. You never know."

Mollified slightly, Tom continued to line up the offending pieces of the changing unit, hoping against hope that Hazel would return with some kind of an implement. If she didn't he'd be still looking at the bits in front of him until the hardware shops opened again on Monday. Hazel, meanwhile, whizzed upstairs to swipe a Juicy Tube across her lips in preparation for her first encounter with the wonderful Shay.

Marcus was always singing his praises. They'd all heard how kind the young accountant had been the morning after Alex was born, doing Marcus a huge breakfast and making himself late for work as a result. Even recently, Marcus had been telling them how interested he was in Alex's progress, at ease discussing the value of breastfeeding and other topics that most young fellas would run a mile from. He rose in Hazel's estimation enormously after this, considering that she only ever met men who were interested in fast cars and making money. She trusted her brother-in-law's judgement, having observed first-hand how calm and together he'd been since Alex had arrived so unexpectedly.

All psyched up for the first meeting with Shay, hair brushed and lipstick on, she was disappointed when the door wasn't answered at the first ring. She waited for a few minutes before pressing the bell again, imagining him in the shower or out the back. Intent on meeting him now that she had a concrete excuse, she rang the bell insistently for a third time, knowing that he was in and convinced that he simply couldn't hear her.

Just as she was about to give up, wondering if he'd left the house without her spotting him, the door swung open. Having eventually decided that he wasn't at home after all, Hazel's opening speech had deserted her.

Particularly when she was greeted with a distracted, "Yeah?"

"I'm Hazel," she managed to get out, "Deirdre's sister." She indicated the house next door. "I'm wondering would you have a medium-sized screwdriver that I could borrow?" Shay was still looking at her quizzically, so she went on to explain that Alex would be coming home in the next few days. "We're just making up his cot and stuff. Everything comes in flat-packs these days."

"No, I'm sorry, I don't have one I'm afraid." Aware that the elegant brunette looked disappointed, Shay apologised again for not being of any help before closing the door.

Hazel was indeed disappointed, having hoped to engage him in conversation. Usually she found it easy enough to deal with men, but she'd failed miserably this time, she berated herself. Tom too was disappointed and rather than ditch the project altogether, decided to try the Co-op store in town as a last resort seeing as in any case Rose wanted to stock up on vegetables from the farmers' market nearby.

44

Leadington

Shay for his part felt guilty once the girl was gone from the door. He knew he'd been downright unfriendly, especially considering all that the couple next door had been through in the past few months.

But the phone-call from Anthony had thrown him. He'd expected it to be his mother again, begging him to get in contact but instead he'd heard a deep, gravelly voice come out over the answering machine. Saying that it would be great if he would call his mother, just to put her mind at rest. And that he really would like to meet Shay sometime "when things settle down a bit".

Shay played the message over a few times to try and get a sense of what his mother's friend was like. He could still only think of him as a "friend", afraid to imagine anything else.

One part of him admitted that his mother was perfectly entitled to have whoever she wanted as a companion, or whatever it was that Anthony could be called. But he couldn't get away from the sense of hurt that his father was being put to one side. All the time that he'd been at home, it had been as if he was just getting to know his father, to know what he was like as a person. Nora had never talked about him like that before to Shay, so it was like discovering a new person, one that he'd begun to like. Then suddenly he'd found out about Anthony and was hit with all sorts of feelings.

He'd been through all this with Will Moore, the counsellor that he'd planned to abandon after a few sessions. But now that Ken was gone and he couldn't bear to look at his mother, Will was proving to be the only person he could talk to about the whole fiasco. Weeks on, the anger was burning itself out a bit but his pride wouldn't let Shay pick up the phone to his mother.

That would mean having to accept the possibility of Anthony being a fixture in his mother's life and hence his own, combined with the whole reality of actually meeting him. He knew he wasn't ready for all that just yet but the tone of Anthony's voice on the answering machine reminded Shay of the worry he was causing to his mother. She probably had visions of him not taking his medication and ending up the way he'd been after the funeral.

Funnily enough, despite the whole Anthony thing, Shay was feeling pretty strong. The idea of going back to work was beginning to seem less daunting since he'd been talking it out with Will. He'd even made a plan to phone his boss on Monday to discuss his return date. He also planned to say, very simply and briefly, that he'd be improving the standard of his work this time, with a short apology for his past behaviour. Hopefully, that would clear the air and allow him to prove his intentions with action after that.

To distract himself from the fact that he'd have to contact his mother sooner rather than later, Shay went out to the small garden shed that housed his lawnmower and the patio furniture and gas barbecue during the winter. Surely there must be some class of a screwdriver among the many gadgets that his mother bought him every Christmas. Eventually his glance alighted on a compact plastic case that housed a dizzying array of screwdrivers of all shapes and sizes. One of them would surely be appropriate for the job in hand.

Shay rang the doorbell over at Number 2, hoping that Deirdre's sister wasn't too put out over his brusqueness earlier. She opened the door looking a bit frazzled but smiled broadly when she saw the bright blue carry-case.

"Brilliant. I was just beginning to panic," she exclaimed. Catching his questioning expression, she went on to explain. "My dad needed one of those to finish the changing unit so he went off to the Co-op to see if they had one. I didn't realise that I'd need one for the cot too. Now there are bits and pieces all over the place."

The usually cool Hazel was now regretting her decision to unpack the components, thinking that she'd have it finished before her father or Marcus arrived home.

"Would it be any good if I gave you a hand? I'm not great at this sort of thing but it must be fairly straightforward."

Hazel didn't know her luck as she ushered him inside, registering him mentally as the first man of her acquaintance, apart from Marcus, who'd admitted to being useless at DIY.

Feeling a bit alarmed at the array of pine legs and spindles spread out on the floor, Shay was slightly heartened by the single-page instruction leaflet. After silently studying the leaflet for a few minutes he decided he'd read enough to make a start. Apart from a few problems with terminology and the omission of a few washers the cot took shape and was standing on all four legs in about half an hour.

"Not bad," he congratulated himself, thrilled that he hadn't made a show of himself in front of Hazel. Although he'd vowed to give dating a rest for a while until he got his life straightened out, he couldn't help noticing how attractive she was. He'd always fancied brunettes more than blondes, so had been immediately taken with the way the rich chestnut curls fell around her face as she knelt on the floor calling out the instructions to him. She was tall too, something else he liked about her.

"God, I can't wait to see Alex in this!" Hazel

enthused. "It'll be huge compared to the one he's in now but he's gone past the Moses basket stage so he'll have to get used to it."

"Should we carry it upstairs, do you think? Otherwise it'll be bunging up the sitting-room until Wednesday."

Pleased at his thoughtfulness, she lifted one end of the cot while Shay lifted the other and they attempted to manoeuvre it through the door. A few minutes later, having tried every conceivable angle, they realised that it wasn't going to happen and accepted that the cot would have to be dismantled and reassembled in the small nursery upstairs.

"Shay, it needn't be done this evening. Dad will give me a hand when he gets back. You've been here for ages as it is."

"This is the first thing I've ever had the pleasure of making and I'm damned if I'm leaving here until it's fully installed!"

Laughing at his determination, Hazel gave in, promising him tea and scones once the job was done.

By the time Rose and Tom arrived back, both the cot and the changing unit were in position and the master craftsmen were enjoying a few of Rose's scones at the kitchen table, the cardboard boxes stacked at the back door for recycling. Tom was impressed that his services were no longer required and went off to inspect the handiwork while Hazel made a fresh pot of tea.

"The cot looks great. Fair play to you for getting it up the stairs," Tom commended as he arrived back into the kitchen. "Had you any bother with it?"

Their eyes catching, Shay and Hazel grinned at each other, thinking of the contortions that they'd been through earlier.

"Not a bit," Hazel fibbed with a wink at Shay, refusing to give in to Tom's notion that DIY was best left to men.

"Well, it was marvellous of you to give a hand, Shay," said Rose. "You must come over some evening and see how Alex likes it."

Rose was smiling at Shay as if he was the most charming man she'd ever set eyes on. She already thought he was the bee's knees since Marcus had told her that he'd been away from his house for a while on account of nursing his mother back to health. She mentioned this now, forcing him to lie through his teeth.

He felt terrible afterwards and cursed his dopiness that day when he and Nora had met Marcus in the driveway and she'd had to cover up for his absence. It made him feel desperate that these people thought he was some kind of latter-day saint when he was nothing short of a dope-head who'd had a fair hand in the death of his friend. It made him feel a complete fraud to hear Tom say that Deirdre and Marcus were blessed to have good neighbours as he left the house. If only they knew.

He was going to have to talk to Will about this whole guilt thing at the next session. Even holding a door open for someone and hearing them say "Thanks" was making him cower with shame, so strong was the sense that he was only masquerading as a normal citizen. Meantime he was going to have to think about phoning his mother and putting things right. She'd be gone to evening Mass by now, he decided, relieved to be able to put it off until Sunday morning.

45

Seefin

Back over in Seefin, Hazel was replaying the evening over in her mind as Rose held forth on Shay's virtues. While wholeheartedly agreeing with her every word, she was deliberately vague when her mother wondered out loud if he was single or not. There was no way that she'd let them see how much she fancied him, knowing that Deirdre and Marcus would give her an awful slagging.

She knew she was picky about men but this time it was different. She had enjoyed Shay's company as they struggled over the baby things and was amazed at how bashful he was when her parents had expressed their thanks for his helping Deirdre and Marcus out now and again. It made a change from the cocky eejits that she so frequently met in nightclubs and pubs around the city. She liked his quiet manner and the blond streaks in his fair hair that definitely hadn't been achieved artificially.

She snapped out of her reverie when Deirdre and Marcus arrived home again, exhilarated by their successful parenting over the previous twenty-four hours.

"We've had orders from the girls in the Neonatal Unit to take you all out for a drink tonight to bribe you into helping once Alex arrives home," said Marcus, relieved that everything had gone so well, and more than ready for a few pints.

"Well, I was going to suggest that yourself and Tom go off to the pub and let the rest of us have a girls' night in," said Rose. "It'll be ages before I have these two to myself again." She was already feeling lonely about going back home after the activity of the past few months, particularly as both Deirdre and Hazel would be tied up with Alex for a while.

"Grand so," Tom agreed readily. "We'll bring ye home a few bags of chips if we're not too late!" He was already pulling on his coat, looking forward to a chat with Marcus over a few drinks.

"Charming," Rose called after him, starting to laugh herself when she saw her daughters giggling at the table.

46

Leadington

Shay liked to think that he would have eventually phoned his mother, even if Anthony hadn't arrived at his door that Sunday morning. He had been putting it off and off but had made a plan to call her after lunch on the Sunday, having felt ashamed of himself following Anthony's phone message the previous day.

When the doorbell had rung, he'd immediately assumed it was his mother and ran to answer it, guilty that he'd forced her to come over and sorry that he hadn't phoned her already. He'd been shocked to find a youngish man, dressed neatly in corduroys and a tweed jacket, standing there.

Shay had known straight away that it was Anthony and stood there spellbound, studying the man who'd so suddenly butted into his life. He was average looking, with thick grey hair that was almost silvery at the temples.

"Shay? I'm Anthony Lewis." Aware that Shay seemed to be unable to speak, he asked gently if he could come inside.

Suddenly coming to, Shay realised that this man must think of him as a complete child. He'd made up his mind the previous night to phone his mother and tell her that seeing someone was her own choice, and that it had just been a bit of a shock for him. He'd figured that he'd have to meet Anthony at some stage and had planned to discuss this with Nora, maybe suggesting that they go out for dinner or something.

He'd finally acknowledged that his mother had dedicated a large part of her life to her son's welfare and that she was perfectly entitled to enjoy the remainder of it in whatever way she wanted. Now Anthony was here, probably to make him see sense, not realising that Shay was already aware of how childish he'd been. Determined that his mother's friend wouldn't think he was a total eejit, Shay decided to be honest with him and see how he fared.

"I was just going to make coffee. Would you like a cup?" He indicated one of the tall barstools lined up by the breakfast bar and Anthony took a seat.

"Thanks, I'd love one. Especially if it's real coffee," he said, noticing that Shay was measuring out coffee beans.

"I only ever do it at the weekends. Not enough time during the week to be waiting for it to brew. Although I've had plenty of time on my hands lately," he added wryly, wanting to draw the conversation around to the reason for Anthony's visit.

"I'm sorry about that. Your mother told me how close you and your friend were. It can't have been easy."

"It's a bit better now," Shay admitted, "but I was in bits for ages. I'm sure Mam told you the state I was in."

He looked up at Anthony as he said this, wanting to know how close his mother and this man really were. He knew his mother was too loyal to talk to someone about the horrific time her son had been through unless she really trusted him.

"She was desperately worried about you. She had to talk to someone. I'm sorry you had to go through all that." Anthony spoke very gently and cautiously, Shay noticed, not at all forcefully or intrusively as he'd imagined he might.

"I'm an awful lot better now. I think I was still a bit borderline when I heard about you. It was a bit of a shock and I lost the head a bit. I was planning to phone Mam when she got home from Mass today." His eyes met Anthony's as he handed him the coffee, wondering if he believed him. Unable to read the expression on the older man's face, Shay went on, "It was your phone call yesterday that made me see how unfair I was being."

"I'm glad you changed your mind, Shay. Your mother's whole life revolves around you. I don't want to damage that or interfere."

"I know that. I think I just reacted badly. I'm sorry for being such an ass about it."

He hoped fervently that Anthony would accept his

apology. There was something about him that suggested that he was the type of man who would never in a million years treat someone the way that he, Shay, had treated his mother. Suddenly, the good opinion of the man sitting across from him at the breakfast bar was important to him.

"I hope it's OK now?" said Anthony. "I don't want to take over your father's place or anything. I'm not sure I'd be very good at it anyway." He smiled as he said this and Shay responded with a grin, happy that Anthony was so ready to move on from where they'd been a short while before.

Shay topped up their coffee cups and they talked a bit more, mainly about Anthony and how he'd known Shay's father in college. He'd spent most of his working life in New York and had retired early in order to settle in Cork. He'd met Nora when he decided to look up some people that he'd known years before and had been shocked to find that Frank had died so young.

"It must have been hard, growing up without him?"

"To be honest, I didn't really know the difference. Mam made sure that I had everything and she always organised for me to go to football and things with Ken's dad, so I hardly noticed that my dad was missing. I think I only realised it when I was staying with Mam after Ken died."

Somehow, knowing that Anthony was aware of how bad he'd been after his friend's death made it easier to talk to him. Apart from his mother and Dr Daly, nobody else knew how low he'd been. It actually gave him a feeling of freedom that he didn't have to hide it.

After an hour or so, Anthony left, thanking Shay for his understanding and wishing him luck with phoning his mother.

Shay stood at the door and watched him leave, waving as his car pulled away. Then he closed the door and picked up the phone.

47

Seefin

"You know you can phone us any time? Just because he's at home doesn't mean you can't phone us for advice if anything crops up." Kim was very much aware that leaving the unit was an enormous step for the parents of a premature baby. Even though they'd been doing most of the hands-on care in the weeks coming up to discharge, it was still daunting to leave the security that had been there from the beginning.

Marcus was struggling with the straps of the baby car-seat, despite having gone through it endlessly over the past few days. Eventually it was tightened to his satisfaction and he laughed at the head of Alex peering out from under a mountain of clothes. It would be his first expedition in the open air and they were terrified he'd get cold. Marcus straightened up and thanked Kim once again for all the hard work, support and kindness to all of them.

"And thank you both for the great gift!" she responded. "We'll be thinking of Alex when we're tucking in."

Deirdre and Marcus had deliberated for ages over what gift they would give the unit staff when Alex was leaving, knowing they could never thank them enough for all that they'd done. It was Hazel's idea to get a voucher for a restaurant in the city so that they could have a night out *en masse.*

Everyone in the unit had gathered to wish them well as they left, with Kim accompanying them as far as the car to ensure that they could manage the car seat. It was this kind of thoughtfulness that impressed them most, the little things that had always made them confident that Alex was getting the best of care.

With a final round of hugs and good luck wishes, they set off, unable to believe that they were heading for Pebble Cove as a family at last.

48

Number 1

"There's no way I'm going. Do you think I want to have all the secretaries giggling and speculating about my social life?"

"Linda, there's nobody speculating," Daniel said, exasperated with his daughter that she wouldn't let go of this thing with Charlie. If anything, it was *she* who was making a big deal out of it. "And you're part of Coltons now so you'll be expected at the Christmas night out."

What was really bothering Linda was the idea that Charlie might turn up with someone else on his arm. If she thought that he was going alone, she'd be able to brazen it out and give the impression that she didn't care. After all, nobody knew what had happened between them. But if Charlie arrived with a new girlfriend in tow, then the immediate assumption would be that he'd left her for someone else.

"I can go next year," she countered. "I'll be much more involved by then because The Sanctuary will be up and running. But I'm definitely not going this year."

As far as Linda was concerned, there was nothing as important as maintaining her dignity. So what that she'd bought the teal Versace dress before her break-up with Charlie with the Christmas party in mind. She'd had visions of the dipped hem showing off her long legs perfectly and the matching sandles that would make her almost as tall as him. It would have been a triumphant night for her, on the cusp of a career as a successful property developer, and beautiful and glamorous to boot.

Now however, Charlie had ruined it all and she certainly wasn't taking the chance of being humiliated in front of the entire Coltons staff to add to it.

"Suit yourself," Daniel sighed, resigned to the fact that his daughter was, in her own way, every bit as stubborn as himself.

49

Leadington

Shay lobbed the bag of golf clubs into the boot of the car and went back inside to pick up a warmer sweater. The air was chilly outside but he didn't want to wrap up too much or he'd be sweltering once they got going.

Christmas Day in Nora's house had been as ordinary and normal as any Christmas Day that he'd ever spent. When his mother had asked him about Christmas and how he'd feel about including Anthony, Shay told her honestly that he'd just presumed that they'd all be spending it together.

It was over dinner that they'd got talking about golf. Shay had finished his ten lessons and was coming on nicely according to the instructor. He'd put himself on the waiting list at the local club and hoped to get started in earnest in the New Year. Anthony had suggested tentatively that Shay come out for a round with him now and again until he joined properly. Shay had been strangely pleased to be asked and had settled immediately on St Stephen's Day, reminding Anthony that he was still a novice without even a handicap to his name.

So much had changed since the day he'd first unearthed his father's old clubs in the attic at home. It had only been a few months ago that he'd found out that Anthony existed at all and now here he was going for a round of golf with him. And if anyone had told him on St Stephen's Day last year that within the year Ken would be dead and buried, Shay would have laughed them off the stage.

Last St Stephen's Day he'd been in bed with a horrendous hangover after a party that had lasted until 6 a.m. He'd barely made it to his mother's house for lunch and even then he hadn't been able to eat more than a few forkfuls.

Shay slammed the door behind him now, glancing at his watch. He was leaving a bit early so that he could shoot a few balls in the Driving Range before Anthony arrived. He was just getting behind the wheel when Hazel pulled in next door. He waved and got out again as he hadn't seen her since Christmas Eve.

Deirdre had invited him in for mince pies and mulled wine and he'd been glad to accept. He'd planned to spend the night over at his mother's house but wasn't expected until later and had started to feel a bit down at the thought of not going out for his usual rip with Ken. He'd stayed for about an hour and had spent most of that chatting to Hazel.

Since the evening that they'd fixed up the cot and

changing unit for Alex, they'd become great friends. Hazel was strong-minded and independent with, it seemed to Shay, a great head for business. As well as running a busy salon, she was renovating the living quarters above it and was already looking about for a second premises for her next salon. She had amazing energy, dashing from work to minding Alex, prodding the builders about her new home in between.

The night that he'd been over at Deirdre and Marcus's house, he'd told Hazel a little about Ken's death and how it had affected him afterwards. She was so practical in her outlook that he didn't feel she was judging him when he spoke about how depressed he'd been. She seemed to think it was a fairly natural response and thought it was better to have dealt with his feelings from the outset rather than covering them up and imploding later. He'd been tempted to tell her about the real reason for Ken's death but had held back on account of his promise to the Roches that he wouldn't broadcast the fact that their son's death had been drug-related. It wasn't that he didn't trust her with the information. It was more that he felt that the least Ken's family deserved was their privacy.

In a weird sort of way, he'd wanted Hazel to know that he was far from perfect. Her family already thought he was Mr Nice Guy, which made him feel like a bit of a fraud. He knew that if their relationship was to go anywhere, she'd have to know everything about what had happened. He wasn't sure what Hazel thought of him beyond being a next-door neighbour and he certainly didn't want to ruin what could be a good friendship by getting the wrong end of the stick.

"Hi there, Shay!" she called now, unloading a colourful rucksack from the passenger seat of the car.

"Hi. Have you started in the gym already?" Shay knew that she'd been planning to join Bodywork and was impressed that she'd started working out already.

"No time like the present. The place was packed with people promising themselves that they'll be a size 8 for next Christmas. It'll probably be like a graveyard by the end of January."

Shay laughed, thinking appreciatively that Hazel had very little need for good intentions as far as her figure was concerned. She looked great in navy jogging pants and a white fitted top that clung to her breasts and small waist.

"So did Christmas Day go alright with Anthony and everything?" she asked, interested because he'd told her a little about his mother's new relationship on Christmas Eve.

"Great. Our Christmas Day is usually fairly quiet so it was actually good to have Anthony there. I even arranged a game of golf with him for today – that's where I'm off to now."

"More good intentions," Hazel laughed.

"How was your Christmas?" He knew that Hazel and her parents had planned to stay with Deirdre and Marcus to celebrate Alex's first Christmas in style.

"Mental. The place was full of toys with every one of them beeping and making noise. It was like an asylum by the time we had the dinner eaten. Alex was hyper from all the attention and wouldn't go to bed."

"He's doing great, isn't he? I saw him out with Deirdre the other day and I couldn't get over the size of him."

"It's amazing. He's almost grown more in the month that he's been home than he did for the whole four months in hospital. Marcus reckons that Deirdre is sitting down all day stuffing him."

"He's even got hair now," Shay commented.

"He would have had hair in hospital too if they hadn't kept shaving bits of his scalp to put IV lines in." Alex now had a sparse covering of the same chestnut hair that his mother and aunt did, although Hazel was disappointed that it seemed to be turning out poker-straight like Deirdre's.

"It's great that it's all turned out so well," Shay observed, knowing how worried they'd been about Alex's progress.

"It's brilliant," Hazel agreed. "Deirdre and Marcus were completely wired over his first Christmas and poor old Alex didn't know what day of the week it was. They had him out of bed the minute he woke to dress him up in his Santa outfit before we arrived. You should have seen him in the hat!"

"Sounds like a good day."

"The night was even better. As soon as Alex was in bed, Mum told Dee and Marcus to have a few drinks and she could get up if Alex needed a feed. You should have seen them," she giggled. "They were like two fourteen-year-olds. They haven't been out much since

Alex arrived so they were mental after three drinks. It was entertainment just being with them."

Her humour was infectious and Shay found himself visualising his inebriated neighbours in amusement. He was still smiling when he got back into the car and headed for the golf club, his good intentions to have a bit of practice before Anthony arrived gone by the wayside.

* * *

That night Shay lay in bed, images of the day reeling slowly through his mind. For the first time in ages he felt content. The afternoon with Anthony had gone really well. They'd played a full eighteen holes and even though Shay's game hadn't picked up until the back nine, he hadn't been at all intimidated by Anthony, who had a handicap of twelve. Shay had found him easy company as they strolled along between shots. They'd talked a lot about Shay's job and how he was getting on after his long absence, and Shay had been surprised at how knowledgeable the older man was about the kind of work he was involved in. Even though his mother had always been interested in his career, it was good to be able to talk to someone who understood the difficulties he encountered. The four hours had passed remarkably quickly, leaving Shay wondering why he'd been fretting over having to make conversation for the duration of the round.

Nora had had the dinner ready when they arrived back and they'd chatted easily until Shay left at seven.

He'd wanted to get home a bit early to get things sorted for work the following day. Since he'd started back, he'd made a determined effort to establish himself as a reliable member of the team and was surprised to find it was easier than he'd imagined.

All the while he'd been out sick, he'd been imagining that he'd have to work twice as hard as he had done in order to regain the good opinion of Joe Kiernan and Michael Murray. The thought of it had overwhelmed him, making him ever more reluctant to face going back. He'd talked about it exhaustively with his counsellor until it finally dawned on him that many of the factors that had previously dogged his ability to perform well at work were now a thing of the past.

Before Ken had died, Shay had arrived at work hung-over most Monday mornings. Fridays had generally been a write-off as well, considering that they had gone out drinking almost every Thursday night. Even mid-week they'd have gone out at the drop of a hat if the opportunity arose, so it was no wonder that his work had been suffering. Talking to Will Moore about his behaviour at work had brought it home to him how little of each day he'd actually spent in productive mode. He'd have thought nothing of spending a whole afternoon e-mailing Ken or phoning some girl that he'd met over the weekend. Looking back, he couldn't believe that he got away with it for so long.

Now that he was no longer drinking so heavily, he was amazed at how much work he could get through in a morning. And with very little effort, now that he had a clear head. He seemed to be able to get to bed at a reasonable hour these days, arriving at work on time as a result. In the past, he'd have spent most of the morning making cups of coffee to wake himself up, then headed to lunch early because he couldn't concentrate. Because he had a natural aptitude for numbers, he'd been able to bluff his way through the day with the minimum of exertion.

Since he'd been moved off the major accounts when he'd arrived at a meeting still drunk, his workload had been high in volume but low in complexity. Now that he was firing on all cylinders, he was flying through it, but was getting bored with the mundane nature of what he was doing. He certainly wasn't going to complain but hoped that Joe Kiernan would eventually realise that he'd settled down enough to be given a bit more responsibility. He knew it would take time for Joe to trust him again so he'd just have to wait it out.

In the meantime, he was going to take advantage of his non-demanding working environment to start weaning himself off his medication. Dr Daly had prescribed a slightly lower dose for him the last time he'd had his prescription renewed. He'd advised him to keep attending the counselling, warning him that some of the feelings that he'd had in the early days would start to come back a little but that he'd be able to deal with this by talking it out with Will. Shay was a bit apprehensive about experiencing the terrifying sense of fear and loss again but trusted his GP's opinion and was prepared for a slightly rocky patch until he was fully off the medication.

It saddened him sometimes when he saw things like coming off the tablets or managing well at work as an achievement. If they hadn't been so stupid, Ken would still be alive. There would have been no need for medication or redeeming himself at work if they'd just behaved like normal people and enjoyed themselves without going overboard. He'd talked about this to Will, about the feeling of heavy sadness that came over him at times. It seemed to be happening a lot less lately but even that in itself made him sad – the thought that he'd eventually stop feeling the terrible sense of loss and forget about Ken altogether.

Will had encouraged him to find something that would always remind him of his friend, something physical and solid that he could look at and hold. Ken's parents had given him a signet ring that they'd given their son on his twenty-first birthday but he couldn't bear to wear it. He kept it in a small silver snuffbox that he'd seen one day in a gift shop. Sometimes he took the ring out, hoping it would conjure up a picture of his friend but it never seemed to work the way he wanted it to. He knew it would take time before he eventually accepted that Ken was gone but right now he didn't even *want* to accept it. Time, it seemed, was going to make everything alright in the end.

* * *

"Anthony?"

Nora had gone out to put the kettle on before the news started and Shay knew he had to ask now or he wouldn't get the opportunity again. His heart was beating a little fast but he continued when Anthony looked up enquiringly from the *Sunday Times*.

"I was wondering about Mam's birthday. If you had anything planned?"

"Well, she said that you two normally go out for a meal so I didn't –"

"I was thinking about that," Shay interrupted nervously. "Maybe she'd like to go somewhere with you this time."

Now that he'd said it, he waited for Anthony's reaction. He'd been thinking about it for ages and had come to the conclusion that it made sense for his mother to want to spend her birthday with Anthony, but he knew he'd have to let her know first that he wasn't upset about it. He realised that Anthony was the main person in her life now, in the same way that he himself would have his own family some day.

"Thanks, Shay. It's really good of you to think of it. But I don't want to change anything, you know. Nora likes having time with you."

"What would you think if we all went? How would that be?"

Shay knew it would mean a lot to his mother to have him accept Anthony as part of their lives and he was determined to let her know how much he'd come to like him.

"I'd love it, if you're sure it's OK with you. I don't want you to feel that I have to be stuck in everything." He smiled slightly as he said this, causing Shay to break into a smile also.

"I think Mam would like it if we both went. Do you think the Granary would be alright? I could book it for eight and I could come over and pick the two of you up here."

"That'd be great, Shay. And thanks," Anthony said sincerely, adding with a grin, "No wonder she's mad about you."

"The lads in school used to say I was treated better than the Baby Jesus," Shay responded, laughing.

Nora arrived back in with the tea tray just then so no more was said about the birthday. Lately, Sunday lunch at Nora's house had become a bit of a routine, with Shay leaving after the *Nine O'Clock News*. He liked the regularity of it. It was sort of comforting, and he sensed that his mother and Anthony liked the fact that Shay was at last comfortable with Anthony's presence around the house.

Nora walked him to the door as she always did when it was time for him to leave. Just before he stepped out into the February chill, Shay said lightly that he'd book the Granary for eight o'clock the following Friday, adding that he'd pick them up at half seven. He kissed her quickly and dashed for the car, leaving her speechless on the doorstep. He knew she'd be delighted but didn't want to make a big deal of the fact that he'd included Anthony in the equation.

443

Shay often felt a bit guilty about how much his mother had missed out on in the months that he was ill and was glad that her relationship with Anthony had survived the strain. In the initial stages, she'd hardly left the house except to pick up groceries or collect Shay's prescriptions.

Whenever he tried to express how sorry he was about how he'd reacted on finding out about Anthony, Nora brushed it off saying that they were over all that now, so Shay knew he'd have to make it up to them by deed rather than word. Tonight had been another step in that direction. Yet if the truth be told, he knew that his acceptance of Anthony wasn't just due to him giving them his blessing to please his mother.

Shay had begun to look forward to seeing Anthony on Sundays. As well as spending Sunday afternoons in Nora's house, the two men had started to play the odd round of golf together on Sunday mornings and had started to get to know each other on a level that was separate to Anthony's relationship with Nora. Proving to be a natural on the course, Shay was only too glad to take advice from Anthony, who had a strangely non-directive way of telling him how to go about a shot or whether to use a wood instead of an iron. As a result, Shay's game had improved to the point where he'd signed up for a team that his company were entering in a charity golf classic on St Patrick's weekend. He'd admitted to Anthony on one occasion that although he was nervous about making a show of himself in front of the more experienced players, he felt that the inevitable social evening afterwards would be an ideal environment for the managing director and Joe Kiernan to see how he'd settled down.

"I agree with you. It's often the out-of-office activities that give the people you work with a real sense of the kind of person you are. It won't be about how well you play at all."

"I've no problem keeping my head down as far as the free drinks are concerned but I wasn't always so sensible," he'd disclosed ruefully.

Anthony had looked at him quizzically as they'd walked to the next tee box, encouraging him to elaborate.

"Before Ken died I wasn't exactly the most reliable at work. I got away with it for ages but I made a few blunders eventually and I was under surveillance a bit before I went out sick. I'm trying to make up for it now, but it'll be a while before they trust me again, I think." He watched Anthony now to see what his reaction to this would be.

He'd talked often with Will Moore about the sense of shame he felt at his former lifestyle and the fact that it had culminated eventually with Ken's death. He'd come to the conclusion that the only way he could regain any shred of self-respect was to come clean with the people whose opinion mattered to him. Anthony was now one of those people, and he already knew about the fact that there had been recreational drugs involved the night that Ken had died. Shay figured that he wouldn't be at all surprised at the way he'd carried on in the past.

"All you can do is to carry out your work as well as you can and behave well as a person. You can't start overworking to prove the point. They'll come around eventually, you know."

"That's what I'm hoping. I haven't told Mam about being in the bad books at work – I thought it'd only worry her. And I'm over the worst of it now so there's no point. But I feel I let her down when I think of her putting me through college and everything."

Anthony looked at him thoughtfully as he said this. "I know she worked hard to have everything right for you. But there can be a lot of pressure involved in trying to keep up with someone else's idea of what you should be like afterwards. Do you think that's why you went off the rails for a while?"

"I'm not blaming Mam, Anthony. I'm thirty years of age, for God's sake. It was time I calmed down a bit." Shay was adamant that Anthony shouldn't think he was trying to make excuses for his behaviour.

"I know you're not blaming her, Shay. I'm just saying that people expected a lot of you because of how hard your mother worked to give you a good education. You were expected to make something of yourself to show people that all her hard work was worth it. *Nora* wouldn't expect it but maybe other people would."

Shay thought about this and realised that there was indeed a grain of truth in what Anthony was saying. He'd been naturally bright at school and had grown up hearing that he was a credit to his mother. Teachers, relations who visited the odd time, his mother's friends, all agreed that Shay would surely be able for law or medicine when he finished his Leaving Cert. He'd excelled in school, mainly because subjects like Maths and Physics came easily to him, allowing him to concentrate fully on his weaker subjects like English and History. Shay couldn't bear to do badly in anything, often turning the bedside light back on again to go over something when he heard his mother's bedroom door closing. He needed to do equally well in all his subjects, knowing that he'd be letting everyone down if he didn't.

"Jesus, Anthony, you're as good as Will Moore," he exclaimed. "I never thought of it like that. It's good to be able to see why I was trying to break out, even though it's no excuse. I suppose I'll just have to move on from it."

"You don't have to get too sensible though. That's as bad as it is good."

Anthony had smiled as he said this, letting Shay know that he accepted that his past was just that and that there was nothing to be gained by wearing a hair shirt forever. Shay had felt an enormous sense of relief that Anthony hadn't been at all judgemental about the way he'd lived his life and had seemed to even understand it in some way.

After that, they became tentative friends, although it would be a long time before either could admit how much that meant to them.

50

Evergreen

"Amy, I'm really sorry but I'm not sure that I'll be able to come in tonight," Carol Hayes snuffled when she'd finally struggled through the night report on the babies in the ICU. Her eyes were red-rimmed and her nose swollen from blowing it for the last twelve hours.

Oh God, this is all I need, Amy thought, starting to panic. Where am I going to get a replacement for Carol before 8 p.m.?

"That's no problem, Carol, just get home as quickly as you can and dose yourself with Lemsip. You'll need a night off to get over your cold," Amy told her, smoothly reassuring her that her shift would be covered.

As soon as the rest of the night staff had dispersed and she'd allocated the day staff to their various tasks, Amy made a beeline for her new office to look at the staff roster. Surely there would be someone willing to

449

do an extra shift.

Five phone calls later, she was beginning to feel exasperated. Why did nobody answer their phone these days? She'd left a series of messages and hoped that she'd get a positive reply from one of her own staff rather than having to phone one of the private nursing agencies looking for someone with neonatal experience.

Noreen stuck her head around the door and grinned supportively.

"Were you able to get anyone?"

"Not yet but there's always the agency."

"Paddy from the pharmacy is after phoning – he's wondering what time you'll have the order form down to him. He says to remind you that they have to fax them in by half ten."

"Thanks Noreen, I'll give him a ring." She hadn't even looked at the order form with all the phone calls about Carol's replacement for the coming night. Swiftly she rifled through the folder that Rhona had thoughtfully left her and found the ten-page pharmacy stock list.

She'd barely reached the drug press, hoping to get started on the order straight away, when the door opened to admit Dr McAllister, the Director of Neonatology, who'd interviewed her for her new job.

"I won't keep you," he greeted her. "I know you're busy but I wanted to offer my congratulations on your first day."

Amy thanked him and made polite conversation for a few minutes, all the while thinking of the time ticking away.

When he eventually left, she got straight down to the pharmacy order and worked diligently for about two minutes until the phone rang to say that there was a twin delivery expected in the next half-hour, at thirty-two weeks gestation.

She abandoned the pharmacy list again, this time to ensure that a pair of open incubators would be available to receive the premature wins.

"If we double up Darren Kelly with Dora Conway we'll be able to put the Carter twins into Cubicle 4," she instructed, assessing the situation confidently. "That'll leave space for two incubators for the new ones. I'll phone and ask them to bring the incubators up."

"Grand, Amy, I'll move the Carters in the meantime."

"Great, Noreen. Will you take the new babies and I'll ask Barbara to take over the Carters?"

"No bother," Noreen smiled. "Good start!"

Amy grinned back at her and immediately phoned the equipment room, aware that they would need time to transport the two incubators upstairs to the unit.

Eventually, with a few more interruptions, she finished the pharmacy order and handed it to Kira, the ward attendant.

"Make sure you give it directly to Paddy," she advised, worried that it might go astray if Kira dropped it on the countertop in the pharmacy.

Next up was the duty rota which needed to be made out for the following week and sent down to the salaries department before the end of the day. Amy pulled out Rhona's folder again, grateful that her predecessor had been kind enough to make notes on what needed to be done in an immediate sense.

She'd just opened the duty roster database when the phone rang.

"Hi, Amy, it's Nuala here. I got your call about filling in tonight but I'm afraid I have something on. Sorry."

"No problem, Nuala. Thanks for getting back to me."

One down, four to go. Hopefully someone would come up trumps.

Almost immediately, the phone rang again.

"Hello, Amy. Christina Kelly here."

It was Christina now, Amy thought in amusement, having always called Matron "Mrs Kelly". Amy greeted her and listened while she outlined a few things that she'd need later in the day.

"And if it's convenient, you can call down to my office before lunch to go through your employment details."

The rest of the day had flown by in a buzz of phone calls, enquiries and the arrival of not only the twins but also of two term babies who'd had traumatic deliveries. Kim finally rang to say that she got Amy's message and that she'd be delighted to cover for Carol that night.

Her head whirling with relief that she didn't have to employ an expensive agency nurse on her first day as unit manager, Amy gratefully checked that everything was running smoothly before leaving the unit at six.

Thankfully, the hospital manager had given in to the idea of her working 8 a.m. to 6 p.m. in order to continue with her course in UCC.

When she'd donned the navy uniform for the first time that morning, her heart had started to beat furiously, making her wonder momentarily if she was up to the challenge at all. She almost pulled the neatly ironed white tunic and trousers out of the hot-press, even though she knew it was definitely too late to change her mind.

Thankfully, the first day had gone reasonably smoothly. Her mind was still buzzing from all the new information that she'd processed throughout the day. Besides what was going on in the unit itself, she discovered all the managerial stuff that needed to be done on a daily or weekly basis, like ordering stocks and medications, sorting out duty rotas and ensuring that the mix of senior and junior staff was at a safe level at all times.

The other thing she hadn't thought about was having to deal with situations under the glare of the unit spotlight. Some of her colleagues had also applied for the job, one of them older and more experienced than herself, so Amy had naturally felt that she was somewhat under surveillance to see how she'd perform. Thankfully, her closest friends hadn't been in the running for the job: Sheila, being a job-sharer, hadn't been eligible, Kim was too recently qualified and Noreen had enough on her plate with three young children.

Amy thought about all of this on the drive home to Pebble Cove, letting her mind unwind as much as she could. She felt comforted as always when she reached Evergreen, closing the front door gratefully and leaning her back against it, sighing deeply. Her first day as unit manager had passed with only a little aggravation but no significant disaster.

Deciding that a long soak was the only remedy to release the tension that had built up over the day, she ran the bath and dosed it with a luxurious bath essence that someone had given her on her last birthday. Abandoning her clothes on the bedroom floor, she tied her hair up and sank into the mass of bubbles that were by now frothing over the edge of the bath. Amy knew that she was always heavy-handed and probably quite wasteful with her collection of bath products. But there was nothing she loved more than to settle in for an hour-long soak, equipped with a book and sometimes even the cordless phone. She rarely had to actually buy any bath oils or lotions herself – she was so renowned among her friends and family that they automatically bought her "smellies" every birthday and Christmas.

Firmly putting work out of her mind for the moment, she stretched her legs and leaned back into the towelling-covered inflatable pillow that her sister Laura had given her on their last holiday. She smiled as she heard the front door opening and the sound of heavy footsteps bounding up the stairs.

"Well, how'd it go? Have you been fired yet?"

Amy heard her brother rummaging around in the

spare room as he yelled into the bathroom at her. Older than her by almost two years, Robert was the most ebullient person she knew. Although he lived in Dublin, he was working in Cork for a few weeks and had elected to stay in Pebble Cove with Amy rather than a hotel in the city.

Even though they'd always been close, she hadn't felt able to talk about Peter to her brother. It wasn't that he wouldn't have been sympathetic. But somehow she felt that it would be hard for him to understand how she felt when he had never laid eyes on Peter and had only ever heard of him from the twins who'd ribbed Amy incessantly about "settling down" since they'd met him at her house the night before their holiday.

"Not so far!" Amy called back now, thinking to herself that just having her brother around the house was comforting in itself. "I'll be out in a minute. Put the kettle on and I'll tell you about it."

Robert was always fascinated by the details of her work and had been almost disappointed when she'd told him she was applying for a managerial post. A teacher in Dublin's inner city, he was enthusiastic about almost everything in life, particularly where there was action involved.

She could hear him clattering around in the kitchen and was amazed that he hadn't smashed anything yet, despite being in residence for five days. She hopped out of the bath and rubbed in the creamy body lotion that matched the bath essence, a sharp memory of Peter assailing her with the familiar scent.

Over the noise of her brother ransacking the kitchen she heard the doorbell ring and hoped that Robert would answer it. Amy knew she was too nice for her own good and was useless at getting rid of the phone salesmen that seemed to target housing developments around tea-time.

On the second ring, Robert *did* answer the door but whoever it was got fairly short shrift as it closed almost immediately after a brief exchange. Wrapping herself in a towelling dressing-gown, Amy headed down to see what her brother had trumped up for their dinner.

"A fellow came to the door to enquire how you got on with the job. I think he was one of the neighbours. I told him you'd only be a few minutes but he said he'd see you again."

"Must have been Marcus from across the way. He knew Rhona was taking leave and that I'd applied for the post. What are we having?"

Amy told Robert a bit about Marcus and the rest of the neighbours over an eclectic collection of food that he'd purchased in the English Market on the way home.

Her brother had only been in Pebble Cove once before, for the housewarming, and hadn't yet had a chance to explore the area. He'd taken a year out to travel around Australia, making it back just in time for her party. Amy was glad of the time to catch up with him and was enjoying having him around the house. She had loads of jobs lined up for the weekend, like hanging pictures and curtain rails as well as getting his help to do some of the heavy digging in her garden. She was planning to visit the garden centre after work on Friday to purchase some ivy plants that would soften the bare fencing, and some low hedging to go between her house and Shay Deegan's at the front.

"What are you doing tonight, by the way," he asked through a mouthful of seafood risotto.

"Nothing. Apart from lying down with a glass of wine to get over the stress of my first day."

"I told some of the lads from college that I'd meet them in town. Will you come? It won't be a late night or anything."

"No, thanks! I know what your early nights are like. Anyway, I'm wrecked so I'd be no company."

"Well, what about Friday night then? We'll go somewhere for a few drinks and a chat, to celebrate the end of your first week in the new job. If you survive it, that is!"

"OK then, but it's not as if you need an excuse. You'd celebrate the opening of an envelope if there was nothing else going on," she laughed, aware that she'd be more than ready for a few drinks at the weekend if indeed she did survive her first week as unit manager.

Later that evening, she lit the fire and settled herself on the couch with her book.

After her stressful day at work she needed something to chill her out so she'd plucked up Maeve Binchy's latest and curled her feet under her. Just as she was getting absorbed in the story the doorbell rang. Figuring that it was yet another evening salesman she hopped up to answer it before the next insistent ring came.

She was delighted to see Sheila on the doorstep. "Oh, hi, Sheila! Come on in!"

Amy and Sheila had become closer since Peter's death and, even though they were of a different generation, Amy felt that Sheila was the only person who truly understood what she was going through. In her heart, Amy knew that she had loved Peter and Sheila had seemed to accept this from the outset without it having to be said out loud. She also seemed to understand Amy's reluctance to show any outward signs of how deeply she felt Peter's loss, feeling that she didn't feel "entitled" to the same sympathy that would have been warranted if she were a wife or fiancée.

"Thanks, Amy. How're things with you? Any major drama?"

Sheila had been off-duty earlier in the day and was dying to hear how Amy had fared.

"Nothing startling," Amy told her, smiling wryly as she ushered her into the living room. "The day flew and my head is still buzzing. Hence the wine. Will you have a glass?" She'd opened a bottle of red earlier so Sheila was just in time to share it.

"I'd love a glass. I'm on the scrounge for your services, actually," Sheila ventured as Amy collected a second glass from the kitchen and poured her a generous measure.

"Oh? Tell me," Amy demanded with interest, sipping her wine contentedly.

"How would you like to be a guinea-pig and get free reflexology sessions at the same time?"

"Sounds good. Tell me more."

Over the years, Sheila had become interested in complementary health therapies and was qualified in aromatherapy and massage. Since she'd started job-sharing, she'd used her free time to take on clients at home and had built a steady practice. Her long-term plan was to retire early from the Neonatal Unit and go into practice full-time.

"For the last year or so I've been thinking about taking up another therapy, so for my birthday Grace and Rachel packed me off to a Mind, Body, Spirit weekend in Wicklow. I'd been looking into reflexology for a while so I had a few sessions and spoke to some of the practitioners before I made up my mind."

"That's pressure points on the feet, isn't it?"

Amy was always amazed at Sheila's attitude to life, having heard from many colleagues how hard she'd worked in the years after her husband's death. Now here she was at fifty, still full of dynamic energy, planning a career change with the same enthusiasm with which she approached almost everything in her life.

Sheila now explained the details of the therapy to Amy, who listened in fascination.

"The course consists of five weekends spread over a year, with projects and essays to cover in between. I've just done my third weekend and they've set us a series of case studies to do. So I'll need to pick five people and do ten sessions on each of them."

"Fifty sessions! You'll be wrecked at the end of it. It

sounds pretty intensive." Amy was impressed.

"It is but I'm loving it. A lot of the people on the course practice other therapies as well, like massage or Reiki, so I'm learning loads about other therapies as well."

"So where do I come in?"

"How would you feel about being one of my case studies? I know ten sessions sounds like a lot but it'll be over the next three months. You might even benefit from it if I'm any good."

"Free reflexology sessions – I'd be thrilled. One of Dad's friends has a bad back and he gets a treatment every couple of weeks. He's always raving about it."

"Brilliant. We can start any time you want. We can pick one night a week or something. I'll leave it up to you."

"Well, how about Tuesdays? We could start tomorrow night if you like. How does it work?"

Sheila explained about the origins of the therapy and its modern form, delighted to display her recently acquired knowledge. As well as Amy, she planned to approach Kim and Noreen from work as they both lived near the hospital so she could call to them on her way home in the evenings. As well as her three work-mates, she'd practise on her daughters at the weekend.

Before they knew it, it was ten o'clock. Amy could hardly believe that they hadn't spent the evening talking about Peter and was strangely glad of the diversion. The reflexology sessions would be something to look forward to now that she had every evening free, evenings that would have included Peter if some horrendous force hadn't decided that he was better off somewhere else.

"God, I'd better let you get to bed. It's all hours. You'll be wrecked before you start your sessions at all," Sheila laughed as Amy showed her out. Promising to return at eight on the dot the following evening, she reversed out of Amy's driveway to make the short journey back to the city.

51

Leadington

Shay closed his eyes and breathed in the scent of the essential oil wafting from the burner in the corner of Will's room. It was a month since they'd talked and he was looking forward to filling him in on the latest news about work. It mightn't seem like a big deal to anyone else, but for Shay it was like the start of yet another new chapter in his life. Since the time that he'd turned up unprepared, unshaven and hung-over for a meeting with Daniel Colton, he'd been strictly office-bound, with almost no contact with the clients. He shuddered now to think of Joe Kiernan describing him as a "liability", but was proud that his months of hard work had paid off and that he'd finally regained some of the trust that had been lost between them.

"That's a huge achievement on your part, Shay," Will congratulated him when he heard about the recent turn of events.

Although he'd been allowed some involvement in the Coltons account of late, Shay felt that he'd never again be permitted to encounter Daniel Colton in person and had been stunned when Joe had asked him to be present at the next scheduled meeting. He'd gone on to explain that Daniel was out of the country and that his daughter, Linda, would be attending with some of the directors instead. Joe said he felt it would be a good opportunity for Shay to become re-involved and allocated a certain portion of the portfolio for Shay to work on in the interim. Shay had been determined to be word perfect on the day and had spent the remainder of the week working on it, even taking it home with him in order that it wouldn't interfere with his other work.

He'd been intent on proving himself to Joe as much as to the Coltons delegation and had been surprised to find that Linda Colton appeared to be pretty new to the financial workings of her father's company, necessitating detailed explanations on a few matters. This had given Shay an opportunity to display his knowledge of the account to his boss, who'd quietly acknowledged Shay's contribution on the way back to the office.

It had been an enormous milestone for Shay, giving him a sense that things were finally falling into place. He said as much to Will, who agreed with him and said that he'd been thinking the same thing himself.

"I know you only come once a month at this stage but how would you feel about stopping off altogether? You've reached a sort of plateau now so it might be good to assimilate things on your own steam."

"I think it'd be good for me to be more independent, to be honest. Coming off the medication was a big step but I think I'm fine with that now. And after last week, I feel that I'm finally getting places at work. I know it'll be a while before I have full rein again but at least I'm getting there."

"And what about Anthony?"

Will had been very much aware of how difficult it had been for Shay to accept that there was a person of importance in his mother's life, although things seemed to be getting better each time a counselling session came around.

"You know, it's weird but I can't imagine life without him now. He's sort of fitted in so well that I think he was always there. I actually enjoy him being there now."

Shay couldn't believe he was saying this but a few weeks previously he'd arrived over on the Sunday to find his mother alone in the house. Anthony had had to go up the country the previous evening to visit an elderly aunt who was dying. Shay couldn't believe how disappointed he'd been, having planned to talk to him about a life assurance plan that was being offered through work. He told this story to Will now as a means of illustrating how far he'd come.

"It's not just that I accept him being there, I actually like him being there, for me as well as for Mam."

"You've overcome a lot in less than a year, Shay. How are you feeling about yourself now compared to before Ken died?"

"I was completely out of control, when I think of it now. I was very close to being totally burnt out from late nights and drinking. I think I might have collapsed eventually, even if Ken hadn't died. It sounds mad but I'm glad something happened to get me back on track. I'm just sorry that it had to be Ken dying, that's all."

"Sometimes it takes something radical."

Shay smiled at this, knowing that Will was right. If Ken had been around, he would just have kept going on as he was, maybe losing his job in the process. For a long time he couldn't accept that it had taken the death of his friend to make him alter what had become a dangerous lifestyle but he'd eventually been able to come to terms with it, with Will's guidance.

"I think I'm ready to go solo now," he said in relation to the counsellor's earlier question.

Will agreed that Shay was indeed well enough to cope with the business of life without the need for ongoing therapy, but reminded him that he could always return if he had any difficulties.

Shay walked out into the sunshine that day like a new man, finally feeling that he was able to face the world and whatever life brought to him.

52

Evergreen

The remainder of the week at work passed without incident, much to Amy's relief. It was enough to have to adapt to an entirely different role, without the added stress of things going wrong. By Friday, the feeling that she was some sort of impostor had left her and she felt at ease directing the rest of the staff in their various roles. It was strange to allocate the neonatal staff to a particular group of infants every morning without taking care of any babies herself, but she knew it was what she'd signed up for. There was a huge amount of work to be done besides the actual care of the infants, something she hadn't fully appreciated before she applied for the job.

Leaving at lunchtime on a Friday was a great bonus. She'd be able to nip into the garden centre on the way home to pick up her plants so that they'd be ready to start on the garden first thing in the morning. Robert had promised to pick up a take-away on his way home, having made it a rule years ago never to cook on Friday evenings. Amy agreed wholeheartedly.

They were going out for a drink with his friend later in the evening so she'd have time to beautify herself. Although she'd never met him, Robert had mentioned that Jason was single and had hinted that he might just be Amy's type. Thinking that if he was anything like her brother he'd be a bit too "hyper" for her taste, she decided she'd make an effort nonetheless. Her brother might be more tuned in than she gave him credit for and she certainly didn't want to turn up looking like The Wreck of the Hesperus.

By half-nine they were struggling through the crowd in The Loft, one of the most popular bars in the city. Robert was glancing around for Jason, his six-foot-two frame towering over many of the heads around him. They'd already picked up a round of drinks at the bar and Amy could feel the Bacardi and coke sloshing over her wrist as yet another inebriated punter bumped into her. She prayed that this Jason had arrived earlier and secured a few seats, as she didn't fancy heaving around all night in this crowd.

Finally she saw Robert waving and he turned to jerk his head towards an alcove that housed one small table. At least we have seats, she thought with some relief, spotting two stools shoved under the table. She presumed the redhead waving them over was Jason as she followed Robert towards the table, but ground to a halt in shock when the person with him stood up to greet them. She hadn't expected to see Charlie here.

"Hi, Amy," he said gruffly, apparently flustered at her sudden appearance. "I didn't know you knew Jason."

"I'm just tagging along," Amy told him, smiling. "I haven't seen you around in ages. How are you?"

"Grand. Here, sit on this before someone else does," he grinned as he pulled one of the stools out from under the table.

Amy thanked him before being commandeered by her brother who was dying to introduce her to Jason. He seemed like a nice guy but Amy was too taken up by seeing Charlie there to concentrate on what her brother's friend was saying.

Not only was Charlie a fine thing, he was a nice guy as well. He was chatting to her brother now which Amy thought was really strange. How could they possibly know each other?

Jason, meantime, was chatting away about Robert's madder escapades from their college days and Amy knew she'd have to tune in or she'd look like a right snotty madam. It wasn't that she didn't want to talk to her brother's friend – it was just that she wasn't concentrating very well generally. With an effort, she focused in on Jason, listening intently to a hilarious tale that ended with Robert waking up in a shed full of goats in Mykonos. It was genuinely funny and one that Amy hadn't heard before. She was laughing when Robert tapped her on the shoulder and indicated that he was heading to the bar again. Jason excused himself to help Robert with the drinks and she found herself next to Charlie.

He couldn't believe the effect she had on him. She looked fantastic in a black top with thin straps that showed off smooth shoulders that still had a hint of summer colour. He'd been watching her as she chatted with Jason earlier and thought that she always seemed to be smiling and vibrant, although she looked somehow more delicate than he remembered.

He was still a bit mortified at having called to her house earlier in the week. He'd been going to ask if she'd like to go out sometime but had got an awful hop when she hadn't opened the door herself. He'd felt like kicking himself for not realising that someone like her would almost definitely be in a relationship and had had to cover up by saying that he'd been passing and was wondering how she'd got on at her interview. He knew it was lame but it was the best he'd been able to come up with at the time. He knew he'd have to mention it sooner or later.

She leaned towards him now to say something and he could get the scent of her perfume, the same one that she'd been wearing the evening he'd met her in the video shop.

"So how do you know my brother, then?" Amy was interested to know where the connection was.

"Your brother?" Charlie looked as if he didn't know who she was on about.

"Robert," she explained, indicating the general area of the bar.

He looked completely at sea now and mumbled something about thinking Robert was her partner when he called to the house.

"When did you call? He never said." Surely Robert would have remembered to tell her if somebody called when she was out?

"Monday evening. I was passing and I wondered how you got on with the interview. You were in the shower, I think."

It dawned on her then that she'd just presumed it was Marcus who had called. Now that she knew it had been Charlie, she was disappointed that she'd missed him.

"Well, thanks for dropping in. I got on well as it happened. I actually started last Monday."

"Brilliant. How is it going so far? The first few days must have been daunting."

They talked for ages about the job before moving on to other things that they had in common.

Charlie was relieved that she didn't appear to have a live-in lover but still couldn't determine whether she was available or not. He wanted to ask her out but it occurred to him that she probably thought he was still seeing Linda. It wasn't something that you could just slip into the conversation, he thought, so he'd just have to bide his time a little.

He was glad he'd agreed to go out with the lads tonight. Jason had phoned him earlier and persuaded him that it'd be great *craic*. They'd been to school together in Gilcrenan and tried to hook up for a drink as often as they could. Since Charlie had broken up with Linda, Jason rang him most weekends to "get him out of himself". This was his friend's way of telling him to start getting out and about with the lads a bit more, especially now that he was free to engage in something as common as a drink on a Friday night.

"Well, Chas, you look happy enough." Amy had left the table a few moments earlier and Jason was over like a flash to see what the story was. "I told you to start getting out more. What's the story with the lovely Amy?"

"No story," Charlie said obstinately, smiling at Jason's incredulous face. "OK, she's gorgeous," he gave in finally, as his friend continued to eyeball him.

"So, are you thinking of asking her out?" Jason had never warmed to Linda, although he wouldn't admit as much to Charlie, who was fiercely loyal and undoubtedly wouldn't hear a word against his ex.

"Jesus, it's like the Spanish Inquisition around here. She could be going out with someone. I don't know."

Jason had never seen his friend so bothered. He was normally very self-contained, even when they'd been younger. He'd noticed earlier the way that Charlie and Amy looked so comfortable talking to each other but felt he should say something about her recent loss in case Charlie upset her by jumping in too quickly.

"Well, she is actually single, but I'm not sure that she'd be ready for dating or anything just yet. Robert was telling me earlier in the week that her boyfriend died a couple of months ago. He got a brain haemorrhage and died later the same day."

Charlie was shocked. He'd noticed that there was something different about her since the last time they'd met. She was more vulnerable looking, he thought, but still as friendly and open as she'd been previously. She was obviously good at putting on a brave face. Charlie thanked his lucky stars that she hadn't actually answered the door when he'd called on Monday – that he hadn't had the opportunity to barge in and ask her out. He felt weak even at the thought of it.

Amy was approaching the table again with a tray of drinks and Charlie stood up to help her. Their hands touched for a moment as he took the tray off her and when their eyes met, he felt the same as he had on the other occasions that he'd met her, as if he was going to lose the run of himself and actually put his arms around her. Confused, he grabbed a few of the drinks off the tray and started to pass them around, glad of the distraction.

Once the drinks were passed around, Amy gratefully commandeered the chair next to Charlie again, relieved that the buoyant Jason was engaged in conversation with her brother. At any other time, she would have enjoyed his lively banter but tonight she found Charlie's gentle, more serious manner a welcome change.

"Amy," he began softly once she'd settled herself beside him, "I'm really sorry that I didn't know earlier about your boyfriend. Jason only said something now. I didn't realise."

Amy looked away, embarrassed in case she'd start to cry in front of him. She'd been pretty much distracted from thinking about Peter all evening so it came as something of a shock for her to have Charlie bring it up, and so suddenly.

"Thanks," she said eventually, not knowing what else to say. She looked up then and saw the expression of distress on Charlie's face and realised how ungracious she'd sounded. Not wanting to make him feel as if he'd upset her by mentioning Peter, she smiled ruefully. "This is Robert's idea of getting me out and about again."

They both smiled then, the noise and rabble around them, each thinking that The Loft was surely the most unlikely place in Cork than anyone could be brought to get over a bereavement.

"That's probably hard," said Charlie, "the going-out-again bit. And not being part of a couple."

"It is, in a way. Even though I didn't know Peter for very long." Amy was anxious that Charlie didn't have the impression that she'd been practically engaged or something.

"That's not what matters. You can be with someone for years and never really know them. It's more about the depth of what you feel." Charlie thought about Linda as he said this, and the strange draw that he felt towards Amy even though he barely knew her.

Amy looked at him almost as if she'd never seen him before, startled that he seemed to have the same attitude as Sheila to the fact that she and Peter weren't formally a couple. Sometimes she felt a bit invisible. Peter's family probably didn't even know she existed and she felt like a fraud accepting any kind of sympathy, even from the gang at work.

Suddenly they were talking easily again, and for once neither Robert nor Jason felt the need to butt in and entertain them. Amy was surprised to hear that Charlie had recently split up with the blonde in the house opposite her, having been too distracted to notice his absence across the road. It intrigued her that, in direct contrast to how guilty she herself felt for being overly upset at losing Peter, Charlie felt an enormous sense of guilt for his own *lack* of distress after his break-up with Linda.

"Don't get me wrong. It's not that I'm delighted about it. It's more that I'm shocked at the fact that we mustn't have been close enough to really miss each other. We still get on well but I keep thinking that I should have more regrets about it."

"Is it awkward at all, working together now?"

"Not at all, that's the strange thing. We got back onto an even keel at work almost straight away. Linda's great at what she does, so it's easy to admire how professional she is."

In a way, Amy was sorry that she wouldn't see much of him around the Cove any more. He was easy to talk to and had much the same outlook on life as she had.

A few minutes later Jason was on his feet suggesting that they leave a bit early in order to grab the taxis that would be queuing outside before the crowds hit. Amy located her jacket and followed the others out of the pub. The night had flown by, even if Robert's subtle plan to distract her with Jason hadn't come to fruition. It had been good for her to get out, she realised now.

Amy leaned back in the darkness of the taxi and closed her eyes, glad that her brother had fallen asleep immediately. The lively atmosphere outside the pub, the jostling for cabs and the hurried goodbyes had suddenly reminded her of what Peter was missing out on. It was such a shame she thought sadly, the wastefulness of him not being in the world any more.

53

Number 1

"I don't care how much he's charging. Just get it sorted before the doors open in the morning!" Seething, Linda stalked away from a stunned Brona, turning momentarily to add, "And if he charges anything more than 10% over the average, strike him off our list of suppliers once the job is done and never use him again. I've had enough of these contractors taking advantage."

Glad that Brona was finally taking a bit of action, she hurtled down the corridor to check that there was at least an "out of order" sign on the shower cubicle in question. Generally speaking, Brona was managing well enough to get the leisure centre, Esprit, off the ground. But having a shower stall out of action for three hours before it was even noticed was beyond the beyond. Although her credentials were excellent and she had a good eye for what the clients wanted, Linda sometimes wondered if Brona was aggressive enough to manage an establishment as large and exclusive as Esprit.

As regards maintaining a solid clientele at Bodywork while establishing a core membership for Esprit, she'd done Trojan work. But now that the latter was up and running, it was essential to keep up the superior standards that they'd sold in the advertising campaign. And if that meant pulling out all the stops in terms of service and, in this case, maintenance, then Brona would just have to get over being nice and start to demand the same high standards from the people they dealt with.

Having given the whole of the shower and changing area the once-over as she was there, she headed for her own office to check on the arrangements for the next phase of the development, the Carnelian Springs holistic centre.

Passing through the link corridor that connected Esprit with the administration block, she noted with satisfaction that the car park was reasonably well-endowed with a selection of vehicles from the top end of the spectrum.

Since Esprit and Ivy Lodge had opened their doors simultaneously almost a month ago, the crunch of tyres on gravel had become reassuringly frequent. The gym and leisure centre was well subscribed already and the healthcare wing, Ivy Lodge, had also taken off well.

Already, the rental from the GP and dentist was generating a considerable income, closely followed by that of the renowned sports physiotherapist, Noel Creedon.

The Guru, as he was popularly known, had been considering moving his practice out of the city centre and Linda had brazenly approached him after reading an interview that he gave to the *Examiner*. Promising him free rein to design the layout of the suite with Charlie's assistance, she courted him relentlessly until he'd capitulated, won over by the idea of having a purpose-built clinic with an abundance of parking and direct access to a gym and swimming pool.

Creedon's presence had raised the profile of the complex no end, plus he put a lot of business the way of Rosa, a young clinical nutritionist who'd bravely taken on the substantial rental of one of the smaller suites in Ivy Lodge.

Of course there was more money in the country than ever before, with over half the population subscribing to private health insurance. And many of the insurers were now covering expenses for complementary therapies like acupuncture, as Linda had pointed out to Roland Blake only yesterday.

"The clients will be only too happy to avail of a treatment if it's covered by their health insurance, Roland," she'd reminded him tartly.

"Are you suggesting that I purposely make referrals to the holistic centre just because it'll benefit The Sanctuary as a whole, Linda?" he'd asked pompously.

"Well, a steady stream of referrals would help to establish a client base for the holistic centre and, likewise, I imagine that they in turn would make referrals to you on anything that they considered medical."

Linda had waved off Roland's monologue about ethics and appropriate referrals. He'd soon know what side his bread was buttered on once his till started jangling.

Dismissing these thoughts from her mind, Linda settled herself at the desk, pulled out the sheaf of application forms that had flooded in throughout the month and settled down to go through them.

Organising the interview procedures was next on her list, now that she had the main body of applications down to twenty practitioners. Aware of her own lack of expertise in the area of holistic health and her limited connections in the field, she'd had Michelle compile a list of the national bodies governing a selection of therapies. She would contact some of the associations over the next few days in order to form an expert body to assist her in verifying the credentials of the chosen applicants, and who might later sit on the interview panel.

Draining her coffee mug, she glanced at the clock, registering that it was gone seven. It was almost a year since she'd first brought up the idea of The Sanctuary and enormous strides had been made so far, mainly at the cost of putting in twelve-hour days chasing between the temporary office at the complex and her office at Coltons, as well as keeping an eye on Bodywork. She rarely got home before half-seven and often spent the evenings poring over her diary, planning the following day's work. There was so much to be done, and time was of the essence if she wanted

The Sanctuary to start paying for itself as soon as possible. It was exhilarating to see the buildings rising before her, a thrill that more than made up for her dwindling social life.

Since her break-up with Charlie, Linda had found herself concentrating solely on work. Her only respite was the occasional meal out with Luke Nolan after work. These outings were mainly an extension of work, but once they'd dispensed with the business side of things, they generally progressed onto lively discussions about all sorts of things, often ending up being ushered out of a restaurant as the Early Bird sitting made way for the main evening trade. Luke was charming and attractive but she'd learned her lesson with Charlie.

While she enjoyed the element of flirtation, Linda was determined that there would be no more workplace affairs.

54

Evergreen

"Now, just lie back and enjoy it. Are you comfortable?"

"Am I what?" Amy giggled, surrounded by pillows and cushions with her feet wrapped in a warm towel. "I'm like the Princess and the Pea."

This was her third reflexology session and she was enjoying it immensely. Sheila tended to go the whole hog, bringing her aromatherapy burner to diffuse the relaxing essential oils and a collection of candles to place around the room for atmosphere. She'd even brought "mood music" to add to the ambience.

Amy was loving it and dreaded the day that the ten sessions would be complete. She'd bought a few of the essential oils herself, lavender and geranium being her favourites, and added them to the bath water as well as using them for the burner. Sheila was so enthusiastic about the idea of natural healing that Amy was becoming more and more interested.

"How are you getting on with writing up the case studies?" Amy asked now as Sheila's fingers slid gently over the soles of her feet.

"Great. The rest of the class are studying for the Anatomy and Physiology exam next week whereas I don't have to make any effort for that, so I'm able to concentrate on writing up the case studies. The benefits of being the only nurse in the class."

"Any more progress on getting up and running full-time? Even though I shouldn't be encouraging you considering how much I'd miss you if you did give up work in the unit."

"The lease on Martin's surgery won't be up for another year so that could hold me up a little. The GP that's there at the moment has started to look around for another premises but it's not easy and I don't want to rush him, although I'd love to get going and renovate the place properly."

Leasing her husband's surgery had been an extra income in the years after his death but now that Sheila's own clientele was steadily building she planned to remodel the rooms for use as a holistic treatment centre. The self-contained unit was attached to her house with its own entrance door and a small bathroom and kitchenette.

"At least you'll have time to finish the reflexology course in the meantime," Amy commented.

"Actually there's a short course in baby massage coming up soon. I was thinking of doing it. A lot of people have phoned lately asking if I practise that as well as the adult massage."

"That'd be interesting. How long is the course?"

"Every Saturday morning for six weeks. I was actually thinking that you might like it. Would you think about doing it with me?"

"It sounds great but would I be any good at it? Where is it on anyway?"

"Clonakilty. I know it's a bit of a drive but it doesn't start until half nine. You could always help me out next year by doing a few sessions if I'm busy."

"I'd love to try it – I'm getting to like this natural healing business."

"I'll bring in all the details to work next week and you can have a look before you decide. Now there you go – all done!" Sheila announced, finishing Amy's treatment with a flourish.

"That was lovely, Sheila, I always sleep like a log on Tuesday nights after the reflexology. Will we have a cuppa?"

Sheila was delighted to hear that Amy was sleeping better. She'd had black circles under her eyes for the past few months, despite putting on a great show of professionalism at work. Managing the neonatal unit was a demanding job, but Amy seemed to be carrying it off easily, her calm capability unusual in one so young. Sheila thought that perhaps the baby massage course would provide a welcome diversion for her young friend for the winter months.

"Here you go!" Amy was back with two mugs of tea and a selection of the creamy cakes that she knew Sheila loved. She flicked on the television to catch the end of the news as they sat back enjoying the lingering scent of the aromatherapy oils.

"God, it's depressing," Amy sighed, switching to another channel as yet another bombing in Iraq was reported. This time her choice was more upbeat and they chatted comfortably while idly watching a documentary, *Great Love Stories of the Twentieth Century*.

"It's all very fine," Sheila commented thoughtfully when a feature on John Lennon and Yoko Ono came up. "Who knows how they would have fared if he'd lived a bit longer?"

Amy thought about that comment long after Sheila had left that night. How would she and Peter have fared if *he'd* lived a bit longer? Would it have been a case of a relationship that would have run its course and fizzled out? She didn't want to believe that that would have been the case.

They'd been so well matched, their sense of humour sparking off each other all the time. Even physically they'd been compatible, their bodies somehow just right together. Amy shivered now as she thought about this, wondering was it possible that the one man who could make her feel as Peter had done was actually gone off the earth. Her eyes closed as she remembered the feel of his hands on her skin and slowly she drifted towards sleep as once again the clock inched its way towards three.

*   *   *

"Hi there, Amy!" Deirdre called across to her, Alex hoisted on her hip as she adjusted the straps of the car seat. The morning was chilly and his head was enveloped in a woolly hat with a large coloured tassel.

Amy made her way over, conscious of the fact that she'd been a little distant with Deirdre and Marcus in the past few months. She'd called over before she left for her parent's house on Christmas Eve to give Alex a small present but she hadn't had a proper chat with either of them in ages.

"Hi," she greeted now, "how are you getting on?" Alex was growing at a rate of knots and looked to Amy as if he was developing along normal lines.

"Great. He'll be having his nine-month developmental check down at the health centre later, so fingers crossed. How's the job going?"

"The same as if I'd always been doing it! Plenty of stress and hassle but I love it. Listen, I'd better go or I'll be sacked. I'd love to catch up this evening if you're around?"

"That'd be great. I'll call around if you like – Marcus can baby-sit and it'll give me a chance at an adult conversation."

Looking forward to a chat with Deirdre in the evening, Amy headed off to work in great form. She had a meeting with the hospital's legal team at nine so she'd already let the girls on the ward know that she wouldn't be in until at least eleven. This was a part of the job that she hadn't anticipated; the many medico-legal cases that all of the country's hospitals had to face on an ongoing basis. The particular case arising now had happened long before Amy had even worked in the unit so she'd have to be briefed in detail by the legal team as any new events arose.

It was almost half eleven by the time she got back to the Neonatal Unit, having missed her coffee break in the process. Collecting a quick cup of tea from the machine in the hospital foyer, she made her way back to the unit, noting with a sigh the huge pile of post placed neatly on her desk.

The phone rang suddenly and she answered it, hoping that it wasn't the labour ward with news of another admission. The unit was packed to capacity as it was.

"Hello. Is this Amy Harkin?" The voice was soft and a little hesitant, alerting her immediately to the fact that it wasn't an ordinary work call. She confirmed that it was indeed her.

"Hello, Amy, I'm Marcella Deasy. Peter's mother?"

Amy could only utter a hoarse acknowledgement, unable to get another word out. The woman continued softly, as if aware that Amy might be a bit stunned to hear from her. "I'm sorry to phone you at work, only I didn't have your home number. And I really should have contacted you before now. I'm afraid I just wasn't able for much until now, to be honest."

"But how did you know . . . I mean, how did you . . . ?" Amy's voice was full of questions but she couldn't quite get the words out.

"There was a photo in Peter's wallet. They gave us

all his things but I couldn't bear to go through them at the time. I only found it afterwards and I remembered you from the funeral. I asked one of the other librarians about you."

"Oh," was all Amy could say in response. She'd never expected to hear from Peter's family and certainly not like this. She felt overwhelmed suddenly, faint almost.

"I'm sorry to land in on you like this. The photo was taken at a dinner dance, I think. He mentioned it actually but I didn't take much notice at the time. I'd love if we could meet, even for a cup of coffee?"

"That'd be lovely," Amy said hoarsely, finding her voice at last. She'd never expected this to happen, for Peter's family to know anything about her. But this woman needed to put all the pieces together. *And so do I*, Amy thought.

"I'm going to be in Cork this evening, in the apartment. Would it be too much for you to meet me there?"

For the remainder of the day, she did precious little in the line of work. What would it be like to stand in Peter's apartment again? Sam, she knew, had moved to Scotland to his girlfriend. Was everything still the same, she wondered, or had it already been sorted out? Where would all his things be?

It dawned on her then, that in the years that she worked as a nurse, she'd been through the bereavement process with many people and had somehow foolishly believed that everyone's grief was the same. Why hadn't it occurred to her that every situation was different, like her own was now?

The meeting with Peter's mother would be difficult for her, but not half as difficult as it would be for Marcella Deasy. She would see that Amy had her whole life ahead of her whereas her own son would never have any more chances at life. She focused on this as she pressed the bell on the ground floor and heard the click from above.

Afterwards, she only remembered the meeting in flashes. Marcella Deasy's thick, dark eyelashes so reminiscent of her son's. The same familiar smell in his home even though he'd been gone for months. Everything being in the same place, not tidied or moved around as she'd expected.

"It's not healthy to leave it like this, I know that. I just needed something to happen before I sort everything out. I knew when I saw the photo in his wallet that I'd have to meet you before I could say he was gone properly."

"I think it might be a bit like that for me too," Amy told her hesitantly. "The whole thing feels more real now. Sometimes I used to wonder did I dream it all, that maybe he was never there at all."

Marcella Deasy smiled for the first time when Amy said this, her eyes crinkling at the corners in the same way that Peter's had. Amy sat there, in the same armchair that she'd tended to sit in before and looked in admiration at her. Could this woman have been my mother-in-law, she'd wondered vaguely.

"I'll walk out to the shop and get some milk for that coffee I promised you," Marcella said then, her way of giving Amy some time alone in the apartment, she realised afterwards.

She sat in Peter's room on the bed, taking deep breaths as if she could somehow breathe in the essence of him. Eventually, hearing Marcella in the hall below, she closed the door softly, knowing that she'd said goodbye to him properly at last.

Later, as she was leaving, Peter's mother asked her if she'd like to take anything, a momento, with her. Amy thanked her, telling her gently that she'd rather remember him in her head.

"I think you're right. You're such a lovely girl, we would have been so proud to see him married to someone like you. But you can't waste your life like that one in *Great Expectations*. Some day, I hope you'll meet someone else. It might be a while, but I hope you do, and that you'll be happy."

Amy had kissed her cheek then and they'd hugged, tears in both their eyes. She wouldn't waste her life like Miss Havisham, sitting there with the clocks stopped, mourning for a lost love. Today, she'd start again, knowing that she'd always remember Peter as a wonderfully special part of her past.

55

Seefin

"This is the life. I won't know what's hit me when I eventually have to go back to work."

Deirdre was curled up in one of the large squishy armchairs in Amy's sitting room, sipping a glass of wine. Amy had put on one of Sheila's CDs and a mixture of lavender and jasmine oil wafted from the burner. The fire was blazing in the hearth and the two women chatted comfortably.

"Do you miss the gang at work at all?"

"I miss the social side of it, dressing up for work and meeting people. But most people in my department have called to see Alex at some stage and Marcus brings home all the news to me. At the moment, I can't imagine leaving Alex with someone else until he gets a bit stronger."

Even though he was surpassing everyone's idea of how well he would develop, Alex was still "behind" on many of the milestones that other babies of his age would achieve.

"So how did he get on at the health centre earlier?" Amy asked now.

Earlier that day, they'd brought him to their local health centre for his nine-month developmental check and watched nervously as their Public Health Nurse, Alison, gave him small tasks in order to assess his development, such as transferring blocks from one hand to the other and picking up a tiny object with his thumb and forefinger. This done, she'd worked through his physical examination, giving them a running commentary on the procedure as she did so.

"At this point, most babies are able to stand holding onto something like a couch or coffee table. As you know, Alex isn't at that stage yet, which is understandable considering that he was so premature. What's important is that his legs can bear his body weight. See what I mean," she said, holding Alex under the arms and allowing him to plant his feet firmly on the examination couch.

"Do you think it'll be much longer before he starts to pull himself up?"

Deirdre had been reading up about the milestones and knew Alex should be learning to walk by now.

"He'll probably start to cruise the furniture over the next four weeks or so but we'll call him back for a recheck to make sure."

Alison now placed Alex in a sitting position, not touching him but holding her arms in a circle around him to make sure he wouldn't fall over. He sat obligingly for her for half a minute or so, wobbling a bit before falling sideways into her arms.

"Sitting-wise he's very good," she told them. "Again he's not sitting for quite as long as he ought at nine months and he's not able to balance himself for long but that's down to his prematurity. He's well able to stop himself falling forward, so he's getting there. Let's have a look at his head control."

As she said this, Alison encouraged Alex to take one of her index fingers in each hand. Slowly, she pulled him from lying flat on his back into a sitting position.

"Watch how he brings his head up along with the rest of his body. His head doesn't lag back at all which is great."

"We've been practising that one," Marcus told her with a proud smile. "The Grow team told us to play with him while he's lying on his tummy to strengthen his neck muscles because he had a bit of head lag the first time they assessed him."

"That's great. Does he try to crawl when he's put on his tummy?"

"He tries," Deirdre said laughing, "but he goes around in circles – backwards!"

"He'll start to go up onto his knees soon. When he gets used to that position you can use a toy to motivate him to crawl towards you."

Alex was still on his tummy as Alison proceeded to check his reflexes. Holding him at the waist she lifted him high above the couch for a moment.

"I want to see if he'll put out his hands to protect himself."

With that, she briskly lowered Alex towards the couch. Deirdre and Marcus were amazed at how rapidly his little arms shot out, his hands landing firmly on the brown leather surface.

"Perfect," Alison pronounced, running a tape measure around Alex's head. This done, she laid him on a measuring mat to record his length. "Now, little fellow, let's see what weight you are."

Alex howled as his bare bottom landed on the plastic surface of the scales. Eventually the digital reading settled at 8.2 kg.

"You can dress him up now while I plot his measurements on the growth chart. We'll be checking his hearing in a minute so you can leave his little coat off."

Alex wriggled magnificently as Deirdre struggled to manoeuvre him back into his clothes, giggling in response to his continuous "Da Da" chant.

"You'd never guess who the one looking after him all day was, would you?" Deirdre looked at Alison, eyebrows raised at the fact that Alex hadn't said "Ma Ma" yet.

"Most babies will say 'Da Da' and 'Ba Ba' first, so you're not alone. The main thing is that he's vocalising and babbling at this stage. Now, have a look at his growth chart."

"God, he's almost at the average. The last time he was checked he was still one level below it."

Marcus was astounded at this. Deirdre had breastfed Alex up to six months and he was now on three bottles of formula every day as well as his solid food. Finally, his growth was coming to a par with other babies of his age, proving to his anxious parents that they were getting it right in terms of feeding.

Alex behaved like a complete angel for the hearing test, turning sharply every time the nurse made a low or high-pitched noise behind him.

At last the developmental test was complete, with Alison assuring them that the areas of development in which Alex was delayed were acceptable, considering how early he'd come into the world.

"I'll send you an appointment in about six weeks to see how he's progressing. He may be slow to reach some of the milestones but as long as he's making good headway within a reasonable timeframe, it's acceptable. The two main areas are the standing and crawling, but we'll recheck everything else as well."

Thrilled that there hadn't been any alarming deficit in Alex's development, Deirdre and Marcus had headed out to The Gallery in Ballycotton for a celebratory lunch. The nine-month assessment was of particular significance to them as Alex's consultant in the Neonatal Unit had told them at one of the outpatient appointments that signs of Cerebral Palsy would generally be present before this age.

So far, all of his limbs seemed to have equal strength, with no signs of weakness or spasticity of the muscles, and his early speech pattern appeared to be normal.

Knowing that they couldn't hope for more, they'd decided to celebrate Alex's achievements and to continue to stimulate his already impressive progress to the best of their ability.

Deirdre replayed the scenes from Alex's developmental check to Amy as she snuggled up in her comfy armchair. Taking the time off work had been the best thing she'd ever done. As well as being able to give her son the extra time and attention he needed to progress as normally as possible, she herself had begun to cultivate a new dimension to her life.

Once Alex had completed his initial set of immunisations, she'd joined the Mother and Toddler swimming group at Bodywork, the local leisure centre. The Grow team had recommended this as a means of therapy for Alex's muscles, but it was proving to be almost as beneficial to Dee as it was to Alex. Getting to know the other new mothers in the Pebble Cove area had been marvellous, and some of them had even started going for coffee and scones in the café afterwards.

"It's amazing how things change in life," she commented now to Amy. "This time last year, I wouldn't have been able to imagine myself at home full-time, with my only social outlet being the Mother and Toddler swimming group. But once Alex came along and I made up my mind about it, I can't believe how I've taken to it."

"I suppose you start to realise that it's different but just as important."

"That's it. I never really looked on parenting as an actual job but in Alex's case, it's the most valuable thing I can do right now. It's not just about sitting at home looking at him – the day flies by."

It occurred to Amy then that Deirdre might be interested in the baby massage course that Sheila had mentioned. It'd be a morning out for Deirdre and would benefit Alex in the long run. And, from Amy's own perspective, it would be a chance to renew her former closeness with Deirdre now that she'd been able to acknowledge Peter's death properly.

"What would you think about doing a baby massage course with myself and Sheila Forde? It'd be great for Alex."

"Baby massage? What's that when it's at home?" Deirdre was intrigued.

"I don't know much about it myself yet, to be honest, but Sheila's been telling me about it. It's basically massage therapy for babies. Some people do the course to practice it as a complementary therapy but some people do it to use on their own children. Apparently it's great for things like colic and constipation."

"And what kind of a course is it? Can you do it in Cork?"

While the idea of massaging Alex's limbs to relax his muscles sounded great, the idea of having to leave him in order to do a course didn't appeal to Deirdre at all.

"I haven't got the full information yet but Sheila will have it tomorrow for me. It's on in the holistic centre in

Clonakilty, every Saturday morning for six weeks."

"It sounds great. Will it definitely be on a Saturday?" Deirdre was already getting excited at the thought of how much Alex would love being massaged with scented oils. Amy had been filling her in on the properties of the aromatherapy oils earlier and she was fascinated. Apart from anything else, the scents were divine and she was already planning to resurrect a burner that she'd been given as a housewarming present. She hadn't known what to do with it at the time but at least she could start with the lavender and jasmine.

"As far as I know, it is. As soon as I get the details from Sheila I'll drop them over and you can have a look. It sounds as if it'd be manageable though."

"Mum and Dad live in the same area as the holistic centre in Clonakilty. I'm sure they'd love to have the three of us for lunch after the course on the Saturdays before we'd head back to Cork."

"That sounds like a plan then," Amy smiled, thrilled that Deirdre was interested.

"You're brilliant to be doing something like this, Amy, considering that work must be hectic."

"Having regular hours is fabulous. You probably wouldn't think twice about having every weekend off, Dee, but in nursing, after years of weekend and night duty, it's a bonus. And it's no harm to have an interest in something different. Sheila finds the complementary stuff really therapeutic. Plus, I could probably do with re-focusing a bit."

Amy gave Deirdre a rueful smile as she said this, wanting to talk a little about why she'd been so distant to her and Marcus in the months since Peter's death. It was easy to do it now, her meeting with Marcella Deasy having placed some kind of closure on what she now saw as a chapter in her life, with a beginning and an end.

Deirdre was glad that Amy was talking so easily now. She and Marcus had been feeling guilty about how little good they'd been to their friend, considering how wonderful she'd been to them at the most difficult and frightening time of their life. Deirdre said this now, but Amy was having none of it, reminding Deirdre that she'd stubbornly refused their many overtures, preferring at the time to go it alone.

"Let's put it behind us now. It can't have been easy for Marcus either. Plus he'd probably be terrified of mentioning the soccer club in front of me," she laughed lightly. "You can tell him I'm able for it now."

"What about the hillwalking?" Deirdre asked her now, aware that Amy had said as much as she wanted to say about Peter. "Have you got back into that at all?"

"That's my next plan. I haven't met the group for ages. They'll think I've gone off the face of the earth. There's a big walking weekend in May but I'd better get in a bit of practice before then."

"Speaking of May, myself and Marcus are planning a little party for Alex's birthday. Nothing big – just family, a few friends and the gang in the houses here. So make sure to keep the Bank Holiday Saturday free."

501

"Sounds great. We might be qualified baby masseurs by then, mind you, so Alex will probably be rubbed away to nothing. He'll be delighted with the fuss of a party."

Deirdre laughed, thrilled to be able to plan a party for her precious Alex, considering the many occasions when they couldn't see as far as a first birthday.

"It's mainly to say thanks to everyone for being so good to us. Poor Alex won't have a clue what's going on but it'll be nice to have everyone over. We never actually had a proper housewarming so it'll kill two birds with the one stone. Three actually," she giggled.

"How do you mean?" Amy was curious now.

"Hazel's mad to hook up with Shay next door. They're always chatting over the fence and they've even gone out for a drink a few times but she reckons she'd have more of a chance if she had an opportunity like a party. Don't let on that I told you though."

"He seems nice. Robert, my brother, was planting the hedge between the two houses a while back and he came out and gave him a hand. He came in for a cuppa afterwards. Robert had great notions that he might be the man for me. He seems to be a bit of a whiz-kid on the financial side of things."

"Seriously? He's definitely the right man for Hazel so."

"Well, I only know because he and Robert got talking about mortgages and life assurance and stuff like that. He was all business about it. When Robert looked into what he'd told him, it transpired that he was spot on. So he's the main man as far as my brother's concerned. Shay's saved him a heap of money, apparently."

"Wait 'til I fill Hazel in on that. She'll have him beatified before ever she gets a date out of him. We'll definitely have to do our best to get them together in May so, as long as Alex doesn't mind his party being hijacked as a dating agency."

"He'll just have to consider it payment for all the baby-sitting she's doing."

"Here, I'd better get going or Marcus will think I've deserted my family and taken up lodgings here," Deirdre laughed. It was almost eleven o'clock but she was thrilled that her friendship with Amy was back on track. "Will you let me know about the Baby Massage course when you get the details? I might phone the liaison nurse at Grow in the morning to make sure that it'd be suitable for Alex. If it is, I'll be raring to go."

"Brilliant. I'll drop over as soon as I have more info. I really enjoyed tonight, Dee."

"Same here," Deirdre smiled back. "See you soon."

* * *

Two days later, Deirdre was sitting at the kitchen table poring over the leaflets that Amy had given her. As regards price, the course was excellent, and it was definitely going to be run on Saturdays, which suited because Marcus would be able to look after Alex. She'd already spoken to Sheila Forde on the phone to find out a little more about it and had been further boosted by the older woman's enthusiasm.

Deirdre had always liked Sheila Forde, having found her warm and reassuring as well as extremely professional, especially in the early days when everything had been so strange and frightening. She was amazed to hear her say now that she planned to leave the Neonatal Unit in the near future and work full-time as a complementary therapist.

"And would you set up at home or something?" Deirdre was impressed that Sheila had so many strings to her bow.

"Eventually, although the rooms that I need to use are occupied at the moment so I might need to go into practice elsewhere for a year or so, to keep my client list up."

"That's great, Sheila, and you've really sold me on the baby massage. I hope you and Amy don't mind me tagging along?"

"The more the merrier," Sheila had informed her. "Anyway, I hear there's a free lunch in it for us in Clonakilty!"

She filled Marcus in on all the details now, trying to weigh up the pros and cons.

"Well, love, as I see it, the reason you took the time off work was to do whatever it took to give Alex the start he needs. If you're happy to do the course and the Grow team think it'll benefit him, then I think you should go ahead with it."

Marcus was always practical when it came to

making decisions, a trait Deirdre loved when she herself was dithering over something. Even though it was only for one morning a week, she was a bit reluctant to spend it away from Alex.

"How about if I took him swimming on the Saturday mornings?" Marcus suggested. "Then you wouldn't feel that he was missing out on his exercises or anything. And it'd be nice to be able to meet your parents for lunch after the course."

Deirdre religiously took Alex to the pool every morning except Sundays and carefully carried out the routine that the physiotherapist had set for him to strengthen his limbs. The baby massage course ran from half nine until two on the Saturdays, so she, Amy and Sheila would have to leave around eight to have time for a coffee before the classes started. It would be mid-evening by the time they'd get back to Pebble Cove. Still, she told herself, it was only for six weeks and Alex would gain from it in the long-term.

"I'll ring in the morning and book in," she declared finally. "And it'll be no harm to get out of the house for a day. You never know, they might even teach us a bit of exotic massage on the side if we're lucky!" She laughed wickedly, happy now that she'd made a decision that would enable her to bring Alex yet another step closer to leading as normal a life as possible.

56

Number 1

Linda glanced at her watch, conscious that she'd left it too late to have lunch as she was due to meet her father and the rest of the directors in twenty minutes. Too bad, she thought, slipping on her jacket and grabbing her car keys.

The initial anxiety about meeting Charlie at work had worn off relatively quickly, particularly when she realised that he was approaching the matter of the end of their relationship as evenly as he dealt with everything else. Linda's big fear had been that people would find out that she had been dispensed with and that she'd look a fool, but nobody seemed to even be aware that they were no longer an item. Either that or they were too cautious to question either of them about it, which Linda thought more likely.

Either way, since the work on The Sanctuary had snowballed, she'd hardly had time to consider the fact that she was single again. However, presuming that Charlie would probably be present at the afternoon meeting, she'd taken extra care with her appearance that morning, choosing a black Yves Saint Laurent trouser suit and a pair of soft leather boots that added to her height considerably. She'd even taken her time over her make-up, wanting to make sure that he'd know what he was missing, though she was way past wanting him back.

Now sitting with her father in the boardroom, she was determined not to allow her eyes to flicker towards the door every time she heard steps approaching along the corridor. When he did arrive, she was glad that it was in the company of Luke Nolan, in that a casual "Hi, guys!" was sufficient as a greeting rather than having to address him directly. Characteristically, her father got down to business straight away, sparing her the need to exchange pleasantries under the watchful eyes of the rest of the gathering.

By half three, they'd thrashed out the main outline for the order of the next phase of the development, as well as running through the progress being made on Phase 2. Adamant that Carnelian Springs would be functional by September, Linda summarised the arrangements that she had made thus far for its staffing. She noted with satisfaction how impressed Charlie appeared to be at her plan to rent the rooms on a sessional basis for the first year, to get a feel for which therapies would generate most interest while ensuring full use of the space.

Towards the close of the meeting, when the main business had been dealt with, Linda took the opportunity to inform the directors that plans for the hair salon and beauty therapy rooms were also underway, reminding them that it was essential that The Sanctuary start turning over a profit with as little delay as possible.

"We may need to think about renting the units to outfits that are already established who are looking to expand. Hair and beauty are definite money-spinners so we'd be able to command a fairly substantial rental deal."

Linda's purpose in bringing their attention to this particular aspect of the development was to let her father see that she was as intent on making money out of the venture as he was, and to allay any concerns that he might have as to her propensity for heavy spending. Especially when she'd have yet another extraordinary expenditure to present to him in the near future, all going well.

"Have you time for a coffee?"

Linda started at finding Charlie's voice so near her shoulder, but she turned and smiled nonetheless.

"Time for a coffee? I haven't even had lunch yet."

"Me neither. Will we go out for a sandwich?"

Linda agreed nonchalantly, wanting to show that she was every bit as cool as he obviously was. Anyway, she was starving.

Five minutes later they were settled in the snug of the nearest pub, their food on order. They chatted away about work until the delicious open sandwiches arrived, pausing then to pour their coffee and tuck in.

"Actually, I was hoping to have a chat with you about something," said Linda suddenly.

Charlie looked up, knowing all too well that Linda's tone of voice meant business. It reinforced yet again for him how different they were and how right he had been to end their relationship when he had.

"Go on."

"I know the drawings are finished and everything but I was thinking about the chalets."

"What about them?" he asked, knowing that he was about to incur further work on a part of the project that he'd thought he was finished with.

"If you think about it, they're a bit isolated from the rest of the complex. Apart from keeping the same limestone finish they're not linked in any way. We're supposed to be drawing the whole thing together as we go along but I feel that there's something missing."

"What have you in mind?" Charlie knew that Linda rarely exposed a problem until she'd actually found the solution to it. In this case he, Charlie, seemed to be part of the solution.

"What would you think about doing some sort of rockery behind the chalets, with a small waterfall that would have a kind of pond at the base. I was thinking it could run into the moat around the Carnelian Springs building. It'd be a fantastic feature."

"More like a fantastic expense. We'd have to pump the water back up from the moat continuously, not to mention actually build the thing."

"We'll be re-doing the marketing brochure next year when the whole thing's finished. It'd look fantastic. We need something a bit exotic to catch people's attention."

"Have you mentioned it to Luke or your father yet?"

"I wanted to see if it was manageable first. What do you think? If money wasn't an object, I mean."

"It shouldn't be too much of a problem. We should start holding onto the topsoil to raise the ground at the back, for a start. And the existing moat would want to be deep enough to hold all of the water volume if the pump failed or was turned off. It sounds good though," he said, admiration evident in his voice.

"To be fair, it's not exactly an original idea. There's something a bit like it at Springfield Manor in Clonakilty. Only the waterfall there is natural, of course. I was thinking we could go and look at it and you could draw something up afterwards. We could show it to Luke then and see what he thinks."

Charlie had to admit that Linda was a hard case. She knew full well that her father would baulk at an added expense that had no practical value. Therefore, she knew that she'd need both Charlie *and* Luke onside before she even mentioned it. It didn't escape his notice that she'd approached him first, knowing that Luke would be bowled over if he saw the plans on paper.

"And when do you propose going to Clonakilty? Friday?" He knew she'd have this figured out as well and that it would be sooner rather than later.

"I've booked meetings with people from the various

holistic organisations for then and I assumed that you'd be full up as well. What would you think about Saturday morning? If you've nothing on, that is," she finished hopefully, aware that she knew little or nothing about his social life now.

Charlie meantime was flicking the idea over in his head. It *would* look great on the brochure. He could have a chat with one of the engineers about the viability of pumping the water to the top of the rockery to create the waterfall. The landscapers would sort out the rest. Rolling his eyes in exasperation, he grinned at her before agreeing, "Go on then, you've sold it."

* * *

The following Friday, Linda belted down the corridor at high speed, her heels clattering noisily. She was meeting the chairperson of the Cork Reflexology Institute in five minutes and she needed to formulate a few questions before the lady in question, Joy Norris, arrived. Thankfully, Linda had everything she needed laid in a neat pile on her desk: copies of all the applicants who were qualified as reflexologists, with a note stuck on to the dual-qualified ones to say what their other therapy was.

Linda planned to question Joy on the popularity of the other therapies in order to whittle down the number of people to be interviewed as far as possible. She'd also confirm the dates for the interviews and try to devise a series of questions for the candidates. Aware of her own limitations in the area of holism, she intended to let Joy and the other panel members ask most of the practice-related questions to ensure that any quacks would be unmasked. The last thing she wanted was some loose canon to slip through the net and tarnish The Sanctuary's reputation.

She had barely gathered her thoughts and got settled when she heard a brisk step approaching down the corridor. Having expected to meet a hippy in flowing skirts, she was taken aback when Michelle introduced a slim, elegant lady in an exquisitely tailored navy trouser suit. Her hair was jet black – natural, Linda thought – and cut in a gamine style that showed off a pair of large dark blue eyes and made her look like a combination of Audrey Hepburn and Bambi.

Twenty minutes later, Linda was fully enlightened as to exactly the kind of people they'd be looking for, with Joy encouraging her to discard many of the applications that she'd been considering.

"Sometimes it's not all about having a huge list of qualifications, it's more about being excellent in at least one area, taking into account that on many occasions people come with intangible things like stress, depression, bereavement or lack of energy. A lot of the time they'll have been checked out by a doctor and may be on medication. Sometimes they'll have been told that there's nothing wrong with them physically, so it might be the interaction with the therapist as well as the treatment that is of benefit."

"So you're saying that someone with twenty

certificates might be a sort of course-hopper, while someone who's excellent at even one therapy and with the social skills to match, would be a better proposition in terms of return business?"

"Possibly."

"In that case I'd better let you have a look at some of the applications I weeded out already."

Linda buzzed Michelle and asked her to resurrect the ones that she'd already sent refusals to, glad that she'd had the foresight to promise to keep their applications on file.

"Look, see this one," Joy pointed out a few minutes later. "She says she has a particular interest in bereavement. I mean, if *I* was suffering from stress and looking for a holistic therapy to help me through it, this one would jump out at me if I'd lost a loved one in the past. Or this one, she's offering aromatherapy massage, reflexology and baby massage. A voucher for a session with her would be an ideal gift for a new mum."

Linda studied both of the applications thoughtfully, glad that she'd had the wit to enlist the help of a few experts to help her decide on those to be interviewed. Both of the candidates that Joy had picked out seemed to be new to some areas of holistic therapy, which was why Linda had discarded them initially. One was a retired teacher while the other was presently working as a nurse, she noted.

"You have to look *through* the CV bit to see what's driving them," said Joy. "Take the teacher, for instance. She might have taken up Indian head massage as a retirement hobby. Or she may actually have had a bereavement herself and then got interested. The fact that she was a teacher means that she probably has a good understanding of human nature. I'd want to find out that at an interview."

"Should we put her on the list then?" Linda couldn't believe how deferential she felt before Joy Norris's competent and assured air. When she agreed, Linda asked about the other applicant that Joy had picked out.

"On the face of it, she seems to have good experience," said Joy, "and the combination that she's practising is good, plus she's working in the health sector, something that a lot of people feel comfortable with. It takes the *'hocus pocus'* fear out of complementary therapy for some people if they feel it's endorsed by a doctor or nurse. We'd need to find out what understanding she has of the concept of holism and whether it's only a pastime, or if she's interested in a long-term career in complementary therapy."

They spent the rest of the morning in this vein, eventually coming up with ten interviewees. Far from being the *au natural* hippie that Linda had expected, Joy seemed to have an acute eye for what the customer would want in terms of selection and choice.

"How would you describe him in a brochure?" she'd ask, forcing Linda to visualise the actual wording to be used in the glossy advertising booklets.

"We certainly need to have a sort of menu," mused Linda, "with a profile of the different practitioners and what they're offering. For instance, we could market people as having particular interest in bereavement, or special needs children in the case of that lady from Macroom who uses the Reiki on her son to ease spasms and relax him."

"Exactly. Women's health is another issue that's big at the moment. Infertility, menopause and that sort of thing. Both the herbalist and the acupuncture fellow seem to do a lot of work in that area. That might be something to look into."

Linda was meeting more of her "experts" the following week, so anything that Joy didn't have a definitive answer on, she listed to ask them. Relieved that she'd have an authoritative panel to ask the relevant questions and decipher the answers accordingly, she added the reflexology/ baby massage/ aromatherapy person to the list, along with the Indian head massage lady and the special needs/ Reiki person.

After Joy left, Linda gave the revised list to Michelle, reminding her to hold off on posting the invitations to interview until she'd met with the director of Chinese Medicine and the fellow from the Society of Herbalists in Ireland. No doubt both of them would be as enlightening as Joy had been. Sorting through her desk, Linda got as much as she could in order for the following week. She was leaving early as she'd be spending the following morning travelling to Clonakilty with Charlie. Hopefully, seeing her idea in the flesh would convince him to add a similar feature to the plans.

* * *

Much as she'd expected, Charlie *had* been impressed with her idea, especially when he saw the real thing at the old country house hotel in Clonakilty. She'd picked him up at eleven, just in case he did have anything on the night before. She'd been a little apprehensive about spending an hour and a half in the car with him but she needn't have worried. She'd forgotten how carried away he got once he was convinced of an idea. He'd spent the previous few days drawing up a series of plans for the rockery, waterfall and a meandering stream that would lead into the moat that surrounded the holistic centre building.

"You can have a look at the drawings when we get there," he told her, having explained each one in painstaking detail. He'd also spoken to one of the civil engineers about it and was satisfied that the whole thing was logistically possible.

They'd walked around the outside of the hotel, examining every aspect of the water feature, with Linda brazenly taking a few photos with the digital camera that she kept in the car for such occasions.

"We may as well have lunch while we're here," she said at last. "It's nearly one and the dining room looks out onto the waterfall. I wonder if we could get a window seat to get an idea of what it looks like from inside."

This was typical of Linda. She had to investigate

everything to make sure that she'd get the very best. Charlie knew that she was going to be enormously successful whenever she took over the reins at Coltons, even though he knew it would be a while before Daniel allowed that to happen.

As it transpired, they did get a window seat, to Linda's satisfaction. Charlie was ravenous and ordered a proper lunch while Linda picked at a Caesar salad as she pored over the drawings that he'd brought. Seeing her idea on paper was exhilarating and she was thrilled that Charlie had been able to envisage the concept almost exactly as she had visualised it.

As she dissected the plans in minute detail, Charlie's eyes wandered around the dining room, taking in the ambience of the old Tudor residence. Then his heart suddenly started to beat furiously as his eyes met those of Amy Harkin across the room. She smiled in surprise and gave a small wave, her eyes averted almost immediately as her attention was diverted by one of the two ladies at the table with her.

Charlie was shocked at the way he seemed to react every time he saw her. After the night that they'd met in The Loft with Jason and her brother, she'd been on his mind constantly. Although he knew where she lived, he was at a loss as to how he could make any further contact. He knew he couldn't just ring the doorbell and ask her out as he'd originally planned, especially after the trauma that she been through the previous summer. He was terrified of frightening her off for good, although at least she looked a bit less delicate than she did the last time he'd seen her.

"How come the water lilies are gone out of the equation?" Linda dragged him back to the present. But he found it difficult to focus on what she was saying, knowing that Amy was only a few yards away.

"The water in the moat will have a much more brisk flow on it if we have the waterfall running into it. We'll have to talk to the landscapers about it."

"And what about the pump? Where will that be?"

Linda shot questions at him for the next twenty minutes, determined now to have her pitch ready for Luke on Monday morning. She'd initially planned to wait a little but seeing as Charlie had done all the groundwork it might be better to move ahead with it. If Luke was in agreement, they could present it to her father on Wednesday. Now that it was down on paper and apparently viable in the technical sense, she was adamant that it would go ahead.

Charlie watched Amy and her companions anxiously, hoping that Linda would run out of steam before they finished their meal and left. Finally she did and called for the bill.

"No, I'll get it," Charlie insisted, getting up from the table. "You're doing all the driving."

"Grand so, thanks. I'll nip to the ladies' before we go."

Charlie hurriedly paid the bill and collected up the roll of drawings before making his way towards Amy's table.

She greeted him with a smile, expressing surprise to

see him so far from Cork city.

"A working lunch of sorts," he explained, hoping that she wouldn't think he was back with Linda. "How about you?"

"We're doing a weekend course in the holistic centre down the road from here. These are my friends, Sheila and Deirdre."

He shook hands with the two girls, asking Deirdre how Alex was doing since he arrived home from hospital. He'd met her and Marcus briefly on a few occasions and knew that Amy had been involved with the baby at work.

"What kind of course are you doing?" he asked then. "Something to do with the Master's?"

Pleased that he'd remembered that she was already studying, Amy laughed. "No, baby massage, even though we only possess one baby between the three of us."

"Interesting. So how do you fit in the hillwalking with all this going on?"

"I've been a bit lazy lately," she admitted, "although I have great plans to get back to it."

Noticing that Linda had returned from the ladies' and was studying some of the old paintings in the foyer, Charlie knew he had to make a move or the moment would be gone. God only knew when he'd meet her again. "I don't suppose you fancy going for an easy walk tomorrow? The forecast is good so I was thinking of doing Musheramore, over near Millstreet. It only takes a couple of hours and it'd be great to have company." He knew he was holding his breath and was conscious of her friends watching him as he waited for her to answer.

"That sounds great. As long as you'll go easy on me – I could be crocked after half a mile."

"I will!" he laughed. "I'll pick you up around nine then, if that's alright?"

"Brilliant. I'll bring the lunch for both of us."

"Don't go overboard or we'll need a Sherpa," he grinned as he left the table, remembering the feast she'd unloaded when he'd met her at the walking festival in Gilcrenan.

"Less of that," Amy shot back, "or you'll get nothing. See you tomorrow."

Out in the foyer, Linda was waiting impatiently.

"What was that about? I didn't know you knew them?"

Although Linda barely acknowledged any of her neighbours, she recognised both Amy and Deirdre and was a bit piqued that Charlie seemed to be on chatting terms with them.

"They're down here doing some sort of massage course, apparently," Charlie told her vaguely as they walked to the car.

"Massage?" Linda looked at him incredulously, thinking that none of the three looked the type to be into something as sensuous as massage.

"Baby massage," Charlie corrected. "Deirdre's the one who has the premature baby." "The other lady works in the Neonatal Unit with Amy, the girl across the road from you."

"Jesus, you're very tuned in," Linda said in a clipped voice, hating that the exclusive area that she'd been raving to live in had turned out to be so insular.

"I've met Amy hillwalking a few times. Her brother's friendly with Jason." Charlie said this as a means of letting Linda know that he was some way friendly with her neighbour, knowing that there was a distinct possibility that he'd one day get around to asking her out on a proper date. He dreaded to think of Linda's reaction to that but she'd just have to put up with it if it did happen.

The very mention of Charlie's best friend was enough to rile Linda further. They'd never clicked and Charlie had simply minimised the contact between them insofar as it was possible. Linda was less than impressed with Jason's lack of interest in any sort of career path, having only a derisory interest in the fact that he was actually principal of a small primary school just outside Cork city. Jason, for his part, loved the parochial element of his job and the fact that he knew all of the children and their parents personally. He could never understand Linda's persistent view that one shouldn't "stagnate" when there were countless opportunities for promotion in the bigger schools around the city.

As they reached the car and got in, Charlie diplomatically brought the conversation back to the subject of the water feature, smoothing her ruffled feathers to some degree. But his mind was on Amy and their outing the following day. He knew he'd have to be fairly restrained and resist rushing in and asking her out, knowing that she was probably only ready for a friendship of sorts. He'd just have to play it by ear and hope for the best.

57

Evergreen

Bumping into Charlie in the hotel in Clonakilty had happened purely by chance. Deirdre's parents, having invited the trio to lunch on one of the Saturdays during the baby massage course, had needed to go up the country to a funeral unexpectedly. Embarrassed at letting Deirdre and her friends down, they'd given them a lunch voucher for Springfield Manor as a treat.

Amy had noticed Charlie and his ex-girlfriend talking intensely as they'd pored over what looked like some sort of plans or drawings, and presumed that they were in Clonakilty on business. She'd been surprised at his invitation to go walking the following day and had jumped at the chance to get back to the outdoors again. She knew he'd be good company and while she knew that Musheramore was a great walk, she'd been working any weekend her own walking group had done it.

Deirdre and Sheila had been fascinated by the relationship between Amy and Charlie, with Sheila calling her a dark horse to have kept such a handsome devil under her hat. Amy agreed that he was handsome in a serious sort of way, but insisted that there was nothing more to it, only that they'd met a few times recently and got on well. They'd both teased her a bit for the rest of the day, glad that she seemed to be getting out and about a little more.

Charlie arrived early to collect her the following morning, catching her as she was just starting her breakfast.

"I haven't even made the lunch yet," she told him in a fluster. "Sit down and have a cuppa and I'll buck myself up."

They chatted easily while Amy finished her breakfast with Charlie filling her in on the route that they'd be taking. It was another half an hour before they got going but neither of them was too concerned as the walk itself was quite short and there would be daylight up to six o'clock.

By the time they reached the outskirts of Millstreet it was almost eleven o'clock. The sun had risen fully and had burned off all traces of the fog that they'd seen enveloping the top of Musheramore as they'd approached. Charlie was navigating, having walked the route many times, so Amy was content to just enjoy the countryside and the fantastic views.

She was surprised at how fit she was, despite having neglected her hobby for months. Although the distance to the summit was short, the climb was steep. Conversation was out of the question as each of them concentrated on the slope ahead of them. Charlie led, stopping occasionally to consult a crumpled map lest any of the more temporary landmarks such as fences had been moved since his last trip. The terrain was heathery with deep pockmarks covering the surface. Amy always found this type of ground hard going and frequently envied the long stride of tall people like Charlie.

Just as she herself liked to do, Charlie tended to stop now and again to survey the wonderful scenery around him and the miniature farms and houses below, rather than just going hell bent for the summit as some of the more ambitious walkers often did. Despite a stiff breeze, there was still a little warmth in the sun and they'd both discarded their outer layers long before they reached the large heap of rocks that marked the summit.

They stood for a few minutes admiring the magnificent views in silence, enjoying the sense of being detached from the bustle of ordinary life. This isolation always struck Amy when she reached the top of a mountain, making her wonder about the necessity of all the things that people packed into each and every day.

After a while they put their jackets back on and tucked themselves in between two large boulders on the sheltered side of the pile, conscious of the fact that they'd soon start to shiver from a combination of the strong wind and their recent exertion.

"I can't wait to see what's in the bag," said Charlie.

"Well, you won't have to wait much longer," Amy responded cheekily, already passing him two small stainless steel Thermos flasks.

Charlie started to undo one of them, watching in amusement as she proceeded to unload two packs of sandwiches, fruit, a bag of chocolate peanuts and another of yoghurt raisins as well as a selection of chocolate bars.

"I used to love picnics when I was small," she said laughing, as he handed her a mug of tea and proceeded to unwrap his sandwiches, smiling at the selection of food that she'd assembled.

"This is what I call living," Charlie announced, turning his face to the sun, his long legs stretched out in front of him. Amy leaned back against the rock and closed her eyes, a sense of peace enveloping her.

"Was Peter into the hillwalking as well?" Charlie asked this gently, obviously mistaking the reason for her reverie.

"Not a chance," Amy laughed. "There wouldn't have been enough time left over for soccer if he was."

They talked a little about Peter then and Amy even surprised herself by telling him about the day that Marcella Deasy had phoned her at work.

"I know the Americans are always on about 'closure' but honestly, it *was* a bit like that."

Charlie's heart had lifted when she said this, but he immediately felt like some sort of predator, trying to swoop in as soon as soon as an opportunity arose. He was unbelievably attracted to her. She looked fantastic, her cheeks flushed from the climb and her hair blowing around her face. Something about her brought out an enormously protective instinct in him, even though he knew that she was well able to mind herself.

The descent was glorious, the route he'd chosen much more gentle than the slope they'd experienced on the way up. It was easier to talk, and Amy felt something new between them that she thought had a lot to do with her need to explain earlier that she wasn't still grieving over Peter. She wanted Charlie to know that – it seemed important somehow.

They stopped off for coffee at a small village pub on the way back to Pebble Cove and Charlie spoke about Linda and the way that their personal relationship had survived their break-up and had reverted to a very professional one.

It was almost dark when they finally arrived back at Amy's house, both exhausted after the strenuous walk. She was vaguely disappointed when he made to leave almost immediately, declining her offer of supper.

"Thanks," he said, sounding slightly regretful, "but I'd better get going. Would you like to go again in a couple of weeks? I could give you a call."

Wary that he'd lose the bit of restraint that he'd had such a fragile hold on for the greater part of the day, Charlie knew that if he didn't leave soon he'd end up asking her out for dinner and making a pig's ear of the whole thing before Amy was really ready for it.

"That'd be great. I really enjoyed today, Charlie."

To her surprise, he kissed her quickly on the cheek and left without a word.

58

Number 1

Linda paced around the office, her mind whirling. Charlie had sat there, cool as a breeze, as if there was no big deal. Granted, he'd backed her up fully on the subject of the waterfall. But why the hell wouldn't he when it was such a good idea? She'd tried to come across as calm as she could but inside she was seething. Almost a week had gone by and she'd met him briefly a few times, but today they'd been in close contact for almost two hours, even having their coffee together, and he'd failed to mention a word about his latest little conquest.

* * *

The previous Sunday morning had really shocked her. She'd slept poorly, having gone out to a charity dinner with her father after she'd dropped Charlie home following the trip to Clonakilty. The dinner had been boring in the extreme, with her father insisting that she meet a collection of tiresome old codgers that he felt would be valuable contacts for her over the coming years. She'd drunk too much and had woken up at eight with her head pounding and her mouth as dry as sandpaper. Knowing that she wasn't going to get back to sleep, she went downstairs and had a cup of strong coffee, half listening to the radio news as she wondered what to do with the day.

Flicking through her work diary, she realised that she'd been so caught up with the waterfall idea on Friday that she'd forgotten all about an accounts meeting that she'd be attending on Monday with her father. He'd expect her to be up to speed if she was eventually going to be appointed to the board of directors.

Suddenly energised, she'd headed upstairs for a shower, coffee mug in hand, planning to look over a few of the accounts so that her father would realise how tuned in she was to all aspects of his business. She'd paused at the door of the *en suite* and decided to turn on the computer in the study first. It always made her impatient to have to wait while it went through the long-winded virus scans before she could get down to work.

Just as she'd turned to leave, she glanced out of the window and noticed a familiar car, Charlie's black BMW, in the driveway opposite. She'd made her way closer to the window, hardly believing what she was seeing. He'd mentioned yesterday that the girl living there, Amy, was friendly with Jason but he bloody well hadn't mentioned anything else.

Glad that her study happened to be at the front of the house and that the slatted Venetian blinds fortuitously allowed her to observe the other house without being caught spying, she sipped her coffee and waited. The curtains were drawn in one of the upstairs windows but Linda wasn't sure if that one was the master bedroom or not, as all of the houses had a different layout.

She waited there for ages, racking her brains to try and think back to whether the car had been there when she'd come home last night. The taxi had dropped her directly to the door and she'd been too inebriated to do anything but lock the door behind her and clean off her make-up before falling unceremoniously into the bed, her clothes discarded on the floor. She cursed herself yet again for having over-indulged, the existing headache intensified by the fact that Charlie had been so blatantly underhand with her. He'd obviously stayed the night with the whey-faced little madam across the way, not even bothering to make any pretence of it by parking out of Linda's view.

After half an hour or so, the door had opened and Charlie had emerged, carrying two jackets over his arm. He stowed these in the boot and went back inside again. Pulling her robe tightly around her, Linda had watched as Amy, dressed in what Linda took to be hillwalking gear, casually packed a tidy rucksack into the boot of Charlie's car, followed by a pair of walking sticks that she'd once heard Charlie refer to as trekking poles. Real jolly hockey-sticks stuff, Linda thought with a sneer, edging back from the window a little when Charlie emerged from the house again.

Feeling a bit like Jessica Fletcher, the annoying old bat in *Murder, She Wrote*, Linda hadn't been able to resist watching the interaction between the two people in the driveway opposite, chatting animatedly as they scurried in and out like ants while the wide-open boot of the BMW grinned across at Linda.

She'd turned away eventually, fuming, as the car pulled out of the driveway.

* * *

Now sitting at her desk with her mind flitting over it again, she was suddenly resentful of all the time that she'd wasted on Charlie. One minute he didn't want to commit, the next he was taking up with her next-door neighbour.

This can't go on, she thought angrily, annoyed that she couldn't get the picture of them setting off together in Charlie's car out of her mind. So fucking what if he and Amy are shagging each other night and day? *I could be at that myself if I wasn't so fucking busy with work.*

Well, there's more to me than just work, she thought decisively, a picture of Luke Nolan springing to mind involuntarily. Ignoring the voice of caution at the back of her mind, she slipped into her jacket, grabbed her car keys and made for the door. It was almost one o'clock. Perhaps he was free for lunch, she thought impulsively, banishing the memory of the intimate smile that Charlie and Amy had shared before banging the doors of the BMW and heading off together.

She focused instead on the mildly flirtatious undertone that pervaded the working lunches and early evening dinners that she'd shared with Luke, and the way he actually appreciated her intelligence and business acumen rather than being threatened by it as Charlie had. This sudden realisation that there *was* actually a spark between them glowed defiantly inside her like some kind of a beacon. Charlie wasn't the only one with a life.

Nearing Luke's office, she slowed to collect her thoughts, planning to ask if he'd like to go out for lunch. She'd decided to add that she was meeting her father at half two, lest he think that she'd come over to Coltons specially. Once she had him alone, she could let him know subtly that their flirting was now acceptable and that she was even ready to progress to something more than just flirting. It would be interesting to see how long it would take for Luke to make a move.

She considered this with satisfaction as she reached the door at the end of the corridor, relieved to hear his voice coming from within, obviously on the phone. As she paused outside for a moment to relish the deep timbre of his voice, some of his conversation drifted out into the corridor.

"And whose fault is that?" He seemed to be teasing,

his words accompanied by a low, intimate laugh.

Linda stood stock still, listening.

"Well, you'll know what to wear the next time. Or else wait in the pub until the game is over. Only then you'd miss out on the sight of me in shorts." He chuckled at the response, a sickeningly cosy tone to his voice.

"I'll bring a woolly hat for you next week," he laughed.

Another low laugh commenced at whatever was being said on the other end of the phone. Linda felt sick.

"I'll hold you to that! Talk to you later, Kelly! Bye!"

Shocked at the probability that Luke was already in a relationship that she wasn't aware of, Linda had to think on her feet, terrified that she'd be discovered lurking outside Luke Nolan's office by someone passing. Briskly, she tapped on the door and walked in as she did so, greeting him with as casual a tone as she was able to muster.

"Sit down," he invited, the remnants of a smile still on his face. "Do you want a coffee?" he added, indicating his own cup and an unfinished sandwich.

Linda refused, saying she was only staying a minute. "I just popped in to see if we could cancel Friday and meet on Thursday morning instead. Something's come up over at Bodywork," she shot off rapidly, using the first excuse that came into her head.

"No bother," Luke answered obligingly. "What time?"

"Would nine be OK?" she asked without thinking,

smiling as professionally as she was able when he nodded in agreement.

She fervently hoped that Michelle hadn't pencilled her in for anything important at 9 a.m. on Thursday. She can bloody well cancel it if she has, Linda swore bitterly to herself, alarmed now at how perilously close she'd come to making a complete fool of herself.

When she finally escaped from the building, she sat in the MG, her head spinning. Desperately, she tried to decide what to do with herself, unable to face the mountain of work waiting for her back at The Sanctuary. Some sanctuary, she cursed, resolving eventually to take the rest of the day off, feeling that it was the least she deserved considering the hours she put in. An afternoon in front of the television would settle her whirring brain and allow her to take stock of the situation. This is all Charlie's fault, she swore resentfully, still appalled at the audacity of Luke Nolan for the way that he'd subtly implied an interest in her while he very obviously was in some sort of relationship.

Emotionally exhausted from it all, she was glad to reach Pebble Cove and see the limestone entrance pillars come into view. She swung into the drive, grateful for a place to hide away for the time being at least. Parking carelessly, she drew her breath in sharply when she noticed that Deirdre next door was out on the front step with the baby on her hip, squealing about something with a self-satisfied Amy. Irritated that Charlie's girlfriend seemed to be under her feet morning, noon and night, Linda cursed under her breath.

Getting out of the MG with all the panache that she possessed, Linda's defiant stare met Amy's level expression across the low limestone wall. Collecting her Hermes handbag and the carton of Darina Allen's chocolate ice cream that she'd picked up along the way, Linda nodded curtly before turning on her heel and making for the safety of her front door with as much dignity as she could muster.

This really is too much. What if this works out? Where would they live? Surely not here in Pebble Cove? Is he purposely trying to make me look like a fool? Bad enough to have to look at Charlie day in, day out at Coltons. But this? No fucking way!

Incensed, Linda looked at the tub of ice cream in her hand and considered flinging it at the floor with as much force as she could muster. She decided against it on the grounds that Charlie bloody Moorehouse had discommoded her quite enough for one day. Serious action was called for now, she vowed resolutely. Determined that she wasn't going to spend the foreseeable future looking across the street at that smug bastard and his picture-perfect Florence Nightingale, she picked up the phone, the ice cream abandoned on the hall table. Enough was enough.

59

Evergreen

"Amy, hi, it's Charlie."

"Oh, hi, Charlie, how are you? Recovered from the walk yet?" Amy was thrilled to hear from him so soon and settled herself into the small antique armchair at the end of the stairs so that she could talk properly.

"I've recovered so well that I was thinking of going again the weekend after next – I'm not sure where though. Would you like to come?"

He sounded a bit hesitant and Amy started to wonder if he was a bit nervous.

"I'd love to. It's great having every weekend off now – I can plan things a bit better than when I was on shift work."

"That's great!" He sounded relieved. "Any ideas on where to head for?"

"I don't mind where we go as long as there's not too much driving involved. Seeing as it's my turn."

"Oh, very nice," he teased. "You don't mind a long trip if I'm the one driving!"

They both laughed over this until Charlie asked her about work and from there the conversation veered off onto anything and everything. They chatted for ages, filling each other in on things that had happened since they'd last met. Amy was amazed at how pleased she was to hear from him, slow to admit, even to herself, how much he'd been on her mind since they'd climbed Musheramore together.

Then, out of the blue, after a slight pause, Charlie said, "Actually, Amy, I wonder would you like to go out for dinner tomorrow night?"

Stunned at the change of subject, she recovered enough to agree, wondering wildly if it was a date.

She spent the whole of the following day wondering if he'd meant the invitation as a romantic evening together or whether it was just a platonic sort of outing. In the end, she decided she'd just have to wing it but dressed up to the nines in case it did lead to something more.

White linen was always good, she decided eventually, teaming the suit with a black sleeveless top and the beaded pendant that she'd worn to the dinner dance in the Mount Vernon.

Charlie had picked her up as planned, oddly shy considering that they'd been completely comfortable with each other on the phone the previous evening.

He'd dressed up as well, she noticed. He looked gorgeous in a dark suit and a white shirt open at the neck. He smell gorgeous too when he kissed her on the cheek in greeting.

They'd made the short drive to The Gallery in Ballycotton in silence, the fresh scent of his aftershave making Amy almost ache to reach out and touch him.

The atmosphere in the restaurant was lively, cutting through the tension that she'd felt between them in the car. They talked animatedly, catching up on the things that they didn't already know about each other's lives. There was a slightly flirtatious edge to their conversation, a sense of anticipation surrounding them that was almost electric.

Charlie couldn't take his eyes off Amy. She looked beautiful in white linen trousers and a black sleeveless top, her hair piled loosely on top of her head. Small bits of it escaped and he longed to reach out and push the silky strands back from her face. Her brown eyes had a sort of smoky look to them tonight, making her more desirable than ever. He hoped that he'd done the right thing by asking her out; the invitation had escaped from him before he'd had time to really think it through.

It was too late for wondering about that now, he decided finally, allowing himself to relax and enjoy Amy's company, whatever the outcome.

The evening flew by, the food fabulous. Like himself, Amy loved good food and had no compunction about ordering from both the dessert trolley and the cheese board. It was late when they finally left, having lingered over a second cup of coffee.

Almost unconsciously, Charlie took her hand as they negotiated the steep path from the restaurant to where his car was parked.

Amy shivered at the feeling of her hand in his. It had been the same last week on the hillwalk. When they reached the car, reluctant to let go of his hand, she turned to him. His name escaped her lips in a whisper. They stood there, almost frozen for a moment, before Charlie slowly bent to kiss her, their lips meeting with a passion that stunned both of them.

60

Leadington

"I suppose two huge favours are out of the question?"

"*You* doing *me* two huge favours? That's a new one." Shay was teasing her, knowing that she was trying to rope him in to help her with Alex's birthday party.

"No," Hazel retorted, flustered, "I want to ask *you* for two favours."

"Two more, you mean! Go on, then. I can't guarantee that I'll be able to help you but there's no harm in begging." He was laughing now at Hazel's expression, and she eventually started to laugh herself, knowing that he probably would help her.

"Catering? For Alex's party? Any takers?"

"Of course I'll come over and help you with the catering. I've already cancelled a round of golf on account of it."

"Oh, Shay, that's brilliant. Come on and I'll show you the list. I hope I have enough food planned."

543

Considering that Hazel never did things by halves, Shay was more worried that there'd be a sausage-roll mountain left over in the middle of the Cove than that a shortage would occur. She was fabulous, fitting more into any one day than should be humanly possible. Her business seemed to be booming, as she had taken on two new stylists in as many months. And the apartment that she was renovating over the salon was taking shape at a rate of knots.

Shay had been over to the building in Dalton Street with her one day when she'd been supervising the installation of the bathroom suite and while he'd been impressed with the whole project, he'd been suddenly alarmed by the speed at which it was progressing. He dreaded the thought of Hazel leaving Pebble Cove and moving back to the city and found himself almost willing the builders to drag their heels. To his frustration, they seemed to be the only builders in the history of the state to actually be working on schedule.

"Hold on, what about the second huge favour?" he asked now.

"We might need a drink for that one," she said seriously. "It's about work."

"Grand so. We'll sort out the party things and you can come over later and we'll open a bottle of wine."

Hazel was deadly serious when it came to work. She'd been looking around for a place to open a second salon, but hadn't found anything suitable up to now. Shay wondered if this was what she wanted to talk about but knew he wouldn't get anything out of her while her mind was focused on glasses and napkins.

Later that evening, Hazel arrived over, a roll of Pringles under one arm and a selection of ledgers and her laptop under the other.

"This looks serious," Shay smiled as he relieved her of some of the load. "I'm not sure the wine will be such a good idea."

Hazel busied herself in the kitchen, pulling out the shallow dish that Shay always used for the Pringles, surreptitiously watching Shay. He looked gorgeous in jeans and a navy T-shirt, his arms and face tanned from the outdoors, making his eyes look bluer than ever. His hair was shorter now than it had been when she'd met him first, but it still had the same streaky blonde colour that it seemed to have all year round. Hazel was drawn to him in a way that she'd never experienced before, but was definitely not going to make a fool of herself if he wasn't interested.

They'd become close lately, with Shay opening up gradually about the events that had led up to his friend's death. Hazel wondered if he wasn't being too hard on himself, unable to imagine him as the hard-drinking, party animal that he described. She admired the fact that he'd been open enough to go to counselling afterwards, even though he'd confessed to being sceptical at the outset.

"So, what's the deal?" Shay was intrigued by the fact that she'd brought over the details of her accounts and was touched that she'd feel comfortable with the idea of him going through them. He wondered again if it would be wise to try and move their relationship onto a more romantic footing, aroused by the scent of her perfume as she leaned over and handed him the bowl of Pringles, her fingers brushing his momentarily.

"You know I've been looking around for somewhere to open up in the city? Well, any places that I've looked at in good locations have been either seriously expensive to rent or, if the rent is reasonable, then they've been in dire need of renovation. Either way, they'd cost too much to start up in."

"So have you come up with something?"

"The Sanctuary, the health spa out in Rochestown, is advertising rental space specifically for a hair salon. I've rang up about it. It'd be fully fitted out, purpose built *and* it'd have a fairly immediate client base from the rest of the complex."

"What would the rent be like?"

Shay knew that the complex was being pitched at the high end of the market and was aware of the Coltons policy of starting to achieve a turnover from the existing components of the health spa as quickly as possible.

"That's the thing. It's pretty high, but not extortionate by city standards. I think I could manage it easily, considering I have no huge overheads in Dalton Street."

Hazel thanked her lucky stars every day that she'd inherited the building, more so since she'd discovered the kind of rent people were paying for much shabbier premises in poorer locations.

"How long would it be fixed for?"

Shay was very much aware that many businesses got caught in the trap of renting premises at low rent for a couple of years but were unable to take the hike that inevitably came when the lease came up for renewal. Reluctant to move an established business, particularly if they were dependent on passing trade, they ended up signing away most of their profits in rent in order to stay in the same place.

"Two years only. God knows what it could rise to after that. It's ideal otherwise though – it'd take off like a bomb."

"So what are you thinking? Offering higher rent in exchange for fixing the lease for a longer period?"

"I'd need to sell it pretty well," Hazel said, thrilled that Shay seemed to be on the same wavelength as her. She loved the way he sat back and asked only a few considered questions, never rushing ahead of her to tell her what she *should* do.

"You're thinking that we'd need to go through the books and figure out how much you could afford over ten years or maybe even fifteen?"

"Would you mind helping me, Shay? Normally Marcus and Dee go through all these things with me but they've enough on their plate at the moment."

"No bother. I presume you'll have to move fairly quickly. Did you arrange a meeting with Linda Colton or whoever's dealing with it?"

"I'm pencilled in to meet her next Friday but I'm not sure if that'll be enough time – with the party the following day, I mean. What do you think?"

"You'll be in plenty of time. You concentrate on the party and I'll tackle the business end of things," Shay told her resolutely. "Only give me over your laptop and go and put the kettle on. We'll need nothing stronger than coffee for the next few nights."

61

Evergreen

Amy woke up, slightly confused at first. It took her a moment to register that it was Saturday. No need to rush to the shower. Relaxing back into the comfy familiarity of her bed, she listened idly to the sound of a car door slamming outside and the echo of voices below. Dee and Marcus were probably up to their eyes getting ready for the party.

An unbelievable contentment settled around her and she curled into a ball to savour the feeling. So much had changed in her life that she felt like a different person to the one that had woken up in Pebble Cove for the first time almost a year ago. She'd started to feel older lately, something to do with being made painfully aware of the fragility of life, she supposed. Plus getting the promotion at work and taking on the extra responsibility that went with it. Even the extra study she'd had to put in to get her thesis finished had weighed more heavily on her than it normally would.

The last month, however, had been like a breath of fresh air.

Everything had changed once Charlie had kissed her outside The Gallery, overlooking Ballycotton Lighthouse. Barely a month had passed yet hardly a day passed that they didn't speak to each other. Charlie had been hesitant at first, reluctant to rush her, but Amy had gradually reassured him that she was more than ready to start again.

She closed her eyes now at the memory of their lovemaking the previous night. Nothing could have prepared her for the way that Charlie's hands had touched her, his lips trailing gently all over her until she'd almost cried. His quiet strength made her feel unbelievably cherished, the sense of trust she felt when he was around her was utterly complete. She listened to him now, clattering around in the kitchen below and felt as close to him as if he was right next to her.

62

One Year Older

Deirdre closed the door of Alex's room as quietly as she could, only half realising how ridiculous it was to be treading so carefully when Alex had actually fallen asleep in the midst of chaos. Thanks to his early days in the neonatal unit he was well able for noise, having been used to people coming and going twenty-four hours a day. Now he was sleeping soundly, despite the lively sound of *Abba Gold* vibrating through the house. The party was hotting up already and she hadn't even had a drink yet.

Stooping to pick up a stray glass that someone had left on the landing, she counted her blessings that Hazel had taken on most of the catering for the evening. Shay from next door appeared to have been drafted in, although Deirdre wasn't sure if he'd actually consented or whether he'd been railroaded by her sister. It was just as well that she'd roped him in, considering how busy she'd been with the proposal for the new salon.

As it stood, he was passing around a selection of seafood hors d'oeuvres that Hazel had spent the whole morning trimming and shaping, so that they were almost a work of art and far too flawless to consider eating.

Hazel had been unusually stressed when she'd arrived back from Talking Heads at twelve, having popped in for an hour to check that things were ticking over. Two of the senior stylists were on maternity leave and Deirdre wondered if she'd run into bother at the salon. It wasn't like her sister to be so quiet in herself, especially when there was a party in the offing. Making a mental note to check in with her as soon as they got a quiet moment together, Deirdre made her way downstairs to join the party.

Passing through the dining-room, she came across Marcus who, instead of keeping an eye that people's drinks were topped up, was extolling the virtues of marriage to Charlie Moorehouse, who looked as if he was about to start taking notes on the subject. Deirdre caught her mother's eye and returned her wink with a roll of her eyes and a wry grin. Any time that he had more than two drinks Marcus tended to start eulogising on what a wonderful wife he had, something that Deirdre's family thought hilarious and teased her constantly about.

Deirdre deftly collected Alex's belongings from where they'd been abandoned when he'd fallen asleep in his grandmother's arms a little earlier, despite being hyped to the nines from all the attention. He'd spent the afternoon pulling the wrapping off his presents and chewing on the paper, discarding the actual contents of the parcels. He'd stayed up a full hour later than his usual bedtime, his cheeks rosy from the exertion of pulling himself into a standing position and then flopping back down on his bottom, knowing that he'd get a clap and a laugh from whoever was watching him.

Quietly, she sneaked up the stairs again, this time to stow the mountain of toys in the spare room where her parents were sleeping for the night. They'd offered to get up during the night if Alex woke to allow Deirdre and Marcus a chance to enjoy the party, especially if it turned into a late night.

Detouring to Alex's room to make sure he was settled, Dee smiled affectionately when she saw the blankets kicked to the bottom of the cot. He was definitely Marcus's son.

It was unbelievable, she reflected, how far they'd come in a year.

This night last year, she'd been in labour, terrified of what was to come. If anyone had told her of the nightmare that was to follow and had given her a choice of whether to face it or not, she was quite sure that she would have been unable to take it on. To think that she'd be expressing breast milk for a baby that wasn't even able to suck a bottle, that would most likely be brain-damaged! That she would learn to do things like inserting the feeding-tube and filling in feeding charts as a matter of course, and that she would cope with these things, would have been beyond the scale of her imagination. She'd read about people in women's magazines whose babies were on life-support machines but she'd never visualised herself as being one of them.

Pictures of Alex in the first days of his life flashed through her mind suddenly. The first time she saw him, covered in bubble-wrap with the horrible tube down his throat breathing for him. The early morning brain scans, with the radiographer squeezing the ultrasound gel onto the soft spot on the top of Alex's head, in order to get a clear view of the haemorrhage that could devastate his already immature brain. She shivered, almost physically sick, as the images of Amy resuscitating him the evening he stopped breathing flittered through her mind. Never before had she felt such icy shock, or such gratitude to another human being, as she had when she'd seen the colour seeping back into Alex's face.

She'd banished these pictures from her mind up to now, too scared to be reminded of the trauma that he'd come through, and the reality of what that trauma could mean to his future development. The staff in the neonatal unit had described these incidents as "insults", explaining that any insult to the body could deprive the brain of oxygen, possibly causing further damage. Nobody could ever tell them the *degree* of damage that might be caused. Just that it was a warning to them to accept that Alex's progress would be slow.

It was only now, when his progress had far surpassed anything that could have been predicted, that Deirdre could allow herself to think about how different it could have been. To see a child standing upright as he clung to the sofa for dear life was a joy to any parent, but to Dee, it was as if Alex was flying. To watch him waving his arms to get her attention when he was ready to come out of the cot in the mornings was as fascinating as if he was about to address the General Assembly at the United Nations.

It made her heart soar to know that she would have loved him dearly anyway, no matter what disabilities he might have had. But to think, finally, that he might lead a normal life, that he wouldn't have to suffer some of the things that they'd envisaged, was truly a miracle. To know that he'd be able to walk, to hear him start to say "Da Da" and feel confident that he would talk and play like every other child was all that they could have wished for.

She heard Marcus come into the room behind her and felt his arms come around her, his lips brushing her temple.

"Imagine, this time last year Alex wasn't even born," he said softly, echoing Deirdre's thoughts.

"I know, I was just thinking the same thing."

"After he was born, when I had to go to the Neonatal Unit with him, I was terrified that I wouldn't be able to cope. That I wouldn't know what to do to help him."

"Of all the things that I was afraid of," Deirdre told him softly, "the one thing that I was sure of was that you'd look after us. I remember how helpless I felt the first night when I couldn't move my legs after the epidural, but I knew if anything was wrong you'd come and get me." She turned and wrapped her arms around him, feeling secure as always when they were together.

"I know it's easy to say now that he's doing so well," said Marcus, "but I know we'd have coped with anything, whatever happened. When people say that they'd never be able for everything that we went through in the last year, they don't see how much we love him, only all the coming and going to the Neonatal Unit and all the scares."

"And that we had each other. That was the thing for me, Marcus – that we were together in everything. And that we had Alex, no matter what."

"I love you, Dee," Marcus told her softly, his arms tightening around her. "Now, come on. If we don't go down soon they'll all go home. Plus we have to find out what the story with the doll next door is," he added wickedly.

"Well, I'm damned if I'm the one who's going to ask," Dee retorted, kissing him smartly before wriggling out of his arms and making for the stairs. "I'm sure we'll find out soon enough."

* * *

Charlie watched Amy chatting animatedly to Hazel and Sheila, her eyes sparkling and her head thrown back laughing. It always struck him how natural and at ease she was with herself, and it came unbidden to his mind how different she was from Linda.

Amy never tried to create an impression – she was just naturally poised and comfortable in any company or situation. There was no ulterior agenda with her; everything was straight and honest and sincere. Even the way she dressed captivated him, the way she always looked great whether it was in shorts and hiking boots or dressed up to go out at night. Whereas Linda's confidence in herself had been overt and dominating, Amy's was somehow quiet and steady. He knew with conviction that he loved her completely, and was somehow certain that she felt just as he did.

Already, their lives had melded together as if they'd always been a couple. For Charlie, it was as if everything had suddenly fallen into place in his life. He thought back to the festival weekend in Gilcrenan when he'd first met Amy, and how confused he'd been about Linda and her plans for The Sanctuary.

Even when his father had revealed that the farm at home would soon be sold and that he would, if he wanted, have the money to invest in Linda's venture, he'd felt more confused than ever. As well as feeling under immense pressure to join forces with Linda in business, there had been the unsettling feeling that the farmhouse in Gilcrenan would no longer be part of his life. Charlie had told his parents a week ago that he'd love to keep the farmhouse after they sold the farm, visualising it now as a holiday retreat for the future.

Somehow, he and Amy seemed to have the same outlook on life, valuing a lifestyle that was easygoing rather than dynamic and fast-paced. They were both ambitious in their own way but never to the point of sacrificing their time with each other for the sake of work. With Linda, socialising had always been about making contacts and being seen in the right places, something that Charlie had tolerated rather than enjoyed, when he thought about it now. Likewise, Linda had been bored with the lively evenings in the local with Charlie's friends and their wives or girlfriends, and in the end he'd stopped inflicting them on her.

He wondered sometimes how he'd let it go on for so long, and what would have happened if he hadn't made a move to finish their relationship. Would Linda have eventually felt the same emptiness that he had? Would they have become the type of married couple that led completely separate lives, with nothing in common? Or become another divorce statistic?

It seemed so far away now, and although he never said it out loud, he couldn't help comparing the vibrancy of his life now to the wooden feeling that he'd had in the past.

Guiltily, he contemplated again the effect that his relationship with Amy had obviously had on Linda, but decided to push it to the back of his mind for the time being at least. He knew things had probably moved a little faster than she might have expected. But, at the end of the day, he couldn't be responsible for such hasty action. Vowing to talk it through with Linda after the weekend in order to get their working relationship back on its former steady footing, he decided to put it out of his head and enjoy the rest of the party.

He smiled as he caught Amy's eye and moved over to where she was still talking with Sheila, having been joined now by Deirdre.

"What are you smirking at?" she questioned with a grin, flushed from the warmth of the room and the Bacardi Breezers that Hazel was doling out.

"Must be the skirt and sexy sandals thing again," he teased, reminding her of the last time that she'd worn that outfit.

Amy giggled, leaning in to him for a kiss, knowing that he'd plant one on the top of her head. "Imagine, this weekend last year we'd just met. So it's an anniversary of sorts really."

Sometimes, Amy felt like she was in the middle of a dream. Everything in her life had suddenly come together, as if she'd been building up to it all along. Buying the house last year had seemed like the best thing that had ever happened, her own little haven in the most fabulous place she could think of.

Meeting Peter then had made it seem as if everything was falling neatly into place. When he'd died, it had felt as if her whole future had been dashed, that the life that had been laid out for her, that she'd started to look forward to, had been suddenly pulled away from her. It was a long time before she was able to remember her grandmother telling her wisely: "What's for you won't pass you by."

Getting to know Charlie had overwhelmed her in a

way that she could never have imagined. Everything about him made her fall more in love with him every time she looked at him. She loved his quiet manner and his thoughtfulness, the way he seemed to fit seamlessly into her life as if he'd always been there. Falling asleep beside him at night and waking up beside him in the morning was the most wonderful feeling, something that she couldn't ever have imagined.

Although their personalities varied greatly, their interests and the things they wanted from life were the same. Friends and family were as important to Charlie as they were to her and they both enjoyed simple things like having friends over or going for a walk together.

Now standing here among their neighbours – friends really – Amy couldn't have been happier. Looking around, she was immensely grateful for all the good things in her life. She loved her home and felt somewhere deep inside her that she and Charlie would start their lives together there. The only fly in the ointment was Linda but there was nothing she could do about that. I can live with the shadow of her hanging over me, Amy thought to herself, but she obviously can't.

As Amy departed towards the dining room with Charlie in search of more of the delicious smoked salmon and cream cheese roulade that Shay had insisted they try earlier, Deirdre and Sheila resumed their earlier conversation.

Sheila had finally made the decision to leave the Neonatal Unit permanently, and would hand her notice to Amy as soon as she had the final dates for starting her new life at Carnelian Springs. Reluctant to pressurise the GP who'd built up his practice in her husband's old surgery, Sheila had jumped at the chance to take on as many hours as she could at the holistic centre. A couple of years working full-time there would allow her to hone her skills and develop a steady clientele, without the overheads that opening her own practice immediately would bring. She'd thought about it for ages before applying, finally deciding that a purpose-built room with a service co-ordinator to sort out appointments would be less stressful than starting from scratch on her own. She could use the next few years to renovate Martin's rooms, if ever they were finally vacated.

The interview at The Sanctuary had been nerve-wracking, especially as she'd been refused one initially. Disappointed at the time, she'd put the idea of regular sessions in an organised setting out of her mind and had started to resign herself to her original plan, when a second letter had arrived from The Sanctuary inviting her for interview the following week.

In spite of her daughters' encouragement and a cocktail of herbal teas and aromatherapy oils to calm her, she'd been nervous on the day, terrified that everything she'd learned in the past few years would suddenly evaporate into thin air.

Although they hadn't actually spoken on the day, she recognised Linda Colton as the haughty blond who'd been having lunch with Charlie in Springfield

Manor in Clonakilty. Sitting with an impressive panel of experts for the interview, Linda gave off an arrogant, imperious aura, her cool blue eyes taking everything in.

The others, one from the Reflexology Institute and the other from the Complementary Therapy Board, went through their questions in an encouraging and friendly fashion but Linda seemed to be almost trying to catch her out, as if there was some kind of fraud to be detected. Her manner had been sharp, particularly in relation to the fact that some of Sheila's qualifications were recently acquired.

Amy and Deirdre, however, had prepared her for this, pointing out that the panel were aware of her lack of experience when they called her for interview, so she had nothing to be defensive about. When the question of how short a time she'd been practicing reflexology had been voiced by Linda Colton in what Sheila considered to be an unreasonably challenging tone, she'd stated calmly that she'd made it as clear as possible in her application form just how recently she'd acquired her qualifications. She then waited serenely for Linda's response, practically clamping her lips shut lest she start to babble in her own defence.

The fellow from the Complementary Therapy board had interjected at that point, asking what her plans would be if she weren't successful at this interview. Again, she'd been prepared, explaining that she'd already established a practice at her home and that she'd hope to expand this gradually if a position at The Sanctuary wasn't offered.

Linda Colton had followed on from this with a series of questions about Sheila's nursing career, noting that she worked in the Neonatal Unit at the city's largest hospital. What was it that had induced such a sudden interest in the world of holism, considering that she was obviously highly motivated in her principal line of work?

Sheila had shrewdly deduced that Linda was a hard-nosed business type who would have little appreciation for the fact that Sheila had used up every personal resource within her in the years after her husband's death, and had started using the various complementary therapies to rejuvenate herself as soon as her daughters had been reared. It would be better to portray herself as having observed the levels of stress in contemporary lifestyles and to have seen it almost as a business opportunity, rather than allow someone like Linda Colton to dismiss her as "airy fairy".

Linda had appeared to be grudgingly satisfied with Sheila's slant on her sudden change of career path and queried if she would eventually plan to work full-time in the Complementary Health Sector, perhaps even working entirely from home.

Thinking that Linda was trying to assess whether Sheila would gain experience at The Sanctuary and then take off with the clients she'd acquired to expand her own business in competition with them, she answered as honestly as she could that at the present time her circumstances would preclude her making any dramatic steps for a number of years. She'd hoped that this was enough to prevent Linda from seeing her as a liability in terms of offering her the sessions at The Sanctuary.

It seemed it had, as she'd received a letter three days ago telling her that she'd been allocated a full-time position in Carnelian Springs, set to open in September.

"That's absolutely brilliant, Sheila," Deirdre said, more impressed with her than ever. Changing career at any age was an enormous step, yet Sheila seemed to have no fear at all about it. She looked elegant tonight in a cream linen trouser suit, teamed with a chocolate-brown top with ethnic-type beading at the V neckline. She always looked so vibrant, Deirdre thought, her wavy chestnut hair perfectly groomed and her make-up done to perfection.

Just then, Deirdre's sister Hazel sashayed up to them, bearing aloft yet another tray of delicacies. "Is it holistic practitioners only in this corner only or can anyone join in?"

Hazel was highly amused that her sister, a serious banker up to a year ago, was now dabbling in massage and aromatherapy, traditionally thought of as being slightly "hippy". Merciless once she got going, she giggled as she waved the tempting array of nibbles under their noses knowing full well that neither of them would put up too much resistance.

"So," Sheila prodded, checking to make sure that nobody was listening, "what about the sexy Shay? Any progress?"

She was fully tuned in to Hazel's feelings for their

single neighbour, having listened attentively to a long list of his virtues every Saturday afternoon when the girls arrived back from the baby massage course.

While their friendship seemed to have progressed satisfactorily since the evening that Shay had helped Hazel to assemble Alex's cot and changing unit, there was still no development on the romantic side of things.

"I'm not sure it's going anywhere to be honest," Hazel admitted, suddenly looking glum and defeated, as if she'd decided to accept that a friendship was all she was ever going to have with Shay.

Sheila, always quick to notice emotional responses in other people, was convinced that Shay *did* have feelings for Hazel but was possibly too shy to express them for fear of a knockback from someone so glamorous and dynamic.

"Why do you say that, Hazel? It was all going to plan last weekend, wasn't it? And he's giving a great hand tonight."

Deirdre, listening to the exchange between her sister and Sheila, was now convinced that something had happened to make Hazel doubt her chances with Shay.

"I know," Hazel sighed. "I'm just wondering whether it's all too complicated."

This defeatist attitude wasn't at all like the Hazel that Sheila had come to know during Alex's early days in the Neonatal Unit. Hazel was simply a frank personality with absolutely no hidden agenda and an incredibly loyal and supportive nature. Her impressive height, translucent skin and the reddish highlights in her rich brunette mane of curls had initially led Sheila to believe that she was a dazzling career woman. She'd since discovered that as well as being ambitious and dynamic, she was full of vigorous energy and mischievous in the extreme with a wicked laugh. Sheila couldn't believe that her innate self-possession could crumble so easily in the face of Shay's apparent disinterest.

"To be honest, Hazel, you might have to let him know that you're interested. Subtly!" she added, knowing how direct Hazel could be when she decided to address something. "What do you think, Dee?"

"He might actually be a bit afraid of you," Deirdre agreed. "Nervous about making a move in case you'd be horrified or something. I *do* think he likes you, though. He's always gazing at you as if you're some film star who landed next to him by mistake."

"Do you think so?" Hazel asked.

Sometimes it *did* seem as if Shay was about to make some sort of move, but in the months that she'd known him, he'd never actually given her any definite indication that he wanted more than just a friend or companion. And after the incident with Polly in Talking Heads earlier in the day, Hazel wasn't so sure what she wanted herself anymore.

They went out together a lot, either with Deirdre and Marcus if Rose and Tom were baby-sitting or with Shay's friends from work. Sometimes he called over in the evenings to keep her company when she was baby-sitting Alex, or occasionally she called over to his house for a chat or to watch a video during the week. They got on like a house on fire, or at least Hazel thought so, particularly since he'd helped her to prepare for her meeting with Linda Colton about opening a salon in The Sanctuary.

"I think Deirdre's right," Sheila commented. "Do you want me to chat him up for a bit and see if I can sus him out?"

"And you're asking *me* to be subtle!"

"Only trying to help," Sheila quipped, heading off in the direction of the kitchen to see if she could lend a hand.

"Is everything alright, Hazey?" Deirdre asked, using her sister's pet name. She'd been so absorbed in her own affairs lately that she wondered if she'd neglected her a bit.

"Oh, just something that happened earlier when I dropped into the salon."

"Tell me," Deirdre demanded, adamant that Hazel wouldn't withhold a worry from her.

Looking around to make sure that there was nobody listening, Hazel began.

"I hadn't said to the girls that I was dropping in this morning. Eileen and Trish were manning the place so I assumed that Polly and Marina were on their coffee break. Everything was under control so I went ahead into the office to make a few calls."

She paused then and sighed.

Deirdre, waiting expectantly, prompted her, "And?"

"I could hear Polly and Marina talking through the

567

partition. Gossiping."

Deirdre knew the layout of the salon well and could visualise the two juniors grousing about their boss in the small kitchen while Hazel sat at the far side of the thin partition wall.

"Hazel, you're their boss. We all give out about our bosses." She was surprised that Hazel was so upset about a bit of bitching, knowing that she usually took the unpleasant bits of managing the salon in her stride.

"They weren't giving out about me. They were talking about Shay."

"How do they know him?" Deirdre was perplexed, knowing that Hazel only socialised with the girls from the salon on rare occasions like the Christmas party.

"As far as I could make out, Polly had seen me in town with Shay and recognised him. He used to go out with one of her friends. He's mentioned her before – Carla."

Poor Hazel looked as if she was going to cry, her eyes anxious. Deirdre couldn't imagine what had been said to hurt her so much.

"So what was the gist of it?" she probed gently.

"Well, it was nothing that Shay hadn't told me himself, to be honest. It was just hearing someone else's view of it that upset me. Polly was saying that Carla finished with Shay because of his drinking and that he took drugs a lot."

"But you knew all this, Hazel. It's not as if he tried to hide it." Deirdre liked Shay and, like Marcus and her parents, admired him for making a fresh start. Hazel too had held this view so her about-turn was disconcerting to say the least.

"I know that but it's just a feeling I got listening to them. Like how badly Shay treated Carla – I think he might have been seen out in pubs and clubs with other women and that. Apparently lots of people told Carla about him after they'd broken up."

"I don't know what to say, Hazel. I'm not sticking up for him or anything but you told me yourself that he'd admitted to treating people badly when Ken was on the go with him."

"It's just that I'm wondering if I'd be making a fool of myself if I got into a relationship with him. I know people can change but . . ."

"You're afraid that he'll start drinking and playing around again?" Now that she was getting to the heart of it, Deirdre could see where Hazel was coming from.

"Something like that," Hazel admitted. "I fancy him like mad but now I'm asking myself if I'm a bit blind about his faults. Like one of these women who think that a man will reform and ends up married to an alcoholic despite all her friends telling her she that she's mad."

"Look, Hazel, you're the only one who can decide on this. But you have to remember that Shay had started to shape up well before you two became friendly. He's had a lot of counselling as well, which means that he's very much aware of his own shortcomings. It's not as if he started to be Little Boy Blue the minute you met him."

"I suppose," Hazel conceded, brightening a little, then adding ironically, "And it's not as if he's exactly pressing me for a decision or anything."

"Well, that's it too – but that can be a positive factor – there's no rush. Just give yourself time. You'll know if it's right."

"And I can always sack that little wagon Polly if I have to!" Hazel grinned as she watched Shay making his way towards them.

"Sorry to interrupt, ladies, but there's the small matter of a batch of Prawn Choux Bundles that seem to be missing their Sweet Chilli Dip."

Shay looked at Hazel as if she had the answer to Big Bang versus Evolution tucked away in her handbag. She and Deirdre exchanged glances, with the latter making to sidle away discreetly. Suddenly, Hazel's eyes widened with panic.

"Jesus!" she shrieked in alarm, darting towards the kitchen. "Is the oven still on? They'll be like dog biscuits by now!"

Shay followed hot on her heels, reassuring her quickly that the small knots of flaky pastry, each containing a jumbo prawn, were cooling on a wire tray. Only the sauce was missing. "Your list says Sweet Chilli Dip. There're two sauces in the fridge but I was afraid to proceed in case I dosed them with Raspberry Coulis."

Hazel's face relaxed immediately and she started to smile at the thought of her Summer Berry Pavlova getting drizzled with Sweet Chilli Dip. This was the

Shay that she'd come to know. Talking to Deirdre had put things in perspective for her.

"What?" Shay demanded, eyebrows raised and a grin spreading across his face.

"Nothing," Hazel responded. "I'm just wondering where I got the idea that I'd be able to manage all of this on my own. If you weren't here I'd be having a knicker-fit by now!"

Shay laughed at her dramatic turn of phrase, turning his attention to arranging the little bundles on a Willow Pattern platter that Hazel's mother had produced for the occasion, answering as lightly as he could. "That's what friends are for. Anyway, I'm actually enjoying it."

Hazel, standing next to him at the worktop ladling the sticky sauce into tiny individual ramekins, blithely ignored all warnings about subtlety. She needed to know where she stood with him or she'd go crazy speculating as she'd done all day.

"Is that it, Shay? Just friends or mates or whatever?"

Her heart was beating furiously but she felt somehow calm at the same time, knowing that she needed to hear it out loud if Shay didn't think of her other than as a friend. Because despite the misgivings that she'd raised with Deirdre, she was still madly attracted to him. And now that she'd spoken out loud about his past, she knew in her heart that she did trust him.

Almost the same height, their eyes met for a second before Shay spoke.

"I thought . . . " he began tentatively. "It's just . . . you know about everything with Ken . . . I thought you'd think I was a bit of a basket case." He sighed deeply. "Someone like you deserves better than that . . ."

"What do you mean 'someone like you'?" she asked quietly. "Do you think that I don't understand how awful it was for you, or that I think it was easy to get your life back on track the way you did? Do you think that all I see is E tablets when we're out for a drink?"

"God, Hazel, I didn't mean it like that. I just meant that . . . I don't know . . . " Shay dropped his eyes and stared intently at the prawn parcels dotted around the blue-patterned platter, before looking back at her again. "Hazel, you're great. You must know that, and you have so much going for you. Your parents would go mad if they knew about Ken and the whole drugs thing."

"Shay, they know about that already," Hazel told him gently. Seeing the look of horror on his face, she continued evenly. "Mum thought you had a bit of a 'hurt' look about you, ages ago, and she asked me if you were just out of a relationship or something. I think she was worried about me getting involved with someone who was on the rebound. As if!" she added wryly, resigned now to the fact that Shay was obviously on a different wavelength. "So I told her."

"What did she say then?"

"She thought it was terrific, the way you were tackling it, I mean. And that you were able to be open about it, not covering it up or blaming everyone else."

Taking a deep breath, Hazel knew it was time to move on from where they were at and try to act normally. It was typical of her to make up her mind on a relationship being a good idea only to find out that Shay didn't fancy her at all. Describing her as "great" was a sure sign.

The noise and chatter filtering through from the rest of the house reminded her that she was supposed to be catering for a party, not having emotional scenes in the kitchen.

"Come on, you bring the tray and I'll get more wine," she said brightly, bumping her shoulder against his the way they did when bickering over a film in the small video shop in the village.

"Hazel, come back! We have to talk about this."

"Shay," she began hesitantly, "It's no good . . ."

"Hazel," he interrupted her, "every time you go home I spend the whole night awake thinking about you. I keep thinking that if only I hadn't been such an eejit, I'd be able to ask you out properly."

Hazel, frozen to the spot with a corkscrew in one hand, stared at him in amazement.

"Say something," he whispered anxiously, moving over to where she stood and extracting the bottle-opener from her hand. When she still said nothing, Shay put his arms around her and held her tightly, his lips stroking her hair. "I'm so afraid of messing this up," he told her quietly, feeling her head relax against his chest.

"Shay, you're the only person I know that I could tell

absolutely anything to and not be afraid of what you'd say. You couldn't mess that up," she said truthfully.

She pulled away a little and looked at him smiling, amazed that they'd got this far without ever having even kissed. Shay, obviously thinking the same thing, brought his lips gently to meet hers, feeling the connection like a jolt of electricity as they touched.

Then the kitchen door burst open and they both started in alarm and jumped guiltily away from each other.

"Don't mind me – I just live here," Marcus sniggered as he made for the fridge and pulled out a bottle of white wine and some cans of beer. Blissfully unaware of his sister-in-law's angst less than an hour ago, he continued to tease Hazel and Shay. "It's just that we hired caterers and they seem to have gone AWOL," he added merrily, grabbing the now cold platter of Prawn Choux Bundles, obviously in his element now that Alex was sound asleep and his parents-in-law were on duty. With that, he skittered giddily back to the party, leaving Shay and Hazel giggling behind him.

"Is that what I have to live up to?" Shay quipped, drawing Hazel back into his arms.

"I hope to God you won't be that daft if you get a few drinks once a year," Hazel said affectionately, nibbling his lower lip playfully.

Then the door opened again, this time to admit a sheepish Amy. "Deirdre and Marcus sent me to enquire about the pavlova," she stuttered obediently, rosy-cheeked now that she'd copped on why they were so anxious to have her go to the kitchen.

"Hounds, all of you!" Hazel scowled, breaking away from Shay yet again. She broke into a smile when she saw the corners of Amy's mouth starting to twitch. "Make yourself useful and grab a few plates, seeing as you're here anyway," she ordered tartly.

To which Amy replied cheekily, "What's that about getting it on a plate?"

She ducked to avoid the tea towel that Hazel flung at her, but obligingly started to open cupboards in search of the said items. Shay, with a menacing Arnold Schwartzenegger accent, promised "I'll – be – back!" before exiting to refill a few wine glasses, leaving the two women grinning at each other across the kitchen table.

"I presume you took the advice about being subtle?"

"What do *you* think?"

Having given an edited account of the proceedings, Hazel re-entered the sitting room with Amy in time to see one of Marcus's colleagues from the bank belt out a rousing rendition of *Johnny Jump Up*, a sure sign that he'd exceeded his usual two pints of Murphys.

A gang of them had arrived earlier, including the senior manager of Marcus's division who had been invited on the spur of the moment when the rest of them had started talking about the party in the coffee-room a few days previously. A confirmed bachelor in his fifties, he was now listening attentively to Sheila Forde who was studiously ignoring the saucy winks that Hazel was directing at her, having emerged from the kitchen like someone who'd just won the Lotto.

"Poor Alex will wake up howling if this continues," Deirdre laughed as Charlie joined in for the final verse.

Amy, whispering urgently that she wasn't sure that her boyfriend could sing at all, was shushed by Rose and Tom who were straining to hear what happened to the hero at the end of the song.

Once the singing had started officially, two of Deirdre's friends from Asset Management took off in earnest, starting with a disjointed version of "*I Will Survive*". Their friend, a bosomy little blonde called Tara, was glued to Marcus's brother Vincent who'd arrived from Arizona the evening before to help celebrate his nephew's birthday.

"I have a feeling that Vincent will be offered an interest-free mortgage before the night is out," Deirdre smirked, winking boldly at her friend who obviously thought Vincent was the catch of the day.

"That's not all he'll be offered, by the looks of it," Marcus responded in alarm as his brother tried to extricate himself but was hampered by the voluminous depths of the squishy leather armchair and the fact that Tara was perched so precariously on the arm of it, leaning in perilously close to him.

"He's well able to mind himself, although I not sure how impressed your mother is," said Deirdre.

Despite Tom and Rose's best attempts to loosen them out, Marcus's parents were lined up like two pillars of salt on the sofa, looking as disapproving as if the assembled revellers were snorting cocaine. Rose had already plied Eileen with as much sherry as was decent in order to get a bit of chat out of her, but she was still smiling the same tight smile as she had at Alex's christening all those months ago.

Joe looked as if he might break out a bit if his wife disappeared into thin air. But as that seemed unlikely, he appeared content to sip a well-watered whiskey and observe the goings-on around him. God only knew what he thought of the brazen Tara whose perky boobs were now hovering terrifyingly close to his younger son's face, Deirdre thought with a frisson of alarm. Still, Marcus had decided to tune out and enjoy himself, so there was no point in her worrying about them, she resolved, as she accepted a top-up from Hazel and joined into the inevitable rendition of *"The Banks of My Own Lovely Lee"*.

63

Number 1

Linda felt like screaming as she slammed the window shut to drown out the raucous sounds of *"The Banks"*. Again and again she wondered how she'd wound up living in such a haven of insularity. Incestuous was what it was, all this neighbourly goodwill with everyone tied up in everyone else's business.

She cast her mind back to the time that her father had first mooted the idea of building a selection of exclusive homes overlooking the harbour. Charlie, who she'd presumed would be a permanent fixture in her life, would design each residence with the same innovation and attention to detail that he did with every project that he got involved in. The five-bedroom show house would be decorated to her own impeccable standards, and would eventually be Charlie's home too.

Where had it all gone wrong? Suddenly, everything

had seemed to go pear-shaped. Linda had envisaged a selection of like-minded individuals as neighbours, the kind of people who would complement the tone of the development and maintain the air of exclusivity that the size and location of the houses demanded.

Somehow, despite the hefty price tags and the enormous interest in the properties, each house had fallen into the hands of the sort of people who wouldn't be out of place in any large suburban development.

The Flemings, next door to her, were the type of people that she'd envisaged lending a bit of class to the address? Both successful bankers, they'd seemed the ideal candidates to reside next to her. While there was nothing flashy about them, she'd noticed immediately that Marcus drove a top-of-the-range Volvo and his wife a brand new, although smallish, Audi.

The birth of their first child, however, had turned Deirdre into the sort of matronly *hausfrau* that it usually took at least five children to achieve. Any time that Linda spotted her outside the house, which in itself was rare enough, she had the baby glued to her hip like a mini-extension of herself. Hardly the sign of ambition, Linda would bitch silently to herself.

Shay Deegan in the middle house had again seemed a likely prospect for the task of upholding the selective tone of the development, but he seemed to have joined the ranks of the *hoi polloi* as soon as he'd got settled in among them. Linda had observed him coming and going with the striking brunette who was apparently a sister of the suddenly earthy Deirdre. She'd been startled to find herself facing the same Hazel when she had started to advertise the salon space at The Sanctuary in the trade journals. Hazel had been surprisingly well able to account for herself, despite having Shay Deegan with her as a financial adviser. Equally surprising was the state of her accounts and her plans to expand her business throughout Cork county. The fact that she actually owned her city centre premises intrigued Linda, who admired the fact that she'd obviously been tuned in to the fact that Dalton Street and the surrounding area was the fastest developing section of Cork city.

Nonetheless, it was galling to find oneself co-habiting as it were with people who were effectively employees, especially considering that Linda had also interviewed an older lady that she'd seen arriving for the party, and who was soon to join the staff at Carnelian Springs. She indeed was yet another erstwhile career woman who appeared to be taking the nature trail.

It seemed to Linda as if the solid white houses were suddenly closing in on her. Amy had been the last straw, or rather Charlie and Amy had been. If someone had prophesied a year ago that Charlie would be practically living with the annoyingly perky nurse in the house opposite her, and that the rest of her acquaintances would have come out of the woodwork as soon as The Sanctuary opened its doors, Linda would have said they were dreaming. Without much warning, she'd found herself living with the kind of people that she'd imagined would be well outside the realm of her existence. Housewives and hairdressers, that typified it. Not to mention the indignity of Charlie taking up with one of them on her doorstep.

Sighing, she closed her eyes and tried to ignore the burst of laughter that exploded at the end of a particularly long version of "*The Boys of Fairhill*". The last of the evening sun slanted in across the plush three-seater, highlighting the rich chestnut sheen of the leather. The two Graham Knuttel women over the marble fireplace stared at her with accusing eyes, as if she'd somehow failed to provide them with the kind of environment that they'd been promised. Even the carefully arranged Masai figures on the hearth glared balefully at her, as if they too were disappointed with their circumstances.

Linda stood abruptly and pulled the blinds, even though the sun had barely started to set. She couldn't bear the sight of Charlie's car in the driveway facing her. She'd expected so much better from him. It wasn't just the fact that he'd left her, but the way he'd gone out and deliberately picked someone who was the exact antithesis of herself. It was as if he were subtly pointing out that all her own attributes were what he was trying to avoid in a life partner, and that he was blatantly disinterested in the things that had once attracted him.

Well, she wouldn't have to put up with it much longer, she thought, her eyes resting on the PE Sheeran brochures that were strewn across the glass-topped coffee table. Every last shred of interest had now dissipated and the house felt like more of an encumbrance than an asset. The lifestyle that she had planned for herself here had failed to materialise and Linda wasn't one to waste time flogging a dead horse.

A quick sale, she'd instructed, ignoring the wheedling of the auctioneer that she'd make a very satisfying profit if she held out and allowed a bidding war to develop. A satisfying commission for himself was more like what he was angling for, she reflected cynically. Profit or no profit, she didn't intend to drag her heels in Pebble Cove for any longer than was strictly necessary.

It occurred to her now that in actual fact there was no reason why she had to remain in the house at all. Swiftly, she ascended the carpeted stairs, her feet sinking into the deep pile. Flinging open the doors of the wardrobe, she located the Louis Vuitton suitcases that her parents had given her the previous Christmas. Taking care to pack only as much as she'd need for a few weeks in her father's recently acquired villa in Marbella, she slipped her passport from the top drawer of the cherrywood nightstand and took a final look around the bedroom. Strangely, she felt nothing, knowing that the shine had gone off the place for her long ago. The removals people could pack the rest of her things once a buyer was settled on.

Linda let herself out as quietly as she could, lest any of the revellers in the next house came out and felt obliged to ask her in. She needn't have worried. The blinds on the Flemings' front windows were still open and she could make out the silhouettes swaying to yet another eighties' pop song. Her resolve strengthened by this further display of vulgarity, Linda slid the two suitcases into the almost non-existent boot of the MG, noting with displeasure the eclectic collection of saloons and hatchbacks parked haphazardly along the grass verge. Silently, she reversed out of the driveway of Number 1, her eyes resting for a moment on the gaudy *"For Sale"* sign that swung gently on its short metal chains.

She didn't look back at all, didn't need to, as the twinkling lights of the harbour opened up before her and she left Pebble Cove behind, its laughter echoing in her wake.

The End